BADLANDS

BADLANDS

A NOVEL OF SUSPENSE

RICHARD | MONTANARI

BALLANTINE BOOKS
NEW YORK

Copyright © 2008 by Richard Montanari

Published in the United States by Ballantine Books, an imprint of The Random House Publishing Group, a division of Random House, Inc., New York.

BALLANTINE and colophon are registered trademarks of Random House, Inc.

Library of Congress Cataloging-in-Publication Data

Montanari, Richard.
Badlands : a novel of suspense / Richard Montanari.
p. cm.
ISBN 978-0-345-49242-5 (acid-free paper)
1. Police—Pennsylvania—Philadelphia—Fiction. 2. Homicide investigation—Fiction. 3. Philadelphia (Pa.)—Fiction. 4. Code and cipher stories. I. Title.

PS3563.05384B33 2008
813'.54—dc22   2008025607

Printed in the United States of America on acid-free paper

www.ballantinebooks.com

9 8 7 6 5 4 3 2 1

First Edition

Book design by Susan Turner

For Darla Jean
Sorella mia, cuore mio

ACKNOWLEDGMENTS

With deepest gratitude to Meg Ruley, Jane Berkey, Peggy Gordijn, Don Cleary, Mike McCormack, Christina Hogrebe, and everyone at the Jane Rotrosen Agency—magicians all; to Linda Marrow, Dana Isaacson, Rachel Kind, Junessa Viloria, and the brilliant team at Ballantine Books; to Kate Elton, Nikola Scott, Chrissy Schwartz, and all my mates at Random House UK; to Detective Michele Kelly, Marco Marangon, and Tom Ewing; to George Snyder of Snyder's Magic Shop, for never showing me how it was done; to my father, Dominic Montanari, for being there when the words were not; and to the city of Philadelphia, for letting me write about its neighborhoods, streets, heroes, and monsters, both real and imagined.

In the darkness, in the deep violet folds of night, he hears whispers: low, plaintive sounds that dart and shudder and scratch behind the wainscoting, the cornice, the parched and wormy wood lath. At first the words seem foreign, as if uttered in another language, but as dusk inches toward dawn he comes to recognize every voice—every pitch, tone, and timbre—as a mother would her child on a crowded playground.

Some nights he hears a solitary scream rage beneath the floorboards, stalking him from room to room, down the grand staircase, across the foyer, through the kitchen and pantry, into the consecrated silence of the cellar. There, below ground, entombed by a thousand centuries of bone and fur, he accepts the gravity of his sins. Perhaps it is the dampness itself that accuses, icy droplets on stone shimmering like tears on a brocade bodice.

As memories flower, he recalls Elise Beausoleil, the girl from Chicago. He recalls her proud manner and capable hands, the way she bargained in those final seconds, as if she were still the prettiest girl at the prom. A Dickensian waif in her high boots and belted coat, Elise Beausoleil liked to read. Jane Austen was her favorite, she said, although she considered Charlotte Brontë a close second. He found a yellowed copy of Villette *in her purse. He kept Elise in the library.*

In time he recalls Monica Renzi, her thick limbs and body hair, the frisson of exhilaration as he enthusiastically raised his hand like one of her contemptuous classmates when she asked why. The daughter of a Scranton shopkeeper, Monica liked to dress in red; shy and wordstruck and virginal. Monica once told him that he reminded her of a young banker in one of those old movies she watched with her grandmother on Saturday nights. Monica's room was the solarium.

He recalls the thrill of the chase, the bitter coffees consumed in rail stations and bus terminals, the heat and noise and dust of amusement parks and Home Days and county fairs, the frigid mornings in the car. He recalls the excitement of driving through the city, his quarry so delicately in hand, the puzzle enticingly engaged.

In time, in that gauzy cleave between shade and light, in that gray confessional of dawn, he remembers it all.

Each morning the house falls silent. Dust settles, shadows depart, voices still.

On this morning he showers and dresses and breakfasts, steps through the front door onto the porch. Daffodils near the sidewalk fence greet him, brazen blonds spiriting through the cold sod. A breeze carries the first breath of spring.

Behind him looms a sprawling Victorian house, a lady of long-faded finery. Her back gardens and side yards are overgrown, her stone paths tufted, her gutters dense with verdigris. She is the very museum of his existence, a house crafted at a time when dwellings of such distinction and character were given names, names that would enter the consciousness of the landscape, the soul of the city, the lore of the region.

In this mad place where walls move and stairways lead nowhere, where closets give onto clandestine workshops and portraits solemnly observe each other in the midday silence, he knows every corridor, every hinge, every sill, sash, and dentil.

This place is called Faerwood. In each of its rooms there dwells a restive soul. In each soul, a secret.

He stands in the center of the crowded shopping mall, taking in the aromas: the food court and its myriad riches; the department store with its lotions and powders and cloying scents; the salt of young women. He surveys the overweight couples in their twenties, urging the laden pram. He laments the invisible elderly.

At ten minutes to nine he slips into a narrow store. It is garishly lit, stocked floor to ceiling with ceramic figurines and rayon roses. Small, shiny balloons dance in the overheated air. An entire wall is devoted to greeting cards.

There is only one other patron in the store. He has been following her all evening, has seen the sadness in her eyes, the weight on her shoulders, the fatigue in her stride.

She is the Drowning Girl.

He eases next to her, selects a few cards from the glittering array, chuckles softly at each, returns them to the rack. He glances around. No one is watching.

It is time.

"You look a little confused," he says.

She glances up. She is tall and thin, magnificently pale. Her ash blond hair is pinned in a messy fashion, held in place by white plastic barrettes. Her neck is carven ivory. She is wears a lilac backpack.

She doesn't respond. He has scared her.

Walk away.

"There are too many choices!" she says animatedly, but not without caution. He expects this. He is, after all, an unknown piece on her game board of strangers. She giggles, chews on a fingernail. Adorable. She is about seventeen. The best age.

"Tell me the occasion," he says. "Maybe I can help."

A flash of distrust now—cat paws on an oven door. She peers around the room, at the publicness of it all. "Well," she begins, "my boyfriend is . . ."

Silence.

He begs the conversation forward. "He's what?"

She doesn't want to say, then she does. "Okay . . . he's not exactly my boyfriend, right? But he's cheating on me." She tucks a filament of hair behind an ear. "Well, not exactly cheating. Not yet." She turns to leave, turns back. "Okay, he asked out my best friend, Courtney. The slut." She reddens, a sheer crimson pall on her flawless skin. "I can't believe I'm telling you this."

He is dressed casually this evening: faded jeans, black linen blazer, loafers, a little extra gel in his hair, a silver ankh around his neck, eyeglasses of a modern style. He looks young enough. Besides, he has the sort of bearing that invites faith. It always has. "The cad," he says.

Wrong word? No. She smiles. Seventeen going on thirty.

"More like a jerk," she says. "A total jerk." Another nervous giggle.

He leans away from her, increasing the distance by mere inches. Important inches. She relaxes. She has decided he is no threat. Like one of her cool teachers.

"Do you think dark humor is appropriate for the occasion?"

She considers this. "Probably," she says. "Maybe. I don't know. I guess."

"Does he make you laugh?"

Boyfriends—boys who become boyfriends—usually do. Even the ones who cheat on achingly beautiful seventeen-year-old girls.

"Yeah," she says. "He's kinda funny. Sometimes." She looks up, making deep eye contact. This moment all but splinters his heart. "But not lately."

"I was looking at this one," he says. "I think it might be just the right sentiment." He lifts a card from the rack, considers it for a moment, hands it over. It is a bit risqué. His hesitation speaks of his respect for the age difference, the fact that they've just met.

She takes the card, opens it, reads the greeting. A moment later she laughs, covering her mouth. A tiny snort escapes. She blushes, embarrassed.

In this instant her image blurs, as it always has, like a face obscured by rain on a shattered windshield.

"This is, like, totally perfect," she says. "Totally. Thanks."

He watches as she glances at the vacant cashier, then at the video camera. She turns her back to the camera, stuffs the card into her bag, looks at him, a smile on her face. If there was a purer love, he could not imagine it.

"I need another card, too," she says. "But I'm not sure you can help me with that one."

"You'd be surprised what I can do."

"It's for my parents." She cocks a hip. Another blush veils her pretty face, then quickly disappears. "It's because I've—"

He holds up a hand, stopping her. It is better this way. "I understand."

"You do?"

"Yes."

"What do you mean?"

He smiles. "I was once your age."

She parts her lips to answer, but instead remains silent.

"It all works out in the end," he adds. "You'll see. It always does."

She looks away for a second. It is as if she has made some sort of decision in this moment, as though a great weight has been lifted from her shoulders. She glances back at him, smiles sadly, and says, "Thanks."

Instead of responding, he just gazes at her with great fondness. The overhead lights cast golden highlights in her hair. In an instant, it comes to him.

He will keep her in the pantry.

Ten minutes later he follows her, unseen, into the parking lot, conscious of the shadow, the light, the carbon blue chiaroscuro of the evening. It has begun to rain, a light drizzle that does not threaten a downpour.

He watches as she crosses the avenue, steps into a shelter. Soon after, she boards the bus, a shuttle to the train station.

He slips a CD into the player. In seconds the sounds of "Vedrai, Carino" fill the car. It regales his soul—once again, exalting this moment, as only Mozart can.

He follows the bus into the city, his heart ablaze, the hunt renewed.

She is Emma Bovary. She is Elizabeth Bennet. She is Cassiopeia and Cosette.

She is his.

SHADOW HOUSE

An echoing, garnish'd house
— but dead, dead, dead.

—WALT WHITMAN

ONE

THE DEAD GIRL SAT INSIDE THE GLASS DISPLAY CASE, A PALE AND DELI-
cate curio placed on a shelf by a madman. In life she had been beautiful, with fine blond hair and cobalt blue eyes. In death her eyes
pleaded for benediction, for the cold symmetry of justice.

The last thing they had seen was a monster.

Her tomb was a stifling basement in an abandoned building in the
Badlands, a five-square-mile area of desolate terrain and destroyed lives
in North Philadelphia, running approximately from Erie Avenue south
to Girard, from Broad Street east to the river.

Her name was Caitlin Alice O'Riordan. On the day of her murder,
the day her brief story came to a close, she was seventeen.

For Detectives Kevin Byrne and Jessica Balzano of the Philadelphia
Police Department's Homicide Unit, Caitlin's story was just beginning.

THERE ARE THREE DIVISIONS in Philly Homicide—the Line Squad,
which handles new cases; the Fugitive Squad; and the Special Investigations Unit, which handles, among other things, cold cases. To the detectives of SIU, all of whom were members of the Five Squad, an elite
group of investigators handpicked by the captain based on their abilities, their closure rates, and their investigative skills, a cold case investigation represented a second chance to right a wrong, an ultimatum to
the killers who arrogantly walked the streets of Philadelphia, a state-

ment that said the Commonwealth of Pennsylvania, and the City of Brotherly Love, were not done with them.

The Caitlin O'Riordan investigation was the first SIU case for Kevin Byrne and Jessica Balzano.

When the detectives arrived at the Eighth Street address there was no yellow tape ringing the property, no sector cars blocking traffic, none of the blue and white Crime Scene Unit vans, no officer guarding the entrance, crime-scene log in hand. All this was long gone.

They had read the reports, seen the autopsy protocol, viewed the photographs and video. But they had not yet followed the path of the killer.

Both detectives believed that their investigation would truly begin the moment they stepped into the room where Caitlin O'Riordan had been found.

THE BUILDING HAD BEEN SEALED four months earlier at the time of the initial investigation, the doors replaced and padlocked, the plywood over the windows secured with lag bolts. Originally a single-family row house, this corner building had been bought and sold many times. Its most recent incarnation was as a small grocery, a narrow, slipshod emporium hawking baby formula, chips, diapers, canned meats, magazines, lottery dreams. Its stock-in-trade, its lifeblood, had been the Holy Trinity of crack addiction: Chore Boy scouring pads, disposable plastic lighters, and individually packaged tea roses. The roses came in long, narrow glass tubes which, within a minute or two of leaving the store, became straight shooters, a fast and easy way to fire up a rock, the ashes from which were caught by the steel wool of the scouring pad. Every convenience store in the Badlands carried tea roses, which probably made this part of North Philly the most romantic place on earth. Hundreds of times a day someone bought a flower.

The bodega had closed more than three years earlier, and no tenant had moved in. The building's façade was still a Day-Glo green, with a strange sign painted over the front window:

OPEN 24 HOURS. DAYS 12 TO 8 PM.

Jessica unlocked the padlock on the corrugated metal door, rolled it up. They stepped inside and were immediately greeted with the unpleasant odor of mold and mildew, the chalky scent of damp plaster. It was late August and the temperature outside was eighty-eight degrees. Inside it had to be nearing a hundred.

The first floor was remarkably clean and tidy, except for a thick layer of dust on everything. Most of the trash had long ago been collected as evidence and removed.

To their left was what was once the counter; behind it, a long row of empty shelves. Above the shelves lingered a few remaining signs—KOOLS, BUDWEISER, SKOAL—along with a menu board offering a half dozen Chinese takeout items.

The stairwell down was at the back of the building on the left. As Jessica and Kevin began to descend the steps they clicked on their Maglites. There was no electricity here, no gas or water, no utilities of any kind. Whatever thin sunlight seeped through the cracks between the sheets of plywood over the windows was instantly swallowed by the darkness.

The room where Caitlin O'Riordan was found was at the basement's far end. Years ago, the small windows at street level had been bricked in. The gloom was absolute.

In the corner of the room was a glass display case, a commercial beverage cooler used at one time for beer and soda and milk. It had stainless steel sides, and stood more than six feet tall. It was in this glass coffin that Caitlin's body had been discovered—sitting on a wooden chair, staring out at the room, eyes wide open. She'd been found by a pair of teenage boys scrapping for copper.

Byrne took out a yellow legal pad and a fine point marker. Holding his flashlight under his arm, he made a detailed sketch of the subterranean room. In homicide work, the investigating detectives were required to make a diagram of every crime scene. Even though photographs and videotape records of the scene were made, it was the investigator's sketch that was most often referred to, even in the trial stage. Byrne usually made the diagram. By her own admission, Jessica couldn't draw a circle with a compass.

"I'll be upstairs if you need me," Jessica said.

Byrne glanced up, the darkness of the room a black shroud around his broad shoulders. "Gee thanks, partner."

JESSICA SPREAD OUT THE FILES on the front counter, grateful for the bright sunlight streaming through the open door, grateful for the slight breeze.

The first page of the binder was a large photograph of Caitlin, a color eight-by-ten. Every time Jessica looked at the photograph she was reminded of the Gene Hackman movie *Hoosiers*, although she would be hard-pressed to explain why. Perhaps it was because the girl in the picture was from rural Pennsylvania. Perhaps it was because there was an openness to the girl's face, a trusting countenance that seemed locked into the world of 1950s America—long before Caitlin's birth, life, and death—a time when girls wore saddle shoes and kneesocks and vest sweaters and shirts with Peter Pan collars.

Girls didn't look like this anymore, Jessica thought. *Did they?*

Not in this time of MySpace and Abercrombie & Fitch catalogs and rainbow parties. Not in this day and age when a girl could buy a bag of Doritos and a Coke, board a bus in Lancaster County, and ninety minutes later emerge in a city that would swallow her whole; a trusting soul who never had a chance.

The estimated time of Caitlin's death was between midnight and 7 AM on May 2, although the medical examiner could not be more precise, given that by the time Caitlin O'Riordan's body had been discovered she had been dead at least forty-eight hours. There were no external wounds on the victim, no lacerations or abrasions, no ligature marks to indicate she may have been restrained, no defensive wounds that would suggest she struggled with an assailant. There had been no skin or any other kind of organic matter beneath her fingernails.

At the time she was discovered, Caitlin had been fully clothed, dressed in frayed blue jeans, Reeboks, black denim jacket, and a white T-shirt. She also wore a lilac nylon backpack. Around her neck had been a sterling silver Claddagh, and although it was not particularly valuable, the fact that she wore it in death did not support any theory that she had been the victim of a robbery gone bad. Nor did the cause of the death.

Caitlin O'Riordan had drowned.

Homicide victims in North Philadelphia were generally not drowned. Shot, stabbed, bludgeoned, sliced and diced with a machete, pummeled with an ax handle, yes. Popped by a rebar, run over with a Hummer, stuck with an ice pick, doused with gasoline and lit ablaze— yeah, all the time. Jessica had once investigated a North Philly homicide committed with a lawn edger. A *rusty* lawn edger.

But drowned? Even if the vic was found floating in the Delaware River, the cause of death was usually one of the above.

Jessica looked at the lab report. The water in Caitlin's lungs had been carefully analyzed. It contained fluoride, chlorine, zinc orthophosphate, ammonia. It also contained trace levels of haloacetic acid. The report contained two pages of graphs and charts. It all went way over Jessica's head, but she had no problem at all understanding the report's conclusion. According to the forensics lab and the medical examiner's office, Caitlin O'Riordan did not drown in the Delaware or Schuylkill River. She did not drown in Wissahickon Creek, nor in any of the fountains for which the City of Brotherly Love was rightly known. She did not drown in a swimming pool, public or private.

Caitlin drowned in ordinary Philadelphia tap water.

The original investigators had contacted the Philadelphia Water Department and were told that, according to the EPA, the water found in Caitlin's lungs was indeed specific to Philadelphia. The three treatment plants at Baxter, Belmont, and Queen Lane had all made specific adjustments to their drinking water processes in March, due to an oil-tanker spill.

There was no running water in this building. There were no bathtubs, plastic tubs, buckets, aquariums, or cans—not a single vessel that could hold enough water to drown a human being.

There was some quiet debate at the Roundhouse, the police administration building at Eighth and Race, about whether or not this was a bona fide homicide. Both Jessica and Byrne believed it was, yet conceded the possibility that Caitlin had accidentally drowned, perhaps in a bathtub, and that her body had been moved to the crime scene after the fact. This would bring about charges of abuse of a corpse, not homicide.

One thing was not in doubt: Caitlin O'Riordan did not arrive here under her own power.

There had been no ID on the victim, no purse or wallet at the scene. Caitlin had been identified by the photograph that circulated via the FBI website. There was no evidence of sexual assault.

CAITLIN O'RIORDAN WAS THE DAUGHTER of Robert and Marilyn O'Riordan of Millersville, Pennsylvania, a town of about 8000, five miles southwest of Lancaster. She had one sister, Lisa, who was two years younger.

Robert O'Riordan owned and operated a small, home-style restaurant on George Street in downtown Millersville. Marilyn was a homemaker, a former Miss Bart Township. Both were active in the church. Although far from wealthy, they maintained a comfortable home on a quiet rural lane.

Caitlin O'Riordan had been a runaway.

On April 1, Robert O'Riordan found a note from his daughter. It was written in red felt tip marker, on stationery that had Scotties along the border. The O'Riordans had two Scottish terriers as pets. The note was taped to the mirror in the girl's bedroom.

Dear Mom and Dad (and Lisa too, sorry Lisey ☺)
I'm sorry, but I have to do this.
I'll be okay. I'll be back. I promise.
I'll send a card.

On April 2, two patrol officers from the Millersville Police Department were sent to the O'Riordan house. When they arrived, Caitlin had been missing for nineteen hours. The two patrolmen found no evidence of kidnapping or violence, no evidence of any foul play. They took statements from the family and the immediate neighbors—which, in that area, were about a quarter mile away on either side—wrote up the report. The case went through the expected channels. In seventy-two hours it was handed off to the Philadelphia field office of the FBI.

Despite a more than modest reward, and the fact that the young woman's photograph was published in local papers and on various websites, two weeks after her disappearance there were no leads regarding the whereabouts or fate of Caitlin O'Riordan. To the world, she had simply vanished.

As April passed, the case grew colder, and authorities suspected that Caitlin O'Riordan might have fallen victim to a violent act.

On May 2, their darkest suspicions were confirmed.

THE ORIGINAL LEAD INVESTIGATOR in the Caitlin O'Riordan case, a man named Rocco Pistone, had retired two months ago. That same month his partner, Freddy Roarke, died of a massive stroke while watching a horse race at Philadelphia Park. Dropped right at the rail, just a few feet from the finish line. The 25-to-1 filly on which Freddy had put twenty dollars—poetically named Heaven's Eternity—won by three lengths. Freddy Roarke never collected.

Pistone and Roarke had visited Millersville, had interviewed Caitlin's schoolmates and friends, her teachers, neighbors, fellow churchgoers. No one recalled Caitlin mentioning a friend or Internet acquaintance or boyfriend in Philadelphia. The detectives also interviewed a seventeen-year-old Millersville boy named Jason Scott. Scott said that when Caitlin went missing, they were casually dating, stressing the word "casually." He said Caitlin had been a lot more serious about the relationship than he was. He also told them that, at the time of Caitlin's murder, he was in Arkansas, visiting his father. Detectives confirmed this, and the case went cold.

As of August 2008 there were no suspects, no leads, and no new evidence. Jessica turned the last page of the file, thinking for the hundredth time in the past two days, *Why had Caitlin O'Riordan come to Philadelphia? Was it simply the allure of the big city? And, more importantly, where had she been for those thirty days?*

At just after 11:00 AM, Jessica's phone rang. It was their boss, Sgt. Dwight Buchanan. Byrne had finished his sketches of the basement and was catching some air on the sidewalk. He came back inside. Jessica put her cell phone on speaker.

"What's up, Sarge?"

"We have a confession," Buchanan said.

"For our job?"

"Yes."

"What are you talking about? How? *Who?*"

"We got a call on the Tip Line. The caller told the CIU officer he killed Caitlin O'Riordan, and he was ready to turn himself in."

The Tip Line was a relatively new initiative of the Criminal Intelligence Unit, a community response program that was part of a Philadelphia Police Department project called Join the Resistance. Its purpose was to provide citizens of Philadelphia with the opportunity to covertly partner with the police without fear of being exposed to the criminal element. Sometimes it was used as a confessional.

"All due respect, Sarge, we get those all the time," Jessica said. "Especially on a case like this."

"This call was a little different."

"How so?"

"Well, for one thing, he had knowledge of the case that was never released. He said there was a button missing from the victim's jacket. Third from the bottom."

Jessica picked up two photographs of the victim in situ. The button on Caitlin's jacket—third from the bottom—was missing.

"Okay, it's missing," Jessica said. "But maybe he saw the crime-scene photos, or knows someone who did. How do we know he has firsthand knowledge?"

"He sent us the button."

Jessica glanced at her partner.

"We got it in the mail this morning," Buchanan continued. "We sent it to the lab. They're processing it now, but Tracy said it's a slam dunk. It's Caitlin's button."

Tracy McGovern was the deputy director of the forensic crime lab. Jessica and Byrne took a second to absorb this development.

"Who's this guy?" Jessica asked.

"He gave his name as Jeremiah Crosley. We ran the name, but there was nothing in the system. He said we could pick him up at Second and Diamond."

"What's the address?"

"He didn't give a street address. He said we would know the place by its red door."

"Red door? What the hell does that mean?"

"I guess you'll find out," Buchanan said. "Call me when you get down there."

TWO

J ESSICA THOUGHT, *AUGUST IS THE CRUELEST MONTH.*

T. S. Eliot believed the cruelest month was April, but he was never a homicide cop in Philly.

In April there was still hope, you see. Flowers. Rain. Birds. The Phillies. *Always* the Phillies. Ten thousand losses and it was still the Phillies. April meant there was, to some extent, a future.

In contrast, the only thing August had to offer was heat. Unrelenting, mind-scrambling, soul-destroying heat; the kind of wet, ugly heat that covered the city like a rotting tarpaulin, coating everything in sweat and stink and cruel and attitude. A fistfight in March was a murder in August.

In her decade on the job—the first four in uniform, working the tough streets of the Third District—Jessica had always found August to be the worst month of the year.

They stood on the corner of Second and Diamond Streets, deep in the Badlands. At least half the buildings on the block were boarded up or in the process of rehab. There was no red door in sight, nothing called the Red Door Tavern, no billboards for Red Lobster or Pella Doors, not a single sign in any window advertising a product with the word *red* or *door* in it.

There was no one standing on the corner waiting for them.

They had already walked two blocks in three directions, then back. The only path left to explore was south on Second.

"Why are we doing this again?" Jessica asked.

"Boss says go, we go, right?"

They walked a half block south on Second Street. More shuttered stores and derelict houses. They passed a used-tire stand, a burned car, a step van on blocks, a Cuban restaurant.

The other side of the street offered a colorless quilt of battered row houses, stitched between hoagie shacks, wig shops, and nail boutiques, some open for business, most shuttered, all with fading, hand-lettered signs, all crosshatched with rusting riot gates. The upper floors were a tic-tac-toe of bedsheet-covered windows with busted panes.

North Philly, Jessica thought. God save North Philly.

As they passed a vacant lot fronted by a shanty wall, Byrne stopped. The wall, a listing barrier made of nailed-together plywood, rusted corrugated metal, and plastic awning panels, was covered in graffiti. On one end was a bright red screen door, wired to a post. The door looked recently painted.

"Jess," Byrne said. "Look."

Jessica took a few steps back. She glanced at the door, then back over her shoulder. They were almost a full block from Diamond Street. "This can't mean anything. Can it?"

"Sarge said the *guy* said 'near Second and Diamond.' And this is definitely a red door. The only red door around here."

They walked a few more feet south, glanced over a low section of the wall. The lot looked like every other vacant lot in Philadelphia— weeds, bricks, tires, plastic bags, broken appliances, the obligatory discarded toilet.

"See any killers lurking?" Jessica asked.

"Not a one."

"Me neither. Ready to go?"

Byrne thought for a few moments. "Tell you what. We'll do one lap. Just to say we went to the fair."

They walked to the corner and circled around behind the vacant lot. At the rear of the property, facing the alley, was a rusted chain-link fence. One corner was clipped and wrestled back. Overhead, three pairs of old sneakers, tied together by their laces, looped over an electrical wire.

Jessica glanced around the lot. Against the wall of the building on the west side, which had once housed a well-known music store, were a few stacks of discarded brick pallets, a stepladder with only three rungs, along with a handful of broken appliances. She resigned herself to getting this over with. Byrne held up the fencing while she ducked underneath. He followed.

The two detectives did a cursory sweep of the parcel. Five minutes later they met in the middle. The sun was high and melting and merciless. It was already past lunchtime. "Nothing?"

"Nothing," Byrne replied.

Jessica took out her cell phone. "Okay," she said. "Now I'm hooked. I want to hear that hotline call."

Twenty minutes later Detective Joshua Bontrager arrived at the scene. He had with him a portable cassette player.

Josh Bontrager had been in the homicide unit less than eighteen months, but had already proven himself a valuable asset. He was young, and brought a young man's energy to the street, but he also had what just about everyone in the department considered to be a unique and oddly effective background. No one in the PPD's homicide division— or probably any homicide division in the country—could claim it.

Joshua Bontrager had grown up in an Amish family.

He had left the church many years earlier, coming to Philadelphia for no other reason than that's what you did when you left Berks or Lancaster County seeking fortune. He joined the force, and spent a number of years in the traffic unit, before being transferred to the homicide unit to assist on an investigation that led up the Schuylkill River into rural Berks. Bontrager was wounded in the course of that investigation, but recovered fully. The bosses decided to keep him on.

Jessica remembered the first time she met him—mismatched pants and suit coat, hair that looked like it had been cut with a butter knife, sturdy, unpolished shoes. Since that time Bontrager had acquired a gold-badge detective's swagger, a Center City haircut, a couple of nice suits.

Still, as urbane as he had become, Josh Bontrager would forever be known throughout the unit as the first *Amishide* cop in Philadelphia history.

Bontrager put the cassette player on top of a rusted grill made from a fifty-gallon drum, an abandoned barbecue sitting in the middle of the vacant lot. A few seconds later he had the tape cued up. "Ready?"

"Hit it," Jessica said.

Bontrager hit PLAY.

"Philadelphia Police Department Hotline," the female officer said.

"Yes, my name is Jeremiah Crosley, and I have information that might be helpful in a murder case you are investigating."

The voice sounded white male, thirties or forties, educated. The accent was Philly, but with something lurking beneath.

"Would you spell your last name for me please, sir?"

The man did.

"May I have your home address?"

"I live at 2097 Dodgson Street."

"And where is that located?"

"In Queen Village. But I am not there now."

"And which case are you calling about?"

"The Caitlin O'Riordan case."

"Go ahead, sir."

"I killed her."

At this point there was a quick intake of breath. It wasn't clear if it was the caller or the officer. Jessica would bet it was the officer. You could be a cop forty years, investigate thousands of cases, and never hear those words.

"And when did you do this, sir?"

"It was in May of this year."

"Do you remember the exact date?"

"It was the second of May, I believe."

"Do you recall the time of day?"

"I do not."

I do not, Jessica thought. No contractions. She made a note.

"If you doubt that I am telling the truth, I can prove it to you."

"How will you do that, sir?"

"I have something of hers."

"You have something?"

"Yes. A button from her jacket. Third from the bottom. I have sent it to you. It will come in the mail today."

"Where are you right now, sir?"

"I will get to that in a second. I just want to have some assurances."

"I can't promise you anything, sir. But I'll listen to whatever it is you have to say."

"We live in a world in which a person's word is no longer valid currency. I have seven girls. I fear for them. I fear for their safety. Do you promise me no harm will come to them?"

Seven girls, Jessica thought.

"If they are in no way responsible for this or any other crime, they will not be involved. I promise you."

One final hesitation.

"I am at a location near Second and Diamond. It is cold here."

It is cold here, Jessica thought. What does *that* mean? The temperature had already topped ninety degrees.

"What's the address?"

"I do not know. But you will know it by its red door."

"Sir, if you'll stay on the line for—"

The line went dead. Josh Bontrager hit STOP.

Jessica glanced at her partner. "What do you think?"

Byrne gave it a few moments. "I'm not sure. Ask me when we get the full report back from the lab on that button."

It was common practice to run a PCIC and NCIC check on anyone who called in with information, especially those who called in to confess to a major crime. According to the boss, there was no record of a Jeremiah Crosley—criminal, DMV, or otherwise—in the city of Philadelphia. His Queen Village address turned out to be nonexistent. There was no Dodgson Street.

"Okay," Jessica finally said. "Where to?"

"Let's go back to the Eighth Street scene," Byrne said. "I want to recanvass. Let's bring the cassette and see if anyone around there recognizes our boy's voice. Maybe after that we can take another ride to Millersville."

A day earlier they had gone to Millersville to speak with Robert and Marilyn O'Riordan. Not to conduct a formal interview—the original team had done that twice—but to assure them that the investigation was moving forward. Robert O'Riordan had been sullen and uncooperative, his wife had been nearly catatonic. They were two people all but incapacitated by the torment of grief, the black hole of an indescribable loss. Jessica had seen it many times, but each time was a fresh arrow in her heart.

"Let's do it." Jessica grabbed the cassette player. "Thanks for bringing this down, Josh."

"No problem."

Before Jessica could turn and head to the car, Byrne put a hand on her arm.

"Jess."

Byrne was pointing at a dilapidated refrigerator against the brick wall of the music store. Or what was left of the refrigerator. It was an ancient model from the 1950s or 1960s, at one time a built-in, but the side paneling had long ago been stripped away. It appeared the appliance had originally been a powder blue or green, but age and rust and soot had darkened it to a deep brown. The refrigerator door hung at a crooked angle.

Along the top, on the skewed freezer door, was a logo. Although the chrome letters were long gone, the discolored outline of the brand name remained.

Crosley.

The brand dated back to the 1920s. Jessica recalled a Crosley fridge in her grandmother's house on Christian Street. They weren't that common anymore.

My name is Jeremiah Crosley.

"Could this be a coincidence?" Jessica asked.

"We can only hope so," Byrne replied, but Jessica could tell he didn't really believe it. The alternative led them down a path nobody wanted to follow.

Byrne reached out, opened the refrigerator door.

Inside, on the one remaining shelf, was a large laboratory specimen jar, half-filled with a filmy red fluid. Something was suspended in the liquid.

Jessica knew what it was. She had been to enough autopsies.

It was a human heart.

Jessica checked the front and back of the book. No inscriptions or writing of any kind. She checked the bottom edge. A red ribbon marked a page, splitting the book in half. She carefully lifted the ribbon. The book fell open.

The Book of Jeremiah.

"Ah, shit," Byrne said. "What the fuck is *this*?"

Jessica squinted at the first page of the Book of Jeremiah. The print was so small she could barely see it. She fished her glasses from her pocket, put them on.

"Josh?" she asked. "You know anything about this part of the Old Testament?"

Joshua Bontrager was the unit's go-to guy for most things Christian.

"A little," he said. "Jeremiah was kind of a doom and gloom fella. Predicted the destruction of Judah, and all. I remember hearing some of his writings quoted."

"For instance?"

" 'The heart is deceitful above all things and beyond cure.' That was one of his biggies. There are a lot of translations of that passage, but that's one of the more popular ones. Nice outlook, huh?"

"He wrote about the heart?" Jessica asked.

"Among other things."

Jessica flipped a page, then another, then another. At Chapter 41, the page had a series of marks on it—three small squares drawn with different pens, yellow, blue, and red. It appeared that one word was highlighted, along with two sets of two numbers each.

The highlighted word was *Shiloh*. Beneath it, along the left hand side of the columns, were two numbers, forty-five and fourteen.

Jessica flipped carefully through the Book of Jeremiah, and glanced through the rest of the Bible. There were no other bookmarked pages, or highlighted words or numbers.

She looked at Byrne. "This mean anything to you?"

Byrne shook his head. Jessica could already see his wheels turning. "Josh?"

Bontrager looked closely at the Bible, eyes scanning the page. "No. Sorry." He looked a little sheepish. "Don't tell my dad, but I haven't picked up the Good Book in a while."

THREE

WHILE THEY WAITED FOR THE CRIME SCENE UNIT TO ARRIVE AND begin processing the scene, Josh Bontrager took digital photographs; of the lot, the graffiti on the shanty wall, the refrigerator, the neighborhood, the gathering rubberneckers. Jessica and Byrne played the recording three more times. Nothing leapt out to identify the caller.

And while there were many things they did not yet understand about what they had just found, they knew these human remains did not belong to their victim. Caitlin O'Riordan had not been mutilated in any way.

It's cold here, Jessica thought. He had been talking about the refrigerator.

"Guys." Bontrager pointed behind the refrigerator. "There's something back here."

"What is it?" Jessica asked.

"No idea." He turned to Byrne. "Give me a hand."

They got on either side of the hulking appliance. When the fridge was a few feet from the wall, Jessica stepped behind it. Years of dust and grunge coated the area where the compressor once was.

In its place was a book of some sort; chunky, with a black cover, no dust jacket. Watermarks dotted the linen finish. Jessica put on a latex glove, gently retrieved the book. It was a hardbound edition of *The New Oxford Bible*.

"Let's run this by Documents," Jessica said. "We were supposed to find this, yes?"

"Yes," Byrne echoed. He sounded none too happy about it.

Jessica kind of wanted an argument about this point. Byrne didn't offer one. Neither did Josh Bontrager. This was not good news.

An hour later, with the scene secured by CSU, they headed back to the Roundhouse. The morning's events—the possibility of an arrest in the murder of Caitlin O'Riordan and the discovery of a human heart in a weed-choked vacant lot in the Badlands—circled one another like blood-bloated flies in the haze of a blistering Philadelphia summer afternoon, all underscored by an ancient name and two cryptic numbers.

Shiloh. Forty-five. Fourteen.

What was the message? Jessica thought hard on it.

She had a dark feeling there would be others.

FOUR

TWO MONTHS EARLIER

E VE GALVEZ KNEW WHAT THE THERAPIST WAS GOING TO SAY BEFORE HE said it. She always did.

How did it make you feel?

"How did it make you feel?" he asked.

He was younger than the others. Better dressed, better looking. And he knew it. Dark hair, a little too long, curling over his collar; eyes a soft, compassionate caramel brown. He wore a black blazer, charcoal slacks, just the right amount of aftershave for daytime. Something Italian, she thought. Expensive. Vain men had never impressed Eve Galvez. In her line of work, she couldn't afford the flutters. In her line of work she couldn't afford a misstep of *any* kind. She pegged him at forty-four. She was good with ages, too.

"It made me feel bad," Eve said.

"Bad is not a feeling." He had an accent that suggested the Main Line, but not by birth. "What I'm talking about is emotion," he added. "What *emotion* did the incident evoke?"

"Okay, then," Eve said, playing the game. "I felt . . . *angry.*"

"Better," he replied. "Angry at whom?"

"Angry at myself for getting into a situation like that in the first place. Angry at the world."

She had gone to Old City one night, after work, alone. Looking.

Again. At thirty-one she was one of the older women in the club, but with her dark hair and eyes, her Pilates-toned body, she attracted her share of advances. Still, in the end, the crowd was too loud, too raucous. She gave the bar her two-drink minimum, then stepped into the night. Later in the evening she stopped by the Omni Hotel Bar, and made the mistake of letting the wrong man buy her a drink. Again. The conversation had been boring, the night dragged. She had excused herself, telling him that she had to go to the ladies' room.

When she walked out of the hotel a few minutes later, she found him waiting on the street. He followed her up Fourth Street for almost three blocks, closing the distance little by little, moving from shadow to shadow.

As luck would have it—and luck was something that played a very small role in Eve Galvez's life—at the moment the man got close enough to lay a hand on her, a police car was trolling slowly by. Eve flagged the officers down. They sent the man packing, but not without a scuffle.

It had been close, and Eve hated herself for it. She was smarter than this. Or so she wanted to believe.

But now she was in her therapist's office, and he was pushing her.

"What do you think he wanted?" he asked.

Pause. "He wanted to fuck."

The word resonated, finding all four corners of the small room. It always did in polite company.

"How do you know that?"

Eve smiled. Not the smile she used for business, or the one she used with friends and colleagues, or even the one she used on the street. This was the other smile. "Women know these things."

"All women?"

"Yes."

"Young and old?"

"And every one in-between."

"I see," he said.

Eve glanced around the room. The office was a gentrified trinity on Wharton Street, between Twelfth and Thirteenth. The first floor was three small rooms, including a cramped anteroom with bleached maple floors, a working fireplace, brass accoutrements. The smoked-glass end tables were populated with recent issues of *Psychology Today*, *In Style*, *People*. Two French doors led to a converted bedroom that served as the office, an office decorated in a faux-Euro style.

In her time on the couch Eve had met all the Pams—clonazepam, diazepam, lorazepam, flurazepam. None helped. Pain—the kind of pain that begins where your childhood comes to a deadening halt—would not be salved. In the end, when night became morning, you stepped out of the shadows, ready or not.

"I'm sorry," she said. "I apologize for my crude language. It's not very becoming."

He didn't chastise or excuse her. She hadn't expected him to. Instead, he glanced down at his lap, studied her chart, flipped a few pages. It was all there. It was one of the downsides to belonging to a health-care system that logged every appointment, every prescription, every physical therapy session, every X-ray—ache, pain, complaint, theory, treatment.

If she had learned anything it was that there were two groups of people you couldn't con. Your doctor and your banker. Both knew the real balance.

"Have you been thinking about Graciella?" he asked.

Eve tried to maintain her focus, her emotions. She put her head back for a few moments, fighting tears, then felt the liquid warmth traverse her cheek to her chin, onto her neck, then on to the fabric of the wing chair. She wondered how many tears had rolled onto this chair, how many sorrowful rivers had flowed through its ticking. "No," she lied.

He put down his pen. "Tell me about the dream."

Eve plucked a few tissues from the box, dabbed her eyes. As she did this she covertly glanced at her watch. Wall clocks were scarce in a shrink's office. They were at minute forty-eight of a fifty-minute session. Her doctor wanted to continue. On his dime.

What was *this* about? Eve wondered. Shrinks never went over the time limit. There was always someone scheduled next, some teenager with an eating disorder, some frigid housewife, some jack-off artist who rode SEPTA looking for little girls in pleated plaid, some OCD who had to circle his house seven times every morning before work just to see if he had left the gas on or had remembered to comb his area-rug fringe a few hundred times.

"Eve?" he repeated. "The dream?"

It wasn't a dream—she knew that, and he knew that. It was a nightmare, a lurid waking horror show that unspooled every night, every noon, every morning, dead center in her mind, her life.

"What do you want to know about it?" she asked, stalling. She felt sick to her stomach.

"I want to hear it all," he said. "Tell me about the dream. Tell me about Mr. Ludo."

EVE GALVEZ LOOKED AT THE OUTFIT on her bed. Collectively, the jeans, cotton blazer, T-shirt, and Nikes represented one-fifth of her wardrobe. She traveled light these days, even though she was once addicted to clothes. And shoes. Back in the day her mailbox had been thick with fashion magazines, her closet impenetrable with suits, blazers, sweaters, blouses, skirts, coats, jeans, slacks, vests, jackets, dresses. Now there was room in her closet for all of her skeletons. And they needed plenty of room.

In addition to her handful of outfits, Eve had one piece of jewelry she cared about, a bracelet she wore only at night. It was one of the few material things she cherished.

This was her fifth apartment in two years, a spare, drafty, three-room affair in Northeast Philadelphia. She had one table, one chair, one bed, one dresser, no paintings or posters on the walls. Although she had a job, a duty, a litany of responsibilities to other people, she sometimes felt like a nomad, a woman unfettered by the shackles of urban life.

Exhibit Number One: in the kitchen, four boxes of Kraft Macaroni & Cheese that expired two years earlier. Every time she opened the cupboard she was reminded that she was relocating with food she would never eat.

IN THE SHOWER she thought about her session with the shrink. She had told him about the dream—not all of it, she would never tell anybody all of it—but certainly more than she had intended. She wondered why.

He was not any more insightful than the others, did not have a special sense that raised him above all of his colleagues in his field.

And yet she had gone further than she ever had.

Maybe she *was* making progress.

She walks up a dark street. It is three o'clock in the morning. Eve knows precisely what time it is because she had glanced up the avenue—a dream-street that had no name or number—and saw the clock in the tower at City Hall.

After a few blocks, the street grows gloomier, even more featureless and long-shadowed, like a vast, silent de Chirico painting. There are abandoned stores on either side of the street, shuttered diners that somehow have customers still at the counters, ice-covered in time, coffee cups poised halfway to their lips.

She comes to an intersection. A streetlight blinks red on all four sides. She sees a doll sitting in a fiddleback chair. It wears a ragged pink dress, soiled at the hem. It has dirty knees and elbows.

Suddenly, Eve knows who she is, and what she has done. The doll is hers. It is a Crissy doll, her favorite when she was a child. She has run away from home. She has come to the city without any money or any plan.

A shadow dances across the wall to her left. She turns to look, and sees a man approaching, fast. He moves as a gust of blistering wind, carved of smoke and moonlight.

He is now behind her. She knows what he did to the others. She knows what he is going to do to her.

"Venga aqui!" comes the booming voice from behind, inches from her ear.

The fear, the sickness, blossoms inside her. She knows the familiar voice, and it forms a dark tornado in her heart. "Venga, Eve! Ahora!"

She closes her eyes. The man spins her around, begins to violently shake her. He pushes her to the ground, but she does not hit the steaming asphalt. Instead she falls through it, tumbling through space, head over heels, freefall, the lights of the city a mad kaleidoscope in her mind.

She crashes through a ceiling onto a filthy mattress. For a few blessed moments the world is silent. Soon she catches her breath, hears the sound of a young girl singing a familiar song in the next room. It is a Spanish lullaby, "A La Nanita Nana."

Seconds later, the door slams open. A bright orange light washes the room. An earsplitting siren rages through her head.

And the real nightmare begins.

Eve stepped out of the shower, toweled off, walked into her bedroom, opened the closet, took out the aluminum case. Inside, secured against the egg-crate foam lining, were four firearms. All the weapons were perfectly maintained, fully loaded. She selected a Glock 17, which she carried in a Chek-Mate security holster on her right hip, along with a Beretta 21, which she wore in an Apache ankle rig.

She slipped into her outfit, buttoned her blazer, checked herself in the full-length mirror. She proclaimed herself ready. Just after 1 AM, she stepped into the hall.

Eve Galvez turned to look at her nearly empty apartment, a rush of icy melancholy overtaking her heart. She had once had so much.

She closed the door, locked the deadbolt, walked down the hallway. A few moments later she crossed the lobby, pushed through the glass doors, and stepped into the warm Philadelphia night.

For the last time.

FIVE

The Forensic Science Center, commonly referred to as the crime lab, was located at Eighth and Poplar streets, just a few blocks from the Roundhouse. The 40,000-square-foot facility was responsible for analysis of all physical evidence collected by the PPD during the course of an investigation. In its various divisions, it performed analysis in three major categories: trace evidence, such as paint, fibers, or gunshot residue; biological evidence, including blood, semen, and hair; and miscellaneous evidence, such as fingerprints, documents, and footwear impressions.

The Philadelphia Police Department's Criminalistics Unit maintained itself as a full-service facility, able to perform a wide variety of testing procedures.

Sergeant Helmut Rohmer was the reigning king of the document section. In his early thirties, Rohmer was a giant, standing about six-four, weighing in at 250 pounds, most of it muscle. He had short-cropped hair, dyed so blond it was almost white. On both arms were an elaborate web of tattoos—many of them a variation on red roses, white roses, and the name Rose. Vegetation and petals snaked around his huge biceps. At PPD functions—especially the Police Athletic League gatherings. Helmut Rohmer was big on PAL—no one had ever seen him with a person named Rose or Rosie or Rosemary, so the subject was scrupulously avoided. His standard outfit was black jeans, Doc Martens, and sleeveless black sweatshirts. Unless he had to go to court.

Then it was a shiny, narrow-lapelled, navy-blue suit from around the time when REO Speedwagon dotted the charts.

No pocket protectors or dingy lab coats here—Helmut Rohmer looked like a roadie for Metallica, or a Frank Miller rendering of a Hell's Angel. But when the sergeant spoke, he sounded like Johnny Mathis. He insisted you call him Hell, even going so far as signing his internal memos "From Hell." No one dared argue or object.

"This is a fairly common edition of the *New Oxford*," Hell said. "It's available everywhere. I have the same edition at home." The book sat on the gleaming stainless table, opened to the copyright page. "This particular publication was printed in the early seventies, but you can find it in just about any used-book store in the country, including college bookstores, Half Price Books, everywhere."

"Is there any way to trace where it may have been purchased?" Jessica asked.

"I'm afraid not."

The book's cover had been dusted for prints. None were found. It would take a lot longer, and prove far more difficult, to check the pages themselves, seeing as there were more than fifteen hundred of them.

"What do you make of the Shiloh message?" Jessica asked.

Hell placed an index finger to his lips. Jessica noticed for the first time that his fingernails were well-manicured, their clear polish reflecting the overhead fluorescents in straight silvery lines. "Well, I ran *Shiloh* through the databases and the search engines. Nothing significant in the databases, but I did get hits on Google and Yahoo, of course. Lots of them. As in tons and tons."

"Such as?" Jessica asked.

"Well, a lot of them had to do with that 1996 kid's movie. It had Rod Steiger in it, and the guy who was in *In Cold Blood*. What was his name?"

"Robert Blake?" Jessica asked.

"No. The other guy in the movie. The light-haired guy. The con man who bounces the check for the suit."

"Scott Wilson," Byrne said.

"Right."

Jessica glanced at Byrne, but he refused to look at her. It was a matter of pop-culture principle, she figured. Sometimes Kevin Byrne's knowledge astounded her. On a bar bet, he once rattled off the entire discography of The Eagles, and Kevin Byrne didn't even care too much for The Eagles. He was a Thin Lizzy, Corrs, Van Morrison man—not to mention his near-slavish devotion to old blues. On the other hand, she'd once caught him singing the first verse of "*La Vie en Rose*" at a crime scene. In French. Kevin Byrne did not speak French.

"Anyway," Hell said. "This *Shiloh* movie was a little schmaltzy, but it was still kind of cute. Beagle-in-jeopardy type thing. We just rented it a few months ago. Scratchy DVD, froze up a few times. Drives me frickin' nuts when that happens. Gotta go Blu-ray and soon. But my daughter loved it."

Jessica thought, *Daughter? Could this be the legendary Rose?* "I didn't know you had a daughter, Hell," she said, probing.

Hell beamed. In a flash, he had out his wallet, flipped open to a photograph of an adorable little blond girl sitting on a park bench, hugging the hell out of a black Labrador puppy. *Crushing* the puppy was more like it. Maybe the kid worked out with her dad.

"This is Donatella," Hell said. "She is my heart."

So much for Rose, Jessica thought. "She's a doll."

Byrne looked at the picture, nodded, smiled. Despite the tough-cop pose, Jessica knew Kevin Byrne was complete mush around little girls. He carried at least four pictures of his daughter Colleen at all times.

Hell slipped the photo back into his wallet, trousered it. "Then there's the Shiloh reference in the Bible, of course."

"What's that about?" Jessica asked.

"Well, if memory serves—and it quite often does—Shiloh was the name of a shrine that Moses built in the wilderness. Lots of wilderness in the Bible." Hell flipped a few pages of his notebook. Jessica noticed that there were hand-drawn roses in the margins. "Then there's the Civil War battle of Shiloh, which was also known as the Battle of Pittsburg Landing."

Jessica glanced once again at her partner. Pittsburgh, Pennsylvania, the second largest city in the commonwealth, was three hundred miles west of Philly. Byrne shook his head, emphasizing to Jessica how little she knew about the Civil War, or American history in general.

"Not what you think," Hell said, picking up on the exchange. "Shiloh is in western Tennessee. Nothing to do with Pittsburgh, PA."

"Anything else pop up?" Jessica asked, anxious to move on.

"Nothing really jumped off the screen. I ran the numbers 4514 and got more than six million hits. Can you believe that? Six *million*. My first thought was that the four numbers could be the last part of a phone number." Hell flipped through a few more of his notes. "I took the first three letters of Shiloh—S-H-I—and used them as a prefix, which is 744 on the phone. There is no Philly phone number using that designation. I widened the search to include area codes in Pennsylvania, Delaware, and New Jersey. Ditto. It's not a phone number."

"But you think it was something we were supposed to find, right?" Jessica asked. This sort of thing was not the purview of CSU, but Hell was one of the brightest people Jessica knew. It never hurt to get a second, third, and fourth opinion.

Hell smiled. "Well, I'm no detective," he began. He glanced at the photographs of the refrigerator and kitchen at the Second Street crime scene. "But if grilled under hot lights and deprived of *Dancing With the Stars* reruns, I would say we were *definitely* supposed to find this. I mean, Jeremiah Crosley? Puh-freakin'-*leeze*. It's clever, but it's not that clever. On the other hand, maybe that's the point. Maybe it's just clever enough to be intriguing, but not so difficult that it would go over the heads of us big dumb cops."

Jessica had, of course, considered this. They were supposed to find this Bible, and the message inside was the second part of the riddle.

"So I'm thinking this might be an address," Hell said.

"A street address?" Jessica asked. "Here in Philly?"

"Yeah," Hell said. "There's a Shiloh Street here, you know."

Jessica glanced at Byrne. Byrne shrugged. Apparently, he had never heard of it either. Philly was a small city in a lot of ways, but there were a hell of a lot streets. You could never know them all.

"Where is this Shiloh Street?" Jessica asked.

"North Philly," Hell said. "Badlands."

Of course, Jessica thought.

Hell typed a few keystrokes on his laptop. His big fingers nimbly flew across the keys. Seconds later Google Maps appeared on the screen. Hell entered the street address. Soon the image began to zoom in, stopping at a map view of North Philly. A few more keystrokes yielded a fairly tight picture of a handful of city blocks just south of Allegheny Avenue between Fourth and Fifth streets. Hell clicked on the small "+" sign in the corner. The image zoomed in again. A green arrow pointed at the triangular rooftop of a small corner building

"There it is," Hell said. "Voy-*la*. 4514 Shiloh Street."

Hell tapped another key, switched to satellite view, which eliminated the street names, rendering a photographic image.

From the aerial view, the address appeared to be either a row house or a commercial space at the end of the block. Gray and ugly and undistinguished. No trees. Jessica rarely saw her city from above. This part looked so desolate her heart ached. She glanced at Byrne. "What do you think?"

Byrne scanned the image, his deep-green eyes roaming the surface of the monitor. "I think we're being worked. I hate being worked."

Hell gently closed the book, then opened it again, flipping open just the front cover. "I ran a hair dryer over the inside front endpaper," he said. "Many times people will open a book with their fingers on the outside, and right thumb on the inside. If the front cover was wiped down—and I believe it was—maybe they forgot to—"

Hell stopped talking. His eyes fixed on a slight bump in the lower left-hand corner of the inside front cover, a right angle that lifted an edge.

"What have we *here*?" Hell said.

He opened a drawer, removed a gleaming pair of stainless steel tweezers, clicked them three times. It seemed like a ritual.

"What is it?" Byrne asked.

"Hang on."

Hell wielded the tweezers like a heart surgeon. He grabbed the endpaper, began to slowly strip it back. Soon, it became apparent that there was something underneath. It appeared that someone had already peeled back the endpaper, inserted something, then re-glued it.

Hell took a deep breath, exhaled, continued to peel back the endpaper. Beneath it was a thin piece of cardboard. Hell gently removed it with the tweezers, put it on the table. It was a white rectangle, about three inches by five inches. The paper had a watermark on it. Hell flipped it over.

The cardboard rectangle was a color photograph. A picture of a teenage girl.

Jessica felt the temperature in the room jump a few degrees, along with the level of anxiety. The mysteries were starting to progress geometrically.

The girl in the picture was white, somewhat overweight, about sixteen. She had long auburn hair, brown eyes, a small cleft in her chin. The photo appeared to be a printout of a digital picture. She wore a red sweater with sequins along the neckline, large hoop earrings, and a striking onyx teardrop pendant necklace.

Hell spun in place, twice, both fists raised in anger, his huge rubber-soled boots squeaking on the tile. "I didn't think to look. I hate that, man," he said, calmly, even as a fiery crimson rose from his neck onto his face like the column in a cheap thermometer.

"No harm no foul," Byrne said. "We have it now."

"Yeah, well, I am still upset. I am really, *really* upset."

Jessica and Byrne had dealt with Hell Rohmer on a number of cases. It was best to wait out moments like this. Eventually, he calmed down, his face cooling to a hot pink.

"Can we get a copy of this?" Byrne finally asked. It was rhetorical, but it was the best way to go.

Hell stared at the Bible, as if the suspect might jump out of the binding, like a figure in a child's pop-up book, and he could choke him to death. It was well-known in the department that you didn't fuck with Helmut Rohmer's psyche. A few seconds later he snapped out of it. "A copy? Oh yeah. Absolutely."

Hell put the photograph in a clear evidence bag, walked it over to the color copying machine. He punched a few buttons—hard—then waited, hands on hips, for the photocopy to emerge, adrift in that place where frustrated criminalists go. A few seconds later, the page presented itself. Hell handed it to Jessica.

Jessica looked closely at the image. The girl in the photograph was not Caitlin O'Riordan. She was someone new. A person who stared out at the world with an innocence that begged for experience. Jessica was overcome by the feeling that this girl never got the chance.

Jessica put the photocopy of the photograph in her portfolio. "Thanks," she said. "Keep us in the loop, okay?"

Hell didn't respond. He was gone, adrift on the tangents of hard evidence, juddering with anger. Criminalists didn't like to be played any more than detectives did. Hell Rohmer even less than most.

Ten minutes later Detectives Jessica Balzano and Kevin Byrne headed to 4514 Shiloh Street, the photograph of the auburn-haired girl on the car seat between them, like a silent passenger.

SIX

Aᴎᴏᴛʜᴇʀ Nᴏʀᴛʜ Pʜɪʟʟʏ ʜᴇʟʟʜᴏʟᴇ; ᴀ ɢʀɪᴍ ᴀɴᴅ ᴅᴇᴄᴀʏɪɴɢ ᴛʜʀᴇᴇ-story building, the corner structure in a block of five.

At the entrance to the left of the Shiloh Street address was a memorial. There were memorials all over North Philly, commemorations of the departed. Some were a simple spray painted "RIP" above the victim's name or nickname. Others were elaborate, highly detailed portraits of the victim, many times in a benevolent pose, sometimes flashing a gang signal, sometimes two or three times actual scale. Almost all honored victims of street violence.

This memorial was to a young child. In the recess of the doorway was a small, delaminating nightstand stuffed with plush teddy bears, rabbits, ducks, birds. It always struck Jessica as odd how, at North Philly memorials, items could be left on the street, items that everyday were shoplifted from Wal-Mart and Rite Aid. They were never stolen from a memorial. Memorials were sacred.

A piece of plywood was nailed over the door of this commemorative display, painted with the words *Descanse en Paz*. Rest in peace. On the wall to the left of the door was a beautiful airbrushed portrait of a smiling Hispanic girl. A silver Christmas garland ringed the painting. Beneath it sat a red plastic juice pitcher full of dusty satin tulips. Above the girl's head was scrawled *Florita Delia Ramos, 2004–2008*.

Four years old, Jessica thought. Unless the city moved in and painted the wall over—an unlikely scenario, seeing as how the memorial was the only vestige of beauty left on this blighted block—the portrait would live longer than its subject did.

Jessica glanced at Byrne. He had his hands in his pockets. He was looking the other way. Jessica understood. Sometimes you had to look away.

RIP Florita.

TWENTY MINUTES LATER, Byrne and a quartet of uniformed officers entered the building and began to clear the structure. While they were inside, Jessica crossed the street to a bodega. She bought a half dozen strong coffees.

When Byrne emerged from the row house, Jessica handed him a cup. The rest of the team found their coffees, and Tastykakes, on the hood of the car.

"Anything?" Jessica asked.

Byrne nodded. "A whole houseful of trash."

"Anything we want to look at?"

Byrne thought for a moment, sipped his coffee. "Probably."

Jessica considered the chain of events, the geography. Here was the dilemma: Do you pull a few officers off other investigations to start searching a building for a needle in a haystack? Were they chasing ghosts, or did this address actually have something to do with the murder of Caitlin O'Riordan?

My name is Jeremiah Crosley.

"What do you think, detective?" Byrne asked.

Jessica looked up at the third floor. She thought of Caitlin dead inside a building not all that different from this one. She thought of the human heart in that specimen jar. She thought of all the evil she had seen, and how it always led to a place of unremitting darkness. A place like this.

The heart is deceitful above all things and beyond cure.

She called for a CSU team.

AN HOUR LATER, while Byrne returned to the Roundhouse to check the photograph of the dark-haired girl against recent missing-persons files,

Jessica stood in the stifling hallway just outside the kitchen at the Shiloh Street address.

Byrne had been right. There was a houseful of junk. Hefty bags and loose garbage were crammed into the corners of the kitchen, bathroom, and dining area, as well as almost filling the three small rooms upstairs.

Strangely, the basement was almost empty. Just a few boxes and a moldy eight-by-ten faux-Persian area rug on the floor, perhaps a 1980s attempt at haute décor. Jessica took pictures of every room.

There had to be ten thousand flies in the house. Maybe more. The buzz was a maddening background hum. Between swatting the flies away and the incessant teeming, it was nearly impossible to think. Jessica began to believe this search was a pointless exercise.

"Detective Balzano?"

Jessica turned. The officer asking the question was a fit and tanned young woman, early twenties, about an inch shorter than Jessica's five-eight. She had clear brown eyes, almost amber. A lock of lustrous brunette hair escaped her cap. In the heat, it was all but plastered to her smooth forehead.

Jessica knew the look, the plight. She'd been there herself, many times, back in the day. It was August—add a Kevlar vest, the dark blue of the uniform, along with what, at times, seemed like a fifty-pound belt—and it was like working in a sauna, clad in medieval armor.

Jessica glanced at the officer's nametag. M. CARUSO.

"What's your first name, Officer Caruso?"

"Maria," the young woman said.

Jessica smiled. She had almost guessed. Maria was Jessica's late mother's name. Jessica had always had a soft spot for anyone named Maria. "What's up?"

"Well, there's a lot of stuff upstairs," she said. "Boxes, trash bags, old suitcases, sacks of dirty clothes, a couple of mattresses, tons of drug paraphernalia."

"No bodies, I hope," Jessica said with what she hoped was a little dark humor. This place was incredibly bleak.

"No bodies *yet*," Officer Caruso replied, matching the tone. She was sharp. "But there is a *lot* of stuff.

"I understand," Jessica said. "We have time."

In situations like this, Jessica was always careful to use the word *we*. She recalled her days in uniform, and how that word—uttered by some ancient detective of thirty or so, usually over some incredibly brutal scene of urban carnage—meant catching the bad guys was a joint effort. It mattered.

For a moment, Officer Maria Caruso looked nervous.

"Is something wrong?" Jessica asked.

"No, ma'am. It's just that I heard you and Detective Byrne were investigating the Caitlin O'Riordan case."

"We are," Jessica said. "Do you recall the case?"

"Quite well, ma'am. I remember when she was found."

Jessica just nodded.

"I have family in Lancaster County," Officer Caruso added. "Caitlin's family lives about forty miles from my aunt and cousins. I remember the picture that was in the paper. I remember the case like yesterday."

Caitlin, Jessica thought. This young officer called the victim by her first name. She wondered just how personal this case was to her.

Jessica took out the photograph of Caitlin O'Riordan, the one Caitlin's family had supplied to the FBI. Over her shoulder was a faded lilac knapsack with pink appliquéd butterflies. "This is the picture you remember?" she asked.

"Yes, ma'am." Officer Caruso turned toward the window for a moment, covering her emotions. Jessica understood. Philly tough.

"Mind if I ask where you're from?" Jessica asked.

"Tenth and Morris."

Jessica nodded. People in Philadelphia were either from neighborhoods or intersections. Mostly both. "South Philly girl."

"*Oh*, yeah. Born and bred."

"I grew up at Sixth and Catharine."

"I know." Officer Caruso adjusted her belt, cleared her throat. She seemed a little embarrassed. "I mean, y'know, I *heard* that."

"Did you go to Goretti?"

"Oh, yeah," she said. "I was a Goretti Gorilla."

Jessica smiled. They had a lot in common. "If you need anything, let me know."

The young woman beamed. She tucked that loose strand of dark hair back into her cap. "Thank you, Detective."

With an energy known only to the young, Officer Maria Caruso turned on her heels, and walked back up the steps.

Jessica watched her, wondering if this life was a good choice or a bad choice for the young woman. Didn't matter really, there was probably no way Maria Caruso could be talked out of it. Once you started catching criminals, Jessica knew, there was little else you were good for.

BYRNE WALKED THROUGH THE FRONT DOOR into the hallway. After returning from the Roundhouse, he had conducted a brief neighborhood survey.

"Anything?" Jessica asked.

Byrne shook his head. "Incredibly, no one on this block has ever seen or heard of a crime being committed at this or any other location."

"And yet there's a memorial to a dead little girl right next door."

"And yet."

"Any hits with missing persons?"

"Nothing so far," Byrne said.

Jessica crossed the kitchen to the other side of the counter. She tapped her fingernails on the worn Formica, just for effect. She was turning into *such* a drama queen of late, taking her cues from her six-year-old daughter. Jessica had stopped chewing her nails a year or so earlier—a bad habit she'd maintained since her childhood—and only recently started to get them done at a Northeast salon called Hands of Time. Her nails were short, they had to be for her job, but they looked good. For once. This month they were amethyst. How girly-girl can you get? Sophie Balzano approved. Kevin Byrne hadn't yet said a word.

A uniformed officer stepped into the row house. "Detective Byrne?"

"Yeah."

"Fax came in for you." He handed Byrne an envelope.

"Thanks." Byrne opened it and pulled out a single sheet fax, read it.

"What's up?" Jessica asked.

"Ready for your day to get a little bit better?"

Jessica's eyes lit up like a toddler hearing a Jack and Jill ice cream truck coming down the street. "We're going swimming?"

"Not *that* much better," Byrne said. "But a slight improvement."

"I'm ready."

"I called Paul DiCarlo and asked if he could put someone at the DA's office on tracking down the ownership of this property."

"What did they find?"

"Nothing. Nobody's paid taxes on the place in years."

"And this is good news why?"

"I'm getting there. Paul reached out to a guy at L & I, and the guy said that once a month, for the last five months, he's gotten an anonymous call about this address. He said the same caller went on and on about how the building should be torn down."

The Philadelphia Department of Licenses and Inspections was responsible for the enforcement of the city's building code. It was also empowered to demolish vacant buildings that posed a threat to public safety.

"Do we have any information on the caller?" Jessica asked.

Byrne handed her the fax. "We do. The guy at L & I had caller ID. After the fifth call he wrote the number down."

Jessica read it. The phone number was registered to a Laura A. Somerville. The address was on Locust Street. From the street number it looked to be in West Philadelphia.

Jessica glanced up the stairs, at the CSU officers who were beginning the slow, arduous task of sifting through what had to be years of trash. She wondered what might be up there, what crimes might be concealed, asking for closure.

She'd be back. Somehow, she was sure of it.

The two detectives signed off the crime-scene log, and headed to West Philly.

SEVEN

EVE ORDERED A CHEESEBURGER AND FRIES AT THE MIDTOWN IV RES-taurant, a 24-hour place on Chestnut, catching glances and lewd looks from the night boys. The air in the room was a mixture of summer sweat, coffee, frying onions. Eve glanced at her watch. It was 2:20. The place was packed. She spun on her stool, considered the crowd. A young couple, early twenties, sat on the same side of a nearby booth. In your twenties you sat on the same side, Eve thought. In your thirties, you sat on opposite sides, but still talked. In your forties and beyond, you brought a newspaper.

At 2:40 a shadow appeared to her right. Eve turned. The girl was about fifteen, still carrying a layer of baby fat. She had an angelic face, street-hardened eyes. She wore faded jeans, a faux-leather jacket with a fake fur collar, and bright white New Balance sneakers, about an hour out of the box.

"Hey," Eve said.

The girl scrutinized her. "Hey."

"Are you Cassandra?"

The girl glanced around. She racked her shoulders, sniffled. "Yeah."

"Nice to meet you." Eve had gotten Cassandra's name from a street kid named Carlito. The word was that Cassandra had been abducted. Eve had dropped a pair of twenties and the word was passed.

"Yeah. Um. You too."

"Want to get a booth?" Eve asked.

The girl shook her head. "I'm not going to be here that long."

"Okay. Are you hungry?"

Another shake of the head, this time with hesitation. She was hungry, but too proud to take a handout.

"Okay." Eve stared at the girl for a few silent moments, the girl stared back, neither of them knowing how to start.

A few seconds later Cassandra slipped onto the stool next to Eve, and began.

CASSANDRA TOLD HER the whole story. More than once Eve got goose flesh. The story was not unlike her own. Different era, different shadows. Same horrors. As the girl talked, Eve stole glances at Cassandra's hands. They were alternately trembling and formed into tight fists.

For the past two months Eve had felt she was getting nearer the truth, but it had always been in her head. Now it was in her heart.

"Can you point out the house to me?" Eve asked.

The girl seemed to shrink away from her. She shook her head. "No. Sorry. I can't do that. I can tell you just about where it is, but I can't show you."

"Why not?"

The girl hesitated. She put her hands in her jacket pockets. Eve wondered what she had in there. "I just . . . can't, that's all. I can't."

"You don't have to be afraid," Eve said. "There's nothing to be afraid of now."

The girl issued a humorless laugh. "I don't think you understand."

"Understand what?"

For a moment, Eve thought the girl was going to leave without another word. Then, haltingly, Cassandra said, "I'm not going back there. I can't *ever* go back there."

Eve studied the girl. Her heart nearly broke. The girl had the haunted look of the ever-vigilant, the ever-cautious, someone who never slept, never let down her guard. She was a mirror image of Eve at the same age.

Eve knew her next question would not be answered. It never was. She asked anyway. "Can I ask why you didn't go to the police?"

Cassandra looked at the floor. "I have my reasons."

"All right," Eve said. "I understand. Trust me. I really do." She reached into her pocket, palmed a fifty, slid it across the counter, lifted a finger.

The girl looked down, stared at the corner of the bill for a few seconds, then glanced up at Eve. "I don't need it."

Eve was shocked. Street kids did not turn down money. Something else was at work here. She could not imagine what it might be. "What are you talking about?"

"I don't want the money. I'm okay."

"Are you sure?"

A long pause. The girl nodded.

Eve put the bill back in her pocket. She glanced around the restaurant. No one was watching. No one ever did at the all-nighters. She glanced back at the girl. "What can I do for you?" she asked. "You have to let me do something for you."

The girl drummed her fingers on the countertop for a few seconds, then picked up Eve's cheeseburger, wrapped it in a paper napkin, shoved it in her pocket. She also grabbed a handful of Equal packets. She spun on her stool, seemingly ready to bolt, then stopped, looked back over her shoulder. "I'll tell you what you can do for me," she said. Her eyes were rimmed with tears. Her face was a mask of fear. Or maybe it was shame.

"What's that?"

"You can kill him."

Three thirty.

The huge house was on a quiet street. It looked just as the girl had described it—overgrown with weeds, tangled with shrubbery, gnarled with dying trees. Vines hung from the gutters; dead ivy clung to the north side like black veins. Three stories in height, clad in dark orange brick, it squatted on a large corner lot, all but hidden from the street. A stone balcony wrapped around the second floor, looming over a crumbling stone porch. Four chimneys probed the night sky like a thumbless hand.

Eve circled the block twice, out of caution, habit, training. She parked fifty feet from the gated driveway, killed the engine and headlights. She listened, waited, watched. Nothing moved on the street.

Three fifty.

Eve flipped open her cell phone, and before she could stop herself she pressed the number, speed-dialing it for the first time. It was a mistake, but she did it anyway. The line rang once, twice. Eve's finger hovered over the red END button.

A few seconds later, the phone on the other end clicked on. A lifetime went by.

"Hi," Eve finally said.

FIVE MINUTES LATER Eve clicked off. She had said much more than she had intended, but she felt good, strong. Cleansed. She tapped her right front jeans pocket, where her courage lived. She took out the pill vial, shook out two Valium. She uncapped the pint of Wild Turkey, sipped from it, capped the bottle, looked around.

This small section of Philadelphia had a neighborhood name, the way almost all sections of Philadelphia did, but this one wouldn't come to her. It was a small enclave of old, hidden houses, just west of the Oak Lane Reservoir.

She stepped out of the car, into the torrid, cloudless night. Philadelphia was quiet. Philadelphia dreamed.

Eve crossed the street, walked down the sidewalk toward the corner, skirting the iron fence. Beyond the fence the huge house loomed in the darkness, its dormers rising into the sky like devil's horns. Tortured trees obscured the walls.

As she got closer she saw lights in the windows on the first floor. She reached a gate, pushed on it. It moaned. It was almost a human sound. She pushed again, slipped through.

When she stepped onto the grounds, the feeling overwhelmed her. She felt it, *smelled* it. Evil dwelled here. Her heart raced.

She slowly made her way through the tall grass, moving ever closer;

the undergrowth, the bushes and weeds and wildflowers, seemed to grow around her. A large evergreen stood twenty feet from the house. She stepped behind it.

The house was massive. It appeared to be a pastiche of architectural styles—Queen Anne, Italianate, Gothic revival. A half-round tower graced the right side. A room on the second floor appeared to be candlelit. Chalky shadows danced on the white sheer curtains. As she drew closer, Eve heard classical music.

She took a few more steps, stopping fifteen feet from the dining room window. The drapes were open. Inside a dozen candles flickered. She could see the buffet and hutch and sideboard, all heavy antiques, all highly polished. On the walls were enormous oil paintings; hellish, Boschian scenes. There were also a pair of large portraits of a dark-haired man with sinister, intense eyes, a Van Dyck goatee. No one stirred.

Eve circled the mansion to the east. There she found a small gazebo, a pair of stone benches covered in ivy; a rusted sundial stood guard on a weed-tufted path. As she rounded the back of the house she paused, listened. There was a sound, a low humming sound. Then a snick of metal on metal.

What was it?

She cocked her head, tuning to the noise. It wasn't coming from the house or the garages to her right. For a moment it reminded her of the old elevators in the building where her father had once had his office. The sound seemed to rattle the ground beneath her feet.

It stopped.

The voice came from behind her.

"Welcome to Faerwood."

Eve drew the Glock, spun around, the weapon leveled in front of her. A man stood in the small gazebo, about twenty feet away. He was in shadows, but Eve saw he wore a long coat. For a few endless moments he did not move or say another word.

Eve slipped her finger inside the trigger guard. Before she could respond, a bright yellow light shimmered overhead. She glanced at the window on the second floor. It was barred. The curtains parted to reveal a silhouette, a girl with narrow shoulders and long hair. Eve looked back at the man.

"It's you, isn't it?" she asked.

The man stepped into the moonlight. He was not as big as she had expected. She had anticipated a hulking ogre. Instead, he was sleek and lithe, almost elegant. "Yes," he answered.

He slowly raised his right hand, palm upward, as if in blessing. In an instant there was a searing flash of flame and a cloud of white smoke.

Eve fired. Round after round pierced the air, the loud reports echoing off the hard brick surface of the old house. She kept pulling the trigger until the magazine was empty.

The night fell still. Eve heard the beating of her heart, felt the horror of what she had just done. She knew she had hit him, dead center in his chest. Four rounds at least. She knew she had to run, but she also knew that she had come too far not to see this to the very end. She holstered her weapon, stepped cautiously to the gazebo. In the moonlight the gun smoke lingered, painting a white haze over this surreal scene. Eve peered over the railing.

He was gone. There was no blood, no torn flesh, no body. It didn't seem possible—it wasn't possible—but the gazebo was empty.

It all began to close in on her. The last two months of her life had been pure madness, a summons to the grave. She understood that now. She turned and ran through the tall weeds and grass.

Moments later she reached the iron gate. She pulled on the handle. It wouldn't budge. It seemed rusted shut. She looked around her, sweat streaming down her face, burning her eyes. Was this where she came in? She couldn't remember. She had gotten turned around and she had lost her bearings. She pulled again on the gate. It finally moved. She might be able to squeeze through, she thought. She tried, ripping her jeans on the latch. She felt the tear of flesh on her right thigh. The pain was excruciating.

One more hard pull, giving it everything she had. The gate swung free.

And that's when she felt the hand on her shoulder.

Eve spun, saw his eyes. At first they flashed liquid silver, mercury in the moonlight, then all the fires of hell burned inside them. They were the eyes of her nightmare.

As Eve Galvez reached for the Beretta in her ankle holster she heard the snap of breaking glass. Then came a strong chemical smell. In the instant before her world went black she knew it had all come to a close.

Mr. Ludo.

He had won the game.

EIGHT

The Denison was a ten-story U-shaped apartment building on Locust Street in West Philadelphia, near Forty-third Street, not far from the main campus of the University of Pennsylvania. The building was an exhaust-ravaged bronze-colored brick, built in the 1930s, with a recently sandblasted white sandstone arched entrance and electric flambeaux flanking its glass front doors. The long flower beds leading up to the doorway were baked and cracked and arid, populated with wilting impatiens, dying salvia, dead begonias, spent lobelia.

Like the old joke went: In Philly, in August, you couldn't just fry an egg on the sidewalk, you could fry the chicken.

Jessica and Byrne entered the building, crossed the lobby. It was five degrees cooler in here, which meant the temperature was a frigid eighty-five degrees or so. They had called the address in, checked the results against the roster of tenants in the lobby. Laura A. Somerville lived in apartment 1015. She did not have a police record or DMV record. In fact, she did not have a record of any kind.

For some reason, Jessica expected Laura Somerville to be a middle-aged career woman, a real estate developer, perhaps a lawyer. When the woman opened the door, Jessica was surprised to find that Laura Somerville was a rather elegant older woman, probably in her late sixties: powdered and lightly perfumed, classically attired in pleated gray cotton slacks and white blouse. Silver-coiffed and graceful, she reminded Jessica of one of those women who had looked fifty at forty, but would look fifty the rest of her life. Lauren Bacall type.

Jessica produced her ID and badge, introduced herself and Kevin.

"Are you Laura A. Somerville?" Jessica asked.

"Yes."

"We'd like to ask you a few questions," Jessica said. "Would that be okay?"

The woman put a hand to her throat. She looked at a point in space somewhere between the two detectives. Her eyes were a clear sapphire. "Is something wrong?"

"No, ma'am," Jessica said, hedging the truth. "Just a few routine questions."

The woman hesitated, then seemed to relax, the tension leaving her shoulders. She nodded, and without another word opened the door fully. She gestured them inside, closed the door behind them.

The apartment was blessedly cool. Almost cold. Jessica wanted to spend the rest of the summer here. Maybe the rest of her life. It smelled of jasmine tea.

"Can I get you something cold to drink?" the woman asked. "Soda? Lemonade?"

"We're fine, thanks," Byrne said.

Jessica glanced around the small, tastefully decorated apartment. It was a room full of older furniture. In one corner was a hutch full of sparkling figurines; the opposite wall held a long bookcase, crowded with books and boxes that appeared to contain games and jigsaw puzzles.

In front of the burgundy leather nailhead couch was an oak coffee table covered with magazines. Not covered exactly, Jessica realized, but *tiled* with magazines. Geometrically precise. Ten magazines, all opened, perfectly arranged, parallel and squared to each other. Two rows: five up, five below. Jessica looked at them a little more closely and discovered they were all crossword puzzle magazines. A pen lay on top of each, crossing the rectangle of off-white paper and black ink at a precise forty-five-degree angle. Ten magazines, ten pens.

"Wow," Jessica began. "You must be a serious crossword puzzle fan."

The woman waved a delicate, long-fingered hand. "*Way* beyond fan, I'm afraid," she said. She crossed the space, eased herself onto the couch. Jessica noticed that the woman's nails were done in the French manicure style. "Beyond addiction, even."

"Beyond addiction?" Jessica asked. As a police officer she had encountered every kind of addict there was—drugs, booze, sex, gambling, porn, food. She didn't know what the next level could be.

The woman nodded. "You see, the word 'addiction' hints at a cure."

Jessica smiled. She stepped closer, and now saw that the magazines were published in what appeared to be ten different languages. All the puzzles were at some stage of completion.

Jessica was stunned. *Who does this?*

She glanced over at her partner, and noticed that Byrne seemed captivated by an elaborate display of brightly colored boxes on the bookshelves.

"I see you are intrigued with my collection," the woman said to Byrne. "It is not very extensive, but it is well-balanced."

"I feel like a kid in here."

Laura Somerville smiled. "As George Bernard Shaw once said, 'We don't stop playing because we grow old, we grow old because we stop playing.' "

Men and games, Jessica thought. Her husband Vincent—a fellow PPD detective working out of Narcotics Field Unit North—was exactly the same way.

"What is this?" Byrne held up a beautiful white box. About six inches square, it appeared to be carved ivory. Whatever it was, it was old and delicate, probably a collectible.

The woman crossed the room, gently took the box from Byrne's big hands—in a manner suggesting that it *was* both rare and expensive—and put it down on a sideboard.

"This is called a tangram puzzle," she said.

Byrne nodded. "Never heard of it."

"It is quite intriguing," the woman said. "One of my passions." She reached over, turned up a small latch on the box, and gently opened it to reveal seven small, intricately carved pieces of ivory, seven geometric shapes snugly tucked inside: five triangles of varying sizes, one square, one rhombus. Or maybe it was a parallelogram. Jessica hadn't done all that well in geometry.

"It's about three thousand years old," she said. "The puzzle," she added with a wink. "Not this edition."

"It's Chinese?" Byrne asked.

"The origin of the puzzle itself is in some doubt," she continued. "It is most *likely* Chinese, although many Oriental games were really invented in Europe, then credited to the Orient in an attempt to make them seem more exotic."

"It's a jigsaw?"

"No, it's what's known as a rearrangement puzzle," the woman said. "Rearrangement puzzles go back to Loculus Archimedes in the third century B.C. Or thereabouts." She took one of the pieces from the box, held it up to the light. The ivory triangle shimmered small rainbows across the room. "This particular set was purchased at the Portobello Road market in London," she added. "By an old suitor."

Jessica saw a pastel glow rise in the woman's cheeks. Old suitors sometimes did that to a woman's memory.

"What's the point of the exercise?" Byrne asked.

Jessica had to smile. Kevin Byrne was an endgame kind of guy. Jessica was all about the rules. It was one of the reasons they clicked as partners.

"The point of the *puzzle* is to solve it, young man," Laura Somerville said. "To rearrange the pieces to match a diagram."

Byrne grinned broadly. "Okay," he said. "I'm game."

The woman stared at Byrne for a moment, as if she had just been challenged. The word *game* seemed to bring her alive. "Are you?"

Byrne blushed a little. It was the Irish curse. Get cornered or challenged, you went red. Even the toughest of the tough.

Jessica wanted to get down to business, but Kevin Byrne was better at gauging when someone was ready to talk. This woman was not a threat. She was, instead, a cog in the wheel of an investigation. They had time. And it was about sixty-five degrees in here.

"I am," Byrne said.

Laura Somerville reached into a drawer, removed a black velvet mat, placed it on the dining room table. She then carefully arranged the ivory tangram pieces on it. She handled them as if they were the bones of saints.

One square, five triangles, one parallelogram.

Laura then retrieved a tall book from a shelf. It was beautifully bound, thick. "This is a book of games," she said. "It includes a history and collection of tangram. The author lives in Chester County." She flipped through the three hundred or so pages. Page after page had a dozen silhouettes of geometrically shaped items on them—buildings, animals, people, flowers. She stopped at a page near the middle. "For instance, here is a page of problems created by Chien-Yun Chi in about 1855. It is a page of tools and household items."

"All of these shapes are made from just these seven pieces?" Byrne asked.

"Yes."

"Wow." Byrne glanced at the diagram, studied it for a few moments.

She tapped a diagram at the bottom of the page. "This problem is a wedding drinking cup."

Byrne glanced at Laura Somerville, then at the carved ivory pieces. "May I?"

"Oh, by all means," she said.

"I'll be careful," Byrne said. For a big man, he was cautious, precise. Meticulous in his actions. When called for.

Byrne picked up the square and one of the large triangles. He stared at them closely, perhaps gauging their size and shape, their relationship to each other, his eyes darting from the diagram to the remaining pieces on the velvet.

He placed the big square on the velvet, the triangle to the right of it. He stared at the arrangement for a few seconds, then turned the triangle. He grasped two of the smaller triangles, held them over the emerging shape. He placed them on the table, moved them. He repeated this three or four times, his eyes roaming the geography of the puzzle.

A few minutes later, he was done. Jessica looked at both the diagram in the book and the arranged ivory pieces on the table. They were identical.

"Very impressive," Laura said.

"Was this a tough one?" Byrne asked.

"Tough enough."

Byrne beamed. He looked like a kid who had just hit a stand-up triple.

Jessica cleared her throat. "Right, *well*," she said. "Way to go, partner." It was time to get down to business. If they didn't, Kevin Byrne would probably play with the puzzle all day.

Laura Somerville hesitated a moment, then gestured to the chairs in the living room. "Please. Sit down," she said.

"This won't take too long," Jessica said. She took out her notebook, clicked a pen. "How long have you lived at this address?"

"Six years come October."

"Do you live alone?"

"Yes," she said.

"Do you know a young woman named Caitlin O'Riordan?"

The woman asked Jessica to repeat the name. She did. Laura Somerville seemed to think about it for a moment. "I'm sorry, the name doesn't ring a bell."

Jessica took out the photograph, handed it to the woman. "This is Caitlin," she said. "Do you recognize her?"

The woman took the photograph from Jessica, slipped on a pair of rose-tinted bifocals, examined the picture in the bright sunlight streaming through the window overlooking Locust Street. "I'm sorry," she said. "I do not."

Jessica put the photograph away. "Are you familiar with a building at 4514 Shiloh Street?"

"Shiloh Street?"

"Yes ma'am."

"I've never heard of it. Where is it?"

"North Philly."

"No," the woman said. "Sorry."

Jessica and Byrne exchanged a glance. "You're saying you're not familiar with the building?"

The woman looked from Jessica, to Byrne, back to Jessica. "Can you please tell me what this is all about?"

Jessica gave the woman a brief account.

For more than a few seconds, the woman stared at Jessica in what seemed like shocked disbelief. "You're saying the young woman was *murdered*? The young woman in the photograph?"

"Yes," Jessica said. "And I'm afraid there is a connection to this building." Jessica held up the faxed document. "According to the Department of Licenses and Inspections, a series of calls have been placed from your telephone number regarding the building at 4514 Shiloh Street."

The woman stared at the paper, but did not put her glasses back on. She wasn't reading it. "I . . . I don't know anything about this. Anything at all."

"Could someone else have called from this number?"

The woman thought for a moment. "I have a woman come to clean once a month. But she is from Honduras. She doesn't speak much English."

Jessica didn't bother writing this down. She was just about to ask one final question when Laura Somerville said, "Can you excuse me for just one moment?"

"Of course."

The woman rose slowly, crossed the room, entered what Jessica figured to be the apartment's solitary bedroom. She closed the door behind her.

Jessica turned, looked at Byrne, shrugged, palms up and out. Byrne knew what she meant. What she meant was, you cross the city—the concrete canyons of Broad and Market streets, the alleys of North and South Philly—and you really had no idea what was going on behind those walls. Sometimes, you ran across someone who smoked crack and kept their children in a closet. Other times you discovered an elegant woman who lived alone in West Philly, a woman who could do crosswords in ten languages, a woman who had beautifully carved ivory puzzles on her bookshelves, puzzles purchased by a mysterious former suitor on London's Portobello Road.

Jessica stared out the window for a moment, at the heat-shimmered expanse of West Philadelphia. In the distance was a hazy iridescent image of the city.

"What do you think?" Byrne asked, sotto voce.

Jessica considered the question. "I think I don't *know* what to think," she said, matching his low volume. "You?"

"I think this woman doesn't have anything to do with the investigation."

"Then how does that explain the phone calls?"

"I don't know," Byrne said. "Let's leave it open with her."

"Okay. I'll just tell her that—"

Jessica was interrupted by the sound of shattering glass coming from the bedroom. It did not sound like someone dropping a tumbler or plate on the floor. It sounded as if a brick had been thrown through a window. Seeing as they were on the tenth floor, this was unlikely.

Byrne fired a glance at Jessica. *The* glance. They'd been partners for years, had been to hell and back, and there was no mistaking the look.

"Mrs. Somerville?" Byrne called out.

Silence.

Byrne waited a few more moments. "Ma'am?" he asked, a little louder this time. His voice seemed to reverberate between the walls, underscored by the low hum of the air conditioning. "Is everything all right?"

No response.

Byrne walked across the living room, put his ear to the bedroom door. He waited a few moments, listening, then looked back at Jessica, shook his head. He called out once more, even louder.

"Ma'am?"

Nothing.

Byrne took a deep breath, counted off a cop's second, then eased the doorknob to the right. He shouldered open the door, hand touching the grip of his weapon, flanked left, stepped into the room. Jessica followed.

As expected, it was a bedroom. Inside was a four-poster bed, 1950s vintage, as well as a dresser and writing desk, both from the same era. In the far corner was a brocade settee. In addition, there were two nightstands, a cheval mirror, one closet.

But no Laura Somerville.

The room was empty.

The window overlooking Locust Street had been shattered. A handful of glass shards sparkled on the worn carpeting. Broiling air roared inside, a hot and feral breath from hell. The smell of carbon and oil and exhaust filled the small space, along with a dozen different city sounds—traffic, shouts, hip-hop music among them. Beneath those sounds, closer, the CD player on the nightstand softly offered "Witchcraft." It was Sinatra's duet version with Anita Baker.

Jessica turned the CD player off, crossed the bedroom, slowly eased open the bedroom's one closet door. A puff of moth cakes and worn leather and sweet perfume leaked out. Inside was clothing on hangers, boxes, luggage, shoes, folded sweaters. On the bottom shelf were a pair of dusty, teal Samsonite suitcases. Above that, neatly stacked woolen blankets and sheets. To the right, on the top shelf, was what looked like a strong box of some sort.

But no people. The closet was empty.

Jessica closed the door, put her back to it. The two detectives then crossed the room, looked out the window. Below them, more than ten stories to the pavement, Laura Somerville lay on the baking sidewalk of Locust Street. Her head was demolished pulp, her body a jigsaw of ragged ends. From this height her form appeared to be a dark crimson Rorschach. A crowd was already collecting around the gruesome display.

Byrne got on his handset, called for an ambulance.

Jessica glanced at the writing desk in the corner. It was old, not quite an antique, worn, but well maintained. It held a Tiffany-style lamp, a pair of small black-and-white photos in a tarnished silver double-frame. It also bore a vintage Scrabble board. When Jessica looked more closely, she saw that the words on the board had been disturbed. They were off-center, not quite in their squares. A few of the tiles were scattered on the chair and the floor beneath the desk, as if someone had taken letters off the board in a hurry.

"Jess."

Byrne pointed at the windowsill. On the sill were four Scrabble tiles. It appeared to be a hastily spelled word, the wooden letters positioned at oblique angles to one another.

In her mind's eye, Jessica saw Laura Somerville enter this room just a few short moments ago, grab four tiles from her Scrabble board, arrange them on the windowsill, then leap to her death. Suddenly, despite the stifling air rushing in, Jessica was cold.

"Do you have any idea what this means?" she asked.

Byrne stared at the strange configuration a few more seconds. "No."

At that moment a siren erupted, just a few blocks away. Jessica glanced again at the Scrabble tiles on the windowsill.

One word glared back.

Ludo.

Byrne retrieved his phone from his pocket and flipped it open, preparing to call their boss. But before he could complete the call Jessica put her hand on his forearm, stopping him. She sniffed the air.

In addition to the fact that a woman had just leapt one hundred feet to her death—a woman who, until the Philadelphia Police Department had knocked on her door was only marginally connected to a four-month-old homicide investigation, if at all, a case that was growing more cryptic by the second—something else was wrong.

In a moment, Jessica knew. The smell of burning cotton and smoldering hardwood suddenly made her gag.

She looked at Byrne. No words were needed.

The two detectives bolted from the bedroom as the flames began to tear up the drapes, and across the living room.

The apartment was on fire.

NINE

Two hours later Joseph Edmund Swann, thirty-eight, stood in the spacious foyer, listening to the sounds of his house, the skittering echoes of his life: the chime of the Freadwin of Exeter clock, the settling of old, dry joists and rafters, the mournful heave of the summer wind in the eaves. It was his nightly ritual, and he never strayed from the custom. He had always believed that Faerwood was a living thing, an entity with a heart and soul and spirit. He had long ago personified its many faces, given life to its raised panels, its slate tiles and brass fittings, its numerous stone hearths.

Swann was lean and muscular, of average height. He had azure blue eyes, fair hair without yet a single strand of gray, a less than prominent nose.

When he was a child of six, a woman in Galveston—an aging circus acrobat with flame-red tresses and ill-fitting teeth, the portly doyenne of a Hungarian gypsy troupe—had called his profile "androgynous." Joseph had been too young to read anything into this, of course, although the word conjured many things dark and disturbing. In his late childhood years he'd had to fend off myriad advances from both men and women alike, all of questionable character and breeding. In his early teens he had succumbed to the enchantments of an exotic dancer in the French Quarter in New Orleans, a young woman who had afterward referred to him as *oiseau féroce*. It was only years later he had learned this meant *fierce bird*, a word play on his last name it seemed; a comment, perhaps, on his sexual prowess. Or so he had hoped.

Swann was nimble without being athletic, far stronger than he appeared. His choices in clothing tended to the well-tailored and classic, his shoes always scrupulously polished. He was rarely seen in public without a tie. Unless he was hunting. Then he could, and quite often did, blend into the scenery; urban denizen, country gentleman, midnight jogger, suburban dad. He had dedicated each of the house's sixteen closets to a different persona.

This evening Faerwood was ominously quiet. For the moment.

At eight o'clock he prepared himself a modest dinner of center-cut pork chops, braised butternut squash, and fresh mango chutney. He considered opening a bottle of wine but resisted. There was much to do.

For dessert he allowed himself a thin slice of a devilish chocolate *ganache* he had picked up on a whim from Miel Patisserie on Seventeenth Street.

As he savored the cake, he thought about Katja. She did not look healthy. He fed her very well, of course, bathed her, smoothed her skin with the finest emollients money could buy, met *all* her needs religiously. And yet she looked sallow, resigned, *older.*

When he finished the cake, he crossed the great room to the kitchen, placed his dish and fork in the sink, then returned. He selected an LP from the shelf, started the turntable, carefully placed the needle. Soon, the strains of Mozart's *Le Nozze di Figaro* filled the room. He always played "*Dove sono*" when things were about to change.

Before he reached the stairs, the voice thundered up from somewhere deep inside him.

"*Joseph.*"

Swann stopped. The hair rippled on his forearms. "Sir?"

"*Where dwells the effect, Joseph?*"

"The effect is in the mind, sir."

"*And the method?*"

For a few agonizing moments, Swann could not recall the drill. It was a simple exchange, as old as his ability to talk.

"*Joseph?*"

It came to him. "The method is in the soul."

A few moments later, fully returned to the moment, he checked the quality of his breath, the order of his hair, the knot in his tie. He took a few seconds, then climbed the stairs, hesitating briefly on each tread.

When he reached the second floor he walked down the hallway, drew the key from his vest pocket, then unlocked and opened the door to Katja's room.

She was sitting on the bed, staring out the barred window, her thin legs dangling over the side. She was growing so pale. Her eyes were blank and vacant, her wrists and arms were stick thin. She wore a pale blue nightdress. Her feet were bare.

Swann stepped into the room, closed the door behind him, locked it.

"Good evening, my love," he said.

She slowly turned her head. She parted her dry lips, but said nothing.

Swann glanced at the tray on the dresser. For lunch he had made her a Salisbury steak and green peas, real mashed potatoes. She had said weeks ago that real mashed potatoes were her favorite. She hated the Hungry Jack type.

The lunch sat untouched.

"You haven't eaten," he said.

For a few moments Katja just stared, as if she did not recognize him. For a further moment he thought she had not even *heard* him. It got that way near the end. The dreamy look, the soiled sheets, the stuttering. Then, weakly, she said: "I want to go home."

"Home?" He tried to say this as innocently as possible, as if it were some sort of revelation. "Why would you want to go home?"

Katja stared at him, *through* him, her face a blank, gessoed canvas. "It's . . . it's my . . ."

He sat on the bed, next to her. "Your parents? Your family?"

Katja just nodded, slowly. There was none of the vibrancy he had seen that first day, none of zest. On that day she had been a whirlpool of teenaged energy, ready for any challenge, any idea.

He took her hand in his. Her palm felt like desiccated parchment.

"But *I* am taking care of you now, dearest." He reached out, gently stroked her hair. It felt damp and greasy between his fingers. Earlier in the day he had reminded himself to give her a bath. Now there hardly seemed any point. He removed a handkerchief from his pocket, wiped his fingers.

She nodded weakly.

"Think of it, Katja. Of all the people in your life, all your family and friends, have I not been the kindest? I read to you, I feed you, I paint your toenails your favorite color."

The truth was, it was *his* favorite color. Persimmon.

Katja looked toward the window, at the shafts of frail sunlight. She remained silent.

"Drink some tea," he said. "You will feel much better." He stood, crossed the room, lifted the insulated pitcher, poured a cup of tea. It was still warm. He dropped into it a sugar cube. He returned to the bed, sat, stirring, the sound of sterling silver on bone china circling the room.

He got Katja's attention, lifted the cup to her lips. She took a small sip. He dabbed her mouth with a linen napkin.

"You're taking care of me," she said.

Poor Katja. He had tried with her. He had tried so hard with them all.

"Come with me, love." He put the cup and saucer down on the nightstand, extended a hand.

"Where are we going?" she asked.

"Somewhere safe."

Swann thought about the precision-crafted device three floors below them, the box and its seven keen blades.

Katja stood, shaking, her thin legs not quite supporting her. Joseph Swann put a strong arm around her waist. She felt brittle.

"Are you taking me home?" she asked.

He looked into her eyes. He found no trace of the firebrand he had met in the park, the young woman who had so willingly accepted his aid and comfort. All without thanks.

Moments later, they descended the stairway. Mozart filled the house. Three floors below the magic box awaited.

"Yes," Swann said. "I am taking you home."

TEN

KEVIN BYRNE SAT ACROSS FROM THE DENISON APARTMENTS. THE TOP floor of the building, the side facing Locust Street, was smoke blackened, charred. Gnarled ebony fingers caressed the brick façade. The air on the entire block was still dense with carbon.

Byrne was exhausted, but exhaustion was an old friend. He glanced at his watch: 2:15 AM.

Byrne had always suffered from some degree of insomnia, but he had rarely slept more than five or six hours a night since he had become a detective. When he was in uniform he had drawn last-out as often as not, and the schedule of working all night was something the body clock never forgot. The routine and rhythms of sitting in a cramped, airless car at three and four and five in the morning, drinking coffee, eating high-sugar, high-fat foods became the usual, not the exception. Sleep became unnatural. Indigestion and sleeplessness the rule. Byrne did not know one detective on the job for more than twenty years who slept well.

Now the insomnia was invasive and seemingly permanent. Since moving over to SIU, the schedule had been a little easier to predict, and that was both the good news and the bad news, at least as far as the victims were concerned. In SIU there wasn't the heat of a new homicide, the buzz of the immediate chase, the drive to get the forensics and witnesses and collateral personnel lined up in a hurry before your doer got 'way. Cold cases were just that—cold. The dead stayed dead.

Still, when you picked up a scent, Byrne had to admit, if only to his partner, it was the same thrill, the same rush that accompanied that first sniff of the chase you encountered when you were a rookie at twenty-two.

Byrne glanced up at the window, at the smoke-blackened bricks of the top floor of the Denison, the area surrounding apartment 1015. In the sodium streetlights the building was bathed in pale blue. The two windows were large eyes staring down at him, defying him to understand what had happened in that apartment.

Because they were able to make the 911 call early—Byrne had phoned the fire department from just outside Laura Somerville's front door—the fire had destroyed less than half of the space. Much of the apartment had been left virtually intact. There was smoke and water damage to the furniture, the bookcases, the walls, but little else.

Byrne had seen quite a bit in his time on the job. He had seen just about everything a human being could do to another human being, had seen just about everything human beings could do to them*selves*, had encountered every weapon, every opportunity, every motive. Despite his experience, he had to admit that Laura Somerville's suicide was as startling as anything he had ever come across.

Byrne had cornered Mickey Dugan, an old friend and PFD captain. Dugan told him that, presumptively—which meant very little at this stage—the Philadelphia Fire Department believed the source of the fire was an oil lamp under the mattress in the bedroom. Moments before Laura Somerville dove through that window, moments after she excused herself from the living room, she had walked into her bedroom, pulled an oil lamp from her closet, lit a match, placed it beneath the bed, and deliberately set her apartment on fire.

What was she trying to conceal by burning down her apartment, her possessions, perhaps the entire building? Not to mention her prized collection of games and puzzles. Could it be that the Philadelphia Police Department had coincidentally shown up on the same day this elegant, cultured woman planned to commit suicide?

Byrne sipped his coffee, a thought circling him, a dark feeling he knew he was not shaking anytime soon. Unvarnished, unwarranted, unearned, yet all too real.

There was no evidence that this was anything other than a suicide. Jessica and Byrne were homicide detectives, and there were plen homicides to go around in the City of Brotherly Love. They had a full day ahead of them. A day belonging to Caitlin O'Riordan. A day Kevin Byrne knew would be haunted by the image of Laura Somerville's demolished body, and one strange word.

Ludo.

ELEVEN

THE BASEMENT WAS A VAST AND SILENT CAVERN, COOL EVEN IN HIGH summer—corridors crosshatching corridors, carved lintels threatening headroom from above each passageway, stone walls unencumbered by paint or memory. Its corners were clean, damp, sunless.

The enormous space was divided into more than a dozen rooms. When Faerwood had been built, around 1900, the basement was used primarily for storage. There was a coal chute, of course, the boiler, an oil heater, a forest of rusted iron support columns.

The original owner—an executive with the Pennsylvania Railroad named Artemus Coleridge, a man who hanged himself from an attic roof beam in the house in 1908—had seven children, and it was in the wide expanse of the main basement that they played their outdoor games in winter, their contests illuminated by scores of gas lamps, hundreds of candles. To this day Swann found small mounds of melted paraffin and blackened wicks in the unlikeliest of places.

As an adult Swann could not picture this house full of happy children, not in this place of his ruined childhood, but as a boy he had often stalked these rooms, imagining voices and bright laughter, conjuring unseen friends, gamboling with ghosts.

Originally there had been only one set of stairs leading to the basement, from a small pantry directly off the main kitchen, a direct route to both the wine and root cellars.

All that changed when Joseph Swann's father bought the house, and the transformation of Faerwood began. Now there were more than ten ways to enter the lower level.

One basement room—perhaps the smallest at a mere six feet by seven—was his dressing room. On one wall was a large mirror, ringed with yellow globe lamps. In the corner was a tall collector's cabinet, its many drawers containing a lifetime collection of items dedicated to the art of makeup. One of these drawers held prosthetic devices used for both concealment and diversion. One was devoted to scabs, wounds, and scars. Another, Swann's favorite, contained hair and character effects. Some of the wigs and mustaches were more than fifty years old, among them some of the finest ever produced.

Yet even the finest of prosthetics and wigs were useless without the true secret of makeup—application.

The tools of this trade were laid out precisely on the clinically clean table—brushes, combs, sponges, pencils, and crayons, along with tubes and jars of powders, matte foundations, paint, glitter, lipsticks, and the increasingly important neutralizers and concealers. Now that he was nearing forty, Swann lamented, he found himself turning to the concealers more and more.

His wig already in place, Swann applied the last of the spirit gum to his chin, and opened the clear plastic box that bore his prized human-hair goatee. He held the beard in place for a few seconds, then smoothed it to the contours of his chin. He had applied the black eyebrows earlier, and settled into his right eye the steel-rimmed monocle made of clear glass.

He stood, slipped on the cutaway coat, adjusted the shoulders, the waist. He tapped the remote in his left pocket, turning on the music. Bach's *Sleepers Awake* began to softly fill the outer rooms.

Moments later Joseph Swann opened the door, and stepped onto his secret stage.

KATJA SAT CROSS-LEGGED in the box, her eyes vacant, distant.

The Sword Box was painted in a lustrous red lacquer. It measured approximately four feet tall, two feet wide, two feet deep. It rested on a short, polished-steel pedestal. The inside was a glossy black enamel.

The box was fitted with a drain hole at the bottom, a portal that fed the iron pipe that emptied into the sanitary sewer running beneath the rear of the house.

Swann emerged from the darkness, his white shirt and scarlet tie a magnificent contrast to the blackness of the room. He stepped into the spotlight, just to the left of the box.

A few feet away watched the eye of the camera, an unblinking silver portal in the gloom.

He glanced at the open box, at Katja's face. She looked young again, in need of tending. Alas, it was too late for that. He reached out, touched her cheek. She tried to shy away, but she could not move, not in the confines of the magnificent Sword Box.

Joseph Swann was ready.

Upstairs, in a room secreted from the rest of Faerwood by a false wall at the top of the grand staircase, secured by steels doors, a television flickered, a monitor carrying this live performance.

"Behold the Sword Box," Swann began, looking directly into the lens, out at the world, into the hearts and minds of those who would soon see this and thus be tasked to solve his puzzle. "And behold the lovely Odette."

He slipped the box's front panel into place, secured it with a quartet of thumbscrews, then turned to the table next to him, the table bearing seven gleaming swords, all keened to a razor sharpness.

Moments later he drew the first sword. In the quietude of the basement the steel sang, finding each threshold, each doorway, each memory, a silver whisper floating through a maddening maze of dreams.

TWELVE

JESSICA WALKED INTO THE DINER AT 7:30 AM. THE MORNING RUSH WAS on. She edged her way to the back, found her partner. Byrne looked up from the *Inquirer*.

"Did you sleep?" Byrne asked.

"Are you kidding?" Jessica sat down, took Byrne's coffee, started drinking it. Byrne motioned to the waitress. She brought him a fresh cup.

Jessica looked her partner over. He looked even worse than she felt. He was wearing the same shirt and tie he had worn yesterday. She wondered if he'd even made it home. She doubted it. "Got a question for you," she said.

"I'll do my best."

"What the hell happened yesterday?"

Byrne shrugged. When the waitress brought his coffee, he tore open a sugar packet, dumped it in. As a rule, Kevin Byrne didn't take sugar in his coffee. If there was one thing you learned early on about your partner in this job, it was how they took their coffee. *He must be running on fumes*, Jessica thought.

"Your guess is as good as mine," he said. "Probably better."

Byrne shifted in his seat, winced, closed his eyes for a moment.

"Your sciatica acting up?" Jessica asked. When Byrne had been shot in the line of duty, almost three years earlier, he had survived a brain injury, had survived a lengthy coma, but his sciatica—a compression of the sciatic nerve that caused excruciating pain in the lower back and legs—persisted. It seemed to flare up twice a year. Byrne tried his Irish macho best to play it down.

"It aches a little," he said. "I'm good."

Jessica knew that, where Kevin Byrne was concerned, *a little* meant it was killing him. She sipped her coffee, picked up the menu. A scan of the first page told her she could get custard-baked French toast with a side order of Philadelphia scrapple. She called the waitress over, ordered.

"Is there anyone we can reach out to in the fire department?" Jessica asked.

"I already did," Byrne said. "Mickey Dugan. He said he'd call as soon as they had something definite. You know Mickey?"

Jessica shook her head.

"Great guy. Got two boys in the Eagles training camp. *Two*. At the *same time*. Can you believe that?"

Jessica said that she could not. On the other hand, if it wasn't boxing—specifically women's boxing, along with the occasional Phillies or Eagles game—she lost all interest, sports-wise. Her husband maintained a rec room full of Flyers and Sixers memorabilia, but those two sports never got under her skin for some reason. "How about that?" she said. "Two boys. Same time. *Huh*."

"Anyway," Byrne said, reading her disinterest. "You want to know what happened yesterday? I'll tell you. What happened yesterday was that an old, very eccentric, very troubled woman jumped out of a window. Simple as that."

"And lucky us, we just happened to be there at the time."

"Lucky us."

"So you think she made these peculiar calls to Licenses & Inspections?"

"I'm not seeing any other explanation. She must have been lying to us."

If you were a police officer, you accepted the fact that people lied all the time. It came with the job. *Wasn't there, don't know him, isn't mine, doesn't ring a bell, can't recall*. On the other hand, given what Laura Somerville did, the woman was clearly disturbed in ways that far outweighed lying to the police.

"Any idea why she would do that?"

"Not a one," Byrne said. "I've been in this business more than twenty years, and I can spot liars 99.9 percent of the time. She had me completely fooled."

Jessica felt the same way. Cops with any time in on the street possessed a confidence—mostly warranted, sometimes even cocky—that they could detect bullshit from a block away. It's a little unnerving to learn you were completely wrong about someone. "It makes you wonder what else she was lying about," Jessica added.

"Yes it does."

"Yeah, well," Jessica began, her thoughts ricocheting around the events of the past twenty-four hours. "I'd still love to get back up there and poke around."

She knew that Byrne understood what she meant. He'd like to poke around Laura Somerville's apartment, too, but today the job was Caitlin O'Riordan. She deserved their full attention.

What was most distressing for Jessica was that Caitlin O'Riordan's murder had been recorded as just another Philadelphia homicide statistic.

The truth was, in Philadelphia, something like twenty-five percent of shooting victims had pending court cases. In the microclimate of North Philly it was probably higher. Because of the national attention to the city's homicide rate, some people believed Philadelphia was a dangerous place. Factually, for the most part, the people doing the shooting and the people being shot tended to overlap. If you didn't live in that small dangerous world, you were not particularly at risk.

But these were, for the most part, the handgun statistics. There was less to go on when it came to drowning victims. Especially drowning victims found on dry land. Jessica had read the most recent FBI report on crime statistics in America. Drowning as a cause of homicide was almost nonexistent.

The waitress brought Jessica's French toast and scrapple. It was a monstrous portion. Jessica drizzled the plate with maple syrup, then artfully dusted the French toast with a generous sprinkling of sugar. She dug in. Nirvana. She'd have to remember this dish at this diner. Nothing like seven thousand calories, all sugar and cholesterol, to give you a boost.

"How can you eat that?" Byrne asked, a dour look on his face.

Jessica wiped her lips, set her napkin down, sipped her coffee. "What?"

"That . . . that *scrapple*."

"It's good. I've been eating it my whole life."

"Yeah, well, do you want to know what's in it?"

Scrapple was the absolute last step in the dismantling of a pig: foreheads, elbows, kneecaps, shins, with a little cayenne and sage thrown in for flavor. Jessica knew this, but she just didn't need to hear at 7:30 AM. "Absolutely not."

"Well, suffice it to say the root word here is *scrap*, okay?"

"Point taken, Detective." With this she sopped the last of the syrup with the last square inch of French toast, topping it with the last dollop of scrapple, then made a dramatic flourish of placing it in her mouth, chewing it with delirious delight. Byrne shook his head and went back to his wheat toast.

A few minutes later Jessica finished her coffee, grabbed the check, and asked, "Where do you want to start?"

"We never did get to recanvass Eighth Street."

Jessica slipped out of the booth. "Let's roll."

THEY SPENT THE ENTIRE MORNING canvassing near the Eighth Street crime scene, learning nothing new. Not much was expected. They spent the afternoon walking every inch of the building in which Caitlin O'Riordan's body was found.

AT 7:00 PM Byrne walked to the block of row houses across the street. The second and third floors of this building were still occupied. The aromas of frying meats and boiling vegetables reminded Byrne they had not stopped for dinner.

At the top of the stairwell he looked across the street at the corner building. The beam of Jessica's flashlight in the gathering gloom cut across the empty space, strobing in the blackness.

Byrne scanned the street, the block. He considered the scenario when Caitlin had been brought to this terrible place. Her killer had chosen this spot well in advance. This was a special place. For some reason. It meant something to him. Most likely he had come in the middle of the night.

A few streets away a sector car's siren suddenly burst to life. Byrne started at the noise. He hadn't realized the street had gone so quiet, hadn't realized the only sound was the beating of his heart.

Time to call it a night.

Byrne reached up to close the window, and the vision all but exploded in his mind. As his fingertips touched the cracked and puttied surface of the sash he knew—knew in a way with which he had been both cursed and blessed since an incident many years earlier, an attack by a homicide suspect that had left him dead for a full minute, a void in his memory that imbued him with a vague second sight—that Caitlin O'Riordan's killer had stood in this very spot.

In Kevin Byrne's mind he knew—

—a man standing at the bottom of the stairs . . . the city street quiet above him . . . the bright white cuff of a dress shirt . . . the sound of a silken cloth snapping in the still air . . . the image of the dead girl framed in the glass display case, the glisten of water leaking from her lips . . . the picture of an old man watching, applauding, his gnarled and feeble hands meeting in a noiseless clash—

—the unclean taste of a murderer's thoughts inside him. Byrne took a few steps back, his head reeling. He exhaled. The air was foul and bitter in his mouth. He spit on the floor.

He took a moment to collect himself. The vision had visited him with a brutal clarity. It had been a while since the last one. Each time it happened he believed it would be the last time.

Kevin Byrne was a man who could sometimes see things. Things he did not want to see.

Years earlier he had been shot by a homicide suspect on the western bank of the Delaware River, in the shadow of the Walt Whitman Bridge. Although the bullet wound to his forehead was not life threatening, the impact forced him backwards, into the frigid water, where he had drifted downward, nearly unconscious, locked in a death battle ⸻ suspect, who had just taken fire from Byrne's partner, the late ⸻urify. When they pulled Byrne from the river, he had to be re- ⸻ According the report he read almost a year later, he had ⸻ for nearly one full minute. Like Caitlin, he had drowned.

For years after, he found that he sometimes had the ability to "read" a crime scene. Not in any psychic sense. He could not lay hands on a weapon or a victim and get a crystal-clear snapshot of the doer.

When he was shot a second time, this time far more seriously, the ability seemed to have disappeared, which was just fine with Kevin Byrne.

Just over a year ago, it returned with a vengeance.

Byrne never shared what he "saw" as investigative findings. To his bosses, to his fellow detectives, he couched his feelings as a hunch, an investigator's gut instinct.

It's not about the victim, it's about the presentation.

Byrne took time to regroup. In the old days he took the visions in stride. He was no longer the man he had been in those days. Too much blood had flowed through his city.

He was just about to head down the stairs when a movement caught his eye, the motion of a silhouette next to the corner building across the street. Byrne stepped back, into the lengthening shadows of the hallway. He peered around the window casing and looked again.

The man was standing in the vacant lot next to the crime-scene house, looking up at him, dressed in dark clothing, hands in pockets. Byrne recognized the man's posture, his bearing. He had seen it many times before.

For a few long moments the two men stood looking at each other, acknowledging each other's role in this agonizing play, deferring, for the time being, to the cover of dusk.

Minutes later, purposely taking his time, Byrne walked down the stairs, stepped out of the building, and crossed the street.

Caitlin's father, Robert O'Riordan, was gone.

THIRTEEN

THEY SAT IN THE PARKING LOT AT THE ROUNDHOUSE, ENGINE IDLING, windows up, AC maxed out to Burger King meat locker. The city was paying for the air conditioning, and they were going to use it.

Kevin Byrne glanced over at his partner. Jessica had her eyes closed, her head back on the seat. It had been a long day for both, but as tired as Byrne was, he felt it was probably worse for Jessica than for him. All Byrne had to do was drive home, drag himself up two flights of stairs, open a bottle of Yuengling, flop onto the couch, and order a pizza.

Jessica had to drive to the Northeast, pick up her daughter, make dinner for her family, put her daughter to bed, take a shower and then maybe, *maybe*, sleep would find her, just a few hours before she had to get up and start it all over again.

Byrne didn't know how she did it. If she was a dental hygienist or paralegal it would be hard enough. Add the stresses and dangers of this job, and the demands had to be off the charts.

Byrne checked the dashboard clock. It was just after 9:00 PM. He had lost track of how long they had been sitting there in the parking lot, not saying a word. His partner finally broke the silence.

"I hate this part," Jessica said.

"Me too."

They were in the doldrums between clue and fact, between suspicion and reality, between idea and truth. Byrne was just about to further lament this fact aloud when his cell phone rang.

Jessica turned to look at him, opened one eye. If she had opened two it would have been overtime. It was that late in the day. "Don't you ever turn that friggin' thing off?"

"I thought I did."

Byrne pulled out his phone, glanced at the caller ID, frowned, flipped it open. It was their boss. Jessica looked over again, both eyes open now. Byrne pointed a finger upward, at the windows of the Roundhouse, telling her all she needed to know. She closed her eyes again.

"Hey, Sarge," Byrne said. "How are you?"

"Like Rosie O'Donnell in a cold bubble bath."

"Okay," Byrne said, not having the slightest idea what his boss meant. But he was fine with that. The visual image was enough to prevent any further inquiries. "What's up?"

A rhetorical question. In this job, if you were on day work, your boss didn't call you after nine o'clock unless it was bad news.

"We've got a body. Fairmount Park."

"We're up on the wheel?" Byrne asked. The "wheel" was the roster of detectives. Whenever you got a new case, you went to the bottom, and steadily moved up the list until it was your turn again. Clearing all your cases before you got a new one was every detective's dream. It never happened in Philly.

"No," Buchanan said. "I need you to back up Nicci and John."

Buchanan was talking about Detectives Nicolette Malone and John Shepherd. Whenever there was a large public crime scene, more than two detectives were called to the site.

"Where?" Byrne replied, pulling out his notebook. He glanced at Jessica. She was listening, but not looking.

Buchanan gave Byrne the location.

THE EVENING WAS A steam bath. White heat shimmered off the streets, the sidewalks, the buildings. Lightning flashed in a deep indigo sky. No rain yet. Soon, though, the radio said. It was going to rain soon. They promised.

Byrne put the car in reverse, then drove across the lot, turned onto Eighth Street. Jessica sighed. Their tour was over, but Philadelphia didn't care.

FOURTEEN

Fairmount Park was one of the largest municipally operated urban parks in the country, covering more than 9200 acres and including more than sixty-three neighborhoods and regional parks. Over the years it had seen its share of mayhem. When there are this many places to hide, there will be crime. Fairmount Park boasted more than 215 miles of winding bike trails.

Jessica and Byrne pulled up onto Belmont Avenue, parked, exited the vehicle. They approached the crime scene, where there was already a flurry of activity. Detective John Shepherd greeted them. Shepherd was a twenty-year man in the homicide unit, soft-spoken, intuitive, as shrewd an investigator as anyone on the force. His specialty was interrogation. Watching him work a suspect in the room was a thing of beauty, almost a clinic. More than once Jessica had seen a half dozen young detectives bunched around the mirror looking into one of the interview rooms while John Shepherd was inside, working his magic. When Jessica had joined the unit, John Shepherd—who was tall and always classically attired, and who would have been a dead ringer for Denzel Washington, if not for his thrice-broken nose—was just going salt-and-pepper. Now his hair was pure silver. His receipt for experience.

"What do we know?" Byrne asked.

"We know it's a human being," Shepherd said. "And we know this human being was buried in a shallow grave, probably within the last sixth months or so. That's about it."

"I take it there was no driver's license or Social Security card sitting on top of the body?"

"You take it right, Detective," Shepherd said. "There's some clothing, a pair of small size running shoes, so I'm guessing a woman, or perhaps an older teenage girl, but that's purely conjecture on my part."

Jessica and Byrne walked to the site of the shallow grave. It was bathed in blue from the tripod police lights.

Detective Nicci Malone walked up.

"Hey," Nicci said. Jessica and Byrne nodded.

Nicolette Malone was in her early thirties, a third-generation Philly police officer. A compact and muscular five-five, she, like Jessica, had come to the job almost out of legacy. A few years on the street, a few more as a divisional detective, Nicci had advanced out of sheer willpower, and God help you if you insinuated she got this job because of her gender. Jessica had worked a few details with Nicci Malone and found her to be smart and resourceful, if not a little rash and hotheaded. They could have been twins.

"Any ID?" Jessica asked.

"Nothing yet," Nicci replied.

In the distance lightning flashed, thunder rumbled. The clouds over the city were pregnant with rain, ready to burst. The CSU team had sheets of plastic ready if needed to cover the body in the eventuality of a downpour.

The four detectives stood at the edge of the grave. The body was partially decomposed. Jessica knew precious little about decomposition rates, despite her classes at Temple University, but she knew that a body that was not embalmed, buried six feet beneath the surface, in ordinary soil without a casket, took about ten years to decay fully into a skeleton.

This grave was only three feet deep, no casket, which meant that the body was exposed to far more oxygen than usual, plus the effects of rain and surface insects.

In Philadelphia, about three hundred bodies or sets of remains arrived at the Medical Examiner's office each year as unknowns. Most were quickly identified, based on the fact that the victim had gone missing at some time within the previous year, often within just a few months. Other identifications took much longer, and called for a more specialized field of study. If needed, they would consult with a forensic anthropologist.

"Who found the body?" Jessica asked.

Nicci pointed to a man standing next to a sector car about twenty feet away on Belmont Avenue. Next to him sat a very nervous, very big dog. The dog, a German shepherd, was panting rapidly, straining against his collar and leash, wanting to get back to the scene.

"The man said he was jogging," Nicci said. She glanced at her notebook. "His name is Gerald Lester. He states that he came up onto the plateau and his dog all but dragged him to this area and started digging."

"The dog went down three feet?" Jessica asked.

"No," Nicci said. "But the man said that the dog used to be on the job in Richmond, Virginia. He said that his wife Leanne used to work the K-9 unit there, and that when the dog retired they adopted him. He said that Demetrius—that's the pooch—was trained as a cadaver dog, and when he fixed on the quarry, and didn't give it up, Lester realized something was awry. At that moment he pulled out his cell and called it in."

Jessica looked around the area. It was a popular spot in Fairmount Park. On the east side of the avenue there were a handful of softball fields and cross-country routes, as well as large open areas for picnics, family reunions, gatherings of all types. The Greek Picnic was held there every year. People came up here every day, often with their dogs, Frisbees, kites, footballs. Jessica wondered why, if this makeshift grave had been here for months, hadn't another dog picked up the scent? Maybe they had, and were yanked back to the trail by their owners, figuring the dog was just jazzing a squirrel in the bushes. Or maybe—and Jessica figured this to be the case—a police-trained cadaver dog, being a special animal who could lead a human being across half a city to find a dead body, was the first of its kind to pass this way since the body had been buried. Jessica had seen cadaver dogs work. They do not give up on their game.

"Do we have all of his information?" Nicci asked John Shepherd.

"We do."

"Tell him we'll be in touch."

"You got it."

Shepherd crossed the field as Jessica, Byrne, and Nicci Malone crouched at the edge of the grave. On the ground around the opening were a patchwork of blue plastic sheets. Battery-operated spotlights on tripods illuminated the scene at either end.

The body was no taller than five-five or five-six. Partially clothed. The upper body had been partially skeletonized. Rotting denim pants, dark colored T-shirt. Sneakers appeared in relatively good shape.

Byrne looked at Nicci, gestured toward the body. "May I?"

"By all means, Detective," Nicci said.

Every detective in the homicide unit had a specialty, often more than one—interrogation, computers, street work, undercover, finances, surveillance. Among his many abilities, Kevin Byrne was very good at a crime scene, and most investigators wisely and gratefully deferred to him.

Byrne snapped on latex gloves, borrowed a large Maglite from one of the officers. He ran the beam of the flashlight slowly over the victim.

Within seconds something flashed, something golden in color. Byrne knelt on the plastic, looked more closely.

"Christ," Byrne said.

"What?"

Byrne took a few moments, then leaned in farther. He took out a pair of pencils, chopstick style, and picked up something that appeared to be jewelry. He held it up to the light. It was a charm bracelet. Five charms dangled from a gold chain. Little golden angels.

"What is it, Kevin?" Jessica asked.

Byrne turned the bracelet over, looked behind the clasp. He shone the flashlight close on the metal. In an instant he went ashen. He dropped the bracelet into an evidence bag without a word.

Jessica looked at her partner, at Nicci. It wasn't often that Kevin Byrne got spooked, or found himself at a loss for words or actions. But Jessica could see that Byrne was taken aback. "What is it?" Jessica asked. "Have you seen this bracelet before?"

Byrne stood up, turned away from the shallow grave. "Yeah," he said. "I've seen it."

When Jessica realized he wasn't going to continue, she pressed "Talk to me, Kevin. Where do you know this bracelet fr

Byrne's green eyes were ebony in the moonlight.

"I gave it to her."

FIFTEEN

J OSEPH SWANN WATCHED THE EVENING NEWS. THEY HAD FOUND A BODY in a shallow grave in Fairmount Park. A helicopter hovered.

Although it had been more than two months ago, Swann recalled the night he buried her as if it were yesterday. He recalled the cerulean sky that evening, the way the moon searched for him. Now, as then, he was a cipher, a man beyond even the reach of the heavens.

He had stood on the west side of Belmont Plateau that night, deep in the bushes and trees, lost in the shadows. He patted the dirt, dumped the bagful of leaves and debris on top of the bare earth. The scene looked undisturbed. The perfect illusion.

He recalled how he took off the gloves, slipped them into a plastic trash bag, how he later burned everything, including the thick plastic sheets that lined the trunk of the car, along with his clothing. It had been a shame to part with his bespoke suit, but it was a small price to pay. He had not been diligent about his visitors all this time to make a simple mistake. In fact, only one had ever gotten away. Sweet Cassandra.

He thought about how he had discovered the woman on the Faerwood grounds that night. She had looked strong, but she also looked manic. She had fired her weapon at him while he was standing in the gazebo, the pergola long ago fitted with the counterweight elevator.

As the police engaged their new mystery, Joseph Swann sipped his tea. He knew it was time to bear down.

The Seven Wonders, he thought.

The game is on.

Minutes later, as he climbed the stairs, he reached into his shirt pocket. He had kept a memento of the dead woman, a small souvenir of their brief time together. A business card. Such a personal thing, he thought, yet something so aloof, something one gives away like a hand-shake, or a compliment:

DETECTIVE GENEVIEVE GALVEZ

SPECIAL INVESTIGATIONS UNIT

OFFICE OF THE PHILADELPHIA DISTRICT ATTORNEY

II

THE SINGING BOY

The past walks here,
noiseless, unasked, alone.

—Virginia Woodward Cloud

IN THE YEARS BEFORE DARKNESS BECAME HIS MISTRESS, AND TIME BECAME an abstract précis, Karl Swann was a student of the masters.

His art was magic.

Born in 1928 to an upper-middle-class family in Hanau, twenty-five kilometers east of Frankfurt, Germany, Karl began his exploration of the dark arts at an early age. His father Martin, a retired army captain from Glasgow, Scotland, had parlayed a small military retirement into a thriving metals business after settling in the area following World War I. Martin married a local girl named Hannah Scholling.

In 1936, when Karl was eight, his father took him to a performance at the Shuman Theater in Frankfurt, a show featuring a well-known magician named Alois Kassner. During this performance Kassner vanished an elephant.

For three nights young Karl could not sleep thinking about the illusion. More than the trick, Karl considered the illusionist himself. He trembled at the thought of the mysterious, dark-haired man.

Over the next year, Karl collected books on magic, as well as biographies of the great American, European, and Asian conjurers. To the dismay of his parents, and the detriment of his studies, this pursuit seemed to consume the boy.

At the age of nine, he began to perform magic tricks at parties for his friends—cups and balls, vanishing silks, linking rings. Although his technique was not dazzling, his hands moved with competence and grace. Within a year he improved substantially, moving his act from the table to the parlor.

As the rumblings of war in Europe began, Martin Swann, over the hysterical objections of his wife, decided to send their only son to live with distant relatives in America. At least until the clouds of conflict blew over.

On October 4, 1938, Karl Swann boarded the USS *Washington* in Le Havre, France. His mother and father stood on the dock, waving good-bye. His mother cried, a white lace handkerchief in her hand, her rich burgundy cashmere coat in stark relief to the gray dawn. Martin Swann stood, shoulders square, eyes dry. It was how he had taught his son to face emotion, and he would not betray that lesson now.

As the ship set to sea, the two silhouettes painted a frozen montage in Karl's mind; his fragile, beautiful mother, his stoic father. It would be how he always remembered them, for he never saw them alive again.

PHILADELPHIA 1938

THE KENSINGTON SECTION OF PHILADELPHIA was a near northeast working-class part of the city, bordering the neighborhoods of Fishtown, Port Richmond, Juniata, and Frankford.

In November 1938 Karl Swann came to live with his distant cousins Nicholas and Vera Ehrlinger. They lived in a narrow row house on Emerald Street. Both of his cousins worked at Craftex Mills. Karl attended Saint Joan of Arc School.

In the late 1930s Philadelphia was a rich and vibrant community for magic and magicians. There were chapters of the International Brotherhood of Magicians, the Society of American Magicians, The Yogi Club, the Houdini Club—an enclave dedicated to preserving the memory of Harry Houdini.

A week after his tenth birthday Karl took the streetcar to Center City with his cousin Nicholas. They were on a mission to locate a tablecloth for Thanksgiving dinner. Karl marveled at the Christmas decorations and displays near Rittenhouse Square. When they reached Thirteenth and Walnut, Nicholas kept walking, but Karl stopped, captivated by the one-sheet poster in the window of Kanter's Magic. Kanter's was the premier magic emporium in Philadelphia, its clientele an amalgam of amateur and professional magicians.

The poster in the window—a bright and bizarre display of doves and grinning harpies—was for a show due to arrive in two weeks, a show the likes of which Karl had never imagined. The star of the show was a man named Harry Blackstone.

FOR THE NEXT TEN DAYS Karl took on every odd job he could. He delivered newspapers, shined shoes, washed automobiles. He finally saved enough money. Three days before the show he went to the theater, and bought his ticket. He spent the next two nights in bed, looking at the voucher in the moonlight.

At last the day arrived.

From his seat in the balcony Karl watched the incredible spectacle unfold. He watched a stunning illusion called the Sepoy Mutiny, a piece of magical theater in which Blackstone was captured by Arabs, strapped to the mouth of a cannon and blown to bits. At more than one performance of this fantastic illusion women had been known to faint, or run screaming from the theater. The fainthearted who fled never got to see that, moments after the cannon fire, the executioner would pull off his turban and beard, only to reveal that it was Blackstone himself!

In another illusion Blackstone passed lighted lightbulbs right through a woman, each pass eliciting shocked gasps from the transfixed audience.

But nothing surpassed Blackstone's version of sawing a woman in half. In Blackstone's rendering, called the Lumbersaw, a woman was strapped facedown on a table, and a large buzz saw ran right through her middle. When Karl saw the illusion it brought tears to his eyes. Not for the woman—of course, she was just fine—but for the power of the ruse. In Blackstone's gifted hands it was a level beyond enchantment, beyond even theater. For Karl Swann, it had reached the level of true magic. Blackstone had done the impossible.

IN THE SUMMER of his fourteenth year, Karl Swann spent every Saturday afternoon at Kanter's, pestering the owner, Mike Kanter, demanding to see every trick beneath the glass. One day Karl wandered behind the store, into what looked and sounded like a machine shop. It was a brass works. He saw a man at a workbench. The man noticed him.

"You should not be here," the man said.

"You are the man who makes the Nickels to Dimes?" The Nickels to Dimes illusion was one where the magician places a stack of nickels on the table, all the while pattering about inflation and the costs of things these days. He passes his hand over the stack, and they turn into dimes.

The man spun on his stool, crossed his arms. "I am."

"I saw the trick today," Karl said.

The man stroked his chin. "And you want to know how it is done." "No."

The man raised a single eyebrow. "And why is that? All boys want to know how magic is done. Why not you?"

"Because I know how it is done. It is not *that* clever."

The man laughed.

"I will work for you," Karl said. "I can sweep. I can run errands."

The man considered Karl for a few moments. "Where are you from?"

"Kensington," Karl said. "From Emerald Street."

"No, I mean where were you born?"

Karl did not know if he should say, the war being the war, still so alive in everyone's mind. He trusted the man, though. He was clearly of German extraction. "Hanau."

The man nodded. "What is your name?"

Karl squared his shoulders, set his feet, just as his father had taught him. He extended his hand. "My name is Karl Swann," he said. "And yours?"

The man took Karl's hand. "I'm Bill Brema."

For the next two years, Karl apprenticed with Bill Brema, working in the brass works, helping to produce some of the finest brass apparatuses in the world.

But the real benefit to working there was the people Karl encountered. Everyone came to Kanter's, and Karl met them all; acquiring moves, pieces of patter, a well-used silk, a battered wand. His magic box grew. His understanding of misdirection flourished.

At twenty, it was time to perform professionally for the first time in the United States. He called himself the Great Cygne.

FOR THE NEXT TEN YEARS the Great Cygne toured the country, performing in towns large and small. Although not a strikingly handsome man, at six-two he was a commanding presence, and his courtly manner and piercing eyes drew women to him in every venue.

In Reading, Pennsylvania, he met a German girl named Greta Huebner. Weary of finding love on the road, Karl proposed to her within one month. Two months later they were married.

Back in Philadelphia, when his father's estate was finally settled, more than fourteen years after the end of the war, Karl received a check for nearly one million dollars. With it he bought a house in North Philadelphia, a sprawling twenty-two-room Victorian mansion called Faerwood. He surrounded it with trees.

For most of the next decade the Great Cygne continued to ply his trade. Childless, the couple had all but given up on a family. Then, at the age of thirty-eight, Greta Swann became pregnant. It was a difficult pregnancy, and on the morning of October 31, 1969, Greta died from complications of childbirth. At 7:00 AM, a weeping midwife handed Karl the swaddled baby.

Karl Swann held his infant son for the first time, and it was in this moment, when the child first opened his eyes, that Karl saw something that chilled him to the bottom of his soul. For a moment, his son's eyes were a blinding silver, eyes that held the very cast of Hell.

It may have been an illusion, he thought a few moments later, a trick of light coming through the high windows at Faerwood, for soon the vision was gone. The baby's eyes were an azure blue, like his father's.

Karl Swann named his son Joseph.

| 1973 |

AT FAERWOOD, JOSEPH'S WORLD was a labyrinth of small, dark rooms and hissing whispers, a place where specters coiled behind the wood lath, and shadows darted and gamboled in the halls. Joseph played his child's games by himself, but he was never alone.

Without a mother, the only woman in young Joseph's life was his father's stage assistant, Odette. Odette cooked for him, bathed him, helped him with his lessons. In the end, it was Odette who knew his talents.

As a young boy Joseph Swann proved to be far more dexterous than other children his age, far more nimble with his hands than even his father had been as a child. At three he was able to perform all the fundamentals of coin magic—palms, switches, vanishes—simply from observation, being particularly adept at *Le Tourniquet*, the classic French drop. At four he mastered the Okito, the small brass box it had taken his father the better part of a decade to perfect. Given a bridge deck—to accommodate his small hands—he could fluidly perform any number of card basics: false shuffles, Hindu shuffles, double lifts, false counts.

In these early years, as Karl Swann struggled to remain relevant in a changing world of magic, as madness began to seed his mind, instead of pride he developed a profound resentment toward his son, a bitterness that at first manifested in abuse, but soon matured into something else.

Something closer to fear.

1975

ONE NIGHT, WHILE on a brief tour of small towns in southern Ohio, Karl Swann locked his five-year-old son in back of the battered step van they used for traveling, leaving the boy to amuse himself with a 250-piece jigsaw, a rather difficult puzzle depicting a pair of eagles high in the clouds. When Karl returned to the van to retrieve a forgotten device, eight minutes later, the puzzle was complete. Joseph stared out the window.

1976

WITH THE SUCCESS of *The Magic Show*—a magic-themed Broadway musical featuring an overly grand, aging alcoholic, a character not all that different from the Great Cygne—the world of parlor and stage magic all but changed forever. It was now the large scale Las Vegas show that the public demanded. For the Great Cygne, the venues got smaller, the road longer.

At the age of seven, it was evident that Joseph, despite his almost preternatural skills, and his integral part in the stage act, had no interest in following in his father's footsteps. His true interest was puzzles—word puzzles, jigsaws, cryptograms, riddles, anagrams, rebuses. If there was a maze, Joseph found its entry, its egress. Deduction, truth, deception, paradox—these were his sacraments.

But if Joseph's mastery of things enigmatic was evident, so had become the darkness which had taken hold of his father. Many nights Karl went down to Faerwood's basement in the middle of the night, constructing partitions, building and erecting walls, making rooms that mirrored the growing divisions in his mind. He once spent six weeks manufacturing a magic apparatus only to set it afire in the middle of the road in front of the house.

Every night, before Joseph went to bed, Karl played an old French film called *The Magic Bricks*. The silent three-minute film, made in 1908, showed a pair of conjurers making people appear and disappear, using boxes, bricks, and other props, mostly with rather crude special effects.

By his tenth birthday Joseph knew every illusion in the film, every trick of the lens, every hand-colored frame. He saw it nearly one thousand times.

| 1979 |

KARL SWANN GLANCED at his image in the gold-veined cheval mirror. They were in a shabby hotel, in a small town in Bell County, Texas.

"Watch," Karl commanded.

He turned with a great flourish of his cape, extended his right hand, and in an instant produced a seemingly endless number of cards, dropping them into a silk hat on a nearby table.

"What did you see, Joseph?"

The ten-year-old Joseph stood at rigid attention. "Nothing, sir." It was a lie. His father had flashed, a term in magic meaning the illusionist had accidentally revealed part of the method. Karl Swann had begun to do it quite a bit of late.

"No flash?"

"No sir."

"Are you certain?"

Joseph hesitated, and thus sealed his fate. "Yes, sir," he said. But it was too late. There came into his father's eyes a tempest of disapproval. Joseph knew this would mean a night of terror.

For his punishment, his father brought him into the bathroom, where he strapped him into a straightjacket. It was an adult straightjacket, and within minutes of his father leaving the room for the hotel bar, Joseph was able to maneuver his arms to the front. He could have easily worked the buckles free, but he dared not.

And thus he sat.

At midnight his father returned and, without a word, unlaced the straightjacket, and carried the sleeping Joseph to his bed. He kissed the boy on the top of the head.

IN THEIR TOURS OF TEXAS, Oklahoma, and Louisiana they would often encounter the young people who drifted along the fringes of the shows, which were mostly county fairs. These were the strays, the unwanted, children who were not missed at home. These runaways, most often girls, became Joseph's playmates during the long hours when his father was drunk, or searching for the local brothel.

Molly Proffitt was twelve years old when she escaped her abusive home in Stillwater, Oklahoma. Slight and agile, a tomboy with cornflower eyes and sandy hair, she joined the Great Cygne's traveling show at a stop in Chickasha, having been on the road herself for more than a month. Karl Swann introduced her to everyone as his niece, and Molly soon became a vital part of the show, helping to dress Odette, cleaning and polishing cabinets, even passing the hat after impromptu performances on town squares.

Karl lavished attention on the girl, as if she were his own. She began to replace Joseph not only in his father's act, but also his life.

Within weeks Molly lobbied for Joseph's spot onstage in a particularly complex illusion called the Sea Horse, an escape trick featuring a large water tank. Every evening, before dinner, she would get on and off the platform hundreds of times, even going so far as to practice her curtsy at the end.

One evening Joseph spied on the girl. He watched her walk up the stairs to the top of the tank, pose, and walk down again. Over and over she practiced her moves. At 7:00 PM she went to dinner—a meager bill of fare consisting of beans and salt pork, eaten in the step van—then returned. She climbed the stairs again. This time, when she reached the top, the platform collapsed.

Molly fell into the tank. On the way down, she hit her head on the sharp edge of the glass, opening a huge gash on her forehead, knocking her unconscious. As she slowly descended to the bottom, Joseph approached the tank, bringing his face to within inches. The sight fascinated him, especially the plait of blood that floated above the girl's head, the undulating scarlet shape that, to Joseph's eye, did not look unlike a sea horse.

Later, long after the air bubbles ceased rising to the surface, long after the water turned a crystalline pink, Joseph climbed the stairs and replaced the four bolts that originally held the platform in place.

At just after midnight he peered out of the hotel window. In the dim streetlight he saw his father and Odette carry a large canvas bag out the back door. They placed it in the trunk of a black sedan, then sped off into the night.

It was the first of many times this scenario was to be repeated. For Joseph there were yet to come myriad rivals to his place in the Great Cygne's show, as well as his father's heart. One by one Joseph saw to it that no one replaced him.

BY 1980, when magic was relegated to television specials and big Las Vegas acts, the Great Cygne had become a relic, a man reduced to roadhouse comedy routines. Karl Swann was drinking heavily, embarrassing himself and Odette onstage, sometimes missing performances altogether.

Then came "The Singing Boy."

| 1982 |

JOSEPH SPENT MOST of the stifling summer in the basement workshop at Faerwood, a spacious room fitted with a lathe, table saw, drill press, as well as a peg-boarded wall of the finest hand and power tools. For more than three months he was not allowed to leave the basement, although every time his father left Faerwood, Joseph picked the locks within seconds and roamed the house at will.

It was during this summer he learned the craft of cabinetry.

THE SINGING BOY was an illusion of Karl Swann's invention, a trick wherein three boxes are rolled onto the stage, each in its own spotlight.

In the illusion, the magician opens each box, showing them all empty. A boy then walks onto the stage, enters the center box. The magician closes the cabinet as the boy begins to sing, muffling the sound. Suddenly the voice is thrown stage left. The magician opens the box on the left to reveal the boy, who continues the song. The illusionist closes the door, and the voice instantly travels to stage right. Again, the boy is seen in the box. The magician closes the door one last time, then waves a hand. In a spectacular flourish, all three boxes collapse to reveal six doves in each, which immediately take flight.

But the singing continues! It comes from the back of the theater where the boy, now dressed in pure white, stands.

AFTER NEARLY EIGHT MONTHS of work, the effect was complete. On a brutally cold January evening, with snow drifts halfway up the windows at Faerwood, Karl Swann entertained two of his friends in the great room. Wilton Cole and Marchand Decasse were other has-beens of the magic world, a pair of third-tier card and coin men. That night they drank their absinthe poured over sugar cubes, shared more than one pipe of opium. Joseph watched them from one of the many hidden passageways at Faerwood.

At midnight the Great Cygne, in full costume, presented the illusion. Joseph—already far too big for the role of the Singing Boy—fulfilled his role. He entered the room, and stuffed his growing body into the center box. His father closed the door.

Joseph waited, his heart racing. The air became close, rich with body smells, dank with fear. He heard a muffled burst of laughter. He heard a loud argument, breaking glass. Time seemed to stall, to rewind.

The bottom of the box would drop any second, as they had rehearsed. He waited, barely able to breathe. He heard sounds drifting in, the two men discussing stealing the illusion from Joseph's father. It seemed the Great Cygne had passed out, and the men found the prospect of the boy spending the night in the box amusing.

An hour later Joseph heard the front door slam. Faerwood fell silent, except for the skipping LP record, a recording of Bach's *Sleepers Awake*.

Blackness became Joseph Swann's world.

When his father opened the box, eleven hours later, the daylight nearly blinded him.

OVER THE NEXT SIX WEEKS, after school, Joseph followed the two men, noting their daily routes and routines. When their houses and places of business were empty, he learned their locks. In late February, Wilton Cole was found by his wife at the bottom of the stairwell in their home, his neck broken, apparently the victim of an accidental fall. Marchand Decasse, who owned a small electrical-appliance repair shop, was found three days later, electrocuted by faulty wiring in a thirteen-inch Magnavox portable television.

Joseph kept the news clippings beneath his pillow for two years.

THE GREAT CYGNE never performed the Singing Boy illusion in front of a live audience. Instead, he sold the drawings and schematics to magicians all over world, claiming exclusivity to each of them. When his ruse was discovered, he became an exile, a recluse no longer welcomed or wanted on any stage. Karl Swann began his final spiral.

He would never set foot outside Faerwood again.

| 1987 |

IT WAS A YEAR of transformation for both Joseph Swann and Faerwood. As the exterior continued to fall into ruin, the interior went through many renovations, changes to which Joseph was not privy. He entered through the kitchen, ate his meals and studied in the dining room, slept on a cot in one of the many rooms in the warren-like basement. Month after month the cacophony was endless—sawing, sanding, nailing, demolition, construction.

Finally, in September, the canvases and temporary partitions came down, and what Joseph saw both excited and confused him. Where there had once been a wall there was now a mirror, a silvered glass panel that turned on a central pivot. Cabinets opened into other rooms. In one of the bedrooms, the switch plate set the walls in motion, forming a separate room, bringing up electric lights outside the frosted windows, giving the room the appearance of being at a seashore, complete with the recorded sounds of gently crashing waves just beyond the glass. In yet another room on the third floor, the movement of a lamp opened a portal in the floor; the movement of a sconce lowered a panel, revealing a round window.

Faerwood had become an echo of the fury swirling inside Karl Swann. On that day Joseph saw his father standing at the top of the stairs, wearing his stage costume for the first time in years. Karl Swann looked like a ghost—his pale skin and dyed hair giving him a funereal look that young Joseph had only seen in horror films.

ON HIS EIGHTEENTH BIRTHDAY, with news of his acceptance to college in hand, Joseph returned to Faerwood to find his father in the attic, hanging from the roof beam. He had used the same noose Artemus Coleridge used nearly eighty years earlier.

Joseph cut his father down, then took a secret staircase to the kitchen.

Faerwood was his.

IT TURNED OUT that his apprenticeship to Karl Swann, building finely crafted magic boxes, served Joseph well. After college he began a small business building one of a kind custom cabinets and furniture. He worked with the finest materials, sometimes not emerging from the workshop for weeks on end. He soon found that his passion for cabinetry and furniture making sprang from his obsession with puzzles, that the elements of joinery—from dovetails to mortise and tenon to dowel joints—all fed his passion for the solving of conundrums, and yet he knew all the while that there was within him a magnum opus, a great and terrible creation yet to come.

JANUARY 2008

Now IN HIS LATE THIRTIES, the dark exhortations of Joseph Swann's youth had passed into the realm of sporadic flame, but he had not forgotten the fascination of that day so many years ago, the shimmering chimera of Molly Proffitt and all who came after her. There were small patches of brown grass and mounded earth on the Faerwood grounds that would attest to this.

In late January, while cleaning the attic, he came across a box he had not seen in many years. Among the books on magic and illusions, beneath his father's many notebooks of gibberish, he found the old eight-millimeter film *The Magic Bricks*. He ran the movie in the attic at Faerwood, not far from where his father had thrown a rope over a roof beam. Tears streamed down his face as he was coaxed down a long corridor of remembrance.

The seminal film had been made in 1908. *One hundred years*, Swann thought. The significance of this centenary was lost on him until, just before dinnertime, the doorbell rang. On the way downstairs he made himself presentable.

On the porch was a girl, a maiden of sixteen or so, soliciting for a nonprofit human-rights group. She had short brown hair and roan eyes. She talked to him, trusted him. They always did. Her name was Elise Beausoleil.

When she stepped inside Faerwood, Joseph Swann saw it all in his mind.

She would be the first of the Seven Wonders.

AUGUST 2008

SWANN'S SHOWROOM was in the Marketplace Design Center at Twenty-Fourth and Market Streets. The building was home to a number of showrooms for the design professional, including Roche-Bobois, Be rice & Martin, Vita DeBellis.

Swann's small, elegant space on the fourth floor was called Galerie Cygne.

From the moment he had leased the space, eight months earlier, he knew he had found a home here. It was part of the vibrancy that was downtown Philadelphia, but not quite in the beating heart of Center City. It was easily accessible from every city on the eastern corridor of the United States—Boston, New York, Baltimore, Washington, DC, Atlanta. Most important, Marketplace Design Center was just across the Schuylkill River from the Thirtieth Street train station, the hub of Philadelphia's rail traffic, the home of Amtrak.

Elise, Monica, Caitlin, Katja. He needed just three more pieces to his puzzle.

One day after the woman was found buried in Fairmount Park, Joseph Swann stood in the gallery, looking out the window, thinking of all the lost children, the night children. They came to the city by the hundreds, filled with hope and fear and promise.

They arrived every hour.

SEVENTEEN

Jessica looked at the file. It was thin, but that was to be expected. The Eve Galvez case had just a day earlier gone from missing person to homicide. It would be a while until they even had a cause of death, if ever.

It wasn't their case, but right now Jessica's curiosity was outrunning her priorities. Especially now that she knew Kevin Byrne had a past with the woman.

Jessica got onto the PPD website and checked the Missing Persons pages. The section was divided into four parts: Missing Children, Other Jurisdiction Missing Persons, Unidentified Persons, and Long-Term Missing Adults. On the Missing Adults page Jessica found a dozen entries, almost half being elderly residents suffering from dementia or Alzheimer's. A few people on the page were missing since 1999. Nearly a *decade*. Jessica considered the strength needed for family members and loved ones to hold out hope for that long. Maybe strength wasn't the word. Maybe it was something more akin to faith.

Eve Galvez's entry was halfway down the web page. The picture was of a striking, exotic woman with dark eyes and hair. Jessica knew the entry would soon be removed, only to be replaced with another mystery, another case number.

She wondered if Eve Galvez's killer had ever visited this web page. She wondered if he came here to see if his handiwork was still a puzzle to the police. She wondered if he scanned the daily newspapers looking for a headline that told him his secret had been uncovered, that a new game was afoot, that a body had been discovered buried in Fairmount Park, and that authorities "had not yet identified the remains," that a new set of adversaries had been conscripted.

Jessica wondered if *he* wondered whether or not he had left a clue behind, a hair or fiber or fingerprint, trace evidence that would bring a knock on his door in the middle of the night, or a phalanx of 9 mm pistols to his car windows as he sat at a red light in Center City, daydreaming of his wretched life.

AT 8:00 AM Kevin Byrne entered the duty room. Jessica walked right by him, through the maze of corridors, into the hallway, not even sparing him a glance or a "good morning." Byrne knew what it meant. He followed. When they were out of earshot of everyone in the room, alone in the hall, Jessica pointed an accusatory finger, said, "We have to talk about this." They had left Fairmount Park around three o'clock that morning, neither having said a word.

Byrne looked at the floor for a moment, then back into her eyes.

Jessica waited. Byrne said nothing. Jessica tossed both hands skyward. *Still* nothing. She pressed. "So, you were seeing her?" she asked, somehow keeping her voice low.

"Yes," Byrne said. "On and off."

"Okay. Was it on or off when she went missing?"

"It was over for a long time by then." Byrne leaned against the wall, hands in pockets. To Jessica, it looked like he hadn't slept a wink. His suit coat was wrinkled, his tie creased. Kevin Byrne was no fashion plate, but Jessica had long ago learned that he felt a sense of responsibility to the image of the job—the history of the people who called themselves Philadelphia police officers—and that sense of responsibility included clean shirts, pressed suits, and shined shoes. Today he was 0 for 3.

"You want the backstory?" he asked.

She didn't and she did. "I do."

Byrne took a moment, fingering the V-shaped scar over his right eye, a scar he had gotten many years earlier, a result of a vicious attack by a homicide suspect. "Well, we both kind of knew early on it wasn't going anywhere," he said. "We probably knew that on the first date. We were polar opposites. We were never exclusive to each other, we always saw other people. By last fall we were pretty much at the 'let's grab some lunch' stage. After that is was Rite Aid greeting cards and drunken voicemails in the middle of the night."

Jessica absorbed the details. The "backstory" Byrne was describing didn't go back far enough. Or deep enough. Not for her. She believed she knew a great deal about her partner—his unyielding love for his daughter Colleen, his commitment to his job, the way he took the grief of a victim's family and made it his own—but she had long ago conceded that there were many parts of his personal life from which she was, and would always be, excluded. For instance, she had never actually been inside his apartment. On the sidewalk directly below his living room window, yes. Parked around the corner, discussing a case, many times. Actually *inside* Kevin Byrne's current living quarters, no.

"Did the FBI contact you when she disappeared?"

"Yeah," Byrne said. "Terry Cahill. Remember him?"

Jessica did. Cahill had consulted with the PPD on a particularly gruesome case a few years earlier. He had nearly gotten killed for his efforts. "Yeah."

"I told him what I knew."

Silence. Jessica wanted to punch him for this. He was making her dig. Maybe it was her penance for asking. "Which was *what*?"

"The who, the what, the where. I told him the truth, Jess. I hadn't seen or talked to Eve Galvez for months."

"When you spoke to Cahill, did he ask your opinion?"

"Yeah," Byrne said. "I told him I thought Eve might have been caught up in the life. I knew she was drinking too much. I didn't think it was serious. Besides, I've had my jags. I'm in no position to judge."

"So, how come I didn't know anything about this?" she asked. "I mean, I knew an investigator from the DA's office had gone missing, but I didn't know you knew her. I didn't know you were interviewed. Why didn't you tell me?" She hoped she didn't sound matronly. On the other hand, she didn't really care. She had an obligation.

Byrne took what seemed like a full minute. "I don't know. I'm sorry, Jess."

"Yeah, well," Jessica said, in lieu of something pithy or clever. She tried to think of something else to ask. She couldn't. Or maybe she realized she had pushed this line of inquiry far enough. She didn't like the position she found herself in. Hell, she had learned 90 percent of what she knew on the job from Kevin Byrne, and here she was putting him on the spot.

At that moment a pair of uniformed officers walked out of the unit, toward the elevators. They made brief eye contact with Jessica and Byrne, nodded a good morning, moved on. They knew what the hallway was for.

"We'll continue this later, right?" Jessica asked.

"I've got a half-day off, remember?"

She had forgotten. Byrne had put in for it a while back. He had also been a little mysterious about it, so she hadn't pressed. "Tomorrow then."

"By the way, have we gotten the lab results on the remains?"

"Just the preliminaries. The heart in the old fridge was human. It belonged to a female, twelve to twenty-five years old."

"How long has it been in that specimen jar?"

"There's no way to tell with any accuracy, not without a hell of a lot more tests," Jessica said. "Preserved is preserved, I guess. ME's office thinks it's less than a year. They also say it was rather inexpertly removed, so this is probably not something that was stolen from a med school laboratory. So, until we find a body to match this organ, the case is going on a shelf."

EIGHTEEN

THEY CAME FROM SCRANTON AND WILKES-BARRE, FROM YORK AND State College and Erie, from points south, west, east, north. They came with the intention of making it big, with the intention of disappearing completely, or with no intention at all. Except, perhaps, finding the love they both ran from and sought. They came with paperbacks and Diet Cokes in hand, with mini Bic lighters in the small change pockets of their jeans, with mysterious female treasures tucked into the folds of their backpacks and purses, raw materials unseen and perplexing to even the brightest of the male species. They got on their buses and trains in Cleveland and Pittsburgh and Youngstown, in Indianapolis and Newark. They hitched rides from Baltimore and D.C. and Richmond. They smelled of the road. They smelled of Daddy and cigarettes and cheap food and even cheaper perfume. They smelled of hunger. Of desire.

They had so many styles—from Goth to grunge, from Barbie to baby doll—yet they seemed to have just one heart, one thing that united them in their differences. They all needed tending. They all needed loving care.

Some, of course, more than others.

JOSEPH SWANN SAT near the periodicals room of the main branch of the Free Library. There were fifty-four branches citywide, but Swann preferred the main branch for its size, for the way it diminished a patron by proportion. He preferred it for its choice.

The library also attracted runaways. It was indeed a free space, and in summer the air-conditioning was splendidly cool. Along the parkway, from City Hall to the art museum, they could often be seen blending in with students and tourists. Locals rarely walked the sidewalks here, along Benjamin Franklin Parkway, a wide tree-lined boulevard fashioned after the Champs-Élysées in Paris. In summer it was packed with sightseers.

Swann was one of the Philadelphians who did come here often. In addition to the library he also frequented the Rodin Museum, the Franklin Institute, the steps of the art museum, which reminded him of the *Scalinata della Trinità dei Monti*, the Spanish Steps in Rome. Here, as there, people lunched on the steps, lingered, romanced, photographed.

But for the night children, the Free Library was a place to spend a few quiet hours. As long as you were relatively quiet, and you looked to be studying or researching something, you were left alone.

And it was for this reason that Swann was rarely unaccompanied in his quest, regardless of the venue. There were others, so many others, he had seen over the years. Men who came for their own dark purposes. Men who lingered too long near restrooms and fast-food restaurants located near middle schools. Men who parked on suburban streets, maps deceptively in hand for cover, side and rearview mirrors adjusted toward sidewalks and playgrounds.

There, right now, stood just such a man. He was younger than Swann, perhaps in his late twenties. He had long, thin hair pulled back into a ponytail, tucked into his shirt. Swann pegged the man by the cant of his lascivious leer, the angle of his hips, the nervous fingers. He was covertly watching a girl at one of the catalog computers. The girl was adorable in her matching pink T-shirt and jeans, but she was far too young. The man may have thought he was invisible to others, especially to the girls themselves, but not to Joseph Swann. Swann could smell the repulsiveness of his soul from across the room. He wanted to put the man in the world of a particularly gruesome illusion called *Strobika*, a deliciously shocking effect that involved sharpened spikes and—

Swann calmed himself. There was no time, nor need, for anything of the sort.

This man was nothing like him. This man was a predator, a ped-erast, a criminal. Few things made Swann angrier.

Over the months, as his mind fit these pieces into his puzzle, he had often wondered about the fates of those he had not chosen, those com-pletely unaware just how close they had come to becoming part of his riddle. How close they had come to becoming part of *history*.

Given his needs, the selection process was easier than one might think. Often, a single stroll through the library's computer center, where patrons could sign on to the Internet, produced interesting re-sults. One glance at what someone was looking at on the Web told him much about the person. If he followed, and was pressed for a topic, he could recall the subject of their search and weave it into conversation. It rarely failed to engage.

Swann glanced at his watch, then across the room, toward the mag-azine racks. Sunlight suddenly streamed through the windows, and he saw her. A new maiden, slouching in the corner armchair. His heart skipped a beat.

This one was about seventeen or so. She had coal black hair. She was Asian-American, perhaps of Japanese descent. She had the slightest overbite, her two front teeth resting on her lower lip as she twirled a strand of hair, deep in concentration on her periodical, biting gently down as the possibilities swirled, all the choices presented to one so young.

He watched her as she idly flipped through the pages. Every so often she glanced at the doorways, out the windows; watching, waiting, hoping. Her fingernails were raw and red. Her hair was three days or more from a shampoo.

At just after 9:20—Swann checked his watch again, these moments were valued in his memory—she put down the magazine, picked up an-other, then gazed across the room, a downy longing to which Swann in-stantly responded.

The girl rose from her table, returned the magazine to its rack, tra-versed the room, the lobby, and stepped onto Vine Street, her nutmeg skin aglow in the Philadelphia summer morning. She believed she had nowhere to go, it seemed, no destination known.

Joseph Swann knew differently.

He had just the place.

NINETEEN

THE SAVOY WAS OPEN FOR BREAKFAST, AND FAIRLY WELL KNOWN FOR ITS three-egg Greek omelets and paprika-laced home fries, but it also served liquor, starting at 7 AM. When Jessica walked in she saw that Detective Jimmy Valentine was taking full advantage of the liquid portion of the menu. He was at a booth near the back.

Jessica traversed the restaurant. As she approached, Valentine rose.

"Nice to meet you, Detective."

"And you," Jessica replied.

They shook hands. Jimmy Valentine was about forty. He had dark Irish good looks, just beginning to crease; black hair tipping silver. He wore a navy suit with subtle gray stripes, decent quality, open white shirt, gold on both wrists. Good-looking in a South Philly way, Jessica thought. He'd had better days than this, though.

"It's Balzano, right?"

"It is."

"I know that name," he said, holding their handshake just a beat too long. "Why do I know that name?"

Jessica was getting used to this. If you were a woman on the job, and married to another cop, you were always in your husband's shadow. Regardless of your own reputation or rank. You could be chief, you could be *commissioner*, and you would still be a half-step behind your spouse. Such was law enforcement. "My husband is on the job."

Valentine let go of Jessica's hand, as if it were suddenly radioactive.

He snapped his fingers. "Vincent," he said. "You're married to Vincent Balzano?"

"For better or worse," Jessica said.

Valentine laughed, winked. In another life, Jessica might have been charmed. "What are you having?" he asked.

"Just coffee."

He caught a waitress's eye. A few moments later Jessica had a cup in front of her.

"Thanks for seeing me," she said.

Valentine mugged. He was a player. "Not a problem. But, like I said on the phone, I already talked to Detective Malone."

"And, like I said on the phone, I appreciate that we're keeping this off the record."

Valentine nodded, tapped out a nervous paradiddle on the table. "What can I do you for, Detective?"

"How long have you been with the DA's office?"

"Nine years," Valentine said. There was an edge to his voice that implied he suddenly found this number to be a long time. Perhaps too long.

"And how long were you partnered with Eve Galvez?"

"Almost three years."

Jessica nodded. "In all that time, did she make many enemies? I mean, more than the usual? Anyone who might have wanted to take the standard shit to the next level?"

Valentine thought. "Nobody stands out. We all get our threats, right? Eve was tough to read."

"So what happened? I mean, when she went missing."

Valentine drained his glass, called for another drink. "Well she had a week coming, right? The following Monday she just doesn't show up. That's about it." He shrugged. "It had happened before."

"Was she troubled?"

Valentine laughed. It was an empty sound. "You know anybody on the job who ain't?"

"Point taken," Jessica said. "When was the last time you saw her?"

Jessica expected some hesitation, some grasping at memory. Valentine did neither. "I can tell you exactly when it was," he said. "I can tell you where and when and why. I can tell you about the weather. I can tell you what I had for breakfast that day. I can even tell you what she was wearing."

Jessica thought about this. She wondered if the relationship between Jimmy Valentine and Eve Galvez went beyond the walls of 3 Penn Square.

"She had on a red dress and a kind of short black jacket," he continued. "The kind that comes to here." Valentine indicated his waist. "You know the kind I mean?"

"Like a bolero jacket?"

"Yeah. Right." He snapped his fingers. "A bolero jacket." The waitress brought his cocktail. He weaved a little bit as he got animated about the story. "We had just shuttled a witness from the airport to that Marriott next to City Hall. We went to the Continental afterward. Had a few drinks, talked about a few of our cases."

"Do you remember which cases?"

"Sure. We had a trial coming up. Remember that kid who got shot on his bicycle in Fishtown? The road-rage kid?"

"Yeah," Jessica said.

Valentine rubbed the heels of his hands into his eyes. "The day she was due back? She didn't show. That's about it. If you knew her, if you worked with her, you expected it."

"What about her car?" Jessica knew this was in the official report. She was pushing.

"They never found it."

Jessica sipped her coffee. She'd finally come to the point. "So, what did you think happened, Jimmy?"

Valentine shrugged. "At first I thought she grabbed her purse and just left town for a few more days. Maybe shacked up somewhere. Said '*Fuck off*, Philly.' " He glanced at the windows, the people passing by. "If you saw her place you'd understand. A couch, a chair, a table. Nothing on the walls. Nothing in the fridge. She was a Spartan."

"And you thought she would just take off without a word? Not even to you?"

Another slow spin of his tumbler. "Yeah, well. I wanted to think we were closer, you know? But I was kidding myself. I don't think anyone ever got to know her. You know the life. Like everyone else, I thought the worst. A cop disappears, you think the worst."

And it was the worst that happened to Eve Galvez.

"There was one case she was obsessed with," Valentine said, unasked.

"What case?"

"She wouldn't tell me. I asked her, went through her desk, even her purse once. Never found a thing. But it was all about some kid."

"Kid?" Jessica asked. "Kid as in child?"

"I don't think so. Not a kid of tender age. A teenager, maybe. I never found out. Eve was good at things like that."

"Good? Good at what?"

Valentine worked the cubes in his glass. "Covering. Diverting. Misdirecting. She was the best liar I've ever met."

Jessica absorbed it all, glanced at her watch. "I have to hit the street," she said. "Once again, I appreciate you reaching out like this."

Jessica stood, dropped a twenty on the table, buying Jimmy Valentine's last two rounds. It did not go unnoticed. They shook hands again.

"Ask you a question, Detective?"

"Sure," Jessica said.

"Are you taking an interest here?"

"An interest?" Jessica replied. It was a freeze. They both knew it. She *was* taking an interest and, except for the obvious reasons, she had no idea why.

TWENTY

SWANN ENJOYED THIS PART MOST OF ALL. THE CARING. THE PREENING. The *tending*.

The girl had been easy. Almost too easy. Had he made a mistake? Was she unworthy of his efforts? When she left the library he followed her in his car for a few blocks on Vine Street. When the traffic behind him urged him forward, he circled the block, twice, having been swept up in center-lane traffic, unable to pull over. At first he thought he had lost her, and had a few anxious moments. When he turned north onto Sixteenth Street he saw her. She was standing at the side of the road, hitchhiking, angling for a ride on the Vine Street Expressway.

He pulled over, all but disbelieving his providence. She got in.

Just like that.

She was not afraid. She was at that age when everything still held adventure, everything was a bold and exciting escapade, an age when it was a certainty that you will never grow old, and that fear and mistrust will never become your mantra.

Had they been seen? Swann didn't know. In a city like Philadelphia, anything was possible. In a city like Philadelphia you could be completely invisible, or you could stand out like a diamond in a dunghill, to borrow a phrase from Thomas Jefferson.

Her name was Patricia Sato. She was from Albany, New York. They talked about music and film. She was a fan of an actor named James McAvoy.

"I thought he was great in *Atonement*," Swann had said. "Perhaps even better in *The Last King of Scotland*."

Patricia Sato was amazed he had ever heard of James McAvoy.

Of course, Swann was well versed in pop culture—music, films, television, fashion. He fastidiously did his research, and had yet to fail to keep up his end of the conversation.

When they reached the entrance to the Schuylkill Expressway, and Patricia realized he was not taking her to Old City as she had asked, she panicked. She tried the doors. She pounded on the windows.

Swann put a hand into the air in front of her. "*Gomen nasai*," he said in apology.

Patricia turned to him quickly, stunned that he spoke Japanese. He snapped the glass chloroform ampoule beneath her nose.

Moments later Patricia Sato was unconscious.

THE SECOND-FLOOR BATHROOM, just off the master suite, was added in 1938. It was clad in ecru tile with oyster accents. The floor was a black-and-white checkerboard pattern. The pedestal sink and claw-foot tub were sparkling white, and featured polished nickel fixtures.

As Swann filled the tub, he poured in two capfuls of Vanilla Shimmer by L'Occitane.

"*What are the six basic types of conjuring effects?*"

Swann ignored the voice. He tried to enjoy the moment. He luxuriated in the rich vanilla fragrance. Soon it would smell of warm girl.

"*Joseph?*"

He turned off the tap, dried his hands. He attempted to fill his head with music, with selections from a recent recording he had purchased, a Telarc recording of Tchaikovsky's *Pathetique*, performed by the Cincinnati Symphony Orchestra.

"*Joseph Edmund Swann!*"

Swann closed his eyes for a moment. He felt the cold steel of the chains against his skin. The terrible licorice smell of absinthe. The voice would not leave him alone. It never did. He began.

"The six types of conjuring effects are as follows," he said.

He crossed the space to the linen closet. He had long ago purchased a set of Turkish cotton towels in peach, just for this day. He took out a bath sheet, draped it over the towel-warmer.

"Number one. Appearance. In which an object appears where it was not." He straightened the bath rug, surveyed his domain. More candles.

"Next!"

"Number two. Vanish. In which an object *disappears* from where it was." He decided on unscented candles. He did not want to overpower the room with any one fragrance. He returned to the linen closet, removed six more tower candles—all white—and began to place them around the bathroom. When he was done, he looked at the overall composition. He was not pleased. He moved two candles closer to the head of the tub. Better.

"I'm listening."

"Number three. Transposition. In which an object changes position in space." Swann removed the lighter from his vest pocket, a slim Dunhill in sterling silver. One by one he lighted the candles. The bubbles in the tub created small rainbows in the soft light.

"Joseph!"

"Number four. Transformation. In which an object changes form." He stepped out of the bathroom, into the bedroom. The girl was sprawled across the bed. He had given her a second ampoule. He needed her to be pliant for her bath. He slipped a thick canvas apron over his head, tied it in the front.

"This will not do, Joseph."

"Number five. Penetration. In which matter passes through matter." He undressed the girl, gently folding her clothes and putting them on the dresser, a nearly perfect Louis XVI Psyche chest he had acquired in Toronto. He took off her shoes. There was a folded five dollar bill in one of them. It was damp with perspiration, flattened with the weight of a hundred miles. He wondered how long it had been in there, what she had sacrificed not to spend it. Joseph Swann took it and put it into the pocket of her jeans.

"I'm waiting."

Swann wanted to discontinue this routine, as he always had, but he knew this was not an option. His one weapon was the irritation of delay. He lifted the girl and carried her into the bathroom. She was feather-light in his arms.

He sat the girl down on the commode, tested the water in the tub. It was perfect. The mirrors and windows were misted with fragrant steam.

"I will strike you down, Singing Boy!"

He closed his eyes, brushed back the rage, waiting defiantly for a reprimand. He was met with silence. A small victory.

"Number six. Restoration," he finally said, in his own time. "In which an object is restored to its original condition."

And then there was stillness. A deep, celestial peace.

Joseph Swann lowered Patricia Sato into the frothy bubbles.

TWENTY-ONE

A T ONE O'CLOCK, JUST AS JESSICA WAS CALLING IN A TAKE-OUT ORDER, the phone rang.

It always did. It was lunchtime.

"Homicide. Balzano."

"Detective Balzano." It was a young woman's voice. Familiar, although Jessica couldn't immediately place it. She usually could.

"This is Officer Caruso," the woman continued. "Maria Caruso."

Of course, Jessica thought. "Yes, Officer. What can I do for you?"

"I'm at the Shiloh Street address."

"What's up?"

Officer Maria Caruso hesitated for a moment. Jessica could tell that the young woman was leading up to something she found difficult to say.

"It's about the rug. The rug in the basement."

"What about it?" Jessica asked.

"Well, we rolled it up and we found something underneath."

"What did you find?"

A crackling on the line covered the pause for a few seconds. "There was a hole cut into the floor."

"A hole?"

"More like a door," Maria Caruso said. "A big square door cut into the wood planking. Maybe three-by-three feet. An access door to a crawlspace."

"Did you open the door?"

"We did."

Time stalled again. For a moment, Jessica wondered if the connection had failed. "Officer?"

"I went down there. It was bad."

It was as flat a statement of fact as Jessica had ever heard. A blank, reluctant declaration, as if the young woman wanted to take it all back. "You went down there?"

"Yes ma'am. And my boss, Sergeant Reed, well, he'll be calling Sergeant Buchanan any second now. I just thought you might want a heads-up on this. I hope I don't get into any trouble."

"You won't," Jessica said, although she could not guarantee this. "A heads-up on what?"

"You should . . . well, you'll see."

"Okay," Jessica said. "Thanks for calling."

"Sure."

Jessica hung up, called Byrne's cell phone, got his voice mail, left a message. A minute later she tried again. Same result.

A big square door cut into the wood planking.

Jessica flipped through Caitlin O'Riordan's case files, rereading some of the witness interviews. There were a number of them. Every so often she'd glance up, waiting for Ike Buchanan to step out of his office, catch her eye.

It was bad.

THE EXTERIOR OF 4514 SHILOH STREET looked essentially the same as it had when they were there the day before, save for the two CSU vans and three sector cars. There were a few more teddy bears at the Florita Ramos memorial next door, a few more flowers. Someone had left a pink panda. It still had the price tag on it. A crowd was assembling across the street.

Byrne still had not called back. For the moment, Jessica was working solo. She hated it.

Having changed from her skirt and blouse into a comfortable pair of Levi's, Jessica exited her car, clipped her badge on her belt, slipped under the bright yellow tape. She was briefed by Sgt. Thad Reed, the day-work commander of the Crime Scene Unit. All Jessica knew was that they had a female DOA in the crawlspace of the building. According to Reed, nothing down there had been disturbed. Photos and video had been taken.

Jessica looked at the sky. The temperature was a tolerable but humid eighty.

Still no rain.

Officer Maria Caruso was off duty, but it appeared that she couldn't bring herself to leave. Jessica understood. When you're young, you get emotionally protective of crime scenes. Every cop had been in that position. If Officer Caruso was ordered off the premises, Jessica had the feeling she would step a few inches past the crime-scene tape and observe, like the ever-growing throng.

Jessica took the young woman lightly by the arm, led her a few doorways south.

"Are you okay?" Jessica asked.

Maria Caruso nodded, a little too forcefully. Jessica wondered whom she was trying to convince.

"I'm good, ma'am."

Officer Caruso looked better than she had sounded on the phone. On the other hand, she'd had twenty minutes or so to suck it up.

"You found the body?"

Officer Caruso nodded again. She took a few quick breaths.

"Did you disturb anything?"

"No ma'am."

"Gloves on?"

"Yes."

Jessica looked at the building, back. She took out her notebook, flipped to a blank page, slipped a rubber band around it. Old habit. She always had a rubber band or two on her somewhere. There was usually one around one of her wrists.

"Was it okay that I called you?" Officer Caruso asked, lowering her voice.

It really wasn't, but Jessica wasn't going to get into that now. The kid would learn. "Don't worry about it." Jessica slipped her notebook back into her pocket.

"Can I ask you something?" Jessica asked.

"Sure."

Jessica wanted this to come out right. It might mean something to this young officer somewhere down the road. She took a second, remembering when she had been asked this very question. "Do you have ambitions on this job?"

"Ambitions?"

"What I mean is, do you see yourself on the force in ten years?"

The look on Officer Caruso's face said that she had indeed given this a lot of thought. On the other hand, it also said that she didn't want to just blurt out the answer. "Yes," she finally said. "I mean, I *do* have ambitions, ma'am. Very much so."

At that moment, in the diffused sunlight of the alleyway, Maria Caruso looked about sixteen. *Take off, kid,* Jessica thought. *Hang up that belt and run. Go be a lawyer or an architect or a surgeon or a country-western singer. Make it to fifty with your sanity and all your parts intact.*

"May I ask what you want to do?" Jessica asked. "What unit you want to work?"

Officer Caruso smiled, blushed. "I want to work homicides, of course," she said. "Just like everybody else. Just like you."

Oh, man, Jessica thought. *No, no, no.* She'd have to get this kid hammered one night at Finnigan's Wake. Explain the ways of the world. For now, she decided to let it go. She glanced at the doorway. "I'd better get in there."

"Sure," Officer Caruso said. She looked at her watch. "I've got to get going anyway. I've got to pick up my daughter."

"You have a little girl?"

Maria Caruso beamed. "Carmen. She's twenty-two months. And counting."

Jessica smiled. *Twenty-two months.* Spoken like a young mother trying to hang on to a child's infancy. Jessica had done the same thing. "Well, thanks again for the good work."

"You're welcome." Officer Caruso stuck out her hand. They shook hands, a little clumsily.

A few seconds later Jessica turned, walked a few feet up the cracked and baking sidewalk. She took out her notebook, glanced at her watch, noted the time, snapped the rubber band. Another old habit.

As she crossed the threshold, she turned, saw Maria Caruso getting into her own car, a ten-year-old Honda Accord. There was rust along the rocker panels, a missing hubcap, a cracked taillight held together with masking tape.

I want to work homicides, of course. Just like everybody else. Just like you.

You might want to think about that a little longer, Maria.

JESSICA LOGGED INTO THE CRIME SCENE, walked into the building. Although she had been there just a day earlier, the interior looked completely different. It was almost presentable. At least to someone thinking about renovating the place. There were still basketball-sized holes in the drywall, still an inch of grease and mold on everything, but a lot of the trash had been removed, and with it seemed to have gone ninety percent of the flies.

Jessica moved down the hallway, then the narrow wooden stairs, into the partial basement, which was now brightly lit with police lights. The floor was not poured concrete, as she might have originally guessed, but rather an old wood planking. It had at one time been painted a deep claret enamel. Before that, as the chipped-away sections told her, something that appeared to be ash gray. The walls were bare concrete block, the ceiling unfinished, just open joists, criss-crossed with one-by-three bridging, dense with cobwebs.

Jessica immediately saw what she was there to see. There was a hole cut into the center of the floor. Next to it lay a plywood square, probably the access door. There was a finger hole drilled near the center. Neither were precisely square.

The rolled-up rug was against the wall.

For the moment, there was only one other person in the basement. An experienced uniformed officer named Stan Keegan. He stood next to the access hole, hands clasped in front of him. He nodded to Jessica.

"Afternoon, Detective."

"Hey, Stanley," she said. "You look good. You losing weight?"

"Twenty-eight ounces in the past twelve days. That's nearly two pounds."

"Awesome," Jessica said. "What's your secret?"

"Fat-free croutons," Keegan said. "You'd be amazed how regular croutons pile on the calories."

"I'll make a note."

Keegan shoved his hands in his pockets, rocked on his heels. "Where's the big man?"

Jessica pulled her hair back, grabbed a rubber band off her wrist, ponytailed her hair. She snapped on a pair of latex gloves. "Detective Byrne has the afternoon off."

"Sweet," Keegan mugged. "Must be nice to have seniority."

Jessica laughed. "What are you talking about? You've been here longer than anyone, Stan. It's you who should be eating Milk Duds at the movies."

It was true. No one really knew how long Stan Keegan had been a Philadelphia police officer. White-haired, potbellied, bowlegged, a face like a just-boiled scampi, he seemed to have come with the city itself. Like an accessory. Keegan often told people he was on William Penn's original security detail.

"Last good movie I saw was *The Quiet Man*," Keegan said.

"What was that, 1950?"

"Won two Oscars. 1952. John Wayne, Maureen O'Hara, Barry Fitzgerald. Directed by John Ford. Greatest film ever made."

Stan Keegan said *fill-um*. Jessica was going to ask him if he knew which Oscars the movie had won, but she figured he did. She stepped closer, glanced into the square hole. She couldn't see much. She wasn't looking forward to this. "Have you been down there?"

Keegan shook his head. "That's above my pay grade, Detective. Plus, I have this unnaturally low tolerance for the sight of dead bodies. Always have."

Jessica recalled her days in uniform, days when she'd had to secure a crime scene. It was always a relief when the detectives showed up. "I understand."

"Does that make me a homophobe?" Keegan asked.

"Only if the dead person is gay, Stan."

"Ah."

Jessica knelt on the floor. There was no ladder, but that didn't seem to be a problem. The crawlspace looked to be only about forty inches deep or so. "You sure I can't promote you, just for the afternoon?" she asked.

Jessica saw the right corner of Stan Keegan's mouth rise a millimeter. For Officer Keegan, this was the equivalent of laughing hysterically. "No thanks."

"All right." Jessica took a few deep breaths. "The sooner I get down there, right?"

"*Dia duit*, Detective."

As far as Jessica knew, this was a Gaelic phrase meaning "God to you." The long tradition of the Irish in law enforcement in most major cities in America infused a lot of Gaelic traditions and language into the department, even if the closest you came to being Irish was drinking Irish coffees. She'd heard many black and Hispanic officers spouting Irish proverbs in the past, albeit usually around last call. "Thanks, Stan."

Jessica swung her legs over the edge, sat on the floor for a moment. Beneath her, the temporary police lights in the crawlspace cast a yellow, ghostlike glow along the hard pack floor. Long shadows filtered across her field of vision.

Shadows of what? Jessica wondered. She looked a little more closely and saw the vague outline of three boxes, their silhouettes elongated by the bright lights.

Three boxes in a crawlspace. One female DOA.

Jessica said a silent prayer, and lowered herself into the ground.

TWENTY-TWO

BYRNE STOOD ON THE CORNER OF TWENTIETH AND MARKET STREETS. As the lunchtime crowd flowed around him, he glanced at his phone. He had turned it off. He wasn't supposed to do this, but he had half a day off, and he was going to take it. He could still think, even when he was off duty, couldn't he? On the other hand, he couldn't recall ever feeling completely off duty, not in the past fifteen years. He once took a week in the Poconos, and found himself mulling over his caseload while sitting in a creaky Adirondack chair, sipping Old Forester out of a jelly jar. Such was the life.

His mind drifted from Caitlin O'Riordan to Laura Somerville to Eve Galvez.

Eve.

Somehow he had always known what happened to her. He hadn't imagined such a gruesome fate, but he had known it was bad. He had always hoped that he was wrong. He knew that they were—

He felt a hand on his arm.

Byrne spun, his heart in his throat. It was his daughter, Colleen.

"Hey, Dad," she signed.

"Hey."

His daughter hugged him, and the world broke out in roses.

THEY WALKED DOWN MARKET STREET, toward the Schuylkill. The sun was high and hot. The lunchtime crowd streamed by.

"You look so good," she signed. "Like, *really* good."

Colleen Siobhan Byrne had been deaf since birth, proficient at American Sign Language since the age of seven. These days she taught it part-time at an inner-city school. Her father was pretty good at it too.

"I'm getting there," Byrne said. It had been a slow climb back since he had been shot three years earlier. He had realized this past spring, on a damp morning when everything, including his eyebrows and ankles and tongue hurt like hell, that he had to do something. He'd had a man-in-the-mirror talk with himself. He knew that if he didn't make a move, at this age, he never would. He was even considering a yoga class, although he would never tell anyone. Even his daughter. He'd even gone so far as to pick up a yoga DVD, and had tried a few of the breathing exercises. He had also been working with weights twice a week, too. Anything to stay out of physical therapy.

"Have you been working out?" she asked.

"A little," Byrne signed.

"A *little*?" She grabbed his upper left arm, squeezed. "Don't get too buff on me, Dad," she signed. "All my girlfriends think you're pretty cute as it is."

Byrne blushed. No one could get to him like his daughter.

Colleen looped her arm through his.

At Twenty-first, a pair of spike-haired boys approached them, boys around seventeen, both wearing torn jeans, black T-shirts bearing some death message. They both leered at Colleen in her white sundress, at Byrne's signing, then back to Colleen. They nudged each other, as if to say that the fact that this hot blond was deaf made her even hotter. The boys smiled at his daughter. Byrne wanted to drop them where they stood. He resisted.

When they stopped, waiting for the light on Twenty-second Street, Byrne knew it was time to ask. He got his daughter's attention.

"So," he began. "What's this all about?"

Two days earlier, Donna Sullivan Byrne, Kevin Byrne's ex-wife, Colleen's mother, had called out of the blue. She said she wanted to see him, to have lunch. Just like that. *Lunch*. It was nearly an alien construct for the two of them.

They hadn't really had lunch since they were courting. Their divorce had been reasonably amicable—if you considered the Crimean

War amicable—but they had tolerated seeing each other over the years for Colleen. The other day, on the phone, Donna had seemed kind of like the *old* Donna. Flirtatious and happy. Happy to talk to *him*. It didn't take the world's greatest detective to know that something was up. Byrne just didn't have a clue what it could be.

Of course, he hadn't slept more than two hours in a row thinking about this.

"I swear I don't know," Colleen signed on the tail of a mysterious smile.

She stopped at a metal box of newspapers, one of a half dozen, and picked up a copy of *The Report*, the sleaziest free weekly in Philly, which was saying something. Even for free it was grossly overpriced. Byrne winced. Colleen laughed. She knew her father's history with the paper. As they walked on, Colleen flipped to page three, halved it, like she knew where she was going. She did. She pointed to the picture of Caitlin O'Riordan.

"This is your case, isn't it?" she signed.

Byrne hated to talk about the ugliness of his job with Colleen, but he had to constantly remind himself of late that she was no longer a child. Far from it. She would be in college before he knew it.

He nodded.

"The girl was a runaway?"

"Yes," Byrne signed. "She was from Lancaster."

Colleen looked at the article for a few moments, then folded the paper and put it into her tote bag.

Byrne thought about how blessed he was, how bright, and capable and resourceful his daughter was. He then thought of Robert O'Riordan, and the four months of hell through which the man had lived. Byrne had no idea if they were ever going to close the O'Riordan case. About this Kevin Byrne had a number of hopes, as well.

When they reached the building, Byrne looked at his daughter, she at him. He must have looked exactly the way he felt.

Colleen rolled her eyes, swatted him on the arm. "You are *such* a baby."

Byrne silently agreed and held open the door.

BYRNE AND COLLEEN were seated at a table at Bistro St. Tropez, near the windows overlooking the Schuylkill River. The sun had come out again, and the water sparkled. They sat without conversing for a while, just enjoying their nearness.

Soon a shadow crossed the table. Byrne looked up. A woman stood next to their table, a butterscotch blond with a slender figure and a beautiful smile. She wore a pale-lemon linen suit.

The woman was his ex-wife, the love of his life. Byrne stood. Donna kissed him on the cheek. She thumbed off her lipstick—an old endearment—and his legs wobbled.

Big city cop, Byrne thought. Real tough guy. He'd been shot, stabbed, and punched more times than he could count. The slightest touch of his wife's thumb and he was down for the count.

THEY SIPPED THEIR WATERS, glanced around at the well-dressed clientele, made their small talk. They perused the menus. Okay, Byrne did. It seemed Donna and Colleen had been here before, and knew what they wanted long before he did. They both ordered salads—one Poulet Moroccan, one Belle Mer—and Byrne ordered the Burger St. Tropez.

No one was surprised.

While they waited for their food, Byrne tried to keep up with the gossip, but he was really lost in a fog. Donna Sullivan was still the most beautiful and vibrant woman he had ever met. From the moment he first laid eyes on her next to a 7-Eleven, when they were both teenagers, he had always been in her thrall. He'd had many affairs since the divorce, had even thought he felt the real thing a few times, but his heart still stuttered every time they met.

Donna had worked as a real-estate agent for the past five years, but had recently joined a small interior design firm. She had always been creative, had taken design courses in college, but had never found the proper outlet. Now, it seemed, she had.

The lunch hour passed far too quickly. At least a dozen times as they ate and talked and laughed, Byrne thought, *I'm with my wife and daughter. I'm actually sitting in a restaurant with the two girls who actually mean something to me on this planet.*

Okay, two of the three. Jessica would kill him.

At just before two o'clock Donna glanced at her watch. She grabbed the check. Byrne objected, but just a little. She made a lot more than he did.

She signed, the leatherette notebook was whisked away, they finished their coffees. She then reached into her bag, pulled out a photo, showed it to Byrne.

"We're redoing a house in Bryn Mawr. They want us to reupholster this couch. Isn't it fabulous?"

Byrne looked at the picture. It was an antique red velvet backless couch, with one end raised. He had no idea how anyone could actually sit on it. "Where's Cate Blanchett?"

Colleen laughed, signed, "You are *so* hip, Dad."

"It's called a fainting couch," Donna said. "I think they paid about fourteen thousand dollars for it."

"I understand the fainting part, then."

"Look, I have to go check out some fabrics for it," Donna said as they were getting ready to leave. "It's just upstairs. Why don't you come up with us? It will be fun."

Fabrics. Fun.

"You know, as much as I would love to do this—you know me and fabrics—I really have to get back," he said.

Byrne made eye contact with Colleen. Colleen's eyes said that she knew he was talking about the Caitlin O'Riordan case. She gave a slight nod, meaning it was okay. She could not only read his lips like an expert, she could read his heart.

Byrne immediately felt bad about taking the rest of the day off. He'd head back to the Roundhouse from here. Either that or lie to his daughter. It was no contest.

"Oh all right, macho man," Donna said. They left the bistro, stood in the fourth floor hallway, waiting for the elevator. Then, completely out of the blue, Donna kissed him. Not on the cheek. Not a two-peck Euro style kiss. It was a full-blown, let's-get-a-room-sailor French kiss, the first in years. *Many* years. Donna pulled back, looked deep into his eyes. Kevin Byrne tumbled, teetered on the edge of saying something stupid, caught himself, then said it anyway.

"Yeah. Well. I didn't feel a thing," he said. "You?"

Donna shrugged. "I think one toe may have curled just a little, but that's about it."

They both laughed.

"We'll walk you down," she said.

Byrne, still reeling, watched his ex-wife and daughter step into the elevator ahead of him. They were the same height now. They looked so much alike that his heart ached. From behind, they were almost indistinguishable. Two women.

In the lobby, Colleen took out her digital camera, took a picture of Byrne and Donna.

Byrne hugged them both again, made his good-byes. Donna walked toward the elevators, cell phone out. Colleen lingered for a moment.

Byrne pushed through the huge doors, into the bright afternoon sun. He took out his handkerchief, wiped his lips. Donna's lipstick glanced seductively back. For some reason he stopped, turned. Colleen was watching him. She was perfectly framed in the lobby's square front window. She smiled her melancholy, teenage smile, held up her hand.

I love you, Dad, she signed.

Byrne's heart flew.

TWENTY-THREE

FROM THE MOMENT JESSICA LOWERED HERSELF INTO THE CRAWLSPACE she was confronted with the smell of old death. All around her she heard vermin scurrying through dry trash.

She thought of Eve Galvez in her shallow grave.

The crawlspace was at one time a storage area for whatever enterprises had occupied the first floor of the building. In the corners were dusty wooden crates, stacks of flattened and twined cardboard boxes, plastic milk crates.

Jessica knelt on the hard dirt floor, ran her Maglite around the corners. The crawlspace measured the approximate size of the building above, that being sixteen by twenty-five or so. Rusted iron pipes and commercial-gauge electrical wire ran overhead. To her left, near the front of the building, was a sanitary stack. Between the joists overhead a spider had spun a silken, silvery web, spanning the trusses. Small carcasses hung from its outer edges.

In the center of the crawlspace were three large wooden boxes.

The boxes were not aligned in a row. The center box was off to one side, forming, from Jessica's perspective, a blocky letter *C*. Each cube measured about thirty inches, each a different color—one yellow, one blue, one red.

The three marks on the page of the Bible, she thought. *The red, blue, and yellow squares.*

She looked at the first box, the one painted yellow. She knew this one had been opened. There was a slight gap between the door on top and the sides, a gap of an inch or so. Jessica was concerned that the person who opened it had been Officer Caruso, a clear breach of procedure. In a situation such as this, all kinds of precautions could have, and should have, been taken.

Jessica eased open the lid. The hinges creaked, echoing off the hard walls. She angled the beam of her flashlight.

Inside was a thing of nightmares.

The partial, long-decayed corpse wore a spangled red sweater, big silver hoop earrings. Around the neck was a distinctive black opal necklace. Jessica had seen it before. She knew who this was. She might have known all along.

It was the girl in the photograph they had found in the Bible. The girl irretrievably connected to Caitlin O'Riordan.

The girl they were supposed to find.

TWENTY-FOUR

H E HAD GIVEN THE GIRL A MUCH-NEEDED BATH, WASHED AND CONDI-
tioned her hair, averting his eyes as much as he could and still do a
proper job, lest the girl find him immodest or, even worse, lecherous.

He used a mint shampoo from Origins.

Restoration, he had thought with a smile. *In which an object is restored
to its original condition.*

When they were finished, he wheeled her down the hall. She was
still a little groggy. He had given her yet another Brisette, one of his
crushable ampoules containing chloroform. In the 1970s his father had
purchased hundreds of them from an English woman who worked as a
midwife. Joseph knew all too well their effect.

"Are you comfortable, my love?"

She turned her head slowly, remained silent.

They entered an upstairs sewing room. It was one of Joseph's favorite rooms. The wallpaper was a blowsy floral in water silk, papered
from the skirting board up to the dado rail. But the room was much
more than beautiful. It was magic. With the touch of a button, located
behind the reproduction of William Beattie-Brown's *Golden Highlands*,
the eastern wall would rise and give onto a small parlor overlooking the
rear of the property. The touch of another button, this one beneath the
spy window overlooking the great room, would release a four-by-four
trapdoor behind the divan. Swann had never found the need to use either.

He positioned her in front of the television and pressed the PLAY button on the remote, starting the video.

"Attend, the Great Cygne," Swann said.

He had transferred all the old film footage—there was precious little of it, reaching back to his father's early performances in 1948—to videocassette years ago. The original 8 mm footage had been brittle, and he had found a company in South Philly that transferred old home movies to CD, DVD, and videocassette.

The first images were of his father as a very young man, perhaps twenty. An entertainer of German extraction, performing in New York City in the late 1940s. What courage it must have taken, Joseph often thought.

A quick cut found his father at about twenty-eight. He now sat at a nightclub table with five others. It was a static, high-angle shot. Vegas, late 1950s. The very best place at the one of the very best times in history. The Great Cygne performed some coin magic to a delighted crowd. He executed Four Coins to a Glass, the Flying Eagles, the Traveling Centavos. In a flourish he grabbed an ice bucket from a passing cart and presented a variation on Miser's Dream.

The next images passed in a blur: a club in Amsterdam, a backyard party in Midland Texas, an appearance at a county fair in Berea, Ohio, a performance for which his father was paid in rolls of quarters.

Image after image, as the tape rolled on, showed a man whose skills and temperament were slowly eroding, a man whose mind was becoming an echoing hollow of horrors, a journeyman illusionist reduced to catalogue tricks: cigarette through a quarter, cut and restored rope, sympathetic cards.

That is why, years earlier, Joseph added a postscript to the tape, a breathtaking coda filmed when his father was in his prime.

The Seven Wonders was a tightly edited, graphic-rich version of a full-length routine his father had performed on a local-access cable channel in Shreveport. Joseph had cut the performance to the sounds of the Lovin' Spoonful's "Do You Believe in Magic?" Hokey, he knew. He had once had thoughts of marketing the event on DVD someday, provided he could get back the rights.

Swann watched for what was perhaps the five hundredth time, his heart racing.

First was the Garden of Flowers, then the Girl Without a Middle, then the Drowning Girl, then the Girl in the Sword Box.

"Watch this," he said to Patricia. "Watch what happens next. This is the Girl in the Sub Tank. This is your part."

When the video was finished, Swann descended the stairs, crossed the great room, allowed himself a glass of sherry. He climbed back upstairs.

"I have a few errands to run, but I will be back, and you and I will have dinner. Maybe we'll even dress. Won't that be fun?"

The girl looked at him. Her velvet gaze was no longer soft. It amazed him again and again how quickly youth faded. He rolled the chair into the guest room and locked the door.

MINUTES LATER, as he prepared to leave, he heard the girl scream. By the time he reached the foyer and slipped into his coat, the sound had receded to a distant echo. By the time he stepped onto the porch, it was only a memory.

The day was bright and sunny, rich with birdsong. Swann singled out a voice. It was a yellow-throated warbler, another lost soul, asking its peculiar questions of the world.

TWENTY-FIVE

Byrne walked to his car, his heart and mind abuzz with the events of the past hour. He still really didn't know what this lunch date with his wife was all about, but he wasn't going to overanalyze it.

Who was he kidding? Besides being one of his most annoying personality quirks, overanalyzing was pretty much what he did for a living.

He took out his phone, fired it up, wincing immediately at the possibility of a dozen angry messages waiting for him. You were never supposed to be completely out of touch with the unit, even if you were off duty, especially if you had active investigations. But in this age of cellular communications, and all its attendant glitches, there was always an excuse.

I couldn't get a signal.
My battery was low.
I had it on Silent.

As soon as the phone went through its boot-up process and found a tower, he got an e-mail. It was from Colleen. She'd sent him the photograph she'd taken in the lobby. It completed his day.

Seconds later his phone rang. Byrne looked at the display. It was Jessica. Even her name looked pissed off. He flipped open the phone, went for bright and cheerful.

"Hey!"

"So *now* you turn your phone off?"

Busted. "I'll explain," Byrne said. "Where are you?"

"Shiloh Street."

"Shiloh Street?" Byrne was a little surprised, a lot intrigued. "Why?"

"We've got a body. Female, mid-teens."

Shit. "Warm or cold?"

"Cold," Jessica said. "Been here for months."

"Inside the house?"

"Yep."

"Where was she?"

"Remember that rug in the basement?" Jessica asked.

"Yeah."

"CSU rolled it up and found a hole cut into the floor. An access hole to the crawlspace."

"She was in the crawlspace?"

"In the crawlspace."

"Any ID on the victim?"

"I haven't been able to confirm it, but my gut tells me we do."

"Why is that?"

"She's wearing the same jewelry as the girl whose picture we found in that Bible."

Byrne's stomach, and mind, began to revolve. This was starting to reach deeper, and further, than he had imagined. And he had imagined something pretty bad. "Go on."

"About an hour ago we got the Missing Person info, so we have a name, but the body is decomposed to the point where a visual ID isn't possible. We're going to have to get dental. Still, I think the clothes and jewelry are a slam."

"We have a COD?"

"We won't know that for a while, but I can make a fairly informed guess," Jessica said.

"What do you mean?"

A moment's hesitation. "You don't want to know."

"It's kinda my job."

Byrne heard his partner clear her throat. It was her usual stall. "She's in pieces, Kevin. In boxes."

"Christ."

"There are three wooden boxes in the crawlspace, but there are only remains in two of them. One box is empty. The one in the middle. And they're painted. Red, blue, and yellow."

"The same colors as those marks in the Bible."

"Yep."

Byrne closed his eyes, recalled the girl in the photograph. She looked so young, so vulnerable. He'd had hopes. Not great hopes, but hopes. "And this is ours?"

"It is."

Byrne took out his notebook, noted the time. "Hit me."

"Presumptively, the victim's name is Monica Louise Renzi," Jessica said, spelling the first and last name. "She was sixteen. From Scranton. Missing for just over six months. Dino and Eric are on the way up just in case."

Jessica was talking about Nick Palladino and Eric Chavez, two experienced detectives from the homicide unit. "Okay."

"This is developing hard and fast, partner," Jessica said. "Ike is down here, and word is that the captain is on his way. Nobody's smoking and everyone's buttoned up. Sarge said he called you three times."

Shit.

"Which one are you going to use?" Jessica asked.

Byrne had to think about it. He didn't want to repeat himself. "I had my phone on silent."

"I like that one," Jessica said. "Get here as fast as you can."

"I'm on the way," Byrne said. He headed toward his car. "One more question for you. Why is this ours again?"

Jessica took a second—a telling second that, between people who know each other well, spoke volumes. Then came the four words Byrne dreaded hearing.

"She was a runaway."

TWENTY-SIX

THE FIRST THING SHE NOTICED WAS THAT THERE WERE A LOT OF FOR-eign people. Foreign people as in Asian, Middle Eastern, African. Not foreign as in folks from three counties over.

The second thing she noticed was that this was, by far, the biggest room she had ever been in. It might have even been too big to classify as a room. It was more like a cathedral. The coffered ceilings had to be fifty feet high, maybe more, offering a dozen or so enormous hanging chandeliers, ringed by the tallest windows she had ever seen. The floors were marble, the hand railings looked like they were made of brass. At one end was a huge bronze statue called the *Angel of the Resurrection*.

As train stations went, she thought, this was probably the Taj Mahal.

She sat on one of the long wooden benches for a while, watching the crowds come and go, listening to the announcements, to the variety of accents and languages, reading—but not really reading—one of the free newspapers. Politics, opinion, reviews, sex ads. Blah, blah, blah. Even the columns on music and movies bored the shit out of her. Which was rare.

Around two o'clock she walked the edges of the huge room a few times, passing by the shops, the ticket machines, the escalators down to the trains. She was still stunned by the scale of the place, still glancing upward every so often. She didn't want to look like a tourist—or even worse, some hick runaway—but she couldn't seem to help herself. The place was that amazing.

At one point she glanced over her shoulder. Three small Mennonite children, perhaps just off the train from Berks County, were looking at the ceiling, too. At least she wasn't alone, she thought. Although, with her tight jeans, Ugg boots, and heavy eye makeup, she was just about the furthest thing from Mennonite she could imagine.

In her experience, the only other place she had ever been that compared to this train station was the King of Prussia mall, the place that had every single store you could imagine, along with a few extra. Burberry, Coach, Eddie Bauer, Louis Vuitton, Hermes. She had visited the mall once when she was about ten. Her aunt had taken her there as a birthday present, but she only came away with a pair of Gap jeans (she preferred Lucky Brand these days) and a bad stomach from something crappy they had eaten at the Ho-Lee Chow or Super Wok or Shang-High or whatever they called the fast-food Chinese restaurant. It was okay, though. Her family was far from rich. Gap was cool back then. Before they left the mall she had found a small discarded shopping bag from Versace and walked around with it at school for three weeks, carrying it like a funky purse. The haters hated, but she didn't care.

According to the brochure she found on the train, the Thirtieth Street station was listed on the National Register of Historic Places, and was 562,000 square feet. Located on Market Street, between Twenty-ninth and Thirtieth, it was one of the busiest intercity passenger facilities in the United States, the brochure went on to say, and it ranked behind only New York's Penn Station and Washington's Union Station in its yearly volume of passengers. In the three previous years there had been 4.4 million people boarding trains in the Thirtieth Street terminal.

Millions, she thought. You'd think there'd be one cute guy. She laughed. She didn't feel like it—there was the rough equivalent of a ball of hot barbed wire in her stomach—but she laughed anyway. The last thing she was doing here was trying to meet cute guys. She was here for something else.

SHE SAT AT ONE OF THE TABLES in the food court, beneath a bright yellow Au Bon Pain umbrella. She tapped her pocket. She was almost broke. When she left the house she'd had sixty-one dollars and change. It seemed like enough money to get through at least a few days on the road.

Knock knock. *Reality calling.*

She dreamed about food. An eight-slice pizza with onions, mushrooms, and red peppers. A double veggie-burger with onion rings. Her taste buds recalled a dish her aunt once made: potato gnocchi with pesto and roasted red potatoes. *God*, she was hungry. But out here there was a well-known equation: runaway = hungry.

It was a truth she had better get used to.

In addition to her rumbling stomach, there was something else she realized that she had better get ready to address. She was on the street, and she needed a street name. She glanced around the room, at the stalls near the doors that led to Thirtieth Street. She watched the people come and go. Every one of them had a name.

Everyone in the world was known by something, she thought. A name, a nickname, an epithet. An *identity*. What were you if you didn't have a name?

Nothing.

Even worse, a number. A Social Security number. A prison number. You couldn't sink much lower than that.

No one knew her here. That was both the good news and the bad news. The good news because she was completely anonymous. The bad news because there was no one she could rely upon, no one to call. She was on her own, a fallen pine cone in a lonely forest.

She watched the ebb and flow of humanity. It did not stop. Tall, fat, short, black, white, scary, normal. She remembered every face. She always had. When she was five years old, the doctors said she had an eidetic memory—the ability to recall images, sounds, or objects with extreme accuracy—and ever since she had never forgotten a face, or place, or photograph.

She noticed a guy at the end of the bench, a sailor with a canvas gym bag bursting at the seams sitting next to him like a dutiful beagle. Every so often he would look over at her, then look away, a flash of hot red guilt on his face. He could not have been more than twenty—kind of cute in his buzz cut and uniform—but she was younger, still bona fide jailbait. She smiled at him anyway, just to make it worse. After that, he got up and walked over to the food court. God, what a bitch she could be.

She glanced at the doors leading to the street. There was a booth selling gifts and flowers. An older couple, perhaps in their thirties, debated over a basket intended for a funeral ceremony. It seemed that the woman wanted to spend a lot of money, seeing as how the dearly departed was her cousin or second cousin, and how they had come all the way from Rochester. The man—a fat guy, a heart attack on a stick, as her aunt used to say—wanted to forget the whole thing. It seemed he was not a big fan of the deceased.

She watched them argue for a while, her eyes roaming the florist's wares. Mylar balloons, ceramic knickknacks, crappy vases, a nice selection of flowers. And it came to her. Just like that. All things considered, as she perused the floral displays, she might have called herself Dahlia or Fern or Iris. Maybe even Daisy.

In the end it became a no-brainer. She may have been a runaway, but now she had a name.

She decided to call herself Lilly.

TWENTY-SEVEN

KEVIN BYRNE CROUCHED IN THE CRAWLSPACE, HIS SCIATICA BESTING the Vicodin in his system. It always did. At his height, just over six-three, he felt entombed by the damp, close walls.

Jessica was directing the scene out front.

Byrne looked at the three brightly colored boxes in front of him. Red. Yellow. Blue. Used-car lot pennant colors. *Happy* colors. The boxes—each had a small bronze doorknob and hinges—were closed now, but he had looked inside each. He wished he hadn't, but he'd been thinking that same thought since the first time he walked onto the scene of a violent homicide on the first night he spent in uniform. That night it was a shotgun triple in Juniata. Brains on the wall, guts on the coffee table, *St. Elsewhere* on the blood-splattered TV. It never got better. A little easier sometimes, but never better.

The wooden boxes were covered in a layer of dust, disturbed only, he hoped, by the gloved hands of the two police officers who had been down here. Jessica and a uniformed officer named Maria Caruso.

Byrne studied the joints, the miters, the construction of these small coffins. They were expertly crafted. There was definitely a great deal of skill at work here.

In a few moments the crime scene unit would begin their collection of evidence in situ, then the victim would be transported to the medical examiner's office. The techs were outside the building now, drinking cold coffee and chatting, waiting for Detective Kevin Byrne's signal.

Byrne wasn't ready yet.

He looked at the placement of the boxes. They were not in a line, but were not placed at random either. They were precisely organized, it seemed, edges all but touching in a staggered pattern. The first box, the yellow one, was closest to the wall on the north side. Byrne made note of this. This was the direction in which the body was facing. He was experienced enough to know that you never knew what might be important, what pathology lurked in the disturbed mind of a psychopathic killer. The second box, the red one, was staggered to the left. The third box, a shade of royal blue, was in line with the first.

He examined the hardpack earth around the base of the wooden cubes. There were no obvious scrape marks indicating the boxes had been dragged. Earlier he had slipped a few gloved fingers under one corner of one of the boxes, tried to lift it. The box was not light. This meant that whoever had brought these boxes down here probably had to duckwalk them across the expanse. That took strength.

One thing was certain: This was not the primary crime scene. The victim had bled out long before she was put into these boxes and moved into this crawlspace. As far as he could tell, there was a small amount of dried blood in the boxes themselves, and none on the floor.

Before coming down, Byrne had borrowed a measuring tape from one of the techs, and measured the opening cut into the floor, then the size of the boxes. The opening was about two inches larger than the boxes in all directions.

Had the opening existed, and then the killer built the boxes to fit? Or was it the other way around? Or was it a lucky coincidence? Byrne doubted it. There were few coincidences in his line of work.

Byrne shifted his weight. His legs were killing him. He tried to straighten them, but he could not stand up more than a few inches, and he wasn't about to kneel down on a dirt floor. This was a relatively new suit. He tried steadying himself on the yellow box and—

—senses the killer coming in from the back. He brings down the boxes one at a time. He has a truck, or a van. He did not assemble the boxes here. They are heavy, cumbersome, but he manages. He has been here before, many times, knew about the access door, knew he would not be discovered. Why?

He brings the girl down in pieces, no middle, the middle is empty, no heart, heartless. He arranges the boxes, meticulous and precise in this dank and confined tomb. She is a runaway, his first? Second? Tenth? He has done this before, has collected a child of the night, long fingers, a man's clever hands on a box of bones, the smoke of a funeral pyre, light my fire . . .

Byrne rocked back on his heels, sat down hard. His head throbbed.

The headaches were returning.

WHEN BYRNE EMERGED from the building he pulled off his latex gloves, dropped them in a trash can. He saw Jessica across the street, leaning against her car, arms crossed. She tapped a finger on her bicep. She looked wired, manic. She wore a pair of amber Serengeti sunglasses.

Before coming out of the crawlspace, Byrne had dry-swallowed a pair of Vicodin, his last two. He'd have to make a call.

The outside air was a mélange of acrid exhaust fumes and the rich tang of barbecue.

Still no rain.

"What do you think?" Jessica asked.

Byrne shrugged, stalling. His head seemed ready to implode. "Did you talk to the officer who discovered the victim?"

"I did."

"Do you think she contaminated the scene in any way?"

Jessica shook her head. "No. She's sharp. She's young, but she knows what she's doing."

Byrne glanced back at the building. "So, why this place? Why here?"

"Good question."

They were being led around North Philadelphia. There was no doubt about that, and few things made detectives angrier. Except, perhaps, having a murderer go underground and never get caught.

Who would do such a thing? After the killer's rage had died, after the fire went out, why not dispose of the remains in plastic bags, or dump them in the river? Hell, Philadelphia had two very usable rivers for such purposes. Not to mention Wissahickon Creek. The PPD fished bodies, and parts of bodies, out of the rivers all the time.

Byrne had run into dismemberment a few times when the victim was killed by one of the various mobs in Philly—the Italians, the Colombians, the Mexicans, the Jamaicans. When it came to hyper-violent gangland homicide, all styles were served in the City of Brotherly Love.

But this had nothing to do with the mob.

Two runaways. One drowned, one dismembered.

Was there enough to tie this to the murder of Caitlin O'Riordan? They were a long way from getting any forensic details—hair, fibers, blood evidence, fingerprints—but the phone call to the CIU hotline and the cryptic clue in the Bible could not be ignored.

"This is one killer."

"We don't know that yet," Byrne said, playing devil's advocate.

Jessica uncrossed her arms, recrossed them. Now she tapped both forefingers on both biceps. "Yeah, well. I know we're in the Badlands, partner, but this is beyond the pale. Way beyond." She took off her sunglasses, tossed them into the car. "That was Monica Renzi's heart. You know it and I know it. The DNA's going to match. It's going to hit the papers, and then hell will break its subterranean bonds."

Byrne just nodded. She was probably right.

"Want to know what happened?" she continued. "I'll tell you what happened. This sick bastard killed Monica, cut her up, stuck her in boxes, then put her heart in a jar and put it in that refrigerator. Then he put his psycho clue in that Bible, hoping we would figure out the Jeremiah Crosley ruse and we would come here to find his little treasure. We did. Now he's out there having a good laugh at how clever he is."

Byrne bought into the entire theory.

"He's targeting runaways, Kevin. Lost kids. First this girl, then Caitlin. He just hid Monica Renzi a little too well. When no one found her, he had to ratchet up the game. He's still out there and he's going to do it again. Fuck him, fuck this job, and fuck this *place*."

Byrne knew that his partner sometimes ran on emotion—she was Italian, it came with the genes—but he rarely saw her get this worked up at a scene. Stress eventually got to everyone. He put a hand on her shoulder. "You okay?"

"Oh, yeah. Top of the world, Ma."

"Look. We're going to get this freak. Let's get the lab work back on this one. There are a million ways to fuck up with a crime like this. This guy may be evil, but he's no genius. They never are."

Jessica stared at the ground for a few moments, simmering, then reached into the car, pulled out a folder. She opened it, retrieved a sheet. "Look at this."

She handed Byrne the paper. It was a photocopy of the activity log for the O'Riordan case.

"What am I looking for?"

She tapped the page. "These three names." She pointed to a trio of names on the log. They were first names, nicknames at that, no last names. Three people who were interviewed on the day after Caitlin O'Riordan's body was found. "I can't believe I didn't see it before."

"What about them?" Byrne asked.

"They were interviewed back in May. Nothing was typed up, and the notes are missing."

Byrne saw that all the interviews were conducted by Detective Freddy Roarke. The late Freddy Roarke. "You checked the binder?" he asked. "There's no notes?"

"Nope. Not for these three people. Everything else is there. These notes are gone."

As a rule, when a detective conducted a neighborhood survey, or an interview in the field, he or she made handwritten notes in their official notebook, which was called their work product. Most detectives also carried a personal notebook, which was not included in the file. The work product, when filled, was put in the binder, which was the official and only file on a homicide case. If a detective wrote notes for two or three different jobs, the pages would be torn out and placed in the corresponding file. If the interviews became important, they were typed up. If not, the notes became the only record of the interview.

"What about Freddy's partner?" Jessica asked. "What was his name?"

"Pistone," Byrne said. "Butchie Pistone."

"*Butchie*. Jesus. You know him well?"

"Not well," Byrne said. "He was kind of a hard-ass. He was a hot-shot when I was coming up, but it all went to shit after he was involved in a questionable shoot. He was comatose near the end. Drinking on the job, chewing Altoids by the case."

"Is he still around?"

"Yeah," Byrne said. "He owns a bar on Lehigh."

Jessica glanced at her watch, at the entrance to 4514 Shiloh Street. CSU was just getting started. "Let's go talk to him."

As they pulled away, a pair of news teams arrived on scene. This was going to make the evening news.

TWENTY-EIGHT

Rocco "Butchie" Pistone had been a Philadelphia police officer for thirty years. In his time he had worked as a patrol officer in the Fifth District, as well as a detective in West Division before coming to homicide. When he retired, two months ago, he bought into the Aragon Bar on Lehigh Avenue, a tavern owned by his brother Ralph, also a retired cop. It was a halfway popular cop stop for the officers in the Twenty-sixth District.

Now in his sixties, Butchie lived above the tavern and, rumor had it, held court in the club a few nights per week, running a medium-stakes poker game in the basement.

Jessica and Byrne parked the car, walked the half block to the bar. The entrance to the apartment on the second floor was a doorway about twenty feet west of the entrance to the tavern.

As they approached, Jessica saw that in front of the door were three beefy white guys in their twenties—knit watch caps, sleeveless T-shirts, fingerless gloves. Two drank from brown paper bags. The smell of pot smoke was thick in the air. Real House of Pain types. A boom box on the sidewalk played some kind of budget white-boy rap. As Jessica and Byrne got closer—and it became clear that they were heading for the doorway—the three guys went a little chesty, like this was their piece of geography, their inch of Google Earth, that needed to be defended.

"Yo. Excuse me. Somethin' I can help you with?" one asked. He was the smallest of the trio, but clearly the alpha male in this pack. Built like a Hummer. Jessica noted that he had a crucifix tattooed on the right side of his neck, just below the ear. The cross was a switchblade with a drop of blood on its tip. Charming.

"*Yo?*" Byrne said. "Who are you, Frank Stallone?"

The kid smirked. "Funny stuff."

"It's a living."

The kid cracked his knuckles, one at a time. "I repeat. Somethin' I can help you with?"

"I don't believe there is," Byrne said. "But thanks for asking."

The biggest of the three, the one wearing a bright orange ski vest in eighty-degree weather, stepped into the doorway, blocking their access. "It wasn't really a question."

"And yet I answered," Byrne said. "Must be my upbringing. Now, if you'll step aside, we'll go about our business, and you can go about yours."

The big guy laughed. It was apparent that this was going to continue. He pushed a stiff finger into Byrne's chest. "I don't think you're hearing me, Mick."

Bad idea, Jessica thought. *Very, very bad idea.* She unbuttoned the front of her blazer, took a few steps back, flanking the other two.

In a flash, Byrne had the big goon by the right wrist. He brought the arm down, twisted it under, turned the young man around, jammed the arm skyward and slammed him face-first into the brick wall. *Hard.* The other two went on alert, but didn't make a move. Not yet. Byrne hauled out the kid's wallet, tearing a pants seam in the process. He tossed the billfold to Jessica. She opened it.

One of the other two thugs took a step toward Jessica. She flipped back the hem of her jacket without looking up. The butt of her Glock was exposed, along with the badge clipped to her belt. The punk backed off, hands out to his sides.

"What are you gonna do? Fuckin' *shoot* me?"

"Just the once," Jessica said. "They have us buying our own bullets now. It's a cutback thing." Jessica tossed the wallet back to Byrne. "This gentleman is one Flavio E. Pistone."

Byrne patted the kid down, spun him back around. Flavio's nose gushed blood. It might have been broken. Byrne stuffed the wallet into Flavio's vest pocket, looked him in the eye. Inches away now. "I'm a police officer. You put your hands on me. That's assault. That's three to five. You don't go home tonight."

The kid tried to maintain eye contact, but he couldn't hold on to Byrne's gaze. Jessica had never seen anyone actually do it.

"My uncle's an ex-cop," Flavio said. The word *cop* came out *gop*. His nose *was* broken.

"He has my condolences," Byrne said. "Now, *Flavio*, I can cuff you right here on the street, in front of your little Eminem social club, haul your ass down to the Roundhouse, or you can step aside." Byrne stepped back, squared off. It was almost as if he wanted the kid to make a move. "Out of respect for your uncle, I'm willing to forget about this. But it's your call. Anything else?"

Flavio smirked, but it didn't play. He was clearly in a world of hurt, but doing his macho best not to show it. He shook his head.

"Good," Byrne said. "It was nice meeting you. A true delight. Now get the fuck out of my way."

Byrne stepped forward. The three thugs nervously shuffled to the side. Byrne opened the door, held it for Jessica. They entered the building, crossed the small lobby and headed up the stairs.

August, Jessica thought. It brings out the best in everybody. "Not bad for a guy with sciatica."

"Yeah, well," Byrne said. "We do what we can."

Butchie Pistone was a short squat man; thick arms and bull neck, navy tats on both forearms. He had a stubbly head and a boozer's eyes, ringed with crimson. Liver spots dotted his hands.

They met in his small living room overlooking Lehigh Avenue. Butchie's chair was right in front of the window. Jessica imagined him looking out onto the street all day, in his retirement, a street he used to patrol, watching the neighborhood go through its throes of change. Cops never strayed too far from the curb.

The room was stacked with cartons of liquor, napkins, swizzle sticks, Beer Nuts, sundry bar supplies. Jessica noticed that the man's coffee table was actually two cases of Johnny Walker Black spanned with a piece of varnished plywood. The place smelled of cigarettes, citrus Glade, frozen dinners. The sounds of the bar drifted up from the floorboards—jukebox, inebriated laughter, ringtones, pool balls clacking.

Byrne introduced Jessica, and the three of them kicked the small talk around for a few minutes.

"Sorry about my nephew," Butchie said. "Got his mother's temper. Rest in peace."

"Don't worry about it," Byrne said.

"She was Irish. No offense."

"None taken."

"And his two cousins down there, eh? Talk about the shallow end of the gene pool."

"They seem like nice young men," Byrne deadpanned.

Butchie laughed, coughed. The sound was a raspy backfire. "They been called a lot of things. Never that." He crossed his legs, wincing with the effort. He was clearly in some discomfort, but the half empty bottle of Bushmills and small forest of amber pill vials on the table next to his chair spoke to the fact that he was working on it. Jessica noticed a cell phone, a cordless phone, a half dozen remotes and a SIG P220 in a leather holster on the table, as well. From his leather La-Z-Boy throne it appeared that Butchie Pistone was ready for just about anything.

"Ike still your boss over there?" Butchie asked.

Byrne nodded.

"Ike Buchanan's a good man. We worked the Fifth when he was on the way up. Give him my regards."

"I sure will," Byrne said. "I appreciate you seeing us."

"No problem at all."

Butchie looked at Jessica, then back, his small talk exhausted. "So, what can I do for you, Detective?"

"I just have a few questions," Byrne said.

"Whatever you need."

Byrne put the picture of Caitlin O'Riordan on the coffee table. It was her missing-person photo, the one in which she was wearing her backpack. "Remember her?" Byrne asked.

Butchie shook a Kool out of a near-empty pack. He lit it. Jessica could see a slight shake in the flame. A tell.

"I remember."

"Back in May Freddy did some interviews." Byrne put the activity log on the table. Pistone barely glanced at it. "He talked to some street kids."

Butchie shrugged. "What about it?"

"The interviews are noted, but nothing was typed up, and the notes are gone."

Another shrug. Another cloud of Kool smoke.

"Any thoughts?" Byrne asked.

"You check the binder? Maybe they got moved around."

"We checked," Byrne said. "We didn't find them."

Butchie waved a hand at his surroundings. "You may have noticed, I'm not on the job anymore."

"Do you remember these interviews?"

"No."

The answer came a little too quickly, Jessica thought. Butchie remembered.

"You continued to work the case for another month," Byrne said.

Pistone coughed again. "I clocked in, did my job. Just like you."

"Not like me," Byrne said. "You mean to tell me that you opened this file another dozen times, and you didn't notice anything missing?"

Pistone stared out the window. He took a long drag on his cigarette, hotboxing it. "I was a cop for thirty fuckin' years in this town. You have any idea the shit I've seen?"

"I've got a pretty good idea," Byrne said.

"That kid was my last case. I was drinking at seven in the morning. I don't remember a thing." He took a sip of his straight Bushmills. "I did her family a favor by pulling the pin. I did the city a favor."

"We may have a compulsive out there. We found a second body today. Young girl. It looks like the same guy."

Butchie's face drained of all color. He hit the Bushmills again.

"Nothing to say?" Byrne asked.

Butchie just stared out the window.

"It's not like we can ask Freddy, can we?"

Butchie's face darkened. "Don't go there, Detective," he said. "Don't even fuckin' go there."

"This is going to go where it goes, Butchie. If you misplaced these notes, or even worse, you lost them, and you didn't make a note about it, it could get bad. Especially if another girl dies. Nothing I can do about it now."

"Sure there is." Pistone put down his cigarette and his drink. He struggled to his feet. Byrne stood up, too. He towered over the man. "You can turn around and walk out that door."

The two men stared at each other. The only sound was the click of the old wind-up alarm clock on Butchie's table, the cacophony of muffled shouts and laughter coming from the bar below. Jessica wanted to say something, but it occurred to her that both of these men may have forgotten that she was even in the room. This was real *High Noon* stuff.

Finally, Byrne reached out, shook the man's hand. Just like that. "Thanks for seeing us, Butchie."

"No problem," Butchie replied, a little surprised.

Byrne was really good at these things, Jessica thought. His philosophy was, always shake a man's hand. That way, when the whip comes down, they never see it coming.

"Any time," Butchie added.

Except this lifetime, Jessica thought.

"I'll pass along your regards to Sergeant Buchanan," Byrne said as they headed to the door, twisting the blade.

"Yeah," Butchie Pistone said. "You do that."

THEY RODE IN RELATIVE SILENCE for a few blocks. When they made a right on Sixth Street, Byrne broke the quiet. It wasn't anything Jessica expected him to say.

"I'd see her sometimes."

"What do you mean?" Jessica asked. "See who?"

"Eve."

Jessica waited for him to continue. A block later, he did.

"After we stopped seeing each other, I'd see her out on the town. Usually all by herself. Different bars, different restaurants. Mostly bars. You know how this job is. We all end up going to the same places. As soon as you find a place where cops don't go, somebody finds out about it and it becomes a cop bar."

Jessica nodded. It was true.

"I always thought about approaching her, seeing if we could just be friends, just have a drink and walk away. I never did."

"How come?"

Byrne shrugged. "I don't know. On the other hand, I never just turned around and walked out, either. I just seemed to sit there and watch her. I loved to look at her. Every man who saw her did, but I had this notion that I had reached her somehow. Maybe I did for just a second."

"Did she ever see you?"

Byrne shook his head. "Not once. If she did, she never let on. Eve had this way of shutting out the world."

They turned onto Callowhill, then onto Eighth Street.

"And here's the crazy part," Byrne said. "Do you know what she was doing most of the time?"

"What?"

"Reading."

It was the last thing Jessica expected him to say. Calf-roping and macramé would have come first. "Reading?"

"Yeah. I'd see her in some pretty rough places—Grays Ferry, Point Breeze, Kensington—and she would just be sitting there, sipping her drinks, and reading a paperback. Usually a novel."

Jessica conjured the image of this beautiful, tough as nails woman, dressed up, sitting in a bar by herself, reading a book. This woman was *something*.

"What did she drink?" Jessica asked.

"What do you mean?"

"What was her cocktail of choice?"

"Wild Turkey, rocks," Byrne said. "Why?"

"Just curious."

BYRNE PUT THE CAR IN PARK, cut the engine. The car clicked and clacked and shuddered. It eventually fell silent.

"What's in those missing notes, partner?" Jessica asked.

"I wish I knew."

"You think they were just misfiled?"

"It's possible," Byrne said. "I'll go rooting around a little tomorrow."

While it was possible the notebook pages were placed into another binder by mistake, it was unlikely. They might never know what was in them.

The activity log did not give full names for these interviewees. Just street names. Byrne felt weary just thinking about the effort needed to try and track down three people without last names, pictures, or Social Security numbers.

The point was, something in those notes might lead to their doer, something that would take him off the streets before he killed again.

"All right," Jessica said. "I'm out. I feel like I've been up for three days straight. After that crawlspace, I want to take a five-hour bath."

"Okay. See you in the morning. Bright and early."

"I'll try to be early," Jessica said. "Don't expect bright."

Jessica got out of the car, began to cross the lot. Byrne watched her go. He rolled down his window.

"Jess."

She turned around. "Yeah?"

"I like your nails."

Jessica smiled, the first time in days.

TWENTY-NINE

As the sun softened into a dusty orange corona over West Philadelphia, Byrne drove to the location where Eve Galvez's body had been found. The crime scene was still taped off, secured by two officers in a sector car. It appeared that the CSU team had not completed its investigation.

Byrne identified himself to the young officers, passed the time of day with them, commiserating over the sheer numbing boredom of such a detail. He had been exactly where they were many times in his early days on the force. He wondered how badly these two guys had fucked up to draw this one. As a patrol officer, Byrne once had to stake out a trash can in a South Philly alley for a full shift, a trash can in which a homicide suspect had dropped a handgun used in a crime. Ostensibly, Byrne was staking out the Rubbermaid on the outside chance the perp might come back for the weapon. Nothing came of it, except for a sore ass, a stiff back, and a career-long empathy for twenty-something uniforms stuck in a beater, drawing a crap tour on a hot summer evening.

A few minutes later Byrne stood at the edge of the now-empty grave, a pall of sadness and anger washing over him. Nobody deserved a fate such as this, especially not a woman like Eve Galvez. He thought of the last time he had seen her. Then immediately flashed on the *first* time he had seen her.

That's all there is, Byrne thought. There are always memories in between, but the landmarks are the first time and the last time. You never get the chance to do those two over.

And you never see either of them coming.

THEY MET AT A WEDDING. The bridegroom was a detective from Central named Reggie Babineaux, an affable, slope-shouldered Cajun in his late thirties who had cut his teeth in the hard Fifth District in New Orleans, pre-Katrina. The ceremony and reception were held at the Mansion on Main Street, a sprawling ornate facility in Voorhees, New Jersey. In addition to a grand spiral staircase, vaulted mural ceilings, and cascading waterfalls, there was also a swan-filled pond and an all-glass ceremony site. To Byrne, it looked like it might have been decorated by Carmela Soprano, but he knew it was all pretty *cher*, as Reggie Babineaux would put it. Reggie had married into new money. His bride was far from a *Vogue* cover girl, but Reggie was still the envy of every mortgage-laden, shrew-burdened male civil servant in the room.

He spotted her as she stood at the bar with a fellow detective from the Philadelphia DA's office. Eve Galvez wore a tight red dress and black heels, a thin strand of pearls. Her silken brunette hair was down around her shoulders, her café au lait skin and dark eyes were incandescent in the soft light of the crystal chandeliers. Byrne couldn't take his eyes off her. He was hardly alone. Every man in the room was sneaking covert glances at the slender, Latina beauty at the bar.

Byrne asked his old friend, Assistant District Attorney Paul DiCarlo, for the details—the 229 as they said in the trade. A 229 report was a basic background form. DiCarlo told Byrne what little he said he knew. Eve Galvez had come to the DA's office three years earlier, had quickly made a reputation for herself as a smart, no-nonsense investigator.

DiCarlo added that just about every man at 1421 Arch Street—where the DA's office was located at the time; it had since moved to 3 Penn Square—unmarried and otherwise, had taken the obligatory run at Eve Galvez. As far as DiCarlo knew, she had rebuffed them all. Rumors abounded, but according to Paul DiCarlo, that's all they were: rumors. A beautiful woman in law enforcement, anywhere in the country, probably anywhere in the world, was subject to the worst nature of men. If they couldn't have her, some felt the need to demean her, to minimize her accomplishments, sometimes to thwart her advancement.

ADA Paul DiCarlo said Eve Galvez had taken it all, and had given most of it back. Despite behaviors that bordered on harassment—incidents that might have called for reprimands, even firings—she had never taken it to the bosses.

That night, at Reggie Babineaux's reception, three bourbons offshore, as the band swung into Robert Palmer's "Simply Irresistible"—a song Byrne would forever associate with that moment—he mustered the courage to approach Eve Galvez.

The attraction was instant, almost visceral. They verbally sparred for a while, until both realized that neither was going to back down, neither was going to have a glove raised in victory. Byrne was older than Eve Galvez by at least ten years, had three times as many years in on the job, but they quickly fell into a rhythm, a comfort zone that surprised them both.

Byrne recalled the way she leaned against the bar, the way she focused on him to the exclusion of everyone else in the room.

Those eyes.

THEY DID NOT MAKE LOVE on their first date. They had dinner at Saloon in South Philly, a nightcap at Overtures. Somehow it became 4 AM. Byrne drove her home, walked her to her door. She did not invite him in. Instead, on the sidewalk in front of the entrance, she leaned into him, and gave him one of the softest, most seductive kisses on the cheek he'd ever received. The kiss promised redemption, if not life eternal.

Byrne stood there for ten minutes after she'd gone inside, staring at the gated door, willing it to open. No such luck.

Their second date was pretty much over before coffee was served. It was almost over before the appetizers. They made it back to Byrne's place—barely. But instead of the animal rutting they both expected, things slowed down rather quickly, and it became the sort of sweet, knowing intimacy you hope for deep into a relationship, the kind of love you make, say, on your fifth anniversary. It was that secret.

On their third date, five days later, Kevin Byrne gave Eve a charm bracelet—a bracelet bearing five small golden angels. He'd had her name engraved behind the clasp. He knew it was far too early in the relationship for jewelry, but when he saw the bracelet in the window of a jewelry store at Eighteenth and Walnut, he couldn't stop himself.

That year, as spring gave way to summer, the crime rate soared. For just about everyone involved in Philadelphia law enforcement, there were three parts to the day: your shift, your overtime, and four hours' sleep. Family obligations and lawns went untended. Relationships waned.

Byrne and Eve Galvez saw each other infrequently over the next few months. Neither could, or was willing to, explain why. The job and its stresses were the prevailing theory, one they both offered and accepted. They ran into each other at the Criminal Justice Center a few times. Once at a Phillies game. Byrne was with his daughter that day. Eve was with a man she introduced as her brother, Enrique. Weekly phone calls became biweekly, then monthly.

They had never promised each other a thing. That's who he was. That's who she was. There was so much he wanted to tell her, so much he *should* have told her.

Byrne turned his face to the sun for a moment, then knelt down. A bright blue tarpaulin was still stretched over this makeshift grave.

A few moments later Byrne touched the grass just inside the crime-scene tape. The vision came back in a brutal rush. For the first time in his life he wanted it to.

In his mind, behind a bloodred curtain of violence, he saw—

—*Eve talking to a man in shadows . . . her hand in his . . . an enormous house surrounded by rusting iron spires . . . the sound of the shovel piercing the soil . . . the jangle of the charms on Eve's bracelet as her body was rolled into the earth . . . a man standing over the grave, a man with silver eyes . . .*

Byrne eased himself to the ground. The grass was warm and dry. The pain in his temples pounded.

He closed his eyes, saw Eve's face. This time it was from the heart of a beautiful memory, not a dark and violent vision. She tossed her head back when she laughed. She would cross her legs, letting one high heel dangle from her toes as she read a newspaper.

Kevin Byrne stood, put his hands in his pockets, looked at the shimmering city.

A man with silver eyes.

He made Eve Galvez his very first promise.

THIRTY

THE ROOF WAS DESERTED. THE WIND BLEW POWDERY WHITE GRIT AND blistering heat across it.

Swann had brought the chair up to the roof a week earlier, had secured it to the roof with a strong construction adhesive. He could not have the chair blowing over, not at a critical moment.

He placed Katja on the chair, secured her feet and arms. She peered out over North Philadelphia like the masthead of a grand sailing vessel, a sea witch, perhaps, or a golden mermaid. Swann took a moment, reveling in the accomplishment of planning and execution. The flourish—the very prestige of the Seven Wonders—was yet to come.

He unraveled the seven swords from the velvet. Repositioning them would be tricky, but he knew the sight of her would secure his place in history when they found her.

A few minutes later, he was finished. He gathered his belongings, walked across the roof to the stairwell, removed the plastic bags from his feet, surveyed the landscape.

Perfect. He glanced at his watch. Patricia Sato was waiting for him at Faerwood.

Five minutes later he pulled out of the garage, into the alley, unseen. He would return home, to his dressing room. He would emerge in a new guise, in the skin of a new man.

He had one more stop to make, and his preparations would be all but complete.

THIRTY-ONE

Antoinette Ruolo hated tuna fish. Especially the kind that had those funky purplish brown streaks in it. Even though the can said "Solid White Albacore," you always got some pieces affected with what Antoinette figured had to be some kind of fish disease.

Some kind of *fatal* fish disease.

And yet she ate tuna fish for lunch once a week. Every Friday. She was raised Catholic and, even though the Pope said you were allowed to eat meat on Friday these days, she never had, not once in her fifty-nine years.

As the elevator climbed upward, she felt the reflux of the sandwich. She wanted to belch, but she dared not. The elevator only held five people, and she figured the four other occupants, all strangers, might not appreciate it.

The car stopped on the forty-fourth floor. They emerged onto the observation deck, and its breathtaking views of Philadelphia. Antoinette took a deep, fishy breath, and continued the tour.

"Originally, it was supposed to be the tallest building in the world at just over 547 feet, but was surpassed by both the Washington Monument and the Eiffel Tower. Both were completed first," she said. She'd been a tour guide at Philadelphia City Hall most of her working life, having started in 1971 as a "City Hall Bunny," a silly promotional gimmick someone had come up with in the 1960s, à la Hugh Hefner, the idea being to hire pretty young things to give distinguished city visitors a personal tour.

It had been a long time since anyone had considered Antoinette Ruolo a pretty young thing.

"It *was* the tallest building in Philadelphia for many years, of course, and was to remain so forever, until the City and Arts Commission broke an eighty-five-year-old 'gentleman's agreement' and allowed the construction of One Liberty Place, which measures 945 feet," Antoinette said. "Since then, of course, the Comcast Center has eclipsed that honor at a height of about 975 feet, making it not only the tallest building in Philadelphia, but in the Commonwealth of Pennsylvania, as well."

As her charges gazed out over the city, Antoinette considered them. Mostly middle-aged, casually dressed.

"Now, the tower of William Penn is a marvel unto itself," she continued by rote. "It stands thirty-seven feet tall and weighs twenty-seven tons. It is still the largest statue on any building in the world."

At this point a man at the back of the group raised his hand, as if he were in junior high school. He carried a huge backpack, the kind hikers carry on long treks.

"I have a question," he said. "If I may."

Wow, Antoinette thought. *A polite person.* "Please."

"Well, I've done a little reading in my Fodor's," he said, holding up the tour book. "The book goes into great detail about the building, but it doesn't say too much about the clock. I've always been fascinated by timepieces."

Antoinette brightened, gave a quick bob to her graying hair. Lord, she needed a perm. "Well, you've come to the right person . . ."

JOSEPH SWANN TUNED the woman out. It was an ability he had developed as a child, listening to his father's well-oiled patter during his close-up routines, the facility to not listen to someone, but still be able to comprehend and recall everything they said.

He realized he was drawing attention to himself by asking questions, but he just couldn't seem to resist. Besides, he had learned the art of makeup and costuming from a master. No one knew what he really looked like, and before they would be able to connect him to the events of the next twenty-four hours, it would be far too late.

The truth was, he knew everything there was to know about the massive timepiece at the base of the tower at Philadelphia City Hall. He knew that the clock had begun running on New Year's Day 1899. He knew that the faces had a diameter of twenty-six feet, and were larger than even those of Big Ben. He knew that each hour hand was twelve and a half feet long.

He also knew that the door he needed to get in was just on the other side of the tower, opposite the elevator. He had taken this tour once before, posing as a much older gentleman, a man with a thick German accent, and knew that the lock on the door was a standard Yale deadbolt. With his skills, it would take him less than ten seconds to open the door. Probably much less.

Swann knew that if anyone noticed he was missing and called security, he would quick-change his clothing and return to the ground level via the south stairwell.

Most important, he knew about the clock's lighting. He had detailed drawings of the schematics, had pored over them for years. Originally, the clock's faces were lit by 552 individual lightbulbs. Now gold-colored fluorescents illuminated them.

Yes, he knew everything Antoinette was going to say about the legendary timepiece that graced architect John McArthur's garish, breathtaking building.

And yet he only cared about one of the clock's *faces*.

The one facing north.

The one facing the Badlands.

". . . WAS A STORY that began in 1906. It seems that so many people relied on these clocks for time, because they could be seen from great distances, that each evening, at 8:57, the lights in the clock tower were turned off," Antoinette prattled. "Do you know why they did that?"

Everyone on the tour exchanged a bemused glance.

"Because three minutes later, when they turned the lights back on, the entire city knew it was exactly nine o'clock!"

Antoinette Ruolo glanced at her watch. "Speaking of time, I'm afraid we have to wrap up this tour in a few minutes." This was her favorite segue. "I'll meet you all back at the elevator in ten minutes."

Antoinette walked over toward the elevator, a low grumbling in her stomach. She sat down on the bench, thought about taking her shoes off and giving herself a quick foot massage, but decided against it. It wouldn't be right for a former City Hall Bunny to be seen with holes in the toes of her support stockings, would it?

TEN MINUTES LATER Antoinette found herself in the lobby, waving good-bye to her last tour of the day.

She looked around the reception area. Had the nice man who had asked about the clock come down with them? Of course he had. Where else would he be?

Antoinette Ruolo signed out, then headed for the exit at the south portal. As she pushed open the door, and stepped into the steaming afternoon, she felt a little better. For at least a dozen reasons, Antoinette was glad it was Friday, one reason eclipsing all others.

No more tuna for a week.

THIRTY-TWO

LILLY SCANNED THE FOOD COURT AT THE TRAIN STATION, MORE WITH her nose than her eyes. She thought back to her last full meal, a $1.99 breakfast special at a roadside diner on Route 61, a tacky plastic place with a water-stained ceiling and prehistoric gum under the stools.

But now, forty-eight hours later, sitting in the food court of the Thirtieth Street station, her stomach rumbled like one of the trains passing beneath her.

This was the life of a runaway. She knew what she had to do.

Desperate times and all . . .

THE MAN WAS WATCHING HER.

Lilly had always had the ability to sense when someone was observing her, even if that person was behind her back, even if they were on the other side of the room or the other side of the street. She registered the feeling as a slight warming of her skin, a minute tingling of the hair at the nape of her neck.

She turned, glanced at the man, then looked away. He could have been thirty, he could have been fifty. He sat two tables away. He moved closer.

"Hi," he said.

Lilly took a moment, playing it out. *Here we go.*

"Hi," Lilly replied.

The man's face lit up. He clearly wasn't expecting a response. He cleared his throat. "Have you just come in by train?"

Lilly nodded.

"Just now?"

She nodded again, a little too animatedly. She felt like a bobblehead doll. She backed off on the act. "Well, just a few minutes ago."

"How exciting," he said. "I *love* train travel."

Oh, yes, how exciting, she thought. Train travel. Let's see: burnt coffee, stale sandwiches, smelly passengers, grimy windows, crappy houses passing by that were so low-rent they were built right on the train tracks. Yeah. This is my dream vacation. This and Cozumel. "It's okay," she said.

"Is this your first time in Philadelphia?"

"Yes, sir."

He arched his eyebrows. *"Sir?"* He laughed, but it sounded phony. "I'm not *that* much older than you are. Am I?"

He clearly was, and it was *so* gross. "No," she said, trying her best to sound sincere. "Not really."

He smiled again. His teeth were the color of old mushrooms.

"Well, seeing as this is your first time in the City of Brotherly Love, I'd be happy to show you around," he said. "If you have the time, of course. It's a great city. Lots of history."

Lilly glanced toward the doors that led to Twenty-ninth Street. It was almost dark. The lights on the street shone in the near distance, a grainy canvas of green and red and turquoise. She looked back at the man, assessing him. He wasn't that much taller than she was, did not look all that strong. She, on the other hand, had played soccer and lacrosse since she was seven. She had strong legs and deceptively strong arms. And she was fast. Lightning fast.

"That would be totally *great*," she said, infusing the word with just enough enthusiasm.

The man looked at his watch, then at the huge area of the food court. The evening commuter rush had long since faded. There were just a few stragglers.

"Tell you what," he began. "I have to make a few calls. I'll meet you at the corner of Twenty-third and Walnut. We can take a stroll."

He didn't want to be seen leaving with her. She understood the play. This told her just about everything she needed to know. "Okay."

"Do you know where that is?"

"I'll find it," Lilly said.

"Are you sure you can?"

Lilly laughed. It sounded creepy, almost sinister, but she was certain this man would not notice. "I found my way to Philadelphia, didn't I?"

The man laughed with her. Those teeth. *Ugh.*

A few moments later the man got up, looked at his watch again, and crossed the huge room toward the Thirtieth Street entrance. She saw him adjust the front of his trousers. She wanted to hurl.

Lilly closed her eyes for a moment—not having any idea how she was going to handle this. She thought about her house, her bedroom, her TV and cell phone, her dog, Rip. Rip was a thirteen-year-old cairn terrier, almost blind. Lilly started to tear up at the thought of Rip and his scuffed white bowl, Rip bumping into door jambs, then retreating, embarrassed. She stopped herself. This was no time for weakness, for sentimentality or dependency on the past. She had something to do.

HE TRIED TO MAKE small talk. He succeeded. It couldn't possibly have been any smaller. "You know, Philadelphia was once the capital of the United States."

She knew this. Every school kid in America knew this. "I didn't know that."

"Do you know who discovered the place?"

Gee, she thought. *Penn and Teller?*

"William Penn, of course." He pointed down Market Street, toward city hall. The statue of William Penn glowed in the dusk.

"Wow."

She felt his hand reach out, try to hold hers. Gross. She reached around to her backpack, covering. She unzipped it, pulled out some gum. She didn't offer him any. He didn't notice. Every time she caught him looking at her he was staring at her chest.

"There's something down here I think you should see," he said. "There's history everywhere."

They walked down the alley, around a corner. They stopped. There was nothing to see.

"You know what?" he asked.

"What?"

"You're very beautiful."

And there it was. On top of it, she knew it was a lie. She looked like crap. She probably smelled, too. She was a runaway. Runaways were skanks. "Thank you," she said.

"Can I ask you a question?"

Lilly almost laughed. "Sure."

"Do you like me? Even, you know, a *little* bit?"

Oh, about as much as a blister or a cold sore, Lilly thought. "Of course," she said. "I'm here, aren't I? Why would you ask me that?"

"Because boys are insecure," he said with gnarled smile.

Boys. She *was* just about ready to puke. Time to get this party started. "You know, you don't strike me as all that insecure."

"I don't?"

"Absolutely not. You strike me more as the Matt Damon type. Older—like my father's age—but still pretty cool."

He smiled again. It was the last thing she wanted.

"You know, I was thinking," he said. "If you're a little short of cash, I could help you out. You being from out of town and all. I did the Jack Kerouac thing myself when I was a little younger. I know how it can be."

"Well, I've never been to Philadelphia before," she said. "I have no idea how much things cost."

"It can be expensive. Not quite like New York, but pricier than, say, Baltimore."

Lilly smiled, winked. "How much do you have, big spender?"

Another laugh, as phony as the others. He reached into his back pocket, extracted a camouflage nylon wallet—pure class. He opened it. It bulged with plastic cards, business cards, ID cards. He pulled them all out, and she got a glimpse: Visa, Macy's, American Express, a Borders gift card. She also saw what looked like a lot of cash. About an inch or so. It might have been all singles, but still.

"Wow," she said. Girls her age were supposed to say "wow" a lot. Like they were all Hannah Montana. "How much is in there?"

"I don't really know," he said. "But I'd be willing to—"

At this moment Lilly turned away, pivoted, and slammed her knee into the man's crotch. Hard, and fast as lightning. He didn't have a chance. The man blew a lungful of sour breath into her face, then folded instantly to the ground.

Lilly looked behind her, to the mouth of the alley, then at the windows of the buildings on either side. All dark. All good. They were completely alone.

"*Why?*" the man managed on a ragged breath. He was curled in a fetal position on the ground, knees to his chest

"*Why?* Are you kidding me? What planet are you from?"

"I don't—"

"You're like a million years old," Lilly said. "And I'm not even legal, dickhead." She picked up his wallet, took his driver's license and the money. "What did you think was going to happen?"

"I thought we might—"

"You thought what?" Lilly asked. "That we were going to fall in love? That we were going to have a romance?"

"No," he said. "It was just . . ."

Lilly got down on the ground next to the man. She lay back, then pulled up her T-shirt, baring her breasts. She worked her right arm around the man's neck, as if they were two drunken people at a wild frat party, or at some tequila-blast on spring break in Panama City. In her left hand she held up her digital camera, the lens facing them. She snapped a picture of the two of them together, then another for good measure: Mr. Mushroom Teeth and his topless teen cohort. Film at eleven.

The flash was bright blue in the darkened alley. It blinded her for a second.

"Now we have a record of our lovely time together," Lilly said, pulling her top back down. She stood up, brushed herself off. "And keep in mind, if you tell anyone about this, if anyone comes looking for me, they'll find this camera, okay?"

The man remained silent. As expected. He was in pain.

"Then later tonight I'm going to take some naked pictures of myself," Lilly continued. "*Full* naked. And all of these pictures will be right in a row." She slipped the camera into her bag, took out a brush, ran it through her hair. When she was done she put away her brush, pulled off the rubber band she always kept on her wrist, snapped her hair into a ponytail. "And your wife, your kids, your boss—the *cops*—they'll see the pictures, too. Think about it. How many of them are going to think you *didn't* take these pictures?" She put her bag over her shoulder, struck a pose. "I'm fourteen, dude. Think about *that*."

It wasn't true. She was older. But she looked fourteen, and she was an unrivalled drama queen to boot.

Lilly stepped back a few feet, waited. She reached into her bag, took out the printed photo she'd carried for two months, turned it toward the man. "This is your house, isn't it?"

The man tried to focus his eyes on the photograph of the big house with the woman standing in front of it. A few seconds later he did. "My . . . my *house*?"

"Yeah. You live here, right?"

"Are you crazy? That's not my house. Who is that woman? Who the hell are *you*?"

Lilly already knew the answer to her own question, but none of this would have made any sense if she didn't ask.

Seconds later, she put the photograph away, took a deep breath, composed herself—after all, she was not used to things like this, even if she had lived it all in her mind for a long time, over and over again—then stepped out of the alley, onto Market Street. No cops. Cool beans. After a block or so she slipped into the shadows, took out the wad of cash, counted it. She had 166 dollars.

Oh, yes.

For a street kid—which was what she was now, officially—it was a fortune. Not Donald Trump big, but big enough.

For tonight.

On Eighteenth Street Lilly slipped into a diner, wolfed a hoagie, gulped a black coffee. Twenty minutes later, back on Market, she raised her hand, flagged a cab. The driver would know an inexpensive hotel, she thought, if there were such a thing in Philly. Right now all she cared about was a clean tub and a soft bed.

A few moments later a cab pulled to the curb. Lilly slipped into the backseat. The driver was from Nigeria. Or maybe it was Uganda. Whichever, he had a wicked bad accent. He told her he knew just the hotel. Cabbies always did. She would tip him well.

He was, like her, a stranger in a strange land.

Lilly sat back, sated, in charge. She fingered the thick roll of cash in her hand. It was still warm. The night air rushing in the window made her sleepy, but not too sleepy to think about the next few days.

Welcome to Philadelphia.

THIRTY-THREE

JESSICA GLANCED AT THE SPEEDOMETER. SHE WAS TWENTY OVER. SHE backed off, but not too much. The day was closing in on her and she wasn't doing a very good job of shutting it out. She usually could.

She remembered when she was small, her father coming home after a tough day, a Philly-cop day. In those days, the days when her mother had already passed and her father, still a patrolman, was juggling his career and two small children, he would drop his cap on the kitchen table, lock his service weapon in the desk in the living room, and circle the Jameson in the hutch.

He always waited until the sun went down. Tough to do in summer. Daylight savings time, and all. Even harder to do in Lent, when he gave it up all together. Once, during Lent, when Jessica was four, and her family was still intact, her father made it all the way to Easter Saturday on the wagon. After dinner he walked down to the corner bar and got tanked. When he got home, and Maria Giovanni saw his condition, she proclaimed that her husband—probably the whole family—was hellbound. She marched Jessica and her brother Michael down to St. Paul's, banged on the rectory door until their pastor came out and blessed them. Somehow, that Easter came and went without the Giovanni family bursting into redemptive flame.

Jessica wanted to call her father, but stopped herself. He'd think something was wrong. He would be right.

SHE GOT IN just after eleven. The house was quiet, save for the sound of the central air, save for her husband Vincent's world-class snoring upstairs. It sounded like a lumberjack competition on ESPN2.

She made herself a sandwich, wrapped more than half of it and put it in the fridge. She cruised the cable channels, twice, then shut off the TV, padded upstairs, looked in on Sophie. Her daughter was awake, staring at the ceiling.

Jessica left the hall light on, the door open slightly. A wedge of gold light spilled across the bedroom. She sat gently on the edge of the bed, smoothed her daughter's hair. It was getting so long.

"Hi, sweetie," Jessica said.

"IIi, Mom." Her daughter's voice was tiny, distant, sleep-thick. She yawned.

"Did I wake you up?"

Sophie shook her head.

"How was school today?"

It was Sophie's third day at school. When Jessica was her daughter's age she recalled starting the new school year well after Labor Day. That was a thing of the past.

"We had a drill."

It took Jessica a moment to realize what she meant. Then it clicked. Grade schools had recently begun to run through lockdown drills with their students. Jessica read about it in one of the school bulletins. She had called the school principal and was told that, for the little ones, they couched the idea in nonthreatening hypothetical terms like, *Suppose a mean dog got loose in the school, and we needed a way to make everyone safe.*

The principal said the kindergarteners usually thought the idea of a dog running through the halls was kind of funny. Parents rarely did.

"We did triangles, too."

"Triangles?"

Sophie nodded. "Eca-laterals and sossalees."

Jessica smiled. "Sounds like fun."

"It was. I like the sossalees best."

"Me too," Jessica said. Her little girl's face was bright and scrubbed. She looked older somehow, like Jessica hadn't seen her in a few months, instead of only about sixteen hours. "How come you're not asleep?"

Sophie shrugged. She was at the phase in her life where she considered every answer very carefully, a stage twice removed from the three-year-old's programmed responses to every question, the juncture where all children are all like miniature witnesses for the prosecution.

We don't want to go into that *store, do we?*

No.

Big girls always bring their dishes to the sink, don't they?

Yes.

Jessica missed that phase. On one hand she wanted her daughter to be the smartest girl ever born, to be clever, inquisitive, resourceful, and successful. On the other hand, she wanted Sophie to remain that sweet, innocent little child who needed help buttoning her cardigans. "Want me to read something?" Jessica asked.

The Junie B. Jones series of novels were Sophie's current rave. On a few nights in the recent past Jessica had caught Sophie reading a Junie B. in bed with a flashlight. She wasn't zipping through the pages yet, but she was definitely ahead of most of the kids in her class when it came to reading and comprehension. In the books, Junie B. was a maverick six-year-old. To Jessica, it seemed like just yesterday that her daughter was into Curious George and Dr. Seuss.

Now it was renegade first-graders.

"I could get out one of the Junie B. books. Want me to do that?" Jessica asked. "Or maybe some Magic Tree House?"

Sophie shrugged again. In the moonlight coming in the window her eyes were fathomless pools. Her lids began to close.

"Maybe tomorrow?"

Sophie Balzano nodded. " 'Kay."

Tomorrow, Jessica thought. You always think there is going to be a tomorrow. Caitlin O'Riordan and Monica Renzi thought there would be a tomorrow.

So did Eve Galvez.

"Okay, my love," Jessica said. "Sleep good." She kissed her daughter on the forehead. In seconds, Sophie closed her eyes. Moments later, she was sound asleep. If there was a more beautiful sight in all the world, Jessica couldn't imagine what it might be.

SHE TOOK A QUICK SHOWER, emerged from the bathroom in a towel. She took a jar of moisturizer from the nightstand. She sat on the edge of the bed. Vincent was still fast asleep, dead to the world.

Jessica tried to rid her mind of the events of the day. She failed utterly.

Three boxes.

Was the number significant? Were the colors important? What about the way the boxes were aligned?

She knew that Dino and Eric had met with the victim's parents, and the parents were on their way to Philly to try and make a positive ID, but there was little doubt in Jessica's mind who the victim was: Monica Louise Renzi, late of Scranton, Pennsylvania.

But there was a bigger question.

If they were being led to these crime scenes, what was coming next?

"Hey."

Jessica jumped a foot. She hadn't heard Vincent stop snoring.

"Sorry," he said.

"It's okay," she lied. Her heart was now lodged somewhere around her upper esophagus.

"Bad day?" Vincent sat up, massaged her shoulders. He knew every knot, every muscle. He gently kissed them all.

"Bad day," Jessica replied. "Yours?"

"Just another day at Black Rock."

Vincent was on an undercover buy-and-bust sting and that scared the hell out of Jessica. A week earlier his team had taken a casualty.

"Let me ask you something," Vincent said.

"Okay."

"Did you get shot today?"

"No," Jessica said. "You?"

"No."

"Then it couldn't have been that bad."

Jessica nodded. Such was the world of a two-badge marriage. You were both allowed to have bad days, but not at the same time. And every day a bullet or a knife didn't enter your body was a good day on the PPD.

"So tell me. Where does it hurt?" Vincent asked.

Jessica put a finger to her forehead, then slowly pointed at her toes.

"So, we're talking the whole robot."

"Yeah," she said.

"Hmmm. Well, then." Vincent gently rolled his wife onto her back. He slipped out of his drawstring scrubs, peeled off her towel, dropped them both on the floor. "As official head of customer service, it looks like my work is cut out for me."

Jessica nodded again.

"Please pay attention to the following five options," Vincent said. "Because our menu has recently changed."

"Okay."

Vincent held up his left hand, fingers spread. "If you like deep, passionate kisses, press one."

Jessica pressed one.

It was the right choice.

IN HER DREAM SHE SAT at the back corner table at the Embers, an old tavern in the Northeast. She was dressed in a tight red dress and black heels, a thin strand of pearls. The clothes were not her own. In front of her was a small tumbler of what looked like Wild Turkey on the rocks.

She glanced down.

In her lap was her wedding album. She hadn't had it out in years. Even before she flipped the cover, she knew what she was going to see. She was going to see herself in the wedding gown that belonged to her mother. She was going to see her aunts and uncles and nieces and friends. She was going to see a hundred drunk cops. She was going to see her aunt Lorrie who had stood up for her at her wedding.

The jukebox at the bar played an old song by Bobby Darin. It sounded like the band at her wedding reception. Pete Simonetta, her sixth-grade crush, sang lead.

She glanced down again. Now the cover of the book was cherry red. In her dream, Jessica flipped open the album.

The woman inside wasn't her. It was someone else wearing her wedding dress, her crucifix, her veil. It was someone else holding her flowers.

It was Eve Galvez.

THIRTY-FOUR

JESSICA CALLED BYRNE ON HIS CELL PHONE AT 7:00 AM. SHE'D BEEN UP since five, had already gone for her run, had already ingested a day's worth of caffeine. Byrne was having breakfast in Old City. He sounded fresh. This was good. She need him to be fresh. She felt anything but.

"We're going to have preliminaries on Monica Renzi at around 10:30," he said.

"Who lit the fire?"

"It came from on high. Zeus-high. Someone is killing runaways and the new administration isn't going to stand for it."

"I'll see you then."

"I think we should—"

She closed her phone with a snap. She knew she had cut him off. She held the phone in her hand, eyes closed, waiting for it to ring, praying it wouldn't. Ten seconds, twenty, thirty. A minute. Nothing.

A half hour later, her daughter fed and lunch-bagged and scrubbed and on the bus, she slipped into her car and headed to Elkins Park.

She had no idea what she was going to say when she got there.

ENRIQUE GALVEZ WAS TALL and slender, in his late twenties. He had dark hair to his shoulders, a model's cheekbones, full lips. He wore a black T-shirt, no logo or message, and worn, frayed, knee-holed Levi's. He was barefoot.

When Jessica pulled up in front of his house, Enrique was trimming a large hydrangea, deadheading the blooms. He was wearing white earbuds, so it appeared that he did not hear her pull into the driveway.

Jessica got out of the car. When Enrique turned and saw her, he put his clippers into his pocket, removed the earphones.

"Mr. Galvez?"

"Yes," he replied. "You are with the police?"

Man, Jessica thought, then wondered. *Is it that obvious?* She produced her ID. "I am," she said. Her gold shield flashed brightly in the morning sun. "I just need a few moments of your time."

Enrique Galvez looked at the ground for a moment, at his flowers. The vibrant bed at his feet was ablaze with color, with life. He looked up. "I have already spoken to the two detectives. It was a Miss Malone and a Mr. . . . ."

"Shepherd," Jessica said. "I know. I have just a few follow-up questions." Now she *was* breaking procedure. Officially. She couldn't seem to stop herself.

"I understand," Enrique said.

The scene froze. Neither spoke. In the near distance Jessica heard a baby crying. Two doors down, perhaps. "May I come in?"

Enrique returned to the moment. "Of course," he said. "Where are my manners? Forgive me." He walked up the steps, onto the porch, opened the screen door wide. "Please."

THE SMALL LIVING ROOM was tidy, decorated in a masculine southwestern style, in shades of brown, rust, cream, and jade. On the walls were well-framed watercolors of various landmarks in Philadelphia, including City Hall, Boathouse Row, Independence Hall, the Betsy Ross house. A parakeet chirped in a cage in the kitchen.

"Who is the artist?" Jessica asked.

"Oh," Enrique said, coloring slightly. "I am the artist. I painted these. Although it was a long time ago."

"They are beautiful," Jessica said.

"Thank you," Enrique replied. He seemed to be humble about his talent. "May I offer you something to drink?"

"I'm fine, thanks."

Enrique gestured toward the couch. "Please sit down."

"I know this is terribly difficult for you," she said. "I'm very sorry for your loss."

"Thank you."

Jessica sat down, adjusted herself on the chair, extracted her notebook. A personal notebook. "When was the last time you saw your sister?"

"As I told the other detectives, we had dinner," Enrique said. "On the day she went missing. At the Palm."

"It was just the two of you?"

"Yes."

"Did Eve say or do anything out of the ordinary?"

Enrique shook his head. "The only thing ordinary about my sister was her potential for the extraordinary."

"Did she mention anything about a case she was working on?"

Enrique thought for a few moments. "Eve never talked much to me about her work. She knew that I found such things quite . . . upsetting."

Jessica shifted tack. "You are originally from Peru?" she asked.

"I am. I was born in a small village near Machu Picchu, as was my sister. We were three and five years old when we came here."

"You came with your parents?"

A moment's hesitation, Jessica noticed. *A family problem?* Enrique glanced out the front window. Jessica followed his gaze. Across the street, a pair of six-year-old girls—clumsy and stick-figured and giggling in their matching lime-green little-girl bikinis—ran back and forth through a sprinkler.

"Yes," he finally said. "My father was an engineer. He worked for TelComCo in Peru. In 1981 they gave him the opportunity to come to America, to Philadelphia, and he took it. He brought his family soon after."

"Did you ever hear from your sister in all the time she was missing?"

Enrique shook his head. "I did not."

It appeared Enrique wanted to continue. Jessica remained silent.

"For these past two months I wondered, of course," he said. "I questioned. And yet it is the kind of thing you know, yes?"

Jessica nodded, despite her best efforts not to.

"It is the kind of thing you *know*," he repeated. "But still, always, you hope it is not true. The hope is something that burns inside of you, a small flame that fights the darkness of what you know in your heart."

"I'm so sorry," Jessica said. She was now afraid the conversation was slipping away. She put her notebook away, glanced once more around the room. "Is there anything else you can think of that might help?"

"Well, I have not touched her apartment. The other detectives were there yesterday, I believe."

"Would it be okay if I stopped by?" Jessica knew she would definitely and irretrievably cross the line if she did this.

"Yes, of course." He crossed the room, opened a drawer, pulled out a single key. He wrote down an address on a small pad, handed both to her. "You can just leave the key there. One day, one day soon, I will . . ."

Enrique stopped. His eyes began to rim with tears.

"I understand," Jessica said, knowing her words were inadequate. "Thank you."

FIVE MINUTES LATER, as Jessica backed into the street, she realized that somehow, in some way, this little visit was going to come back and haunt her. If Ike Buchanan found out that she had come here to talk to a victim's brother without logging the interview, or clearing it with the primary detectives on the case, she would get her ears boxed, or worse. No detective liked an interloper on their patch. Homicide detectives especially.

As she drove away she turned to look at the small house one last time. Before she reached the corner she saw that the porch light was on. It was probably habit, she thought, one that Enrique Galvez was not ready to break.

A small flame that fights the darkness of what you know in your heart.

Enrique Galvez was still waiting for his sister.

THIRTY-FIVE

SWANN SAT ON THE PARK BENCH. IT WAS A GLORIOUS MORNING. HE nibbled on a raspberry scone he had purchased from a new bakery on Pine Street.

Across his knees was a metal detector, a Bounty Hunter Tracker II.

HE WATCHED THEM for the better part of an hour. Five teenagers, a strange number for many reasons. Two boys and three girls. At this age, there was always a peculiar dynamic at play with an odd number. Loud, physical, bounding with energy, they challenged each other. There would always be a hierarchy established at times like this, a ladder based on the reason they had assembled in the first place. Later on it would be money and power and position. But in Swann's experience, at this age, it was usually beauty and strength that won the day.

Their vehicle was a red minivan, doors open, music playing at a respectful level. They teased for a while, shared cigarettes and soda. Eventually watches were consulted, goodbyes uttered, trash thrown into receptacles.

When the van left, it was as he expected. One girl was left behind. To his eyes she was by far the prettiest, but she did not belong to this group for other reasons. She was clearly a stray.

As the van rounded a bend, the girl waved, tossed a finger, a smile. But Swann could see desolation in her smile. Alone now, the girl drank from her water bottle, even though she knew it was empty. Girls her age often repeated tasks like that. The energy had to go somewhere.

Swann got up from the bench, turned on the detector. It was showtime. He walked along the side of the road, brow furrowed, deep in concentration. When he positioned himself about twenty yards behind the girl, the detector alerted him. She heard, turned to watch.

"Yes!" he exclaimed loud enough for the girl to hear. "Oh yes, yes, yes."

Out of the corner of his eye he saw her considering him. Who was this strange man with this strange machine? Her teenage curiosity could not resist.

"Did you find something?" she asked.

He looked up, around, as if trying to determine from where the voice had come. He found her, pointed to the ground near his feet. "Eureka!"

Swann bent over, picked up a necklace. The necklace was cheap gold. It had been palmed in his hand the whole time. "I struck gold!"

He held it up. The necklace glittered in the morning sun. The girl got up to take a closer look. They always did.

"Oh man. Sweet," she said. "Very cool." Her eyes went from the necklace to the emblem on his jumpsuit. The patch looked official, as if he were part of the park service. Closer scrutiny would reveal nothing of the kind.

"You didn't lose this by any chance, did you?" he asked, slight disappointment edging his voice.

The girl hesitated for a moment—Swann would have been deeply disappointed if she had not, the longer she hesitated the longer she had been on the road—then shook her head. "No. I *wish*. It's really nice."

Swann put the necklace into his bag. "You'd be amazed what I've been able to find over the years."

"I'll bet." She shoved her hands into her jeans pockets. She wanted to talk. She was lonely. "What kinds of stuff?"

"Gosh, let's see. Rings, bracelets, coins, barrettes. Lots and *lots* of barrettes."

The girl laughed. "Kids."

"Tell me about it. I buy my daughters barrettes by the case. They are always losing them." He turned off the machine. "My name's Ludo, by the way."

"Ludo? Cool name. Mine's Claire." They shook hands. He did not remove his gloves. "Do you work here?" she asked.

"As little as possible."

The girl laughed again. Swann turned the machine back on, stepped away, then stepped back. "Want to try?"

The girl shook her head. Shy now. "I don't think I'd be any good at it."

"Sure you would. Of *course* you would. There's really nothing to it. If I can do it, you can do it."

"You think?"

"Absolutely. And I'll tell you what."

"What?"

"Whatever you find you can keep."

Her eyes lit up. It was like the best offer she'd ever had. "For real?"

Swann gave her a brief demonstration. She took the detector from him.

"Try near the entrance to the path," he said, pointing to the asphalt-paved lane leading into the forest of trees. "A lot of times people will pull things out of their pockets right there—sweatbands, sunglasses, mosquito spray—and things can fly out and get lost in the leaves. It can be a real gold mine."

"Okay. I don't know. I'm not really . . . okay." The girl began to scan where he told her to look. She waved the machine back and forth, back and forth, like a divining rod, settling the weight.

"A little slower," he said.

"Okay."

Left, left, left, Swann thought. Stop.

"Right around here?"

"Yes."

More to the left. Stop. Right. Stop.

The machine beeped.

Yes.

"Hey! I think I found something! Does this mean I found something?" she asked.

"It does indeed."

"What do I do?"

"I'll show you."

She modeled the bangle. "So this is really mine?"

"Finders, keepers."

The paste jewelry sparkled in the sun. To the girl, it was a Tiffany tennis bracelet.

He glanced at his watch. "Well, I've got to get back to work. They only let me do this on my break. It was nice to meet you, Claire." He pointed to the bracelet. "Very cool find, by the way. I think you're a natural sleuth."

He put the detector over one shoulder, and began to walk away.

" 'Scuse me."

Joseph Swann stopped, turned. "Yes?"

"I was wondering something."

"Okay."

"Is there, I mean, do you guys have, like, campgrounds around here?"

"Campgrounds? Sure," he said. "About a mile up this way. Nice, too."

"I'm not with . . ." she trailed off, pointing back over her shoulder. She meant she was not with anybody. She meant she was alone. He knew this already.

"Don't worry," Swann said. "It's okay. I'll tell them you're my cousin or something. You won't even need ID. I've got a little juice around here. It's a really nice place. Safe, too."

"Cool."

Claire Finneran smiled. Joseph Swann smiled back.

"It's right up here," he said. "C'mon. I'll show you."

No hesitation now. She grabbed her bag.

They walked into the woods.

THIRTY-SIX

Byrne sat in the car, watching. The man stood across the vacant lot, leaning against a half-demolished brick wall. The man had been there every day at the same time for the past three days, probably long before that. He wore the same clothes. He wore the same hat, the same expression. To Byrne he looked emptied, as if someone had scooped out everything that made him human and left just the shell, a brittle shell at that.

This had become Robert O'Riordan's vigil, the same as a death-watch, even though his daughter had already died. Or perhaps she had not, in his mind. Perhaps he expected her to appear in one of the windows, like some spectral Juliet. Or maybe his desires were more earth-bound, and practical. Maybe he expected Caitlin's killer to return to the scene of the crime, as killers were wont to do.

What would he then do? Byrne wondered. Was he armed? Did Caitlin's father have the nerve to pull the trigger or launch the blade, based on a suspicion?

Byrne had talked to hundreds of fathers in his time on the job, men who had lost a son or daughter to violence. Each faced the darkness in his own way.

Byrne glanced at the man. There was no reaching him. Not now.

He started the car. But before he could pull out into traffic his phone rang. It was Jessica.

"We've got something," she said. "Meet me at the lab."

THIRTY-SEVEN

Tracy McGovern was deputy director of the crime lab. A tall, slender woman of fifty, she had silver, shoulder-length hair, blunt-cut bangs. She favored shapeless black suits, rock-and-roll T-shirts, and Ecco walkers. Tracy had spent nearly ten years working with the FBI's Mitochondrial DNA Unit—a division that examines items of evidence associated with cold cases, as well as small pieces of evidence containing little biological material—before returning to her hometown of Philadelphia. According to her colleagues, she had the unique ability to sleep three twenty-minute stretches per twenty-four-hour period, right at her desk, and continue working on a case until the perpetrator was caught. Tracy McGovern was not so much a bloodhound as she was a greyhound.

The three boxes from the Shiloh Street crime scene were on the floor. In the harsh light of the lab they looked even brighter, more colorful. It was hard to reconcile this with the purpose for which they had been used.

"There were no prints on the boxes," Tracy said. "They've been rather thoroughly wiped down with a common household cleaning so-lution."

Byrne again noted the craftsmanship that went into the design and construction of these boxes. The mitered edges were almost invisible.

"These hinges look expensive," Byrne said.

"They are," Tracy said. "They're made by an Austrian company called Grass. They're available from only a few dozen companies on the Internet. You might want to check them out." Tracy handed Byrne a printout of specialty hardware websites.

"We're still collecting trace evidence from the boxes, but there is something else I wanted to show you."

Tracy walked across the lab, returned with a large paper evidence bag. "I didn't work on this last time, so I thought I'd give it a look."

She reached in the evidence bag and removed Caitlin O'Riordan's backpack.

"Detective Pistone emptied the bag on scene, brought everything back in pieces, I'm afraid. I hate to speak ill of the retired, but it was sloppy work. The exterior got dusted, the interior vacuumed and cleared, and then it got stuck on a shelf. We've reprocessed the bag for prints only," Tracy said. "The only exemplars belong to Miss O'Riordan. We'll get on hair and fiber again later today."

Tracy unzipped the bag.

"I went poking around inside," she said. "There's a plastic insert on the bottom that flips up."

Tracy turned the backpack inside out. The inside flap was torn along one edge. "I looked inside here and found something. It was a section of a magazine cover."

"It was underneath?" Jessica asked.

"It was slid inside along this tear," Tracy said, pointing to the seam. The plastic lining had come away from the hard cardboard insert. "I'm inclined to believe Miss O'Riordan may have put it in there for safe-keeping."

"Where is the magazine cover now?" Jessica asked.

"It's being processed for prints." Tracy took out two photocopies of photographs, front and back of the evidence.

The images were of about a third of a page of a magazine cover, torn diagonally. It was *Seventeen Magazine*, the May 2008 issue. Written on the back was a phone number. The last five numbers were obscured, perhaps with water damage, but the area code was clear enough.

"Has Hell Rohmer seen this?" Jessica asked.

"He gets it next," Tracy said. "He's already pacing upstairs."

Jessica picked up the photocopy, angled it toward the light.

"Eight-five-six area code," she said.

"Eight-five-six," Byrne echoed. "Camden."

THE FINGERPRINT LAB found three distinct sets of prints on the glossy surface of the magazine cover. One belonged to Caitlin O'Riordan. One exemplar was not in the system. One set—thumb and forefinger— were ten point exemplars. They ran the prints through a local database, as well as AFIS. The Automated Fingerprint Identification System was a national database used to match unknown prints against known, using either the newer Live Scan technologies—which employed a laser scanning device—or the old method of prints taken in ink.

The third set rang every bell in the system. It belonged to a man named Ignacio Sanz. The detectives checked his name on PCIC and NCIC and found that Ignacio had a long sheet, had twice been ar- rested, tried, and convicted for gross sexual imposition and contribut- ing to the delinquency of a minor. He had done two stretches at Curran-Fromhold, the last being eighteen months, a sentence ending this past April.

Jessica glanced at Byrne as they read the sheet. They were defi- nitely of the same mind: Ignacio Sanz was a creep, a deviant, and he was on the street right around the time Caitlin O'Riordan was murdered in May.

Byrne got on the phone, reached out to Sanz's parole officer. Within an hour they had a home address and a work address.

THIRTY-EIGHT

THE SHRIMP DOCK WAS A SEAFOOD TAKE-OUT RESTAURANT IN EAST Camden, New Jersey, a slanted grease-box scaled in salmon-colored tile and torn, sea green awnings, nestled between a boarded-up Dunkin' Donuts and a Dominican barber shop.

Jessica and Byrne walked in, scanned the restaurant, then the area behind the counter. There was no sign of Ignacio Sanz. He wasn't working the register, nor was he bussing tables or sweeping up.

The service window was double-thick security plastic. Behind it stood a pretty young Hispanic girl in a blue and red tricot uniform and hat, looking about as bored as a human being could look and still register a pulse. She snapped her gum. Byrne showed her tin, even though it was unnecessary.

"Ignacio around?" Byrne asked.

The girl didn't answer. That would've required the expending of energy. Instead, she nodded to a door next to the counter, the one marked EM   YE S   ON Y.

Twenty seconds later, sufficient time to remind Byrne and Jessica just where they were, the girl buzzed them back.

IGNACIO SANZ WASN'T on anybody's list of babysitters. Now in his late twenties, a two-time loser, he was allegedly on the path to respectability. The state had gotten him a job working the fry baskets at the Shrimp Dock, and a room at a halfway house nearby.

When Jessica and Byrne stepped into the back room of the restaurant, the first thing they noticed was that the door was wide open. The second thing they noticed was that a man—without question, Ignacio Sanz—was running across the back parking lot, full tilt.

Jessica, who had dressed in one of her better suits—a nice two-button Tahari she had gotten from Macy's—looked at her partner.

Byrne pointed to his right leg. "Sciatica."

"Ah, *shit.*"

By the time Jessica tackled Ignacio Sanz, he was halfway to Atlantic City.

They were in a small, cramped space at the rear of the Shrimp Dock, in what passed for an employee break room. On the walls were curling posters for the tempting bill of fare: light blue haddock, gray coleslaw, hoary fries.

Iggy was short and spindly, with a caved chest and acne-pitted cheeks. He seemed to be coated in a slick film of fish grease, giving his skin an unnatural sheen. He also had the smallest feet Jessica had ever seen on a grown man. He wore neon aqua cross-trainers and black silk dress socks. Jessica wondered if he was wearing women's shoes.

He also sported the same red and blue tricot smock the girl out front was wearing, but instead of a hat he wore a hairnet that reached down to just over his eyebrows. All of which was now covered with dust and gravel, due to his recent visit to the ground, courtesy of the Philadelphia Police Department.

Byrne sat across from him. Jessica stood behind him. This did not sit well with Ignacio. He was afraid of Jessica. With good reason.

"My name is Detective Byrne. I'm with Philly Homicide." He pointed over Ignacio's shoulder. "This is my partner, Detective Balzano. You may remember her. She's the one who bodychecked you against that Chevy van."

Ignacio sat stock-still.

"I want you to give her twenty dollars," Byrne said.

Iggy looked punched. "What?"

"You owe her a pair of pantyhose. Give her twenty dollars."

Jessica looked down. When she flipped Iggy onto the ground she tore a big hole in the right knee of her hose.

"Pantyhose cost twenty *dollars*?" Iggy asked.

Byrne stuck his face an inch from Iggy's face. Iggy shrunk measurably. "Are you saying my partner doesn't deserve the best?"

Trembling, without another word, Iggy dug around in his pockets, came up with a wad of damp bills, counted them out. Fourteen dollars. He flattened them on the table, stacked them, then handed them to Jessica, who took them without hesitation, even though she wondered where the hell they had recently been.

"You could, you know, come back for the rest later," Iggy said. "I get paid today. I'll have the rest later."

"Come back?" Byrne said. "What makes you think you're not coming with us?"

This had not occurred to Iggy. "But I didn't *do* nothing."

Byrne laughed. "You think that matters to someone like me?"

This also had not occurred to him. But the implications were far more serious. Iggy stared at the floor, remained silent.

"Now, my partner is going to speak to you," Byrne said. "I want you to give her your full attention and your full respect."

Byrne stood up, held the chair. Jessica sat down, her right knee poking through her torn pantyhose, thinking, *Does anything look skankier than this?*

"I'm going to ask you some simple questions," Jessica said. "And you're going to tell me the truth. Right, Iggy?"

It was clear that Ignacio Sanz had no idea what was coming his way. After a lifetime of crime, courts, cops, public defenders, jail, parole, probation, and rehab, it could be anything. "Yes, ma'am."

Jessica reached into her portfolio, put a folder on her lap.

"First of all, we know all about you and Caitlin O'Riordan," Jessica said. "So don't even think about insulting our intelligence with a denial." The truth was, they didn't know anything of the sort. But with people like Iggy, this was the best approach. "This is not even an option."

"Who?"

Jessica took out a photograph of Caitlin. She showed it to Iggy. "Caitlin Alice O'Riordan. Remember her?"

Iggy looked at the picture. "I don't know this girl."

"Look a little more closely."

Iggy did, opening his eyes wide, perhaps believing this would let in more information. He shook his head again. "No. I've never seen her. She could be anybody."

"No she can't. That's not possible. She has to be *this person*. She *is* this person. Or at least she was. You follow me?"

Iggy bug-eyed for a few seconds, then nodded slowly.

"Good. Here's the 411. We have you, Iggy. We have you in Philly in May, out on the street. And the icing, the part with the little candy sprinkles, is that we also have a beautiful set of your fingerprints on something Caitlin had in her backpack."

Iggy reacted as if he had just grabbed a hot copper wire. He rose slowly from his chair, shuddering with panic. "Whatever she says I did, I didn't do it, man," he pleaded. "I swear on my mother's eyes. My mother's *grave*."

"Caitlin's not saying anything. That's because she's dead. She's been dead for four months. But you already know that, right?"

"*What?*" Iggy screamed. "Oh *no, no, no, no. Uh-uh.*"

"Well, here's what I'm willing to do for you, Iggy. First off, I'm willing to cut your hospital stay by a hundred percent."

Iggy, already hyperventilating, began to breathe even faster. "My hospital stay?"

"Yeah," Jessica said. "What I mean by that is, if you don't sit down right now, I'm going to break both of your arms. Sit . . . the fuck . . . *down*."

Iggy complied. Jessica picked up the magazine cover in the clear plastic evidence envelope. She held it up.

"Tell me why your prints are on this magazine, Iggy. Start right now."

Iggy's eyes darted side to side, vibrating, like a lemur's. "Okay, okay," he said. "I remember. It's embezzled in my mind."

"Embezzled?"

"Yeah. I found that magazine."

Jessica laughed. "So, let me ask you, did you find it in the big pile of guns, knives, crack, jewelry, and wallets, or the small one?"

Iggy mangled his face again. *Huh?*

"Where did you find it, Iggy?"

"I found it in my house. It was my mother's."

"This was your mother's magazine?"

Iggy shook his head. "It was her *house*. It was my *sister's* magazine."

"This magazine belonged to your sister? She gave it to you?"

"Well, no," he said. "But we share, you know? We family and everything. I like to look at this magazine."

"Because there are teenaged girls in it?"

Iggy just stared.

"How did this magazine get into Caitlin O'Riordan's backpack?"

Iggy took a few moments, apparently calculating that this next answer was going to be crucial. The smell of hot, fishy grease began to fill the back room. The Shrimp Dock was gearing up for lunch. "I don't know."

"We're going to need to talk to your sister."

"I can help you with that," Iggy said, snapping his fingers, suddenly full of vigor. "I can most *definitely* help you with that."

Jessica glanced at Byrne, wondering if they would spend the rest of the day driving around Camden in ninety-degree heat, looking for a phantom.

"You're saying you know where we can find your sister right now?" Jessica asked.

"Absolutely," Iggy said. He smiled. Jessica immediately wished he hadn't. In addition to the five-car pileup that was his dental work, she caught a blast of his breath: a combo of menthol cigarettes and deep fried hush puppies. "She's standing right behind you."

THIRTY-NINE

FRANCESCA SANZ WAS THE GIRL THEY HAD SEEN AT THE FRONT COUNTER. Standing closer to her, Jessica could now see she was not a mid-teenager, but rather eighteen or so. Coral lipstick, blue eye shadow. Street pretty. She was also four or five months pregnant.

Jessica told the young woman why they were there, giving her the bare minimum of details. Jessica then showed her a picture of Caitlin O'Riordan. While Byrne called in a request for Francesca Sanz's wants and warrants, Jessica and the young woman sat across from each other in a booth.

"Have you ever met this girl?" Jessica asked.

Francesca scrutinized the photo for a few moments. "Yeah. I met her."

"How do you know her?"

Francesca chipped at a nail. "We were friends."

"You mean school friends? She was from the neighborhood? Something like that?"

"Nah. Not like that."

Francesca did not elaborate. Jessica pressed. "Then like *what*?"

A hesitation. "We met at the train station."

"Here in Camden?"

"Nah," she said. "In Philly. That real big one."

"Thirtieth Street?"

"Yeah."

"When was this?"

"I don't know. A couple of months ago, I guess."

"A couple?"

"Yeah," she said. Jessica noticed that the girl had a tattoo on her right wrist, a tattoo of a white dove. "You know. A couple. Maybe more."

"I need you to be a little more specific about this, Francesca. It's very important. Was it June? April?"

Silence.

"Could it have been May?"

"Yeah," Francesca said. "You know. It could have been." She did a little air math—counting something with her fingers in front of her face. "Yeah. May sounds right."

"So you're saying you met her at the Thirtieth Street station in May of this year?"

"Yeah."

"Okay," Jessica said. "Why were you at the train station? Were you going somewhere, coming from somewhere?"

Francesca brewed an answer. "I was just getting something to eat."

"Do you have friends in that part of Philly? Family?"

"No," she said. "Not really."

"So, let me get this straight," Jessica said. "You went down to the river, crossed the Ben Franklin Bridge, made your way all the way across the city of Philadelphia, thirty or so blocks, just to get a hoagie and some Boardwalk fries? Is this what you're saying?"

Francesca nodded, but she would not make eye contact with Jessica. "What do you want me to say?"

"The truth would be good."

Another few seconds. Francesca tapped her long nails on the scuffed Formica. Finally: "I was on the street, okay?"

"You ran away from home?"

"Yeah."

"Okay," Jessica said. She took a moment, giving the girl some space. "I'm not judging, I'm asking."

"And I was using. I don't do it no more, 'cause of the baby. But I had heard that kids used to hang around the station."

"Runaways?"

"Yeah," she said. "I figured I could hook up."

Jessica put her notebook down. Francesca was starting to open up, and a cop making notes was intimidating. "Can I ask why you ran away from home?"

Francesca laughed a wintry laugh. She worried the edge of a table menu, peeling back the plastic. "I don't know. Why does anyone run away?"

"There are a lot of possibilities," Jessica said, knowing that there were really only a handful.

"My mother, right? My mother is *loca*. To this *day*. Her and her pipehead boyfriends. That house is hell. She found out I was pregnant and she hit me."

"You were abused?"

Another laugh. This one laced with irony. "I'm from East Camden, okay? I was *born* abused."

Jessica tapped the photograph of Caitlin. "Did your brother know her?"

"That girl? No. At least, I don't think he did. I hope not."

"You hope not? Why do you say that?"

"You came here to talk to him, so I figure you know his record, right?"

"We do."

"So you know what I'm talking about."

"Okay," Jessica said, trudging on. "So tell me, how did this girl come to be in possession of this magazine cover?"

Francesca leaned back, crossed her arms, resting them on her swelling belly. Defensive, now. "I was reading the magazine, that's all. We started talking. She said she decided to go home. She kinda talked me into it, too. So I wrote down my number and gave it to her. I thought maybe we could talk sometime."

Jessica tapped the magazine cover. "This is your number?"

"Yeah."

"What happened after that?"

"What happened? Nothing. She just walked out."

"And you never saw her again?"

Francesca looked out the window. In this light, Jessica saw her as a middle-aged woman, a woman with all her bad decisions behind her. "I saw her outside."

"Outside the station?"

"Yeah. I called a friend of mine and he came to pick me up. On my way out I saw her. She was talking to a well-dressed man."

"A man? White, black?"

"White."

"Well-dressed how?"

"Not like in a suit, but nice. Expensive."

"Can you describe him?"

"Not really. He had his back to me. It was dark."

"Did you see her get into a car or on a bus with this man?"

"Yeah. She got into his car. I thought maybe he was her father."

"Do you remember what kind of car?"

"No. Sorry."

"After that day at the Thirtieth Street station, did you ever see this girl again?"

Francesca thought about this, weighing her answer. "No," she said. "I never saw her again."

Jessica glanced at Byrne. He shook his head. No questions. She clicked her pen, put it away. They were done. For now. "We may need to talk to you again."

A shrug. "I'll be here."

Jessica started to pack up to leave. "When are you due?"

Francesca beamed. "They tell me December twentieth."

Jessica felt a pang of envy. A Christmas baby. Was there anything better than a Christmas baby? She and Vincent had been trying to get pregnant for the past year or so. There was a close call the previous winter, but no baby. "Good luck."

"Thank you."

They looked at each other for a few seconds in silence, two women at different ends of everything. Except motherhood.

Jessica took out a business card, handed it to the young woman. "If you think of anything else that might help, please give me a call."

Francesca took the card, stood—with no small amount of difficulty—and made her way toward the ladies' restroom door. At the door Francesca stopped, turned. "That girl?"

"What about her?"

A grave look veiled Francesca's young face, a weariness far older than her years. "She's dead, isn't she?"

Jessica could find no reason not to tell the truth. "Yes."

Francesca chipped at another nail for a moment. "Could you tell her family something for me?"

"Sure."

"Tell them . . . tell them I'm sorry for their grief." Francesca placed a hand on her belly, a gesture of defiance to this angel of death who walked the streets, a gesture of defense. "Tell them it's not their fault."

"I will."

Francesca nodded, perhaps thinking about the past, the future, realizing she had only the present. Without another word, she opened the door and stepped through.

IGGY SANZ WAS NOT OUT of the woods yet, but whatever enthusiasm the detectives had on the way over the Ben Franklin Bridge had waned considerably by the time they made their way back. He had no real violence on his sheet. Both detectives were reasonably sure that Ignacio was telling the truth, perhaps for the first time in his life. He may have been a creep and a lowlife, but he was not a killer.

They drove back to Philly.

FORTY

OUR DETECTIVES MET IN THE DUTY ROOM OF THE HOMICIDE UNIT. The second tour had started a few hours earlier, and the last-out detectives had to find somewhere to talk. Desks in the unit were shared— you were lucky to get a drawer in a file cabinet these days. That cop-show myth about how every gold-badge detective had their own desk with a cheap vase with a flower in it and two or three framed photos of their kids was just that, a myth. The reality was, once a tour ended, the next group of detectives took over the desks, and if you were still working you had to find somewhere else fast. Theoretically, every detective cared about every other detective's case, but Roundhouse reality was all about geography.

If it's my tour, my ass is entitled to the real estate.

There was no whiteboard, no chalkboard. Just four detectives crammed into one of the alcoves off the main hallway. A dozen photographs graced one of the desks, a desk hastily cleared of coffee cups, éclairs, muffins.

Jessica, Byrne, Josh Bontrager, and Josh's partner Andre Curtis.

Every homicide unit in the country had a detective who wore hats—homburgs, porkpies, Borsalinos—and Dre Curtis was PPD Homicide's resident lid man. Finding the right hat for his mood was a ritual with him, but he only wore his hat in the elevator and corridors, never in the office. Jessica had once watched him take ten minutes to get the brim right on his beloved grey Rosellini Luauro fedora.

Josh Bontrager was probably partnered with Dre Curtis for no other reason than that they could not have been more different. A kid who had grown up Amish in rural Pennsylvania, and a smooth-talking homeboy, a former gangbanger, from the Richard Allen Homes in North Philly. So far, they had been an effective team.

Byrne let everyone settle in. He got their attention, then recapped both cases, including their visit to Laura Somerville's apartment, and her suicide, and their visit with Iggy Sanz.

"Do we have any forensics tying the two victims together?" Dre Curtis asked.

"We do not," Byrne said. "Not yet. But we just got the preliminary DNA results back on the remains found on Second Street. The heart in the specimen jar belonged to Monica Renzi."

Byrne held up a document. It was the activity log from the Caitlin O'Riordan file.

"There are three interviews missing from the O'Riordan binder. These interviews were conducted by Detective Roarke on May third. We don't have full names on these witnesses, just their street names— Daria, Govinda, and Starlight. It's not much, but it's an entry point."

"What about the detective's notes?" Bontrager asked.

"Missing," Byrne said. "But just the notes for these three. The interviews are logged on the activity sheet, but there's no paper for them." He placed the activity log back into the binder. "All the runaway shelters in Philly have been notified and briefed."

Runaways *from* Philadelphia were handled by the divisional detectives. They were never called runaways officially. They were always referred to as missing persons. When a runaway was missing from another city, and it was reported to the police there, the information went on NCIC. Sometimes the information was posted to the FBI website.

"Detective Park is collating FBI sheets on active runaways over the last year from Pennsylvania, New York, New Jersey, Maryland, and Ohio. He is also assembling reports of any DOA Jane Does from the past three years between the ages of twelve and twenty."

Byrne pulled up a city map on the computer screen. "Let's go where runaways congregate." he said. "The bus station, the train station, the malls, the parks, South Street. Let's make sure we hit Penn Treaty Park."

Penn Treaty Park, where William Penn signed a peace treaty with the chief of the Lenape clan, was a small park on the western bank of the Delaware River in Fishtown. It was somewhat secluded, and therefore a popular destination for runaways and drug transactions.

"Unfortunately, there's a good chance that the kids who were on the streets six months ago have moved on or have gone home, but we all know there's a network out there. Somebody saw these girls. They came into town and they never left." Byrne looked up. "Any questions?"

No one spoke.

"We meet downstairs in an hour."

FORTY-ONE

LILLY HAD SPENT THE NIGHT AT A CHEAP, NOISY PLACE THAT WAS REALLY nothing more than a hostel. It was only fifty dollars. A chunk of money to her, but not to her wallet, a wallet recently fattened by Mr. Mushroom Teeth.

She was out of bed at 6:30 AM, courtesy of the traffic noise and the rolling boom boxes. Didn't this place ever *sleep*? She supposed not.

Welcome to the road, Lilly.

THE GIRL FROM WISCONSIN had heavy metalwork in her lips, her nose, and ears. Her name was Tatiana. Or so she said. She had a foreign accent, so maybe it was her real name after all. She was hefty in the upper body, but had nice legs, legs wrapped in thick black tights.

They were all sitting in the back of a tricked-out Escalade. Lilly had met them near Reading Terminal Market. They asked her if she wanted to get high.

Duh.

"It was like God sneezed, grabbed a tissue with me in it, and threw us both away," Tatiana said.

They all looked at each other, four pairs of eyes meeting for a moment. They'd all had experience with really religious types. If you didn't buy in, you tolerated, nodding your head, agreeing when it was possible. No one really knew what the hell Tatiana was talking about.

After leaving the market they drove around the city for about an hour. The driver was a young Jamaican guy named Niles. He had amazing pot. Two-toke. Lilly was flying.

"I mean, what are you supposed to do? You can't apply for a job, because you can't use your real name," Tatiana said. "The only way to eat is to steal something or go on the game."

Lilly knew what she meant. The first time she had run away from home, at the ripe old age of twelve, she was gone for three weeks. The first few nights were great. She had a few dollars to party, met some cool kids. After that it was hell. She slept behind a grocery store on Wallace Avenue. She got up at 4 AM, just before the delivery trucks would roll in. She got day-old bread and brown vegetables from the Dumpster, half-smoked cigarettes from the gutter. Who says life on the road ain't glamorous?

Then one morning she woke up with a flashlight in her eyes. It was the cops.

She refused to tell them her name. She refused to say *anything*. She spent four days in Juvie, and they had no choice but to let her go. The entire time, she didn't say a single word. But they did fingerprint her and take a few pictures, so she knew that everything had changed there and then.

This time it was different.

She looked out the window. Because they had cruised for a while, she wasn't quite sure where she was. It seemed like South Philly. She couldn't be sure.

"My dad is *such* a fucking Cro," Tatiana said. "I swear to God, if I stayed around, I would have caught him chewing on his toenails one day."

Lilly assumed she meant "Cro-Magnon." Who could tell with these people? She wasn't from around these parts. She wasn't insufferably hip.

Niles fired up another joint, passed it back. It was time to start asking questions. Pretty soon these people would be circling Saturn.

"Can I show you guys something?" Lilly asked.

They all looked at her; stoned, wondering, waiting, as if to say, *Why not?*

Lilly reached into her bag, pulled out the photo. It was pretty wrinkled by now. It was kind of fuzzy to begin with. She smoothed it out on the seat. "Anybody ever been here?"

She passed the photo around. Everyone nodded at the sheer magnitude of the place. Nobody copped to knowing it.

"*Dude*. Who lives here?" Thom asked. "The Addams Family?"

Thom was from Akron, Ohio. He really was kind of cute—curly brown hair, long lashes, pug nose. He reminded her of Frodo, but without the big hairy feet. In another life she might have let him make a move on her.

"I don't know," Lilly said, thinking that it might have been the first thing she'd said in a long time that wasn't a lie. "I really don't know."

FOR THE REST OF THE MORNING she hung out at the Greyhound Station at Tenth and Filbert. She bummed a cup of coffee from a pair of kids from Syracuse, smoked a little weed in an alley. She spent a half hour or so on the Net at a nearby cybercafe, until she was kicked out.

She asked a lot of questions, showed the picture to everyone. Some of the kids were suspicious, as if Lilly were a narc.

Through the course of the morning she talked to more than twenty street kids, swapping horror stories, triumphs, near misses, jail time, cops. Always the cops. If you were a runaway you knew all about cops.

One girl she met—a runaway from Buffalo, a girl who called herself Starlight—told her of an experience she'd had in New York City. Starlight was a force of nature, all hands and hips and flying red hair when she told a tale, a story about how she was almost gang-raped. Lilly hoped for the best for her, didn't expect it. Starlight said she'd been on the street in Philly since last Christmas.

Lilly realized they all had a story of alienation or neglect or mistreatment, a fear of the future. To a person, they all had a saga of woe—abusive mothers, abusive fathers, abusive siblings, abusive life.

They had no idea how bad life could get.

"HEY," THE KID SAID.

Lilly turned around but not too quickly. They were standing near the corner of Ninth and Filbert, outside the BigK.

The kid was a street rat. Lilly didn't like the looks of him. Tall and skinny, dirty blond hair, greasy skin, red Tony Hawk T-shirt. Skateboard grunge had never been her thing. She ignored him, glanced at her watch. A few moments passed. He didn't leave.

"I said *hey*, bitch."

Here we go, Lilly thought. Fucking *boys*. She'd been here before, of course, stuck on a street corner, harassed by some punk. They all had a line they thought was magic, a smile they felt God-given. Then it turned ugly. But it was always on her turf, her hometown. This was an alien landscape.

She tensed, glanced over her shoulder. She was less than a block from the bus station. She could make it back inside in a few seconds. She was that fast. But there was a principle at work here. She wasn't about to be run off the street by some low-rent spod. She turned to face him.

"I'm sorry, what did you call me?"

The kid smirked, took a step closer. Lilly now saw that he was not all that skinny after all. He was muscular. "I think you heard me, Snow White."

He grabbed her arm. She tried to wrestle free. She couldn't. He was strong.

"Let go of me!"

He laughed. "Or what?"

Lilly planted her left foot, shifted her weight. It was a familiar move. She tried to knee him but he turned, blocking it. He laughed again.

"Damn, girl. Why would you want to go and do something like that?" The kid grabbed her other wrist. "You don't want to make me mad."

"I said let *go* of me!"

Lilly tried to break free. She could not.

The kid glanced up the alley, smiled again. He was going to drag her up there. She couldn't let him do that.

But before he could make a move a shadow fell across the sidewalk. They both turned. There was a man standing there. He seemed to appear out of nowhere. He was in his thirties, maybe, wearing a dark blue suit and a burgundy tie.

What was *this* about?

"I think you should leave," the man said, soft-spoken, authoritative.

Lilly's head spun with this weird development. The board boy let go of her arms. She backed up a few steps, but she didn't run.

"I'm sorry," the kid said, turning fully to deal with the man. "Are you addressing me?"

"I am."

The kid planted himself. He racked his shoulders. "What did you say? I mean, you know, exactly."

"Exactly?" the man asked. "Would you like that verbatim? Or would you like me to distill the essence?"

The kid smirked, but there didn't seem to be a lot of confidence behind it.

"What the *fuck* are you talking about?"

"I believe the young lady would like you to leave."

The kid laughed. Psycho shrill. "And who are you, her *father*?"

The man smiled. Lilly felt a little charge run through her. It wasn't that the guy was so good-looking or anything, but there was something about that smile that said she had nothing to worry about.

"Just a friend."

"Well, I'm gonna fuck you up, friend-o. I'm gonna fuck you up big time. This is *my* corner."

The man made a move, a quick shift of his right hand, almost too fast to see. To Lilly it was a like a bird had flown between them, flapped its wings, then flown away. Time stood still for a few seconds. Then, in the next instant, Lilly felt a rush of warm air.

She glanced first at the man. He was still standing there, hands at his sides, his blue eyes sparkling in the afternoon sun, his expression unreadable. She then looked at the kid, and saw something she never expected to see, something horrifying.

The kid's face was on fire. But just for a second. Lilly instantly smelled singed flesh and burnt hair.

"What . . . what the *fuck*, man!" The kid recoiled, his hands to his face. He took five or six steps backward, out into the street. A car almost hit him. When he pulled his hands away Lilly could see that his face was bright pink.

"What the fuck did you do to me?" the kid yelled. "What did you *do*?"

"I asked you to leave," the man said.

The kid pulled a bandanna from his back pocket, began to blot his face. His nose was runny, his eyes were tearing up. Lilly noticed that his eyelashes were gone.

"You are a dead man," the kid yelled. "You are . . . you are *so* fucking dead."

Lilly watched in stunned silence as the kid backed up, turned, ran the length of the block, then disappeared around the corner. She discovered that she hadn't taken a breath in maybe a minute or so.

What the hell had just happened?

She knew the basics. She had been hanging on the corner. A board rat had approached her, threatened her, *grabbed* her. A man appeared out of nowhere and set the kid's face on fire.

Somehow. Like magic.

She looked up Filbert Street, saw a police car trolling. It looked like they hadn't seen what happened. She turned to ask the man his version of the events, to say thank you, but he had vanished.

FORTY-TWO

Jessica got on the computer. For the past two days she'd been trying to block out an hour or so to run some things. If their killer was playing a sick game with the department, the city, then there was a chance that there were things they were not seeing, pieces of the puzzle that did not quite fit. Yet.

She made a list of names, references, places, possibilities, and impossibilities.

She knew that sometimes a search engine could make a connection you might never think of. Sometimes the result of a search was so far off it got you thinking in a new direction.

Forty minutes later she had answers. She knew Byrne was down in the cafeteria. Unable to wait for the elevator, she ran down the stairs.

Byrne was nursing a cold coffee, a wooden Danish, skimming the *Daily News*.

"You're not going to believe this," Jessica said.

"Man, do I love it when conversations begin this way."

Jessica pulled out a chair, sat down. "I ran everything I could think of through a few search engines, along with a couple of things I never thought would click."

Byrne folded the paper. "Okay. What do we have?"

"Well, I think we know what game he was playing with the name Jeremiah Crosley. Nonetheless, I ran a search regarding the Book of

Jeremiah. Interesting guy, but not one of the biggies. Josh was right. Jeremiah was no ray of sunshine. Nothing jumped.

"Next, our guy said he lived at 2917 Dodgson Street. As we know, there is no Dodgson Street in Philly, right?"

"Can't argue with the folks at MapQuest."

"I have issues with MapQuest. They always seem to lead me right into construction. But that's for later. Anyway, I found a Dodgson Street in Lancashire, England, but I figured that would be one hell of a commute, even for a psycho. There are, however, a number of other references. The one that stuck out was a person's name. Charles Lutwidge Dodgson. Ever heard of him?"

Byrne shook his head.

"That's because he was much better known by another name: Lewis Carroll, author of *Alice's Adventures in Wonderland.* Turns out he was also a fanatical game and puzzle enthusiast. Plus, I discovered there's something called the Alice in Wonderland syndrome, also known as micropsia, which causes a person to perceive large objects as being much smaller."

"The big red, yellow, and blue boxes in that crawlspace, and the small colored squares in the Bible," Byrne said.

"It might be a stretch, but yeah, it crossed my mind." Jessica pulled up another chair, put her feet up on it. "Next I ran *ludo.* Guess what it means?"

"You're going to make me guess everything, aren't you?"

"Yes."

"I have no idea what it means."

Jessica held up a color printout. It was a graphic of a game board: a large square marked with a cross. Each arm of the cross was divided into three columns; each column was divided into six smaller squares. The large squares were brightly colored. "Ludo."

"It's colored squares," Byrne said. "Again."

"Yeah, but there are four of them, not three."

"Is it possible we missed something down there?"

"In that crawlspace? Not a thing," Jessica said. "I also looked up the origin of *ludo,* as in, the origin of the word. Guess where it comes from?"

"Greek."

"Latin," Jessica said. "It gets its name from the word *ludus.*"

"Which means?"

Jessica put both hands out, palms up, in her best ta-da fashion. "It means *game*."

Byrne turned to the window. He tapped his coffee stirrer on the rim of his cup. Jessica let him absorb the details.

"I think we can safely assume that the old woman was completely certifiable, yes?" he finally said.

"Yes."

"And deeply involved in this somehow."

"Up to her broken neck."

Byrne turned back to the table. "Remember that puzzle I did? The one with the geometric shapes?"

"Tangram."

"Right. She had that book about tangram and other games. The one with all the diagrams in it."

"What about it?"

"I think we should find a copy of that book."

"She said the author lived in Chester County."

"Even better."

BYRNE CALLED Chester County Books & Music. He got the store manager on the line, identified himself.

"What can I do for you?" the man asked.

"We're trying to locate a local author."

"Sure. What's the name?"

"That I don't know, but I believe he lives in Chester County. He wrote a book about games and puzzles, and in it were a lot of—"

"David Sinclair," the man said, interrupting him. "He's written a few books on the subject. He's done some signings here."

"Do you know how to get hold of him?"

"I'm sure I have his number somewhere."

"Could you ask him to give us a call? As soon as possible if you can. It's very important."

"Sure. No problem."

Byrne gave the man his cell phone number, thanked him, hung up. Since the story broke on the murder and mutilation of Monica

Renzi, the PPD's press office had held a news conference. The official word was that it was still not known if the murder of Monica Renzi was connected to the murder of Caitlin O'Riordan, but that did not stop the mainstream press from speculation, or the alternative press from simply saying so.

In typical journalistic fashion, they had to pin a name on this case. A "unnamed source" within the police department told a reporter that there was a man who was taking girls off the street, keeping them in custody for a while before killing them. The newspaper referred to the killer as "The Collector."

Byrne figured no one at the paper, a birdcage liner called *The Report*, had ever read *The Collector* by John Fowles—a novel about a young man, a butterfly collector, who kidnaps a woman and keeps her in his basement—but that didn't matter. It would only be a matter of time before the mainstream press picked up on it, then the public, and eventually it would find its way into police department memos.

The four detectives met in the lobby of the Roundhouse. They were all dressed in casual clothes. The strategy being, if they were going to talk to runaways and homeless kids, they wanted to look like anything but authority figures. Byrne and Andre Curtis were pretty much hopeless in this area. They both looked like cops. Jessica and Josh Bontrager were a little more likely to gain their confidence.

Jessica wore jeans and a white T-shirt and running shoes. She could almost pass for a college student, Byrne thought. Byrne wore a black polo shirt and chinos. He looked like an off duty cop trying to blend in. But he was surprised to see that this shirt fit. It had been getting a little tight. Maybe he was getting in shape after all.

Jessica briefed Josh Bontrager and Dre Curtis on what she had found online. They made their notes and headed out.

A few minutes later Jessica and Byrne walked out of the Roundhouse. The air was a blast furnace. Still no rain.

"Ready to revisit your misspent youth?" Byrne asked as they slipped into the Taurus.

"What are you talking about?" Jessica said. "I'm still misspending it."

WHILE JOSH BONTRAGER and Dre Curtis went to Penn Treaty Park, Jessica and Byrne started on South Street. They parked on Columbus Boulevard and took the South Street pedestrian bridge over I-95.

South Street was part of the Queen Village neighborhood, one of the oldest sections of Philadelphia. Its business district ran from Front Street to around Ninth Street.

On the way to South Philly they had decided that it would be best for Jessica to ask the questions. Byrne would shadow her from the other side of the street.

They began at Front Street, in front of Downey's, and slowly worked their way west. This section of South was crammed with pubs, restaurants, clubs, bookstores, record stores, piercing and tattoo parlors, pizza shops, and even one large condom specialty store. It was a magnet for young people of all styles—Goth, punk, hip-hop, skateboarders, collegiates, Jersey Boys—as well as a thriving tourist trade. There wasn't too much you couldn't find on this street; legal, otherwise, and every stop in between. To a lot of people, South was the beating heart of Philly.

Between Second and Third, Jessica talked to a group of teenagers; three boys and two girls. Byrne always marveled at how good she was at things like this. They had to identify themselves as police officers of course, and the few kids Byrne tried to approach on his own just took off once Byrne produced his ID. Not so for Jessica. People opened up to her.

All of the kids said they were either from Philly, or in town visiting relatives. Nobody was ever a runaway.

At the corner of Fourth and South, Jessica talked to a young girl. The girl, about fifteen, had her blond hair in pigtails, and wore a tie-dyed tank top and denim skirt. She had a half dozen piercings in her nose, lips, and ears. Byrne was out of earshot, but he saw that when Jessica showed the girl a photograph, the girl studied it, then nodded. A minute later Jessica handed the girl a card, moved on.

It turned out to be a dead end. The girl said she had heard of a girl named Starlight, but had never met her, and had no idea where she might be.

By the time they got to Tenth Street, where the shopping and hangout spots dropped off, they had talked to fifty or sixty teenagers, about two dozen shop owners. No one remembered seeing either Caitlin O'Riordan or Monica Renzi. No one knew anything about anything.

Jessica and Byrne grabbed lunch at Jim's Steaks, and headed to the train station.

FORTY-THREE

LILLY SAT ON THE GROUND NEAR THE FRANKLIN INSTITUTE, HER BACK against the low stone wall. She was still high, crashing fast, and still a little freaked out about the incident on the corner. Had the kid's face really been on fire?

Regardless, all of that was rearview mirror. She was broke, she had nowhere to stay, and everybody she met was worse off than her.

But she would not give up. She had made a promise, and that was something she rarely did. It *would* be honored.

Before she could formulate a new plan, she looked up to see a man coming toward her. He walked all the way across the street, motoring fast, his eyes on her the whole time. She looked away a few times, but every time she glanced back he was staring at her. And getting closer.

He was dressed in a white shirt and black pants. He was blond, had pretty cool hair, light blue eyes, a nice face. He stopped right in front of her, smiled. He was kind of cute, actually.

But he was still a stranger.

"Hi," he said.

Lilly didn't answer. The guy didn't leave. Instead, he waited a few seconds, then reached into his back pocket.

Now what? Lilly thought. Jehovah's Witness? Human resource director for a strip club?

"My name is Josh Bontrager," he said. "I'm with the Philadelphia Police department."

He showed her a gold badge and ID card, but Lilly didn't really see it. She felt the blood rushing in her ears, felt her heart start beating like a racehorse. This was it, she thought. This was how it was going to end. She had come to Philadelphia with a purpose, and now she was going to jail. All she could see was that sick twist, Mr. Mushroom Teeth, laying in that alley, drooling on the pavement.

"What's your name?" he asked.

His voice brought her spiraling back to reality. She looked around, a little surprised to see all the people. She had forgotten where she was for a moment.

"Lilly."

Her voice sounded small, even from the inside. She sounded like a wounded mouse.

"I'm sorry?"

"Lilly."

"Ah, okay. Nice to meet you, Lilly. Great day, huh?"

Lilly just stared at the ground.

"Right. Well. I'd like to talk to you for a few seconds, if that's okay."

She looked up. He didn't look mad, or threatening or anything. Actually, he looked a little bit like a farm boy at a school dance. "What about?" she asked.

He put his badge back into his pocket, held up an envelope. "I won't take up too much of your time. I promise."

He got on the ground next to her, sat down, back against the wall. He put his feet out in front of him, crossed his legs. If he was going to arrest her, put her in handcuffs and haul her away, this was a pretty friggin' weird way of going about it. They never played it this way on *Law & Order.* Not even on *COPS.*

"Now, first off, I'm not going to ask you anything about your life, okay? I'm not going to ask you where you're from, why you're here, or what you're doing. I'm not even going to ask you your last name. Deal?"

For some reason, this made Lilly even more nervous. But getting up and running didn't really seem like an option. This guy looked to be in pretty good shape. He'd catch her for sure. Whatever this was about, she would have to play along.

"I guess."

"Good. I just want you to know that you're not in any trouble, and you're not going to get *into* any trouble for anything you tell me."

He opened the envelope, took out a pair of pictures.

"I just want to ask you if you recognize a couple of people. If you could do that, it would really help me out."

He was lying to her. She *knew* it. All that business about not getting into trouble was bullshit. He was going to show her a picture of Mr. Mushroom Teeth, and a picture of that skateboard asshole by the bus station. She was going to get arrested for kneeing some pervert in the balls and burning that kid's face, too. And she didn't even do that one. *Double* assault and battery. She was going away for life.

When he flipped over the first picture, Lilly felt a cool breeze blowing across her heart. It wasn't Mr. Mushroom Teeth in all his creepy glory after all. It was a picture of a girl. Kind of heavyset, but she had on a pair of great hoop earrings and a killer necklace.

"Do you recognize this girl?" he asked. "Her name is Monica."

Lilly took the picture from him, looked closely. The girl in the photograph looked like a girl she had gone to school with, Trish Carbone, but Trish had smaller eyes. Snake eyes. She didn't like Trish Carbone. "No," she said. "I don't recognize her. Sorry."

"No sweat." He put the picture back into the envelope, flipped over the other picture. This one was of a blond girl. She was really pretty. Like *model* pretty.

"What about her?" he asked. "Have you ever seen her before?"

Lilly scanned the photo. She didn't know too many girls this pretty. Sure, there were girls at her school who looked good—rich girls from Rivercrest and Pine Hollow—but they were all haters. Mean Girls, Inc. This girl looked like someone she could hang out with. "No. Sorry again."

"That's okay. You tried, and I appreciate it."

He slipped the second picture into the envelope, closed the clasp.

"Just one more thing, and I'll leave you to this beautiful day," he said. "I want to give you a few names, see if they sound familiar."

"Okay."

"Daria."

Lilly shook her head.

"Starlight."

"No," she said, absolutely positive her face would give her away. It didn't.

"Govinda."

"Is that a girl?"

"I think so."

Lilly shrugged. "Don't know her either."

"Okay."

He gathered his things together, preparing to leave.

"I wasn't much help, was I?"

"Don't worry about it. You did great," he said. "Some people won't even talk to me."

"Well that's just plain rude."

He laughed. He had dimples. "It surely is. Back in Berks County, where I'm from? People are more than happy to conversate. Well, maybe not in Reading so much, but in Bechtelsville you can't shut them up."

This guy is from Berks, Lilly thought. She knew there was something farm boy about him. She'd always been a sucker for farm boys. For a second she wanted him to stay and talk to her, but she knew that wasn't going to happen.

He stood up, brushed off his pants. "Well, thanks again. It is most appreciated." He reached into his pocket and took out a little black wallet. He pulled out a card, handed it to her. "If you remember anything, or run into anyone who might have known these girls, please give me a call."

"I will."

He smiled, turned, and walked across the sidewalk. He waited for the light.

"What was her name?" Lilly asked.

Detective Joshua Bontrager spun around. "I'm sorry?"

"The girl in the picture. The blond girl. You never told me her name."

"Oh," he said. "Sorry. Great cop I am. It was Caitlin. Her name was Caitlin O'Riordan."

Lilly felt dizzy. It felt as if the earth was falling away beneath her, as if she had just chugged a fifth of bad whiskey and gotten on a Til

Whirl. And he was going to notice. He was going to notice something was wrong and ask her if she was okay and she was going to blurt everything out. Then she was going to jail for sure.

But that's not what happened. Although it felt as if her ears were jammed with wet cotton, it sounded like he said, "Have a great day."

She watched him walk away. There were a pair of teenage boys in the small park across North Twentieth Street. He was going to start all over with them.

Lilly took a pair of deep, slow breaths. She felt like she was at the top of the first hill on a roller coaster, about to plunge toward the earth.

Caitlin O'Riordan.

They knew. And they would be watching her. She would have to act fast.

She would have to trust somebody.

FORTY-FOUR

THEY'D STRUCK OUT. BETWEEN SOUTH STREET AND THE BUS STATION they had talked to more than a hundred teenagers, passed out over a hundred cards. On their way out of the station Byrne saw four cards in the trash. He saw three more on the sidewalk.

Street work paid off more than it didn't, but it was exhausting. And sometimes, on days like this, fruitless. Byrne hadn't expected much, and that's what they got.

ON THE WAY BACK to the Roundhouse, Byrne's cell phone rang.

"Byrne."

"Detective Byrne, my name is David Sinclair."

Byrne rummaged his memory. Then it clicked. "The author."

"Yes sir."

"I appreciate you getting back to us."

"Well, it's not every day I'm asked to call the police. How can I help you?"

"We'd like to meet with you if we could. We have a few questions about your books that we think may impact on a case we're working on."

Silence. "My books?"

"I'll explain more when we meet."

"Okay. Sure. When would you like to get together?"

"Today, if possible."

"Wow. Okay, I can meet you at Chester County Books if you like. Do you know it?"

"We'll find it."

"I can be there in an hour," Sinclair said.

"That will be fine." Byrne glanced at his watch. "Before I let you go, can I ask if you know a woman named Laura Somerville?"

"Somerville?"

"That's right."

A few silent seconds. "No, I'm afraid it doesn't ring a bell."

"Okay. We'll see you in an hour."

Byrne called the boss, got the go-ahead. He and Jessica decided to split up for the afternoon. Jessica was going to continue her canvass on a few of the college campuses. They decided to meet in Manayunk in a few hours. Byrne dropped Jessica off at the Roundhouse, then headed toward Chester County.

CHESTER COUNTY, along with Philadelphia and Bucks, was one of the three original counties created by William Penn in 1682. Although originally named for Cheshire, England, it had long been known around these parts as Chesco.

The bookstore, on Paoli Pike, was one of the largest independent bookstores in the country, covering more than 38,000 square feet and stocking over a quarter million titles. It also featured the Magnolia Grill, a New Orleans fare restaurant.

SINCLAIR WAS WAITING at one of the tables in the Magnolia Grill when Byrne arrived. When he saw Byrne enter, he stood up, waved him over. Byrne guessed he really did look like a cop, even in his trust-us-we're-the-good-guys attire.

Byrne didn't know what to expect, physically, of David Sinclair. He hadn't met too many authors. Perhaps he expected someone about sixty or so, someone who looked like Albert Finney or Michael Caine, somebody in corduroy or tweed, a man who wore vest sweaters and Oxford button-down shirts and horizontally striped knit ties. Someone who smoked a meerschaum.

Instead, Sinclair was about thirty-five, and wore Levi's, a leather blazer, and a Ramones *Gabba Gabba Hey* T-shirt. Along with a New York Yankees cap.

"David Sinclair," the man said, extending a hand.

"Kevin Byrne." They shook hands. "I appreciate you coming."

Sinclair smiled. "Well, I have to admit, I'm intrigued."

They sat down. Byrne glanced at the menu. He resisted, even though the aromas coming from the kitchen were maddeningly enticing—crawfish étouffée, shrimp Creole, jambalaya. He ordered coffee.

"I'm afraid I can't tell you too much at this time," Byrne said.

"I understand."

"What I'd like to do is get an overview of what you do, and who your readers are."

Sinclair looked at Byrne, his eyes firing up. Here was a police officer asking an author to talk about his books. His face all but inquired: How much time do you have?

"Wow. Okay," Sinclair said. "I'm not sure where to start. What I mean is, the world of games and puzzles is huge. Not to mention ancient. Where would you like me to begin?"

"Why do people pick certain games and not others?"

"That's hard to say. I believe people like to be good at what they do, especially in the pursuit of leisure. I think we're drawn to the challenges we have at least a chance of winning. For example, I've been playing golf my whole life and, quite honestly, I've never gotten any better at it. But each time out I hit one or two great shots, and it keeps me coming back. I think we all enjoy a contest that grows and evolves, something that is not fully understood too easily."

"Why do people play games to begin with?"

"People have a gaming instinct, I believe. Even if you rule out professional sports, and I often do—there is a fine line between what is a sporting contest and what is a game—there are thousands upon thousands of ways to challenge a person's mind and hands. Crosswords, Rubik's cubes, video games, backgammon, poker, jigsaw puzzles, chess, darts, cribbage, croquet, billiards. It's virtually endless. Look at the Su-doku madness. Look at *Vegas*. I read recently that Hollywood is making feature-length films based on Monopoly, Candy Land, and Battleship. We are a game-obsessed culture."

"How far back do organized games go?"

"As far back as language itself. Maybe farther. The best-selling book of the entire medieval period was the *Book of Games*, commis-sioned by King Alfonso X. In fact, the first IQ test was a puzzle. The Riddle of the Sphinx. If you wanted to enter Thebes, you had to answer the riddle correctly. If not, the Sphinx killed you on the spot."

"What was the riddle?"

"You want to play?"

"Sure."

"The Riddle of the Sphinx: What is it that has four feet in the morning, two at noon, and three at night?"

Sinclair looked at Byrne, his eyes sparkling with the game.

"Is there a time limit?" Byrne asked.

Sinclair smiled. "The riddle is probably five thousand years old. I can give you a few minutes."

Byrne took thirty seconds. "The answer is 'man.' He crawls on all fours as a baby, walks on two legs as an adult and—"

"Walks with the aid of a cane in old age. *Very* good."

Byrne shrugged. "I had a foot patrol in Thebes back in the day."

Sinclair laughed. Byrne sipped his coffee. It had gotten cold.

"Who designs games and puzzles?" Byrne asked. "I mean, who makes these things up?"

"They come from all walks, really. Some games are based on de-sign, some on logic, some on bringing order out of chaos. Most can be boiled down to the language arts or math sciences. Look at billiards. Pure geometry. There is a game called *Wei Qi*, or Go as its known here, and it is the most mathematically elegant game ever invented. Far more complex than chess. Millions of people play it every day."

"What about tangram?"

"Once again, pure geometry." Sinclair smiled. "Are you a fan?"

"I've really just done one puzzle," Byrne said.

"Do you remember the problem?"

"The problem?

"In tangram, the diagram is called the problem."

"Ah, okay. I believe it was something called a wedding drinking cup."

Sinclair nodded enthusiastically. "I know it well. Fairly complex. Did you solve it?"

"Yes."

"Most impressive," Sinclair said. "Oddly enough, Philadelphia has a role in the history of tangram."

"How so?"

"The tangram puzzle first came to the US in 1816, courtesy of Captain Edward Donnaldson and his ship *Trader.* The first American tangram book was published here the next year."

"How many people are into it?"

"Oh, gosh. It's known all over the world. It was a craze for a while. Kind of like Trivial Pursuit was. Tangram enthusiasts included Edgar Allan Poe, Napoleon, John Quincy Adams, Lewis Carroll—"

"Lewis Carroll?" Byrne asked. "The author?"

"Oh, yeah. Carroll was a big fan."

Byrne thought, *2917 Dodgson Street.* He made a few notes.

For the next half hour, David Sinclair gave Byrne an overview of the history of tangram, from the earliest incarnations to the modern, computerized versions. Not for the first time, Byrne was astounded that there were so many areas of life, so many subcultures about which he was not, and never would be, knowledgeable.

Byrne closed his notebook, glanced at his watch. "I have one more question, if that's okay."

"Sure."

"Is there a dark side to all this?"

"A dark side?"

"What I mean is, is there a history of people who have taken games or puzzles and twisted their meanings? Their purpose?"

Sinclair thought about this for a few moments. "I imagine so. People will twist anything, won't they? Of course, board games like Risk and Stratego are *based* on warfare strategies. And God knows how many video games are predicated on violence."

Byrne grabbed the check, stood. "Once again, I really your time."

"It was my pleasure. I could talk about this stuff all day. I have, in fact."

"I might have a few more questions," Byrne said. "Would it be all right if I called you?"

"Absolutely," Sinclair said. Byrne handed him his notebook, his pen. David Sinclair wrote his number. "This is my cell phone. You can always reach me on it."

"Thanks." Byrne put his notebook away. "By the way, are your books available here?"

Sinclair smiled. "They are."

Ten minutes later, as Byrne stood at the register, buying three of David Sinclair's books, he glanced back at the table. Sinclair was working on the *New York Times* crossword puzzle. He didn't look up.

JESSICA WAITED for Byrne at a Manayunk pub called Kildare's. The place was lively, a little too loud for them to have a discussion about the day's findings. They decided to have one beer and move on.

Byrne slipped onto a stool. He briefly told Jessica what he had learned from David Sinclair.

"I cruised a couple of the college campuses," Jessica said. "Man, did I feel old."

"Any hits?"

"Not a one."

They both watched the baseball game on the flat-screen TV, neither really seeing it. Phillies up on the Dodgers, six to one.

"All these gaming and puzzle references can't be coincidence," Byrne said.

"You think our guy has a fetish?" Jessica asked. "You think that's what this is all about?"

"I don't know. I mean, if he drowned Caitlin O'Riordan and dismembered Monica Renzi as part of a plan, I'm not seeing the connection. The profile on these guys says their MO is always similar. Until we know either where he's meeting these girls, or what twisted plan he's basing this on, I don't think we have a chance at predicting what's next."

Jessica made a finger gun, fired it. "Until he fucks up."

"Until he fucks up." Byrne unknotted his tie, pulled it off, unbuttoned his collar. "Order me a Guinness. I'll be right back."

"You got it."

Jessica flagged a waitress, ordered, spun her napkin around. She folded it in half, making a rectangle, unfolded it, refolded it. She pressed it into the damp bar surface, making a rectangular shape in the condensation. She then turned the napkin ninety degrees. It reminded her of the cross shape in the game Ludo, which reminded her of the old game Parcheesi.

Jessica looked at the flat-screen TV against the far wall. It was a news break-in, a helicopter shot over the city, cutting into the baseball game. The graphic at the bottom of the screen said "Ninth Street."

The shot showed a rooftop, a building in North Philly. Near the edge of the roof, just a few feet in, was a white plastic tent, the kind PPD used to shield a scene from the elements. Jessica saw the CSU windbreakers on the people milling around.

She turned. Byrne stood behind her, watching the screen, along with everyone else in the pub. She glanced back at the TV. There was now a legend at the bottom of the screen.

THE COLLECTOR COLLECTS AGAIN?

There was no doubt in Jessica's mind.

Within seconds, her phone rang.

FORTY-FIVE

AT SIX THIRTY LILLY WALKED INTO THE THIRTIETH STREET TRAIN STA-tion. She wandered over to the food court, scanned the area for Mr. Mushroom Teeth, thinking he might have come back looking for her. Not seeing him, she walked around the station, went into Faber Books, read a few magazines off the rack until the guy at the register gave her the eye. He'd probably seen his share of runaways.

She hit the ladies' room, freshened up, or as much as possible with paper towels and liquid soap in a cramped toilet stall. She hoped she didn't smell.

When she returned to the food court there was a man sitting at one of the tables. She had to look twice to make sure she wasn't hallucinat-ing. She wasn't.

It was the man from outside the BigK.

Her savior.

"Oh my God! It's you!"

The man looked up from the paper. At first he didn't seem to rec-ognize her, then recollection dawned.

"Hello again," the man said.

"Hi," Lilly replied. "I can't . . . I can't believe, well, *hello*." She turned in place. Twice. She felt like a schnauzer. She felt like an *idiot*. "Right, okay. I just want to say thanks. You know. For helping me with that guy."

"That is quite all right," he said. "I've never been able to counte-nance bullies."

"Small world, huh?"

"Indeed." The man gestured to the second half of the cheesesteak in front of him. "Look, I'm never going to finish this," he said. "And you strike me as being a hungry and weary traveler. Are you?"

Against her better judgment—her stomach ruling her mind for the moment, as it just might do for some time to come—Lilly said, "Kinda."

The man's eyes shone, as if he understood. Maybe he did. Despite his expensive-looking suit and gold watch, maybe he had once been in her shoes. Maybe he had once been a "hungry and weary traveler" himself.

"Would you like the other half of this sandwich?" he asked.

"No thank you," Lilly said. "That's okay."

"I understand," he said. He went back to his paper. Then, a few moments later, as a coda: "But it's terribly good. Unfortunately, at my age, one's eyes are bigger than one's stomach."

Lilly looked a little more closely at the man. He wasn't so old. "You're sure you're not going to eat it?"

The man gently patted his stomach. "Positive." He glanced at his watch. It looked old and expensive. It might have been real gold. He wore cuff links, too. Lilly had never met anyone who actually wore cuff links. Hell, back home you were lucky if they wore shirts at all.

"Plus I'm meeting my wife for an early dinner," he added. "She'll absolutely *flay* me if I'm not hungry as a wolf. Or at least give the appearance."

Lilly looked around the immediate area. Even though they were in a public place, and no one was paying attention, she still felt as if people might be watching her, as if she were some sort of charity case, as if she were the only one in the city who was hungry or needed shelter. Like a homeless person. Which she was most certainly *not*.

"This is great," she said, grabbing the sandwich. "Thanks."

The man didn't respond. He just winked. *Help yourself,* his eyes said.

For an older guy, he was kind of cool.

THE SANDWICH WAS DELICIOUS. She wanted another one, or fries, or something, but she would never ask. Asking meant invitation. She'd been *there*.

A few minutes later the man folded the paper, glanced at his watch, glanced at her. "At the risk of being terribly forward, may I ask your name?" he asked.

Lilly wiped her lips with a paper napkin, swallowed the last bite of the sandwich. She sat a little straighter in her chair. She had always done this when she was getting ready to lie. "It's Lilly," she said, a little surprised at how easily it rolled off her tongue now, as if she'd been saying it for years.

The man looked surprised and delighted. "I have a *daughter* named Lilly," he said. "She's only three months old." He reached into his suit coat, pulled out a beautiful wallet. He opened it, took out a photograph. "This is she."

The picture was of the most adorable, apple-cheeked, blue-eyed baby she'd ever seen. "Oh my God! What a beautiful little girl."

"Thank you. I would like to say she takes after her father, but I know this would be self-flattery." He put the photograph away, looked at his watch. "Well, I'm afraid I must be off." He stood, took his brief-case off the chair next to him. "Thank you *so* much for the chat. It was very nice to meet you."

"You too."

"And beware scary boys on street corners."

"I will."

With that the man gave her a slight bow, turned, and walked toward the Thirtieth Street entrance. In a moment, he was gone.

Lilly knew what she was going to do. Somehow, she wasn't afraid.

He was a *father*.

She got up from the table and ran across the station. She found him on the corner.

She told him everything.

FORTY-SIX

THE WHITE TENT SAT NEAR THE EDGE OF THE ROOF, SHIELDING THE MUR-
der victim from the sun, and the prying eyes of the media hovering
overhead like red-tail hawks. There were no fewer than thirty people on
the roof: detectives, supervisors, crime-scene technicians, investigators
from the medical examiner's office. Photographs were taken, measure-
ments recorded, surfaces dusted.

When Jessica and Byrne arrived, the other personnel deferred to
them. This could only mean one thing. The homicide that had occurred here was clearly connected to their investigations.

When Jessica opened the flap on the plastic tent, she knew it to be
true. She felt the gorge rise in her throat. In front of her was a girl, no
more than seventeen, with long dark hair, deep hazel eyes. She wore a
thin black sweater and blue jeans, a pair of sandals on her small feet.
None of this made her much different from any of the other young
murder victims Jessica had seen in her career. What set this girl apart,
what tied her irrevocably to the case she and her partner were working
on, was the manner in which she was killed.

Protruding from the girl's chest and abdomen were seven steel
swords.

JESSICA STARED at the girl's pallid face. It was clear that in life she had
been exotically pretty, but here, on a blistering rooftop in North
Philadelphia, drained of all her blood, she looked almost mummified.

The good news, for the investigators, was that according to the ME's office this victim had been dead little more than twenty-four hours. It was the closest they had come to the Collector. This was no cold case. This time they could amass evidence unadulterated by time. The very scent and presence of the murderer lingered.

Jessica snapped on a pair of gloves, stepped closer to the body. She gently examined the girl's hands. Her nails had recently been manicured and painted. The color was a deep red. Jessica looked at her own nails through the latex, and wondered if she and the victim had been sitting in a manicurist's chair at the same time.

Even though she was seated, Jessica determined that the girl was about five-three, less than a hundred pounds. She sniffed the girl's hair. It smelled of mint. It had been recently shampooed.

Nicci Malone stepped onto the roof, saw Jessica.

"We've got an ID," Nicci said.

She handed Jessica an FBI printout. The girl's name was Katja Dovic. She was seventeen. She had last been seen at her house in New Canaan, Connecticut, on June twenty-sixth.

Dr. Tom Weyrich approached.

"I take it this is not the primary scene," Jessica said.

Weyrich shook his head. "No. Wherever she was killed she bled out, and was cleaned up. The hearts stops, that's it. The dead don't bleed." He paused for a moment. Jessica knew him to be a man not given to hyperbole or arch comment. "And, as bad as that is, it gets worse." He pointed to one of the slices in the girl's sweater. "It looks like she was run through with these swords at the primary scene, they were removed, and reinserted here. This guy re-created the murder on this rooftop."

Jessica tried to wrap her mind around the image of someone stabbing this girl with seven swords, removing them, transporting the body, and doing it all over again.

While Nicci went off to advise the other investigators on the ID, Byrne sidled silently next to Jessica. They stood this way while the mechanics of a murder investigation swirled around them.

"Why is he doing this, Kevin?"

"There's a reason," Byrne said. "There's a pattern. It looks random, but it isn't. We'll find it, and we'll fucking put him down."

"Now there's three girls. Three methods. Three different dump sites."

"All in the Badlands, though. All runaways."

Jessica shook her head. "How do we warn these kids when they don't want to be found?"

There was no answer.

FORTY-SEVEN

LILLY HAD STARTED TALKING AND SHE JUST COULDN'T SEEM TO STOP herself. When she stopped, she felt five pounds lighter. She also felt like crying. She probably did. She couldn't remember. It was kind of a fog.

Lilly had expected one of two reactions from the man. She expected him either to turn on his heels and walk away from her, or call the police.

He did neither. Instead, he was silent for a few moments.

He said he would help her, but only if this was something she really wanted to do. He told her to sleep on it, but only for one night. He said the best decisions in life are made after waiting twenty-four hours, never longer. He then gave her one hundred dollars and his phone number. She promised to call him one way or another. She never broke a promise.

She went back to the hostel. It was as good a place as any.

Despite the early hour, despite the insanity of her day, for the first time in as long as she could remember, she put her head down on a pillow and fell fast asleep.

FORTY-EIGHT

Jessica stood outside Eve Galvez's apartment. It was a small suite on the third floor of a nondescript, blocky brick building on Bustleton Avenue.

She stepped inside, and almost turned the lights on. But then she thought that doing so might be disrespectful. The last time Eve left these rooms she had every intention of returning.

Jessica danced the beam of the flashlight around the space. There was a card table in the dining area, one folding chair, a loveseat in the living room, a pair of end tables. There were no prints or framed posters on the wall, no houseplants, no area rugs. Black fingerprint powder claimed every surface.

She stepped into the bedroom. There was a double bed on a frame, no footboard or headboard. There was a dresser, but no mirror. Jimmy Valentine was right. Eve was a Spartan. The nightstand next to the bed held a cheap lamp and what looked like a photo cube. Jessica glanced in the closet: a pair of dresses, a pair of skirts. Black and navy blue. A pair of white blouses. They'd all been taken off the hangers, searched, and carelessly replaced. Jessica reached inside, smoothed the clothing, more out of habit than anything else.

The entire apartment was tidy, almost sterile. It seemed that Eve Galvez didn't so much live here as stay here.

Jessica crossed the bedroom, picked up the photo cube. There were pictures on all six sides. One photo showed a picture of Eve at five or so, standing next to her brother on a beach. There was another that had to be Eve's mother. They had the same eyes, the same cheekbones. One looked like Eve in, perhaps, eleventh grade. She was heavier in this snapshot than the others. Jessica turned it over, looked again at all sides. There were no photographs of Eve's father.

Out of habit, or training, or just nosiness that had at least something to do with her becoming a police officer to begin with, Jessica shook the cube. Something inside rattled. She shook it again. The rattle was louder. There *was* something inside.

It took a few moments, but she found the way to open it. Inside was a ball of tissue and a plastic object, perhaps two inches long by a half inch wide. Jessica put her flashlight beam on it.

It was a USB flash drive, the kind that plugs into a port on a computer. It was not labeled or marked in any way. Jessica saw the print powder on the cube, so she knew someone at CSU had touched this. She looked inside the cube again. The flash drive had been wrapped in the tissue. Jessica understood. Eve had hidden it in there and put in the tissue so it would not rattle. She had done this for the possibility of a moment just such as this.

Against her better judgment—in fact, against all the judgment she had—she slipped the flash drive into her pocket, and clicked off her flashlight.

Five minutes later, leaving the apartment virtually the way she had found it, she headed home.

AN HOUR LATER Jessica sat in the bathtub.

It was Saturday. Vincent had two days off. He had taken Sophie to visit his parents. They would be back Sunday afternoon.

The house had been ghostly quiet, so she had taken her iPod into the tub. When she'd gotten home she'd plugged Eve's flash drive into her desktop computer, and found that there were a few dozen mp3s on it, mostly songs by artists of whom Jessica had never heard. She added some them to her iTunes library.

Her Glock sat on the edge of the sink, right next to the tumbler containing three inches of Wild Turkey.

Jessica turned the hot water on again. It was already almost scalding in the tub, but she couldn't seem to get it hot enough. She wanted the memory of Katja Dovic, and Monica Renzi, and Caitlin O'Riordan to wash off. She felt as if she would never be clean again.

EVE GALVEZ'S MUSIC was a mix of pop, salsa, *tejano*, *danzón*—a sort of old-time formal Cuban dance music—and something called *huayño*. Good stuff. New stuff. *Different* stuff. Jessica listened to a few songs by someone named Marisa Monte. She decided to add the rest of the songs to her iPod.

She got out of the tub, threw on her big fluffy robe and went into the small room off the kitchen they used as a computer room. And it was small. Room enough for a table, chair, and a G5 computer. She poured herself another inch, sat down, selected the flash drive. It was then that she noticed a folder she hadn't seen, a folder labeled *vademe-cum*. She double-clicked it.

A few moments later, the screen displayed more than two hundred files. These were not system files, nor were they music files. They were Eve Galvez's personal files. Jessica looked at the extensions. All of them were .jpg files. Graphics.

None of the files were named, just numbered, starting with one hundred.

Jessica clicked on the first file. She found that she was holding her breath as the hard drive turned, launching Preview, the default graphic display program she used on her computer. This was, after all, a picture of some kind, and she wasn't all that sure it was something she wanted to see. Or should see.

A moment later, when the graphic showed up the screen, it was probably the last thing Jessica expected. It was the scanned image of a piece of paper, a yellowed, three-holed piece of notebook paper with blue lines, something akin to a leaf from a child's school composition book. On it was a young woman's back-slanted, loopy handwriting.

Jessica scrolled to the top of the file. When she saw the handwritten date, her heart began to race.

SEPTEMBER 3, 1988.

It was Eve Galvez's diary.

FORTY-NINE

SEPTEMBER 3, 1988

I hide.

I hide because I know his anger. I hide because it took more than six months to heal the last time I saw this much rage in his eyes. The bones in my right arm, even now, tell me of a coming rainstorm. I hide because my mother cannot help me, not with her pills and her lovers; nor can my brother, my sweet brother who once stood up to him and paid so dearly. I hide because, not to hide, could very easily mean the end of me, the final punctuation of my short story.

I hear him in the foyer of the house, now, his huge boots on the quarry tile. He does not know about this secret place, this rabbit hole which has been my salvation so many times, this dusty sanctuary beneath the stairs. He does not know about this diary. If he ever found these words, I don't know what he would do.

The drink has taken over his mind, and made it a house of red mirrors where he cannot see me. He can only see himself, his own monstrous face in the glass, reflected a thousand times over like some uncontrollable army.

I hear him walking up the stairs, just above me, calling my name. It won't be long until he finds me. No secret can remain so forever.

I am afraid. I am afraid of Arturo Emmanuel Galvez. My father.

I may never make another entry in this journal.

And, dearest diary, if I do not, if I never speak to you again, I just wanted you to know why I do what I do.

I hide.

AUGUST 1, 1990

There is a place I go, a place that exists only behind my eyes. It all started when I was ten years old. A light in the heavens. More like a yellow moon, perhaps, a soft yellow moon in an aluminum sky. Heaven's porch light.

Soon the moon becomes a face. A devil's face.

JANUARY 22, 1992

I left yesterday. I hitchhiked along Frankford Avenue for awhile, caught a few good rides. One guy wanted to take me to Florida with him. If he hadn't looked like Freddy Krueger I might have considered it. Even still I considered it. Anything to get away from Dad.

I am sitting on the steps at the art museum. It is hard to believe that I have lived in Philadelphia most of my life, and I have never been here. It is another world.

Enrique will be in this place one day. He will paint pictures that will make the world laugh and think and cry. He will be famous.

JULY 23, 1995

I still hide. I hide from my life, my obligations. I watch from afar.

Those tiny fingers. Those dark eyes.

These are my days of grace.

MAY 3, 2006

Nobody who is truly happy is an alcoholic or a drug addict. These things are mutually exclusive. Drugs are what you do instead of loving someone.

JUNE 2, 2008

I walk the Badlands. The nights here are made of broken glass, broken people. I carry two firearms now—one is my service weapon, a Glock 17. Full mag, plus a round in the chamber. There is no safety. I carry it in a holster on my hip.

The other weapon is a .25-caliber Beretta. I have an ankle rig for it, but it fits nicely into the palm of my hand. I do not enter a convenience store without it palmed. I do not walk the streets without my finger on the trigger. When I drive, even through Center City, its weight is familiar on my right thigh. It is always within reach. It is part of me now.

I am drinking too much. I am not sleeping. The alarm sounds at six. A shot before I can face the shower, the coffee, the mirror. No breakfast. Remember breakfast? Bagels and juice with Jimmy Valentine? Remember laughter?

All I want is one good night's sleep. I would trade everything I have for one night's sleep. I would trade my life for the sanctity of slumber, the sanction of rest.

Graciella *mi amor*. I have nothing. Not anymore.

I walk the Badlands, searching, dying, asking.

I am asking to be found.

Find me.

FIFTY

T HE RAIN CAME AT MIDNIGHT. AT FIRST IT WAS AN UNREPENTANT
downpour, thick bulbs of water smashing against the pavement, the
buildings, the grateful city. In time, it relented. It was now a thin drizzle. The asphalt steamed. With the pitted road, the rusted and abandoned hulks of old vehicles, the flickering neon, it looked like an alien
landscape. Traffic was light on Kensington, the few cars taking advantage of the free car wash, the removal of the dust of a hot, dry August.
Five styles of rap pounded in the distance.

Jessica had read more than twenty of Eve Galvez's diary entries.
She discovered early on in her reading that the files were not in any
order. Eve as a child, Eve as an adult, Eve as a teenager. Jessica read
them in the order in which they were scanned. There were still at least
a hundred more.

Jessica's tears had come after reading just a few. She couldn't seem
to stop herself. Eve was abused. Her father was monstrous. Eve was a
runaway.

It was all a continuum of death—Monica Renzi, Caitlin O'Riordan,
Katja Dovic, Eve Galvez.

Jessica stood in a doorway, surveyed the area. It was one of the
worst parts of the city. Eve Galvez had walked these streets at night.
Had she paid the price for it?

Jessica put the earbuds in her ears. She looked at the backlighted
LCD screen, scrolled down, selected a song. The beat began to build.

She felt the comforting weight of the Tomcat 32 in her pancake holster. Eve Galvez had carried two weapons. It was probably not a bad idea.

Jessica pulled up the hood on her rain slicker. She looked left, right. She was alone. For the moment.

Sophie, my love. *Graciella, mi amor.*

The music matched her heartbeat. She stepped out onto the sidewalk, and began to run.

Into the Badlands.

FIFTY-ONE

THE TENTH FLOOR OF THE DENISON SMELLED LIKE WET SMOKE, WET lumber, wet dog. Byrne was six bourbons into his plot, and should be home. He should be *sleeping*.

But here he was. At Laura Somerville's apartment. The walls in the hallway were still warm. The wallpaper was peeled and cracked, some of it charred.

He pulled out his knife, slit the seal on the door, picked the lock, and entered the apartment.

The odor of burned upholstery and paper was overwhelming. Byrne put his tie over his mouth and nose. He had an old friend, Bobby Dotrice, who had retired from the PFD fifteen years earlier, and Byrne would swear under oath that man still smelled like smoke. Bobby had all new clothes, a new car, a new wife, even a new house. It never left you.

Byrne wondered if he smelled like the dead.

Even though the tenants of the building had been reassured there was no structural damage, Byrne stepped lightly through the space, his Maglite bouncing on overturned tables, chairs, bookcases. He wondered what had done more damage, the fire or the fire brigade.

He stood before the partially opened bedroom door. It seemed a lifetime ago he had been there. He pushed into the bedroom.

The window had been boarded up. The mattress and box spring were gone, as was the dresser. He saw blackened Scrabble tiles all over the room.

He opened the closet. It was mostly untouched, except for the water damage. On one side was a canvas garment bag. Byrne unzipped it, peered inside. Old dresses. *Very* old, very *theatrical*. She—

—*sees the countryside from a cracked and taped truck window . . . she knows . . .*

Byrne shut his eyes to the pain in his head.

She knows . . .

HE LOOKED at the top shelf. The strongbox was still there. He put his flashlight under his arm, took down the box. It was warm. There was no latch. The box was perfectly smooth. He shook it. Something shifted inside. It sounded like paper.

When Byrne left the apartment, just a few minutes later, he took the box with him. Out in the hallway he closed the door, reached into his pocket, took out a fresh police seal. He peeled off the back, smoothed it over the doorjamb, and pocketed the backing.

He drove back to South Philly.

As HE STEPPED onto the sidewalk in front of his apartment building his phone beeped. It was a text message. Before reading the message, Byrne looked at his watch. It was 2:45 AM. Just about the only person who sent him text messages was Colleen. But not in the middle of the night.

He retrieved the message, looked at the LCD screen.

It read: 910 JHOME.

Byrne knew what it meant. It was a little-used code he had established a long time ago with Jessica. JHOME meant she was at her house; 910 meant that she needed him, but it was not an emergency.

That would be 911.

Byrne got back into his car and headed to the Northeast.

FIFTY-TWO

SWANN AWOKE AT 3 AM. HE COULD NOT SLEEP. IT HAD BEEN THE SAME since he was a child. On the night before he and his father were to go on a tour, or even move between venues on a sunrise train, he found the anticipation to be overwhelming. Sleep would not find him.

This would be such a day.

He showered and shaved, dressed casually—perhaps an engineer preparing a survey in some wooded expanse, perhaps a junior high school principal about to give a holiday speech.

He parked near Tacony Creek Park, in a small lot off Wyoming Avenue. They would be arriving at first light. Some may have even spent the night in the park.

He looked at the screen of his cell phone. It was dark. Lilly would call. He was sure of it. But still, he had to be prepared if she did not.

FIFTY-THREE

Jᴇssɪᴄᴀ sᴀᴛ ᴏɴ ʜᴇʀ ᴘᴏʀᴄʜ. Bᴇʜɪɴᴅ ʜᴇʀ, ᴇᴠᴇʀʏ ʟɪɢʜᴛ ɪɴ ᴛʜᴇ ʜᴏᴜsᴇ was blazing. The stereo inside blasted the Go-Gos.

"Hey, partner!" she yelled.

Oh, boy, Byrne thought. *She's hammered.* The Go-Gos proved it. "Hey."

"You got my text message? That is *so* cool. God, I love technology."

"You okay?"

Jessica butterflied a hand. "Pain-free."

"I can see that. Family okay?"

"Vincent and Sophie are up at Vincent's father's house. I talked to them earlier. They went swimming. Sophie went off the low diving board. Her first time." Jessica's eyes misted. "I missed it."

There was a pint bottle of bourbon between her feet. It was two-thirds full. Byrne knew she hadn't gotten this plastered on two drinks.

"There's got to be another casualty around here somewhere," he said.

Jessica hesitated for a moment, then pointed at the hedges to the left of the porch. A glint of moonlight shimmered off an empty bottle of Wild Turkey. Byrne plucked it from the shadows, stood it on the porch.

"You know . . . you know how people say 'life sucks,' and how someone always says, right after that, 'No one ever said life is supposed to be fair'?"

"Yeah," Byrne said. "I think I've heard that one."

"Well it's fucking bullshit."

Byrne agreed, but he had to ask. "What do you mean?"

"What I mean is, people say life is fair all the *time*. Right? When you're a kid they tell you that you can be anything you want to be. They tell you that if you work hard, the world is your oyster. You can overcome anything. Buckle down! Hang in there! Stay with it!"

Byrne didn't have much of an argument for this. "Well, yeah. They do say that."

Jessica went south, her mind veering into some new area. She took another slow sip. "What did these girls do to deserve this, Kevin?"

"I don't know." Byrne wasn't used to this dynamic. *He* was the melancholy drunk. She was the sane one. More than once—actually, more times than he could count—Jessica had listened to his inebriated ramblings, standing on some freezing street corner, standing on the banks of the river, standing in some steaming parking lot in Northern Liberties. He owed her. In many more ways than this. He listened.

"I mean, they ran away from home? Is that what this is all about? *That* was their crime? Shit, I ran away once."

Byrne was shocked. Little Jessica Giovanni had run away from home? Strict Catholic, straight-A student, daughter of one of the most decorated cops in PPD history Jessica? "You did?"

"Oh you bet I did, buddy. You fucking *bet* I did." She took another dramatic, *Days of Wine and Roses* swig from the bottle, wiped off her mouth with her wrist. "I only got as far as Tenth and Washington," she added. "But I *did* it."

She offered the pint to Byrne. He took it. For two reasons. One was that he didn't mind having a drink. Two, it was probably a good idea to get the bottle away from Jessica. They fell silent for a while.

"Why the hell do we do this?" Jessica finally asked, loud and clear.

And there it was, Byrne thought. *The* question. Every homicide cop on the face of the earth asked it at one time or another. Some asked every day.

"I don't know," Byrne said. "I guess it's because we're no good for anything else."

"Okay. Okay. Okay. I'll buy that. But how do you know when it's time to quit? That's what I want to know. Huh? Is that in the handbook?"

Byrne looked off into the night. He took a healthy quaff. He needed it for what he was about to say. "Last story of the night. Okay?"

Jessica sat up straight, mimicking a five-year-old. A *story*.

"Do you know a cop named Tommy Delgado?" Byrne asked.

Jessica shook her head. "Never met him. I've heard the name, though. Vincent has brought him up a few times. Homicide?"

Byrne nodded. "In the blood. One of the best ever. Remember the Manny Utrillo case?"

"Oh yeah."

"Tommy cracked it. Walked into the unit one day with the piece of shit killer in irons. Walked him in like a prom date. Eight detectives were working the phones, tracking down leads on the case, Tommy Delgado walks the fucker in. Brought Danish for everyone in the other hand."

Byrne hit the Wild Turkey again, capped it.

"So, anyway, we get called to a scene in Frankford. We weren't the primaries, we were there to back up Tommy and his partner Mitch Driscoll. I was working with Jimmy then. I was in the unit for maybe three years. Still wet. I was still calling the scumbags 'sir.' "

Jessica laughed. She had only given up that practice recently. "Okay."

"This place was ugly. Job was even worse. The victim was an eighteen-month-old baby. Her so-called father had strangled her with a lamp cord."

"Jesus."

"Jesus wasn't there that day, partner." Byrne sat down next to Jessica. "Two hours in we're wrapping it up. I mean, the guy copped to it on the scene. Not too much intrigue. Now, Jimmy and I are keeping a close eye on Tommy, because he's looking a little shaky, right? Like he's going to burn down the whole block, like he's going to cap the first addict he sees on the street, just for drawing air. We're standing on the porch, and I see Tommy staring at something on the ground. Mesmerized. I look down and I see what he's looking at. Know what it was?"

Jessica tried to imagine. Based on what Byrne had told her about the job, it couldn't be a crucial piece of evidence—a shell casing, a bloody footprint. "What?"

"A Cheerio."

At first Jessica thought she hadn't heard him right, then soon real-ized she had. She nodded. She knew what he meant, knew where this was going. Cheerios were the universal toddler pacifiers. Cheerios were baby crack.

"One Cheerio was sitting on this shitty, Astroturf porch, and Tommy Delgado can't take his eyes off it. Now, keep in mind, here was a man who had seen it all. Two tours in Nam, twenty-five plus on the job. A few minutes later he walks to the back of the building, crying his eyes out. I checked on him, just to make sure he didn't have his piece out, but there he was, just sitting on this bench, sobbing. Broke my heart, but I didn't approach him.

"That one thing snapped him in half, Jess. One Cheerio. He was never the same after that."

"Do you know what happened to him?"

Byrne took a few moments, shrugged. "He worked another few years, took his thirty. But he was just sleepwalking the job, you know? Bringing up the rear, hauling water."

They fell silent for a full minute.

"When did it all go to crap, Kevin?"

Byrne had his ideas on this. "I think it was when boxes of pasta went from sixteen ounces to twelve ounces and nobody told us."

Jessica looked fallen. "They did?"

Byrne nodded.

"Son of a *bitch*. No wonder I'm always hungry."

Byrne glanced at his watch. "Want to get some breakfast?"

Jessica looked at the black, star-dotted sky. "At night?"

"Coffee first." He helped Jessica to her feet, and marched her into the kitchen.

FIFTY-FOUR

LILLY WALKED THE STREETS. HER STOMACH RUMBLED. SHE HAD NEVER been this exhausted in her life. And still she walked. Spruce, Walnut, Locust, Sansom, Chestnut, Market. Up and down and across. She lingered for a while on Rittenhouse Square. She watched the city yawn and stretch and come awake. She watched the medical personnel arriving at Jefferson, the delivery trucks bringing the day's news, the day's bagels; she watched the homeless stir in doorways; she watched the cabs and the cops, two groups who knew no time.

She walked, her treasure in hand.

When she was twelve or so she had gone to a house party. As she was about to leave, her friend Roz slipped her a huge bud of weed, but she'd had nowhere to put it, no foil or plastic or anything. So she walked all the way home with it pinched between her thumb and forefinger, hanging on to it for dear life. She was not going to lose it. She walked more than two miles, cutting through Culver Park, across the reservoir, across the tracks. Somehow she made it home, her riches intact and whole, and dropped it into an empty pill vial with no small hum of accomplishment.

She had something even more important than that in her hand now. She couldn't even bring herself to put it in her pocket. She needed the feel of it against her skin.

She had his phone number. He was going to help her.

And so she walked, from Front Street to Broad Street, until she could walk no more. She sat on one of those big concrete planters.

She waited for the sun.

FIFTY-FIVE

THE MURDERS WERE THE LEAD STORY OF THE DAY. IT WAS ABOVE THE fold in the *Inquirer*, on the front page of the *Daily News*. It led all three network affiliate television broadcasts. It was featured on every local news website.

The lab was fast-tracking every piece of forensic evidence. A partial shoe print had been lifted off the roof where Katja had been posed on the wooden chair. The chair itself had yielded a number of friction ridge prints, which were being fed through AFIS. The swords were identified as a homemade version of a double-wide épée, the type commonly used in fencing. They yielded no prints.

Katja's mother, Birta Dovic, was driving in from Connecticut. Two investigators from the Connecticut state police were interviewing Katja's friends and classmates. Photographs of the three victims were now on the dashboards of every sector car in the city. Patrol officers were instructed to ask everyone they encountered if they had ever seen them.

The investigation had reached a whirlwind pace, but the one thing it had not produced, the one thing they all sought, was still eluding them.

They needed a name.

AT JUST AFTER 8:00 AM Josh Bontrager came running into the duty room, out of breath.

"What's up?" Jessica asked. Her head felt like it was made of cast iron. She'd gotten three hours' sleep and driven into the city in a fog. It reminded her of her college days.

Bontrager held up a hand. He couldn't catch his wind.

"Take it easy, Josh."

Bontrager nodded.

"Water?"

Another nod.

Jessica handed him a bottle. He chugged a full bottle of Aquafina. Deep breath. Then: "A woman called 911. She was in the park."

"What park? Fairmount Park?" Byrne asked.

"Tacony Creek," Josh said, nearly recovered. "You know the one I mean?"

Everyone did. Tacony Creek Park, which was technically part of the Fairmount Park system, was a 300-acre park that ran along the Tacony Creek, connecting Frankford Creek in the south to Cheltenham Township in the north. It skirted a very densely populated area in North Philadelphia.

"Anyway, the woman calls in, says she saw a man—a well-dressed white man—let a teenage girl get into his car. It was a black Acura. She said the whole thing looked a little funny, so she kept watching them. After a few seconds, she said she saw the man and the girl fighting in the car."

"What happened then?"

"Well, I guess while the woman was on the line with 911 a sector car drove by. She hung up, flagged it down, told the officer what was going on."

"Did she get a plate?"

"Better than that. She said the car went up an alley and the sector car blocked it in. It's a dead end."

"What are you saying, we have the car?" Jessica asked.

"Not only do we have the car," Bontrager said. He raised his empty bottle of spring water, like a toast. "We've got the *guy*."

FIFTY-SIX

Swann sat on the curb. He calmed himself. As a boy he had been in chains many times.

He reached over with his left hand, slid over the back of his watch, removed the thin steel needle. Nearby, the girl sat crying in the back of the patrol car. A very nervous young officer leaned against the trunk.

Swann rocked gently to one side, then the other. "Officer, I'm afraid you've gotten these cuffs on far too tightly. I'm losing the feeling in both my arms."

At first the officer pretended not to hear him.

"Officer?"

The young man looked up the alleyway, then reluctantly walked over, unsnapping his holster. "If you try anything, I swear to God I will mace you in the face. Are we clear?"

"Yes, sir."

"Roll onto your knees and stand up."

In one graceful move Swann rose. He dropped the handcuffs to the ground, then pulled the officer's weapon out of its holster. He leveled it at the young man's head.

"Don't!" the officer screamed. *"Oh God Jesus don't."* He closed his eyes, waiting for the click, the pain, the dark.

"Cuff yourself to the front wheel. Do it now."

The young man grabbed the cuffs, did as he was told. The girl in the back seat began to cry. Swann took the handcuff keys from the officer's belt, then took a few steps away. He ejected the magazine from the weapon, racked the slide. Empty now. He threw the magazine and keys as far as he could. He leaned close to the young man's ear. "I'm sorry for all this. I would never have hurt you."

He held up the weapon. "You will find this in a sewer on Castor Avenue."

Swann smoothed his clothing. He grabbed his bag from the back-seat of the black car, walked up the alley, and was gone.

FIFTY-SEVEN

TWO SECTOR CARS AND TWO DETECTIVE CARS ROARED TO A HALT AT THE
same moment. Jessica and Byrne hit the ground running. Behind
them were Josh Bontrager and Dre Curtis.

They arrived to find a disturbing tableau. A sector car was at the
mouth of the alley between two blocks of row houses. In front of it was
a black Acura TSX. A young officer was handcuffed to one of the
spokes of the right front aluminum alloy wheel. In the backseat of the
Acura was a young girl, perhaps sixteen. Her face was streaked with
mascara tears.

All four detectives drew their weapons, held them at their sides.

"Where is he?" Byrne asked the officer.

"He's gone." The young man's shame was palpable. He slammed
his free hand into the front fender.

"Which way?"

The officer pointed east, toward Castor Avenue.

"How long ago?"

"Two minutes, max."

"Describe him."

The officer described the man as a white male, thirties, blue and
brown, thick mustache, medium build, no distinguishing marks or
scars. He wore a tan windbreaker, black Docker-style pants, black hikers.

"Is he armed?" Byrne asked.

"He took my weapon. He said he was going to dump it on Castor. He ejected the mag first."

Byrne glanced at two of the four uniformed officers. He pointed them in the opposite direction. If their guy said he'd go east, he'd go west. They were off in an instant.

While Jessica got out her keys and unlocked the handcuffs, Dre Curtis got on his handset. "Suspect is not in custody," he said. "Repeat, suspect is *not* 10-15."

"Put in a call to K-9," Byrne said.

"We need some warm bodies down here," Dre Curtis continued. "We need a search team now. We need K-9."

The officer, a two-year rookie named Randy Sweetin, described what happened. He said he was patrolling, and a woman came across Wyoming Avenue, waving her hands. She told him that she saw a man talking to a teenage girl. She thought it looked funny, so she flagged him down.

"You're saying the cuffs on him were secure?" Byrne asked.

"They were secure. I'm sure of it."

Josh Bontrager approached. "I called in the plates. Stolen off a black Acura in long-term parking at the airport."

"When?" Byrne asked.

"Three days ago."

"*Shit.*"

They would have to identify the vehicle by its VIN.

THE GIRL HAD STOPPED CRYING for the moment. She sat on the back of a detective car, a ball of damp tissues in her hands. Someone had brought her a can of Mountain Dew. It sat unopened next to her.

She said her name was Abigail Noonan. She was sixteen. They had not yet pressed her on ID, address, or Social Security number. As a rule, street kids were only truthful about one out of three.

"Are you okay?" Jessica asked.

The girl nodded.

"Is there anything else we can get you right now?"

The girl shook her head.

"Tell me what happened."

"I don't know. He was just, like, parked there, listening to the radio, okay?"

"Do you remember what station?"

"I don't know too much about which radio stations play what. I'm not, you know, from around here."

"I understand," Jessica said. "Do you remember what song he was listening to?"

"Yeah. He was listening to 'When You Look Me in the Eyes.' That song by the Jonas Brothers. You know them?"

Jessica didn't know the Jonas Brothers from the Wright Brothers. "Sure."

"Anyway, I was on the bench over there, and I heard the music. I wasn't sure where it was coming from. I looked around and I saw this guy in his car. He looked over and saw me."

"What did he do?"

"Do? He didn't do anything."

"I mean, did he smile, did he wave, did he call you over?"

"He might have smiled. I don't really remember. It looked like he was reading a little book of some kind. More like a booklet."

"What kind of booklet?"

"Well, when I walked by, I saw that he was holding the booklet in one hand, and this cool video iPod in the other, so I guess it was the manual. He looked a little confused."

"Did he start talking to you?"

The girl looked at the ground. She began to color. "No," she said. "I started talking to him."

"What did he say to you?"

"He said he just bought his daughter a new iPod, and he was having trouble with it. He said he wanted to download a lot of stuff she liked before he gave it to her. He asked me if I knew anything about iPods."

"Do you?"

"Of course."

"What happened then?"

"I was so stupid. I walked around and got in the car."

"Did he touch you?"

"No," she said. "Not right then. I thought everything was cool until I looked in the backseat, and I saw it."

"You saw it? What did you see?"

"The newspaper. It was opened to the story about that guy who was kidnapping girls off the street. I looked at him. He knew that I saw the newspaper. When our eyes met, we both knew. I *freaked*."

"Did he strike you? Or try to detain you?"

"No. But when I saw that I couldn't get out I started yelling my ass off."

They had checked the interior of the Acura. The inside handle on the passenger's door had been removed. Jessica made a few notes. She put a hand on the young girl's shoulder. "I'm afraid we're going to have to contact your parents. You know that, right?"

The girl nodded. Fresh tears followed.

A few minutes later a K-9 officer arrived with his dog. The officer ran the dog—a German shepherd tracking dog named Oliver— through the driver's side of the Acura, and then around the perimeter of the car. He then walked the dog over to the tree line across the street. Almost instantly the dog alerted to a path. The two disappeared into the trees, followed by Josh Bontrager, Dre Curtis, and a pair of uniformed officers.

Jessica glanced at her watch. If this was their killer, he had a pretty good lead. But she had worked with the K-9 Unit many times. If their man was still in the area, they would find him.

FIFTY-EIGHT

THERE WERE SIRENS EVERYWHERE. SWANN HAD DOUBLED BACK, CIRCLING through the trees near Greenwood Cemetery. He found a row of three unoccupied porta-potties near a construction site.

Once inside, even though the quarters were tight, he worked quickly. He unzipped his bag, put the foam rubber around his waist. He put on a gray wig already tied into a ponytail. He slipped buck teeth over his own. He stepped into a dark blue jumpsuit with the city's water-department logo on the back.

In less than thirty seconds he had gained forty pounds, aged fifteen years, and changed into an outfit as different from the man they sought as could be. He stuffed his old clothes down into the toilet, along with the young officer's weapon. There was probably a wealth of forensic evidence to be found on his discards, but he couldn't think about that now.

He emerged from the portable toilet and made his way south. When he reached the circle at Castor and Wyoming, two sector cars came flashing by.

Moments later Swann flagged a cab. He hated to lose the car, but it was all right. He had four other vehicles.

FIFTY-NINE

THEY MET IN THE DUTY ROOM. A SUSPECT SKETCH WAS BEING RUN OFF at that moment, and would be distributed to every sector car in the division on the next shift. They would not be releasing it to the media for a while, but that did not mean it wouldn't leak.

The K-9 officer and his dog had tracked to a bank of portable toilets. There, in one of the stalls, they found a pile of men's clothing stuck into the holding tank, along with what appeared to be the young officer's service weapon. A CSU team was en route to the site to begin the unenviable task of collecting evidence.

AT JUST AFTER NOON, a detective walked into the unit. It was Tony Park. Park was in his late forties, one of only a handful of Korean-American detectives in the department. There were few people better with a database or spreadsheet. No one was better on the Internet.

"I've been running missing persons of an age along with unidentified DOAs. The DOA data was slim, but, as you might imagine, the missing-person files were huge. Why do so many kids want to come to Philly? Why not New York?"

"Got to be the cheesesteaks," someone said. Then, as expected, from around the room:

"Which means John's Roast Pork."

"Which means Sonny's Famous."

"Which means Tony Luke's."

Park shook his head. "Every friggin' time, the same argument," he said. "Anyway, one of the files jumped high. Last December, a sixteen-year-old girl from Chicago went missing. Her name was Elise Beausoleil. Elise told one of her friends that she was coming to Philadelphia. Her father, who owns a multinational company called Sunshine Technologies—and also happens to be golfing buddies with the governor of Illinois—makes a call to the governor, who in turn calls his friend, the governor of our fair commonwealth, who in turn puts pressure on the mayor and the commissioner to turn over every rock and bucket to find this kid. You guys remember this case, don't you?"

The homicide detectives look at each other, shrugged. The truth was, homicide was a fairly insulated unit. If it wasn't a dead body, you pretty much didn't see it.

"Anyway, detectives in East division discovered that Elise got a part-time job doing door-to-door surveys for some human-rights group. They interviewed the director and some of the people who worked there. They remembered Elise. They turned up a route she worked. They said that after New Year's Day she never showed up again. They all just figured she went home. Her father put on some private detectives, but they turned up zilch."

"Philly guys?" Byrne asked.

"Two from Philly, two from Chicago."

"When did he call them in?"

"Around March."

"Was she on the FBI site?"

"Oh, yeah." Park reached into the folder, pulled out a photograph. "This is her."

He put the picture on the desk. The girl was a beauty—almond-shaped eyes, cropped dark hair, a long swanlike neck.

The detectives looked at the route Elise had taken on her surveys.

"How deep was the canvass?" Jessica asked.

"Like the Mariana Trench. I think they hit six hundred doors."

"I take it there were no leads."

"Not a one."

The Collector, Jessica thought, a little dismayed that the nickname had seeped into her consciousness. She looked at Elise Beausoleil's beautiful dark eyes, wondering if the last person this girl had seen was the man they so desperately sought.

SIXTY

SWANN SAT AT HIS KITCHEN TABLE. HE WAS STILL DRESSED IN HIS DIS-guise.

On the way back to the house he saw the FedEx truck three blocks over. He was waiting for a delivery, a set of antique bronze drawer pulls he had all but stolen on eBay.

A few minutes earlier he had seen on TV the sketch of the man wanted for the attempted abduction of a girl near Tacony Park. It looked no more like him than did the man in the moon. The media was referring to him as "the Collector." He was pleased with both developments.

He hoped the young officer did not have nightmares.

Now that he was so close to the end, to his grand finale, he found his mind drifting back to the place where it all began. It was the same time of day, as he recalled, this lilac-hued hour between the time when he arrived home and his first aperitif. He recalled that he had just watched *The Magic Bricks* in the attic, when the doorbell rang. He thought about Elise sitting at this very table, one leg curled beneath her, the background seeming to dissolve away. She was so bright, so alive, a pixie with a gamine body and close-cropped hair.

She had come from money, of that he was sure. The quality of her boots and jewelry spoke of it; her manner and vocabulary all but confirmed it. She had about her an air of aristocracy, but it was not something by birthright. She was new money. She wore it like a mantle of pride.

Elise had strolled the great room that day, picking up a few of his *objets d'art* on the way. She had seemed particularly interested in the Tiffany crystal and brass carriage clock. It was one of his favorites. This moved him. She also liked—

The doorbell rang. It was FedEx.

Swann crossed the foyer, peered through curtains. It was not the FedEx delivery man after all. Instead it was a very attractive woman. She had silken shoulder-length hair, wore a smart navy suit, white blouse.

"Recall the man in Metairie, Joseph. The one who owned the haberdashery. They know your voice here. Beware."

Swann smoothed his long gray wig. He opened the door.

"Hello," he said. His voice now carried the slightest accent. It was a French intonation, but native to Louisiana.

"Hi," the woman replied. She held up a gold badge. "My name is Detective Jessica Balzano. I'm with the Philadelphia Police Department. I'd like to ask you a few questions, if you don't mind."

Swann steadied himself against the doorjamb. "Of course."

"May I ask your name?"

"Jake," Swann said. "Jake Myers. Would you like to come inside?"

The woman made a note. "Thanks."

He opened the door wide. She stepped in.

"Wow," she said. "This is some place."

"Thank you," he said. "It's been in my family for years." He gestured. "Would you like to sit in the parlor?"

"No," she said. "I'm fine. This shouldn't take too long."

Swann glanced at the stairs. The stairs leading up to Claire's room. He had given her another ampoule, but that was an hour ago. Just a few minutes earlier he thought she had stirred. Patricia was fast asleep in the basement.

"Get her into the kitchen, Joseph."

"Would you like something to drink? I've just made fresh coffee. Kenya."

"No thank you," she said. "We're talking to everyone in the neighborhood."

"I see."

"Do you live here alone?" she asked.

"Oh my goodness, no. I live here with my family."

"Are they home now?"

"My daughters are out, and I'm afraid my wife is a bit under the weather." He gestured to the sideboard, which held a number of photos. His phantom family. He wondered if she would notice that all the photos were solo.

"I'm sorry to hear that," the detective replied. "I hope she feels better soon."

"Most kind of you to say."

"They are going to stop you, Joseph. You cannot allow this to happen."

The detective produced a photograph. "Do you recognize this girl?"

She presented a photograph of Elise Beausoleil. It was one he had seen before. He gave it its proper time, its owing. "Yes. I believe I do, but I cannot remember from where or when."

"Her name is Elise Beausoleil."

"Yes, of course. I remember now. A pair of detectives came around making inquiries. They spoke to my wife and eldest daughter about this young lady. I happened to be in the garden at the time. They stopped and asked me about her as well. I had not seen her."

"Were these city detectives or private detectives?"

"I'm afraid I don't know. What is the difference exactly?"

"Did they have gold badges?"

"Yes. I believe they did. In fact, I am certain of it."

"They were the police," she said. "Has anyone been around here since, inquiring about this girl?"

"She knows, Joseph. You cannot allow her to leave."

Swann feigned deep thought. "I don't think so."

The detective made a note in her book. Swann angled to see it, but couldn't. He put a hand into his pocket, palmed a chloroform ampoule. He would take her in the foyer.

"Once again, I appreciate your time." She handed him a card. "If you think of anything that might help us, I'd appreciate a call."

Swann removed his hand from his pocket. "By all means."

He opened the front door. The pretty detective stepped out onto the porch, just as the FedEx man arrived. The two of them smiled at each other, made room.

Swann took the package, thanked the deliveryman. The drawer pulls no longer mattered. He closed the door, his heart fit to burst.

Upstairs, Claire screamed. It was an unearthly sound.

Swann closed his eyes, certain that the police officer had heard. He peeked through blinds. The woman was walking to her car, her chestnut hair luminous in the late afternoon sun. She was already talking into her cell phone.

And then she was gone.

SIXTY-ONE

A T JUST AFTER SEVEN O'CLOCK, SIX DETECTIVES AND TWELVE PATROL officers returned to the Roundhouse after having done a sweep canvass of the neighborhoods where Elise Beausoleil had been seen the previous January.

They distributed a few hundred photographs, talked to a few hundred people. Some recalled the first time the police came around looking for the girl. Most did not. None admitted to ever having seen her.

Before they got their coats off, a call came in from the communications unit.

.They had a break in the case.

THEY GATHERED AROUND a thirty-inch high-definition LCD monitor in the communications center. Six detectives, as well as Hell Rohmer and Lieutenant John Hurley, commanding officer of the unit. Tony Park sat at the computer keyboard.

"We found this about twenty minutes ago," Hurley said.

Jessica looked at the monitor. It was a splash page, an entry to something called GothOde.

"What's GothOde?" Josh Bontrager asked.

"It's like YouTube," Hell Rohmer said. "It's nowhere near as big, but it's ten times more demented. There are videos of every movie murder ever filmed, pseudo-snuff films, homemade perversions of every stripe. I'm thinking GothOde is a play on the word cathode, but don't quote me. We followed that link and ran the top video. When we saw where it was going we shut it down, made the call."

Park looked at Byrne. "You ready?"

"Yeah," Byrne said.

Park clicked the entry link. Instantly the browser window opened a new web page. To Jessica it looked almost identical to a YouTube page—a main video on top, with linked videos along the side. Unlike YouTube, the background was black, and the logo, scrawled along the top, was written in a blood red.

Park clicked on the play button. Immediately a soundtrack started. It sounded like a string quartet.

"Does anyone know this music?" Jessica asked the room.

"Bach," Hell Rohmer said. "J. S. Bach. *Sleepers Awake*. Cantata 140."

The screen stayed black for the moment. The music continued.

"Any significance here?" Jessica asked, still unsure what this was all about. "Any relevance?"

Hell thought for a few seconds. "I think it's about the assurance of salvation."

"Josh? Anything to add?"

Jessica glanced at Bontrager. Bontrager took his right hand, palm down and sent it slicing the air over his head, meaning just that—this was way over his head.

A few seconds later a title faded up. White letters on a black background, a classic serif type, written in one line.

THE SEVEN WONDERS

"*I have seven girls,*" Byrne quoted. "*I fear for them. I fear for their safety.*" He pointed at the monitor. "Seven girls, seven wonders."

Another fade to black, then a second screen, a graphic of red velvet curtains. Over it, another title.

PART ONE: THE GARDEN OF FLOWERS

Soon the curtains parted, showing a small stage with a spotlight in the center. Seconds later a man stepped into the spotlight. He wore a black cutaway tuxedo, white shirt, red bow tie, a monocle. He stopped center stage. He looked to be in his forties, although the video was grainy and it was hard to discern details. He sported a Van Dyck goatee.

"Behold . . . the Garden of Flowers," the man said. He had a slight German accent. He picked up a large woolen shawl, draped it over an arm, and began producing bouquets of flowers from beneath it, flinging them individually onto the stage. The bouquets appeared to be weighted, and have darts protruding from the bottom. One by one they stuck in the stage floor. When he had created a full circle, he gestured offstage. "And behold the lovely Odette."

A young woman walked tentatively onto the small stage, and stepped into the circle of flowers. The girl was slight, pale, dark-haired. She was terribly frightened.

The girl was Elise Beausoleil.

Without another word, a large fabric cone descended over the girl. A few seconds later it was raised. The girl was now lying in the center of a gigantic floral mass, her head twisted at an unnatural angle. She didn't move.

On-screen the man bowed. The curtains closed. The music faded out.

The detectives waited, but there was nothing else to see.

"Have you played the second video?" Byrne asked.

"No," Park said.

"Play it."

Park hovered the mouse over the second video, clicked.

PART TWO: THE GIRL WITHOUT A MIDDLE

Sleepers Awake was again the sound track. The curtains parted, revealing the same stage. Again a spotlight came up. Center stage were three brightly colored boxes similar to the ones they had found in the crawlspace of 4514 Shiloh Street. They were stacked. All three doors were open.

The man appeared. He was dressed exactly the same.

"Behold . . . the Girl Without a Middle." He held out his hand. A heavyset girl walked onto the stage. It was Monica Renzi. "And behold the lovely Odette."

Monica was crying. She stepped into the boxes. The illusionist closed all three doors. He picked up a thin metal plate and shoved it between the top two boxes.

"My God," someone said. "My God."

There were no other words.

"Click on the next one," Byrne said, his anger clearly rising.

Moments later, the third video began.

PART THREE: THE DROWNING GIRL

This time the curtain parted to show a large, empty glass tank. It looked similar to the glass display case in the Eighth Street crime scene. There was a girl sitting inside.

"It's Caitlin," Jessica said.

Within seconds the tank began to fill. Caitlin just sat there, as if she was accepting this fate. A diaphanous drape was lowered, hiding the tank. There was just the sound of the water beneath the heart-rending music of J. S. Bach.

Tony park clicked on the fourth video.

PART FOUR: THE GIRL IN THE SWORD BOX

It was Katja Dovic in the Sword Box, a red lacquered box with slits cut into the top and sides. The vision of the swords being pushed into the closed container was as horrifying as anything they had ever witnessed.

Tony Park clicked on the remaining three screens, but none of them launched a video.

For a long time no one in the room said a word. It appeared that the killer's kidnap attempt that morning had been thwarted, but there were a lot more girls from which he could choose.

"Can we find out where this is coming from?" Byrne asked.

"It's my understanding that this GothOde is based in Romania," Hell said. "Unfortunately, there's no way for us to know from where these videos have been uploaded. He could be doing it from a cyber-cafe."

"What about the FBI?" Dre Curtis asked.

"I put in a call and forwarded everything to the Computer Crimes Task Force," Hurley said. "They have a forensic examiner on it now, although it will probably take a handful of court orders and three federal agencies to get anything done in a foreign country."

It was then that Jessica noticed something at the bottom of the screen. "What's this?" she asked, pointing to it.

There was a single word beneath the last video. *Corollarium*. It looked to be an active link. Before clicking on the link, Park navigated to an online Latin to English dictionary. He entered the word. The page displayed:

corollarium -i n. [a garland of flowers; a present, gratuity]

Park returned to the GothOde page, clicked the link. A small window opened. It was a still photograph of a room with rotting plaster and broken shelves. In the middle of the room, amid the debris, was what looked a like a large package, wrapped in thin green paper. Out of the top came a variety of fresh-cut flowers.

Through the window beyond the box was visible a vacant lot, partially covered in snow. At the other side of the lot was a mural covering a whole wall, an elaborate rendering that included a man blowing a ribbon of smoke over a city skyline.

"This is Philly," Jessica said. "I know that mural. I know where this is."

They all knew where it was. It was across from a corner building near Fifth and Cambria.

Jessica ran out of the room.

By the time the other detectives got to the parking lot she was gone.

JESSICA PACED IN FRONT of the address. The front door was padlocked. Across the street was the mural in the still photograph.

Byrne, Josh Bontrager, and Dre Curtis approached.

"Take the door down," Jessica said.

"Jess," Byrne said. "We should wait. We could—"

"Take it . . . the fuck . . . *down*!"

Bontrager looked to Byrne for direction. Byrne nodded. Bontrager went into the trunk of his departmental sedan, came out with an iron pry bar. He handed it to Byrne.

Byrne took the door off the hinges with the massive lever. Josh Bontrager and Dre Curtis hauled it out of the way. Jessica and Byrne, weapons drawn, entered the space. The area they had seen in the photograph was now piled with more trash. But the view out the barred window was the same.

Jessica holstered her weapon and stormed across the room. She began pulling trash off the huge pile of debris in the center.

"Jess," Byrne said.

She didn't hear him. If she did, she did not acknowledge him. Soon she uncovered the thing she sought, the thing she knew would still be there, the thing that had been placed in this precise spot, waiting for them.

"It's a crime scene, Jess," Byrne said. "You have to stop."

She turned to look at him. Her eyes stood with tears. Byrne had never seen her like this.

"I can't."

Moments later she had all the trash thrown aside. In front of her lay a body wrapped in green paper, the same kind of green paper used by florists.

The Garden of Flowers.

The dead girl was his bouquet.

Jessica tore open the paper. The scent of dried flora and putrefying flesh was overwhelming. Even in this decayed state it was obvious that the girl's neck had been broken. For a moment, Jessica did not move.

Then she fell to her knees.

SIXTY-TWO

They stood in the punishing heat. Around them buzzed yet another CSU team. Around them stretched another circle of yellow tape.

"This isn't going to stop until he's done all seven," Jessica said. "There are three more girls out there who are going to die."

Byrne had no response. Nothing he could say.

"The Seven Wonders. What the fuck is this all about, Kevin? What's next?"

"Tony's on it now," Byrne said. "If the answer is out there he'll find it. You know that."

Until now, all four of these girls had lived in two dimensions. Photographs on paper, a graphic file on a computer screen, myriad details on a police activity log or an FBI sheet. But now they had seen them alive. All four girls had been breathing on those videos. Elise Beausoleil, Caitlin O'Riordan, Monica Renzi, Katja Dovic. All four of them had entered that chamber of horrors and never left. And if that was not enough, this madman had to apply a special brand of indignity by putting them on display, for the whole city to see.

Jessica had never wanted someone dead so badly in her life. And, God forgive her, she wanted to be the one who pulled the switch.

"Jessica?"

She turned. It was JoAnn Johnson, commander of the Auto Squad. The Auto Squad had citywide jurisdiction to locate vehicle chop shops, investigate car-theft rings, and coordinate investigations with the insurance industry. Jessica had worked in the unit, now a part of Major Crimes, for almost three years.

"Hey, JoAnn." Jessica wiped her eyes. She could just imagine what she looked like. A crazed raccoon, maybe. JoAnn didn't react in the least.

"Got a minute?"

Jessica and JoAnn stepped away. JoAnn handed her the preliminary report on the Acura.

They had towed the car to the police garage at McAllister and Whitaker, just a few blocks from the Twenty-Fourth District station. The order was to hold for prints and processing, so it was held inside. They had identified the owner.

JESSICA STEPPED BACK to where Byrne stood, report in hand.

"We have a hit on the car's VIN," she said.

The VIN, or vehicle identification number, was the seventeen-character number used to uniquely identify American vehicles, post-1980.

"What do we have?" Byrne asked.

Jessica looked at the ground, the buildings, the sky. Everywhere but at her partner.

"What is it, Jess?"

Jessica finally looked him in the eye. She didn't want to, but she had no choice.

"The car belonged to Eve Galvez."

SIXTY-THREE

THEY REFERRED TO IT AS THE WIRE. IT WAS FLEXIBLE, MALLEABLE, NEED not run in a straight line. In fact, it most often did not. It could snake beneath things, coil itself around other things, bury itself beneath a wide variety of surfaces. It was not tangible, but it was felt.

For all the homicides that had ever been committed, from the moment Cain raised his hand to Abel, there had been a wire. A time, a place, a weapon, a motive, a killer. It wasn't always obvious—indeed, all too often it was never discovered—but it was always there.

As detectives Jessica Balzano and Kevin Byrne stood in the duty room of the homicide unit, the wire revealed itself. Jessica held one end. She spoke first.

She spoke of her meeting with Jimmy Valentine. She spoke of her growing obsession with Eve Galvez. Not just Eve's case, but the woman herself. She spoke of visiting Enrique Galvez, and her admittedly insane visit to the Badlands the night before. She spoke of Eve's diary, and her own tears.

Byrne listened. He did not judge her. He held the other end of the wire.

"Did you read all the files?" he asked.

"No."

"Do you have the flash drive with you?"

"Yes."

Moments later Jessica had the drive hooked up to a laptop. She navigated to the folder containing the scanned files.

"How many of these have you read?"

"Less than half," Jessica said. "I couldn't take much more."

"These are all her files?"

"Yes."

"Open the last two."

Jessica clicked on the next to last file.

SIXTY-FOUR

JUNE 30, 2008

They call him Mr. Ludo; though no one can describe him. I've been a detective for years. How is this possible? Is he a ghost? A shadow?

No. Everyone can be found. Every secret can be discovered. Think of the word "discover." It means to take off the cover. To reveal.

One girl said she knew a girl who had been to Mr. Ludo's house once and escaped. Someone named Cassandra.

I am going to meet Cassandra tomorrow.

The picture is on my wall. She was just another statistic, another cold body, another victim. Killadelphia some call it. I don't believe it. This is my city. This was someone's daughter. She was an innocent.

Perhaps it is because she was from a small town. Perhaps it is because she wears a lilac backpack. My favorite color.

She was just a child. Like me. She *was* me.

Caitlin O'Riordan.

I cannot let this rest.

I will not let this rest.

SIXTY-FIVE

EVEN BEFORE THEY OPENED THE LAST FILE, THEY KNEW WHAT IT WAS going to be. The file contained the scanned copies of the three missing interviews from the O'Riordan case binder. Eve Galvez had taken Freddy Roarke's notes from the binder, scanned them, kept the file on her flash drive, along with the rest of her life.

"The case Jimmy Valentine was talking about," Jessica said. "The case he told me Eve was obsessed with. It was the Caitlin O'Riordan case. Eve stole the notes out of the binder. She was investigating it on her own. She was tracking him. He got to her first."

Byrne turned twice, fists raised, looking for something to slam, something to break.

"Eve was a runaway," Jessica said. "She'd lived the life. I guess she saw Caitlin's murder as one too many. She went deep-end on it."

They'd both seen it before. A detective who had taken a case too personally. They'd both been there themselves.

They read the missing interviews. Starlight, Govinda, and Daria. All three kids said they had met a man. A man who had tried to bring them back to his house. A man who identified himself by a strange name.

Mr. Ludo.

BYRNE TOLD HIS STORY, his end of the wire. When he was done, he left the room.

Minutes later he was back upstairs with the strongbox he had taken from Laura Somerville's apartment. In the other hand he had a cordless drill, courtesy of one of the crew working on the renovation on the first floor. In moments he had the box open.

Inside was a sheaf of papers. Postcards, ticket stubs in at least ten languages, going back fifty years. And photographs.

They were photographs of a magician on a stage. The man looked like the man in the videos, but thinner, taller. Many of the photographs were yellowed with age. Byrne flipped one over. In a woman's handwriting it read *Vienna, 1959*. Another photo, this of the man with three large linking steel rings. *Detroit, 1961*.

In each photo a beautiful young woman stood next to the man.

"*Behold the lovely Odette,*" the man on the video had said.

The photographs in the strongbox made it clear. Odette was his stage assistant.

Odette was Laura Somerville.

SIXTY-SIX

Swann drove to Center City. He would not deny that Lilly had stirred him in a way that he had not felt in a long time. He'd had his share of lovers in his time, but they had never been to Faerwood, they had never glimpsed his soul.

He did not think of Lilly as a potential paramour. Not really. She was Odette. She was his assistant and confederate. One could not go through life without confederates.

He had been terribly afraid he would never see her again. But he knew that the night children were creatures of habit. He knew there were only so many places where she could blend in, even in a city as large as Philadelphia.

When she told him her story, and he offered to help her, he knew that she would be his. When he saw her standing on the corner of Eighth and Walnut, he knew it was destiny.

And now that she was in his car, he began to relax. She would be his finale after all.

As they got onto the boulevard, Swann took out his cell phone, hit a speed-dial button, put it to his ear. Earlier he had put the phone on silent, in case he got a call at such a crucial moment as this. He could not have his phone ringing while he was supposed to be talking on it.

He reached forward, turned down the music.

"Hello, my darling," he said to silence. "Yes . . . yes. No, I have not forgotten. I will be home in just a few minutes." Swann turned and looked at the girl, rolled his eyes. She smiled.

"The reason I'm calling is to tell you we have a guest. Yes. A young lady named Lilly." He laughed. "I know. The very same name. Yes, she has a bit of a problem, and I told her we would be most willing to help her solve it."

He covered the mouthpiece.

"My wife loves intrigue."

Lilly smiled.

Swann clicked off.

When they turned onto Tenth Street he reached into his coat pocket, and palmed the glass ampoule.

It would not be long now.

SIXTY-SEVEN

AT 11:45 PM, THE TEAM STARTED ASSEMBLING IN THE DUTY ROOM. In addition to the homicide detectives, a call had gone out to off-duty members of the Five Squad. They also had a call in to a man named Arthur Lake, president of the Philadelphia chapter of the International Brotherhood of Magicians.

TONY PARK HAD BEEN WORKING the computer for more than four hours.

"Detectives."

Jessica and Byrne crossed the room.

"What's up, Tony?"

"There's a new video on his GothOde page."

"Have you run it?"

"I have not. I was waiting for you."

They gathered around a computer terminal. Tony Park clicked on the last image. The screen changed to an individual page.

"This last one was uploaded twenty minutes ago," Park said. "It already has two hundred viewings. This guy has a following."

"Play it."

Park turned up the volume, clicked on the video. It was the same man in the other videos, dressed in an identical manner. But this time he was standing on a dark street. Behind him was City Hall.

"Life is a puzzle, *n'est-ce pas?*" he began, speaking directly to the camera. "If you are watching this, then you know the game is on.

"You have seen the first four illusions. There are three to go. Seven Wonders in all."

On the video, there was a special effect. Three smaller screens appeared below him. On the smaller screens were three teenage girls. All sat in darkened rooms.

"One illusion at 2:00 AM. One illusion at 4:00 AM. And the grand finale at 6:00 AM. This is going to be spectacular. It will light up the night." The man leaned forward slightly. "Can you solve the puzzle in time? Can you find the maidens? Are you *good enough*?"

One by one the small screens went black.

"Here is a clue," the man said. "He flies between Begichev and Geltser."

The man then turned and pointed toward City Hall.

"Watch the clock. The dance begins at midnight."

He waved a hand, and disappeared. The video ended.

"What does he mean, watch the clock?" Jessica asked.

BYRNE SLAMMED on the brakes as he pulled the car over into the center of the intersection of North Broad and Arch streets, about a block away from city hall. It was approximately the same vantage point as the killer in the last video.

He and Jessica got out of the car. The flashing dashboard light strobed across the tall buildings. There was nothing out of the ordinary about the clock tower at City Hall. Not at first.

Then it happened.

At the stroke of midnight the huge clock face turned bloodred.

"Oh my God," Jessica said.

The sky over Philadelphia flashed with lightning. Detective Kevin Byrne looked at his partner, at his watch.

It was just after midnight. If this monster was telling the truth— and there was absolutely no reason to doubt him—they had less than two hours to save the first girl.

III

DEATH CLOCK

In the cool of the night time
The clocks pick off the points...
—CARL SANDBURG, Interior

Twenty-two detectives from the Philadelphia Police Department's homicide unit met in the briefing room on the first floor of the Roundhouse. They ranged in age from thirty-one to sixty-three, in experience from just a few months in the unit to more than thirty years. Eight of these detectives had been on duty for more than fourteen hours—including Kevin Byrne and Jessica Balzano. Six had been called from home. The other ten were already on last-out, but were no longer working cases or leads. Half of this raucous group had to be called in from the street.

For these twenty-two men and women there was only one case at the moment.

An unidentified man with four confirmed kills was threatening the lives of three other people; three females who investigators believed to be under the age of eighteen.

They did not yet have ID on any of the potential victims.

The whiteboard was divided into seven columns. From left to right:

> Elise Beausoleil. The Garden of Flowers.
> Monica Renzi. The Girl Without a Middle.
> Caitlin O'Riordan. The Drowning Girl.
> Katja Dovic. The Girl in the Sword Box.

The next three columns were blank.

AT 12:35 AM Captain Lee Chapman walked into the briefing room. A man stood next to him.

"This is Mr. Arthur Lake," Chapman said. "He is the president of the Philadelphia chapter of the International Brotherhood of Magicians. He has graciously agreed to help us."

In his early sixties, Arthur Lake was well-dressed in a tan cotton blazer, dark chocolate slacks, polished loafers. His hair was a little long, a pewter gray. In addition to his duties at the IBM, he was an investment counselor at Wachovia.

After the introductions were made, Byrne asked, "Have you seen the videos?"

"I have," Lake said. "I found them most disturbing."

He would get no argument from anyone in the room.

"I'll be happy to answer any and all questions you may have," Lake added. "But I need to say something first."

"By all means, sir."

Lake took a moment. "My hope is that this . . . these *events* do not reflect on my profession, my community, or any of the people within it."

Byrne knew where the man was going. He understood. "I can assure you: no one in this room thinks that. No one in the department thinks that."

Lake nodded. He seemed a little more at ease. For the moment.

"What can you tell us about what you've seen on these videos?" Byrne asked.

"Two things, really," Lake said. "One I think will help at this moment, the other I'm afraid will not."

"Good news first."

"Well, first off, I recognize all four illusions, of course. There's nothing really different or exotic going on here. Blackstone's Garden of Flowers, Houdini's Water Torture Cell, or a variation on it, the Sword Box, the Girl Without a Middle. They've been known by different names, have had many variations over the years, but the effects are very similar. They are performed all over the world. From small cabarets and clubs to the biggest venues in Las Vegas."

"Do you recognize any of the devices?" Byrne asked. "What I mean by that is, do you know any of them by manufacturer?"

"I'd have to see the videos a few more times to tell you that. Bear in mind, almost all of the larger stage illusions are manufactured by rather small specialty companies. As you might imagine, there is not a lot of call for them, so they are not mass produced. When you get into smaller devices—devices used for coin, card, and silk magic, the staples of close-up—the demand grows. Stage magic devices are quite often extremely sophisticated, manufactured to highly detailed blueprints and exacting specifications. They are made in relatively small wood and machine shops all over the world."

"Do any of these smaller manufacturers come to mind?" Byrne asked.

Lake rattled off four or five names. Tony Park and Hell Rohmer immediately began Internet searches.

"And the bad news?" Byrne asked.

"The bad news is that I cannot identify the illusionist. At least not yet."

"What do you mean?"

"The world of magic is a vast but tightly knit network, Detective. In a short amount of time I can be in touch with magicians all over the world. There are hundreds of archivists in this network. If this person is or was a performer, someone will know him. In fact, there is a man here in Philadelphia who has one of the largest archives of Philadelphia magic history in the world."

"Is there a magician working today that has all of these illusions in one act?"

Lake thought for a few moments. "No one comes to mind. Most of the well-known acts today are either full scale Vegas or television acts—David Blaine, Criss Angel, Lance Burton. On the stage, high-tech is the order of the day."

"What about the term 'The Seven Wonders?'" Byrne asked. "Have you heard of this?"

"The Seven Wonders does ring a bell, but I can't place it. If it was an act, it was a small one."

"So, after seeing these four illusions, are you saying that there is no way you can predict what might be next? What the next three might be?"

"I'm afraid not. I can make a list of other well-known illusions, but it would be many more than three. It would be in the dozens. Probably more."

Byrne nodded. "One more thing. He said 'Here's a clue. He flies between Begichev and Geltser.' Do these names mean anything to anyone?"

Everyone shook their heads, including Arthur Lake.

"Any idea how to spell those names?" Tony Park asked.

"No," Byrne said.

Park began to key in possibilities on the computer.

"Let me make a few calls, send a few e-mails," Lake said. "I'll get you some answers. Is there somewhere I can do that?"

"Absolutely," Byrne said. "But are you sure you'll be able to make contact at this hour?"

Arthur Lake smiled. "Magicians tend to be creatures of the night."

Byrne nodded, glanced at Hell Rohmer, who shot to his feet.

"Right this way, sir."

While Hell Rohmer led Lake to an office, Ike Buchanan stepped forward.

Wiry and thin, gray-haired, he was now a thirty-five year veteran. He'd been wounded in the late seventies, a working-class kid who had clawed his way up to a command. He had more than once gone to bat for Jessica. She was both happy and saddened that Sgt. Dwight Buchanan was going to retire in less than a month. He could have coasted to the end, but here he was in the midst of battle, as always. He held in his hands an evidence bag. Inside was Monica Renzi's necklace. Jessica wondered if this was Ike Buchanan's Cheerio.

He stood in front a large blowup map of North Philadelphia, specifically the area known as the Badlands.

"I want ten detective teams on the street," Buchanan said. He pinned ten pushpins on the map. "The first five teams will be deployed at the four corners of the Badlands—North Broad and Spring Garden, North Broad and Erie, Erie and Front Street, Front Street and Spring Garden, along with a team near Norris Square. The other five teams will ring the center.

"If this is going down in East Division, I want gold badges at the scene in ninety seconds or less. Sector cars from the Twenty-fourth and Twenty-fifth will be patrolling and monitoring J-Band. Detective Park and Sergeant Rohmer will work the computers. Any request for information should go directly to them. AV Unit will have eyes glued to the cams."

Buchanan scanned the sea of anxious faces, looking for questions, comments. None came.

"It looks like there are three girls in jeopardy out there," he said. "They are our responsibility now. Find them. Find this man. Shut him down."

SIXTY-NINE

THE SOUNDS CAME TO HER IN WAVES. AT FIRST SHE THOUGHT IT WAS Rip. When her dog had been a puppy he got out of his small plaid bed every morning at dawn, parked himself at the foot of her bed, tail in motion, thumping the side of the box spring. If that didn't wake her, he jumped onto her bed and positioned himself, paws out front, right by her ear. He wouldn't bark, wouldn't growl, wouldn't whine, but the sound of his breathing—not to mention the aroma of puppy breath— would eventually wake her up.

Lilly realized it wasn't Rip. She wasn't home.

She was in Hell.

The last thing she remembered was getting in the man's car. He called his wife. Then there was a strong chemical smell, and everything went black. Had they been in an accident? She did a quick inventory of arms and limbs. She wasn't hurt.

Opening her eyes, the first thing she saw was a bronze chandelier hanging from some sort of plaster medallion on the ceiling. She was in a bed, covered with a white down comforter. The room was dim and hot. It felt like night. She threw off the covers, tried to sit up. Her head felt ready to fall off. She lay back down, and it all came back to her. He had drugged her somehow. She had trusted him, and he had drugged her. She felt the nausea rise in her throat, but battled it back.

She looked around the room, gauging distances, heights. The two windows were both covered in dark green drapes. There were also two doors. One had locks. The other must be a closet. There was a dresser with a mirror, two nightstands, one lamp. A big painting on the wall. That was it.

She was about to try sitting up once again when she heard quick-moving footsteps outside the door. She pulled the comforter up to her neck, half-closed her eyes.

Keys turned in the locks. Moments later, he entered the room, turned on a lamp. It cast the room in a warm ginger glow. Lilly did not stir. She wanted him to think she was still out of it.

When his back was to her, she risked opening her eyes. She watched him fuss and straighten things—the vase on the dresser, the hem of the down comforter, the pleats of the drapes. He adjusted the painting for what seemed like the dozenth time. She wanted to jump from the bed, claw his fucking eyes out, but she was far too weak to try anything at the moment. She needed a clear head. She needed to think straight. She might only get one shot.

She kept her breathing slow and steady, her eyes almost completely shut. He stood at the foot of the bed for the longest time, just watching her. It was so quiet she could hear her heartbeat in the down pillow.

After a few minutes, he checked his appearance in the mirror, opened the door, stepped through, and closed it. Lilly heard a key turn in a lock, then a second key. Footsteps padding down the hall.

Then, silence.

| 12:59 AM |

Pᴇᴏᴘʟᴇ ʟɪɴᴇᴅ ᴛʜᴇ sᴛʀᴇᴇᴛs ᴏғ Nᴏʀᴛʜ Pʜɪʟʟʏ. Rᴀɪɴ ᴡᴀs ɪɴᴛᴇʀᴍɪᴛ-
tent, mosquitoes swarmed in dense clouds, music played on car
stereos, blunts were cupped and hidden. Those gathered on Broad
Street, some with binoculars in hand, would every so often point at the
bright red clock face on the City Hall tower. What *next*, Philly?

The story had been splashed across all the local television stations,
starting with a break-in during the late-night talk shows. Two stations
had set up three cameras each, with a live feed to their websites. Every
so often there would be a cutaway shot to the red clock on the tower at
City Hall. It was like a demented version of New Year's Eve with Dick
Clark.

Jessica was always amazed at how fast the media got the down and
dirty on things. She wondered how glib and hip these reporters and an-
nouncers would be if it were their daughters out there in the hands of a
vicious psychopath, just how willing they would be then to play their
stupid and dangerous ratings games.

They drove north on Fifth Street, past Callowhill and Spring Garden, past Fairmount, Poplar, and Girard. Jessica scanned the corners,
the faces, the hands.

Was he among them? Was their killer standing on a street corner,
blending into the urban canvas, awaiting the precise moment for his

next play? Had he already *made* his play, and was simply planning his reveal? And if this was the case, how was he going to let them know?

A representative of the mayor's office, along with the police commissioner, the chief inspector of the homicide unit, and the district attorney herself had met in an emergency session at the Roundhouse, discussing, first and foremost, the advisability of shutting down power to the clock. A technician was standing by at City Hall, waiting for word.

Until the girls were found, the consensus was to leave the clock alone. If this madman was in North Philadelphia, and he could see the tower, there was no telling what horrors might be triggered if his plan went awry.

However, there had yet to be any indication that he wanted anything—other than an audience. There had been no demands for ransom, no demands for acquiescence of any kind. Until there was, or until he was identified, there could be no avenue of negotiation.

This was certainly not about money. It was about a compulsive murderer plying his terrible craft.

Security at City Hall had been tripled. SWAT had been deployed, the bomb unit was standing by. K-9 officers and their dogs were in the process of walking every square inch of the building. It was a large task. There were more than 700 rooms at City Hall. Traffic was rerouted on both Broad and Market streets. A police helicopter, one of three headquartered at Northeast Philadelphia Airport, was being prepped, manned, and scrambled.

Initial reports stated that it appeared the intruder had gained access to the clock tower by picking a lock on the access door on the forty-fourth floor. His method of deploying the red face on the clock was a series of red acetate panels connected to a small electric motor, triggered by a wireless transmitter. There was no telling how long the mechanism had been in place, although a longtime City Hall employee—a woman named Antoinette Ruolo—had phoned the police when she saw the news story break, offering a description of a man she said might have stayed behind on one of her tours the previous Friday afternoon. Police artists were in the process of putting together a composite based on her description.

There was still no word from the FBI's Computer Crimes Task Force.

THEY CONTINUED NORTH on Fifth Street until they reached Cumberland, where they pulled over. Whereas all of the patrol cars in the PPD were equipped with laptop computers, the detective cars were not. Before leaving the Roundhouse, Jessica ran down to the AV Unit and grabbed their highest-tech laptop. As they began their search of North Philadelphia, she fired up the computer, opening all the programs she thought they might need to use, then minimized them. Thankfully, the battery was fully charged.

Getting online was another story. Philadelphia did not yet have citywide wi-fi, but there were hotspots all over town.

JESSICA AND BYRNE got out of the car. Byrne took off his tie and jacket, rolled up his sleeves. Jessica doffed her blazer. A few calls went out over police radio. One was a domestic disturbance in Juniata. Another a possible carjacking on Third. Crime goes on.

"This is maddening," Jessica said. "This is absolutely fucking maddening."

Inside the car, Byrne dug around in the backseat, emerging with a large SEPTA map of Philadelphia. He spread it across the hood of the vehicle.

"Okay. Caitlin O'Riordan was here." He circled the area on North Eighth Street where Caitlin's body had been found. "Monica Renzi." He circled Shiloh Street. "Katja Dovic." Ninth Street. "Elise Beausoleil." Cambria. "What's the relationship between these scenes? Not the killings. But the crime scenes."

Jessica had been staring at these map locations for days. Nothing clicked. "We need to see this from above," she said.

"Can we get a wi-fi signal here?"

Jessica took the laptop out of the car, opened it, launched a web browser. She clicked on a bookmark. It was slow, but it came in. "Yeah," she said. "We're hot."

Byrne got on the phone to Hell Rohmer.

"Can you send us a graphic of the overhead map of North Philly?"

"All of North Philly?"

"No," Byrne said. "Just isolate the areas where the victims were found. I want a good look at all the buildings together."

"You got it. Two minutes."

Byrne clicked off. They watched the streets. They scanned the channels. They paced. They waited.

SEVENTY-ONE

Swann knew Lilly had been awake. He always knew. It was a game
she had often played himself as a child. His father would have his
small conclaves at Faerwood, finding himself in need of a foil or an object of ridicule at two and three and four in the morning. Swann had
even studied techniques—mostly of Eastern origin—to slow down
one's breath and pulse to further the outward appearance of sleep,
coma, or even death.

He fingered the goatee into place, held it, the smell of the spirit
gum drawing him back to his childhood. He recalled a small club near
Boston, 1978. The dressing room chair had tape on one leg. There
were crumpled McDonald's bags in the corner. His father played to an
audience of ten people.

Swann tied his tie, put on an older raincoat. After all, he could not
be glimpsed in North Philadelphia looking like the master of cere-
monies at a bizarre gathering of aging conjurers.

He flipped off the makeup mirror lights. The lights slowly died, as
did the memories.

The van sat waiting for him in the garage. In the back was Patricia
Sato, his lovely Odette. She was the girl in the Sub Trunk. He had built
it to exacting specs. There was no air inside.

Moments later, observing all traffic laws, Joseph Swann—also known as the Collector—drove to the Badlands.

SEVENTY-TWO

THEY RECEIVED THE FILE VIA E-MAIL. JESSICA OPENED THE GRAPHIC PRO-
gram on the laptop. Moments later the screen showed a section of
North Philadelphia. It was an aerial photograph of a zone that included
all the crime scenes.

What tied these four buildings together? What had made their
killer choose these locations?

They were all abandoned properties. Two numbered streets; two
named streets. Earlier, Tony Park had run the street addresses. He had
tried a hundred permutations. Nothing had leapt out.

They looked at the front elevation of the crime scenes. All four
were three stories tall; three were brick, one wood. One, the Eighth
Street address—where Caitlin O'Riordan had been found—had a corrugated metal roll door. All had boarded up windows on the first floors,
all were covered in graffiti. *Different* graffiti. Three had rusted air con-
ditioners lag-bolted next to the front windows.

"Ninth Street and Cambria have panel doors," Jessica said.

Byrne circled the doors on the digital photographs of the buildings.
Two buildings had steps, three had awnings. He circled these, too. Element by architectural element they compared the buildings. None of
the structures were exactly alike, none were completely different. Different colors, different materials, different locations, different eleva-
tions.

Jessica looked at the support pole in front of the door on Eighth Street. A *support* pole. She looked at the other buildings. All three had at one time had support columns in front of the entrance, but now only had sagging, slanted rooms above the entry. It hit her. "Kevin, they're all corner buildings."

Byrne put four photographs on the hood of the car in front of the laptop. Each crime scene was at least part of a corner building in a block of four or more structures. He compared the photographs to the overhead shot on the LCD screen.

Pure geometry.

"Four triangles," Byrne said. "Four buildings that appear to be triangles from above."

"It's the city," Jessica said.

"It's the city," Byrne echoed. "He's making a tangram puzzle out of the city of Philadelphia."

SEVENTY-THREE

L ILLY HAD HEARD THE VEHICLE PULL AWAY FROM THE HOUSE, BUT SHE dared not move. She counted off three minutes. When she heard nothing else she slipped out of bed. Her shoes were neatly arranged at the footboard. She put them on.

Her legs were a little wobbly, but she soon recovered her balance.

She moved to the window, gently pushing aside the velvet curtain. Beyond the iron bars she saw streetlights through the trees, but little else. She wondered what time it was. Outside was pitch-black. It could be 10:00 PM or 4:00 AM. It suddenly occurred to her that, for her whole life, she had always known where she was and what time it was. Not knowing these two simple things was as unsettling as any of part of this predicament.

Lilly turned, got a better look at the room. It was small, but nicely decorated. Everything looked like an antique. There were two drawers in the nightstand nearest to her. She pulled on the handle of the top drawer, but the drawer didn't move. Must be stuck, she thought. She pulled again, a little harder. Nothing. She tried the drawer below, with the same result. She walked around the bed to the other nightstand. The drawers were all nailed or glued shut. She gently shook the table, but she heard nothing inside.

It was as if she were in a zoo, or a museum replica of a bedroom. Everything was fake. Nothing was real, nothing worked. Fear wormed its way up from her stomach. Taking a few deep breaths, she tried to calm herself, then stepped up to the door and pounded on it with the heel of her hand. She put her ear to the surface.

Silence.

She looked at the bed. It was a single with a polished brass head-board. She lifted the down comforter and sheets. The frame was metal. If she could get the frame apart somehow, she could break the windows and start screaming. She didn't think she was close enough to another house to be heard, but you never knew. Besides, if she could get off one of the slats, she could use it as a weapon. She got down on her knees, felt beneath the bed. It all seemed to be welded together into one solid piece.

Fuck.

She sat on the nightstand and looked at the large painting next to her. It was of some castle on a hillside, surrounded by lush forest and flocking birds. Must be nice, she thought. The painting was crooked again. She must have brushed up against it. Without getting up from the nightstand, she reached out, pushed on the edge of the huge gilded frame.

She heard a noise, a low reverberating sound. She ran to the window. No headlights slicing through the darkness, coming or going. Either he had already pulled into the driveway and garage, or it was not a vehicle. The sound continued, growing a little louder. It was not a car. It was in the *room.*

Suddenly it stopped. Lilly glanced back at the wall opposite the door, and saw a passageway. A small door in the middle of the wall.

Lilly rubbed her eyes and looked again. She was not hallucinating.

No way it had been there before. Cautiously approaching, Lilly stopped at the door first, listened to the hallway. Still quiet. A loud noise made her jump.

The passageway was gone. Closed up.

She felt along the paneled wall, but there was no catch, no seam. It had vanished.

IT TOOK HER TEN MINUTES to figure out the sequence of events that led to the noise and the revelation of the door in the wall.

She had been sitting on the edge of the nightstand, her feet on the floor. She had reached over and pushed on the edge of the painting.

She did it all again, exactly the same way. A few seconds later the panel raised, and there was the little door again. It seemed to lead into a dark room, a dark space, a dark corridor, but none of that really mattered to Lilly. What mattered was that it was big enough for her to crawl through.

This time, she did not hesitate.

Before the panel could slide shut again, she crossed the room. She propped her shoes in the opening, entered the portal, and slipped into the blackness beyond.

SEVENTY-FOUR

1:40 AM

Tangram puzzles were five triangles, one square, and one paral-lelogram. According to the book, these pieces could be arranged into a virtually endless number of shapes. If the Collector was making a tangram puzzle out of the rooftops of North Philadelphia, which problem was he using?

All four of the crime scenes were corner buildings—essentially triangles. A parallelogram could be seen as a diamond. If their theory was correct, it would leave one more triangle, one square, and one diamond.

If they could piece together the first four crimes scenes in some sort of a coherent order, based on their geographic location and relevance to each other—in an order that corresponded to a particular tangram problem—they might be able to predict the location of the next three. It was a huge long shot—but at the moment it was all they had.

Byrne raised Josh Bontrager and Dre Curtis on the radio. They needed more eyes on this.

Byrne stared at the screen, at the map, his eyes roaming the shapes of the buildings, their relationships to one another. He closed his eyes for a moment, recalling the puzzle pieces in Laura Somerville's apartment, the feel of the ivory.

Moments later, Bontrager and Dre Curtis pulled up, exited their car.

"What's up?" Bontrager asked.

Byrne gave them a quick rundown. Bontrager reacted with a young man's enthusiasm for the theory. Curtis, although accepting, was more skeptical.

"Let's hear some ideas," Byrne said. "Some words or concepts that might apply. Something that might relate to the puzzle he's making."

"He's a magician," Bontrager said. "An illusionist, a conjuror, a trickster."

Jessica reached into the back of the car. She retrieved the three books by David Sinclair that Byrne had purchased from Chester County Books. She opened the book of tangram and began to run through the index. There were no problems that related to magicians.

"Cape, wizard, wand, top hat," Curtis said. "Cards, coins, silks."

Jessica flipped pages of the index, shook her head. "Nothing even close."

"How about a castle?" Bontrager asked. "Isn't there a Magic Castle somewhere?"

"Here's a castle," Jessica said. She found the page in short order, flipped the book open. The tangram problem, in silhouette, looked to be a tall pagoda, with a tiered tower and multiple eaves. If the first four crime scenes represented the bottom of the problem, it could not be this diagram. There had to be at least two triangles at the top.

"What about the illusions themselves?" Curtis asked. "The Sword Box, the Garden of Flowers, the Water Tank?"

Jessica scanned the index again. "Nothing like that."

Byrne thought for a moment, poring over the map. "Let's work backwards. Let's start with the shapes themselves, see if they match a pattern."

Jessica tore the center section from the book, handed each of the other detectives ten or so pages of problems. They gathered around the map they had received from Hell Rohmer, eyes searching, matching shapes. Every so often, each of the detectives glanced at their watches. Time was passing.

BYRNE STEPPED AWAY from the car. Rain fell again. The other detectives grabbed everything from the car, crossed the street, and entered an all but empty twenty-four-hour diner called Pearl's. They set up on the counter in front of an apprehensive fry cook.

Soon after, Byrne walked in. He finger-walked his notebook, finding David Sinclair's cell phone number, and punched it in. Sinclair answered. Identifying himself, Byrne apologized for the late hour. Sinclair said it was fine, he was awake.

"Where are you?" Byrne asked.

"I'm in Atlanta. I have a book signing tomorrow."

"Do you have e-mail access right now?"

"I do. I'm in my hotel room. They have high-speed access here. Why, do you want to—"

"What's your e-mail address?"

David Sinclair gave it to him.

"Can you hang on one minute?" Byrne asked.

"Sure."

Byrne raised Hell Rohmer on the handset. He gave him David Sinclair's e-mail address. "Can you make a composite of the four buildings, and outline them in some way?"

"I'll drag it into PhotoShop and put a red line around the edges. Will that work?"

"That'll work," Byrne said. "Can you save it as a file and e-mail it to this guy?"

Byrne gave him the address.

"I'm on it," Hell said. "Shouldn't take more than two minutes."

Back on his cell, Byrne told David Sinclair to expect the file.

"If you don't get the file in five minutes, I'd like you to call me back at this number," Byrne said. "I'll also give you a second number if, for some reason, you don't reach me." Byrne gave the man his and Jessica's cell numbers.

"Got them. One question."

"Go."

"This is about the breaking news story out of Philly, isn't it? It's on CNN."

There was no point in dancing around it. They needed this man's help. "Yes."

Sinclair was silent for a few moments. Byrne heard him draw a deep breath, release it. "Okay," he said. "One more question."

"I'm listening."

"What exactly am I looking for?"

"A developing pattern," Byrne said. "A problem. A tangram problem."

"Okay. Let me look at it. I'll get back to you."

Byrne clicked off. He turned his attention to the man behind the counter. "You have today's paper?" he asked the wide-eyed fry cook.

No response. The man was all but catatonic.

"The paper. Today's *Inquirer*?"

The man slowly shook his head. Byrne looked to the back of the diner. There was only one customer. He was reading the *Daily News*. Byrne stormed to the rear, grabbed it out of the man's hands.

"Hey!" the man said. "I was reading that."

Byrne dropped a five on the table. If everyone got out of this alive he would consider it a bargain. He handed each of the detectives a pair of sheets and a pair of shapes to create. He kept one. In a few moments they had all seven shapes.

Josh Bontrager's cell phone rang. He stepped outside.

Byrne put the pieces on the floor. Five triangles, one square, one diamond. Jessica put the torn pages from the tangram book along the length of the counter.

Page after page of tangram problems, all categorized by country of origin and puzzle designer. There were jewelry, vessels, tools, animals, musical instruments, buildings. One page was devoted to plants. Another to mountains.

"The first four crime scenes were here." Byrne pushed the newspaper triangles together in the relative placement to each other. All put together, the overall shape looked like a capsized boat. Or a mountain range. He moved two shapes up, two down. Now it resembled a clock or bell tower.

Bontrager stepped back inside. "I just talked to Lieutenant Hurley. He heard back from the FBI."

"What do we have?" Byrne asked.

"They said they're closing in on a location for the GothOde server. It looks like it's not in Romania after all. It's in New York."

"When do they think they might have it?"

"They said sometime in the next two hours or so."

Byrne looked at his partner, then at his watch, then at his cell phone.

They had less than twenty minutes.

SEVENTY-FIVE

L ILLY WAS IN A LONG, DARK SHAFT. IT WAS BIG ENOUGH FOR HER TO crawl through, but not by much. The walls were made of wood. It was not a heat duct of any sort.

Lilly was not particularly claustrophobic, but the combination of utter darkness and the thick, hot air of the passageway made her feel entombed. She did not know how far she had gone, nor did she see any end. More than once she thought it would be best to go back to the room and take her chances there, but the passageway was not large enough for her to turn around. She'd have to back up all the way. In the end, the decision was a no-brainer.

She continued forward, stopping every so often, listening. Music came from somewhere. Classical music. She heard no voices. She had no sense of time.

After what felt like minutes of edging through the passage she came to a sharp right turn, and felt a breeze. Thin light spilled down from above. Lilly looked up and saw an even narrower passage, too small to pass through. It led to an iron grate. She tried to reach it but it was just beyond her fingertips.

And that was when she heard the crying.

The grate appeared to be a floor register. The crying seemed to be coming from that room. Lilly banged on the wall of the shaft, listened. Nothing. She banged harder, and the crying stopped.

There *was* someone in there.

"Hello?" Lilly whispered.

Silence. Then the rustling of material, the padding of footsteps.

"Hello?" Lilly repeated, this time louder.

Suddenly, the register went dark. Lilly looked up. She came face-to-face with a girl.

"Oh my God," the girl said. "Oh my God!"

"Not so loud," Lilly said.

The girl calmed herself. Her crying faded to the occasional sob. "My name is Claire. Who are you?"

"I'm Lilly. Are you hurt?"

The girl didn't answer right away. Lilly supposed "hurt" was a relative thing. If this girl had been kidnapped, like Lilly had been, it was bad enough.

"I'm . . . I'm okay," Claire said. "Can you get me out of here?"

The girl looked about sixteen or seventeen. She had long strawberry-blond hair, fine features. Her eyes were puffed and red. "Have you searched the room?" Lilly asked. "Have you looked for a key?"

"I tried, but all the drawers are glued shut."

Tell me about it, Lilly thought. She glanced ahead. The endless, ink-black shaft glared back. She looked at Claire. "Do you have any idea where we are?"

"No," Claire said. She started sobbing again. "I just met this guy in the park. He told me there was a campsite nearby. I walked with him through the woods, and the next thing I knew I was in bed. In this room."

My God, Lilly thought. How many girls were here? "Look," she whispered. "I'm going to get us out of here."

"How?"

Lilly had no frigging idea. Not at the moment. "I'll try to find a way."

"I'm scared. He came in before. I pretended I was still knocked out. He left a dress in the room."

"What kind of dress?"

Claire hesitated. Her tears returned in full. "It looks like a wedding dress. An old wedding dress."

Jesus, Lilly thought. *What the hell is* that *about?* "Okay. Hold tight."

"You're not leaving me, are you?"

"I'll be back," Lilly said.

"Don't go!"

"I have to. I'll be back. Don't make any noise."

Lilly hesitated for a few moments, not really wanting to leave, then continued forward. If her bearings were right, she was heading toward the back of the house. She hadn't sensed an incline or a decline, so she was probably still on the second floor. The sound of the classical music had faded to silence, and all Lilly could hear now was the scrape of her knees along the floor of the shaft, and the sound of her own breathing. The air was getting hotter.

She took a break, the sweat pouring off her. She lifted her T-shirt, wiped her face. After a full minute, she started moving again. Before she got ten feet she sensed another opening above her. It wasn't anything dramatic, just a change in the atmosphere. She ran her hand along the ceiling of the shaft, and felt—

A ladder?

Lilly slowly stood up. Her knees popped, and in the confines of the space, the sound was like gunfire. She reached out. It *was* a ladder. There were only five or six rungs. Above them, something solid. She gently pushed on it. It lifted an inch. She eased it all the way open, took a deep breath, then climbed the ladder. The rush of fresh air was dizzying. She lifted herself out of the hole, into another nearly pitch-black space. She had no idea how large a room it was. The air was cool and damp, and there was a sour smell of licorice and body odor. It took some time to allow her eyes to adjust to the scant light. She made out a few shadows—an armoire, perhaps; a cheval mirror.

Suddenly, there was a sound behind her. Heavy footsteps on a bare floor. Each step was punctuated with something that sounded like the screech of a wheel that needed oil.

Clump, squeak, clump, squeak.

Lilly couldn't see a thing. The sounds drew closer.

Clump, squeak, clump, squeak.

Someone was walking across the dark room.

Lilly felt her way, crawling through the blackness. She came across something that might have been a bed, or a large sofa. She crawled beneath it, and held her breath.

Clump, squeak.

SEVENTY-SIX

JESSICA STOOD ON THE SIDEWALK IN FRONT OF THE DINER. THE RAIN had backed off, but the sidewalk steamed. Watching a pair of sector cars troll up the street, she wished she could be in one of them, just a rookie again. There would be none of the weight, none of the responsibility. She glanced at her watch. They would never make it. She had never felt this angry or frustrated in her life.

Byrne banged on the window, beckoning her inside. Jessica nearly jumped. She stepped inside the restaurant.

All seven pieces of the puzzle were close to each other on the floor. Next to them was the SEPTA map. Byrne tapped a location on the map. "Here's where we are in relation to the first four crime scenes." He pointed to the triangle on the lower left. "Slide it up, Josh."

Bontrager slid the triangle northeast.

"A lot of these problems combine two of the triangles to make a square, right?" Byrne asked.

"Right," Jessica said.

"So, let's assume for a second he is saving the real square for last." North Philly had a lot of squares—Norris, Fotterall, Fairhill. The city at large had dozens. "If it's a triangle, and it fits here, it can only be two places." Byrne knelt down, picked up the map, circled two corner buildings with a felt tip pen. "These are the only two corner triangular buildings in this whole area. What do you think?"

Jessica looked at the shapes as they related to the whole. It was a possibility. "I agree, if his next move is another triangle it would have to be one of these two."

Byrne shot to his feet. "Let's move."

The eight detectives spilt into two groups of four. Seconds later, they sped off into the rain.

THIS AREA OF JEFFERSON was blighted and bleak. There were only a few lights on in the scattered freestanding blocks of row houses. Gentrification came slowly to this part of the city, if at all. The block was dotted with boarded up structures, separated by weed-blotted lots, abandoned cars.

At just after 2 AM, two teams pulled up to the address. Byrne checked the street number, then checked it again.

It was a vacant lot. The overhead map showed a building, but there was no telling how old the photograph was. This *had* been a corner building, almost a perfect triangle. They hurried out of their vehicles, scanned the block, the nearby buildings, the empty parcel. And saw it. There, against a low stone wall, at the back of the lot, amid the debris and wild flowers sat a Chinese red lacquer box, decorated with gold dragons.

Josh Bontrager hit the ground at a run. He bolted across the lot, opened the box.

Byrne glanced at his watch. It was 2:02.

Bontrager turned back, and the look on his face told them everything they needed to know. They were too late.

The next piece of the tangram had been placed.

| 2:13 AM |

LILLY CRINGED IN THE DARKNESS. THE FOOTSTEPS HAD DRAWN TO within ten feet or so, and then stopped. She had no idea how much time had passed. Ten minutes, maybe more. She had held her breath as long as she could.

Where had he gone? Had he left this room? Was he in the room with Claire? Had Lilly abandoned the girl and now something bad was happening to her? Unable to wait any longer, Lilly slowly crept out from beneath the bed, got to her feet. She did not know what she was walking into, but could not stay where she had been, just waiting for her terrible fate.

She felt like a blind person. She took a few small steps, feeling the air in front of her. She reached something that felt like a mirror— smooth, cool to the touch.

And that's when the overhead lights came on.

Lilly looked up. She was in an enormous room. The high ceiling was gilded, coffered, but covered in cobwebs. Overhead was a huge bronze chandelier missing half its bulbs.

"Odette."

Lilly spun around. An old man stood behind her. An *ancient* man, next to a portable oxygen unit. His skin was gray, stretched over a skeletal skull. He wore an old silken bathrobe, crusted with food, stained with urine.

In the faint light, Lilly saw the deep red welt around his neck.

She fainted.

SEVENTY-EIGHT

FIVE DETECTIVES STOOD ON THE CORNER, BLANK-FACED. THE SIXTH DE-tective, Kevin Byrne, paced like a wild animal. There was no consoling him. EMS had arrived at the scene, as had an investigator from the medical examiner's office. The girl was pronounced dead at 2:18. There had been no air in the red lacquer trunk. She had most likely suffocated.

They had just over ninety minutes to find the next girl.

Jessica took the laptop out and clicked on the killer's GothOde web page. There were still only four performance videos on the page. The fifth video, the one with the killer in front of City Hall, had been deleted.

"Anything?" Byrne asked.

"Nothing yet."

"We have to think like he does," Bontrager said. "We have to get inside his head. There's one diamond, and one square left."

"I'm open to suggestions here," Byrne said.

The homicide division was an investigative unit that ran on interviews, forensic data, time inside an interrogation room. Everything was quantifiable, except the whims of a madman.

Jessica refreshed the page, over and over again. Finally, there was change.

"There's another one," she said.

Everyone crowded around the laptop.

THE GIRL IN THE SUB TRUNK

The video opened with the same curtains as the first four videos.

This time, center stage, was the Chinese red lacquer box covered with gold dragons. The box was on a pedestal. After a few moments the killer stepped into frame. He wore the same cutaway tuxedo, the same goatee, the same monocle. He stood no closer to the camera.

"Behold the Sub Trunk," he said. He gestured offstage. Moments later a teenage Asian-American girl stepped onto the stage, and then on top of the box. She reached down, picked up a large hoop of silken fabric. She looked terribly frightened. Her hands were shaking. "And behold the lovely Odette," the man said.

The killer walked offstage. The girl lifted the fabric to just beneath her chin. From off camera a shout could be heard.

"One, two, three!"

On three the girl lifted the hoop over her head, then immediately dropped it. It was now the killer standing on the trunk.

Fade to black.

There was no doubt in anyone's mind that the girl in the video was the girl they had just found in the box.

Byrne raised Hell Rohmer on radio. "You watching this?" he asked.

"I'm watching it."

"I want hard copies of that girl's face in every sector car in East Division as fast as possible."

"You got it."

Byrne's phone rang. He belted his handset, answered. It was David Sinclair.

"I'm going to put you on speaker," Byrne said. He put the cell phone on the hood of the car.

"I got your e-mail," Sinclair said. "I think I know what's going on here."

"What is it?"

"This is a pretty famous tangram. The puzzle is in the shape of a bird. A problem invented by Sang-hsia-k'o."

Byrne told Sinclair of the most recent crime scene. He left out the gruesome details.

"Was this anywhere near the other buildings?"

"Yes," Byrne said. "Another corner building."

"Is it northwest of the Shiloh Street address?"

"It is."

"East of Fifth?"

"Just."

"So that makes five triangles."

"Yes."

"And this was the largest so far, so I'm thinking it is the central part of the problem."

Suddenly, the night fell quiet. For a few electrifying moments there was no music, no traffic, no barking dogs, just the sound of a distant barge on the river, just the buzz of the streetlamps overhead. Byrne looked at Jessica. Their eyes met in wordless understanding, and they knew.

They were on the phone with the killer.

The man who called himself David Sinclair was Mr. Ludo.

Jessica walked quickly away, out of earshot. She opened her cell phone, dialed the communications unit. They would begin to triangulate this call.

The killer spoke first.

"In the world of magic, do you know what a flash is, Detective Byrne?"

Byrne remained silent. He let the man continue.

"A flash is where the audience has seen something it was not supposed to see. I know that I just flashed. You did not give me the address of the latest crime scene, so I could not have known it was the largest. Don't pretend you don't know what I'm talking about just so you can buy some time to trace this call. If you do, I will kill the next girl now, while you're listening."

"Okay." Byrne thought of the man sitting across from him at the Magnolia Grill in Chester County. His anger built. He fought it. "What do you want?"

There was no hesitation. "What does any puzzle master want? To be solved. But only by the best and the brightest. Are you the best and brightest?"

Byrne had to keep the man talking. "Hardly. I'm just another flat-foot."

"I doubt that. A flatfoot wound not have seen the Jeremiah Crosley clue and followed it to the Girl Without a Middle."

Thunder rumbled above. A second later, Byrne heard the thunder on the cell phone. The killer was not in Atlanta. The killer was in North Philadelphia.

"Did you see the clock tower?"

"I did," Byrne said. "Nice trick."

The man drew a short breath. There was a nerve here somewhere. Byrne had found it. The first crack.

"Trick?"

"Yeah," Byrne said. "Like that stuff we used to see on the commercials during those late night horror movies. Remember those? The deck of cards that turn into all aces. The multiplying little foam bunnies. 'Tricks anyone can do,' the guy said. 'Magic is easy, once *you* know the secret.' I bought that cheap plastic wand that turns into a flower. It fell apart."

There was a long moment of hesitation. Good and bad. Good because Byrne was getting to the man. Bad because he was unpredictable. And he held all the cards.

"And this is what you think I've done? A trick?"

Byrne glanced at Jessica. She twirled a finger in the air. Keep him talking.

"Pretty much."

"And yet you are there, and I am here. Between us, pretty maids all in a row."

"You have us there," Byrne said. "No argument."

"The question is, can you solve the puzzle in time, Detective? Can you save the last two maidens?"

The man's composure was back.

"Why don't you just tell me where they are, and you and I can meet somewhere, work this out?" Byrne asked.

"What, and give up show business?"

Byrne heard a loud hiss, a crackle in the connection. The storm was moving in.

Jessica took out her pad, wrote on it, dropped it on the car.

It's a land line. We have him.

"By the way. You said the puzzle was a bird. What sort of bird?" Byrne asked.

"The sort that can fly away," the killer said. "Can you hang on for a second? I have to produce a flower."

The man laughed, and the line went dead.

| 2:38 AM |

THE ADDRESS WAS A SMALL, RUN-DOWN FLORIST ON FRANKFORD. A HALF dozen sector cars arrived at the same time. Four departmental cars, eight detectives, Jessica and Byrne among them. In less than a minute they flanked the stand-alone building. It was dark inside. When Jessica and Byrne went around back, they saw the back door wide open. With plenty of probable cause to enter, they did.

Soon the small building was clear. No one was inside. The team stood down.

In a small back room, which doubled as an office and a prep area, was a huge oak desk and an old style desk phone. The receiver was off the hook, lying on its side.

Next to the phone, a flower.

A white lily.

THE OWNER OF THE SHOP, a man named Ernest Haas, looked like he was going to vibrate to death. Despite the number of ADT stickers on doors and windows—stickers he readily admitted he had color-copied and put on the windows, hoping they looked authentic enough to fool burglars—he had no security system, no cameras. They had rousted him and his wife in their small apartment over the shop. Ernest and Ruth Ann Haas had no idea what was going on just below them.

The killer had simply picked the lock on the back door and used the phone. There were myriad prints on the receiver and glass doors that led to the cooler containing the lilies. They had been dusted and rushed back to the crime lab.

Before leaving the Jefferson Street scene Byrne had contacted the communications unit. The phone number "David Sinclair" had given him was a disposable cell phone. Untraceable. Byrne had also given Tony Park the information on Sinclair's publisher. Park was tracking it down now.

JESSICA AND BYRNE STOOD on the corner of Frankford and Lehigh. Byrne's cell rang. It was Hell Rohmer.

"I've been monitoring the GothOde page. There have been another four hundred viewings of the last video. This thing has gone viral. There've also been a few comments, mostly nutcases. What's new, eh? I'm not sure this one guy who posted is any different, but he responded to the 'here's a clue' line."

"What was it?"

"The commenter on the page wrote 'Begichev and Geltser? *Swan Lake?* This guy rox!' It was signed phillybadbwoi. I looked it up. He was right. Begichev and Geltser collaborated with Tchaikovsky on *Swan Lake.* And the lead part in the ballet?"

"What about it?" Byrne asked.

"Her name is Odette."

AT 2:50, IKE BUCHANAN'S CAR drove up in front of the florist shop. Arthur Lake stepped out. He had a handful of e-mail printouts.

"I've contacted a number of my colleagues," Lake said. "The man in the video is known by reputation to some of my contemporaries here in Philadelphia. I've only been in the city about five years. I'm afraid I'd never heard of him."

"What did you learn?"

"Well, for one, as I suspected, this is someone mimicking the look and style of another man who performed in the fifties and sixties. That magician himself would be much, much older now."

"Do you know his name?"

"Not his real name. I have a call in to a man who might know. Onstage he went by the Great Cygne."

The man pronounced the word *seen-yeh.*

"And this older magician was from Philly?" Byrne asked.

"I believe so, although I could not find any specific information on that."

Lake handed Byrne a faded color image of a tall, slender man in a cutaway tuxedo. "This is the only photo I could find. It was downloaded from a German website."

Byrne reached into the car. He took out a pair of photos he found in Laura Somerville's strongbox and compared them to the downloaded photograph. They were identical.

"Rumor was that the Great Cygne was a little unstable," Lake said. "And that he was pretty much shunned by the community at large."

"Why is that?"

"Years ago he invented an illusion called 'The Singing Boy' and sold it to a number of top magicians—claiming exclusivity to each of them—for a great deal of money. When word got out, he was persona non grata in magic circles. No one really saw him after that, I gather."

"The Great Cygne. Can you spell that for me?" Byrne asked.

The man did. It hit Byrne like a sledgehammer.

"If I'm not mistaken," Lake continued, "in French, the word *cygne* means—"

"Swan," Byrne said.

Swan Lake. The puzzle is in the shape of a bird.

"He's building a swan."

EIGHTY

2:55 AM

LILLY SAT IN A CHAIR IN THE CANDLELIT ROOM. THE OLD MAN STROKED her hair, his fingers ice cold. A few moments earlier she had heard something loud—it might have been a slamming door or a backfire—but she dared not ask about it.

She had never been more frightened in her life.

When she looked up at the old man, he was staring at her.

"Who are you?" she asked.

The man looked at her as if she were crazy. He put his shoulders back, lifted his chin. "I am the Great Cygne."

"You called me a name before. What was it?"

"Odette, of course."

"And what is this place?"

Another incredulous look. "This is Faerwood."

"Do you live here?"

The old man got a faraway look. For a moment it appeared as if he might be falling asleep. Then he told Lilly an incredible story.

He told her that his real name was Karl Swann, and that he was once a world-renowned magician, student of the masters, mentor to the greats. He told her that many years ago he'd had a mishap during one of his stage illusions, and accidentally hanged himself. He told her that his son, Joseph, had kept him in this room for more than twenty years, but now he was much better, and was ready to perform all over the world again. He told her that this night would be the Great Cygne's greatest triumph, something called the Fire Grotto.

Lilly tried to digest it all. *Twenty years.* She looked around. The room was crowded with steamer trunks, wooden crates, broken furniture. At one end was an enormous hospital bed with filthy sheets. On the dressers were stacks of food-littered trays. Everywhere were tattered silks, bent linking rings, rusted cups, torn playing cards. The walls were covered with old posters and yellowed news clippings.

"Do you remember the time we played Tulsa?" he asked. "Do you remember Harwelden?"

Lilly shook her head. The man faded in and out. Coherent one moment, gone the next. Earlier she had wandered over to the door, and covertly tried the knob behind her back. It was locked.

"Do you remember Blackstone?" he asked.

Lilly looked at the wall. On it was a framed poster of a man, in caricature, with two small devils at his feet, and another on his shoulder. The name BLACKSTONE was emblazoned across the bottom. There was a smaller legend there, too. Lilly quoted it aloud.

"Blackstone?" she asked. "The greatest necromantic extravaganza on earth?"

The man seemed to come alive. Color rose in his cheeks.

"Yes!" he said. "The greatest magician the world has ever known." The old man struggled to his feet. "It is time to prepare for the stage." He held out his fragile hand. Lilly took it, helping him up.

"What's the Fire Grotto?" Lilly asked.

He assessed her with his milky eyes. "I'll show you."

He crossed the room to a small table, pulled out the drawer, slid it back in. Next to the table a wall panel slid up, revealing a number of wooden file cabinets. There had to be twenty in all.

The old man contemplated the labels for a while, then opened a drawer. He rifled the contents. He soon found an envelope full of photos.

"Here you are at the fair in Baton Rouge," he said.

He showed her an old photograph, a picture of a young woman in a scarlet gown standing next to a box with seven swords sticking out of it. A man in a cape and top hat stood to her right. The man was clearly Karl Swann. A fair-haired young boy stood off to the side. He looked to be about five years old. Lilly recognized his eyes. It was her captor's eyes.

The old man produced a second photograph. "This is Faerwood on the day we moved in. It was earlier this year. Isn't it magnificent?"

Karl Swann proffered a picture of himself and his young son. In the photograph the old man looked young and strong. His son looked sullen.

Earlier this year, Lilly thought. He *is* gone. She turned the photograph to the candlelight, looked at it carefully. It took her breath away. It wasn't the expressions of the man and boy, or the way they seemed to be standing in two different worlds, it was the house itself. The tower, the huge porch, the four chimneys rising into the sky like tortured, barren trees.

Lilly had lived with this image, frozen in her mind, for months.

It's him, she thought. My God, *it's him*. His name is Joseph Swann. She had told him everything, and he had kidnapped her and brought her here.

Lilly steadied herself by putting a hand on the table. She felt nauseated.

"Behold the Garden of Flowers."

Lilly looked at the old man. He was still busy with the file cabinet. He hadn't said a word. The sound had come from behind her. Lilly spun around. The television was now on. On the screen she saw seven rectangles. Six different video feeds playing. In the upper left was something called the Garden of Flowers. Next to it was an illusion called the Girl Without a Middle. When Lilly looked at the third video her heart nearly stopped. She knew the girl in the large water tank. She felt lightheaded again. When she looked back at the screen the last video was playing. There was a girl in a bridal gown being led to a big box. The girl in the video was Claire.

Joseph Swann was a murderer. He was dressing up like his father, and killing girls in a chamber of horrors.

There was one video left on the screen. It was black. For now. Lilly knew exactly who it was for.

Karl Swann rummaged through another drawer. He extracted a folder. Inside the folder were pages and pages of drawings and brittle diagrams, scribbled blueprints. He extracted a single page.

"This," he said, "is the Fire Grotto."

The drawing was of a large box, a cage made of steel and smoked glass. As Lilly ran her eyes over the drawing, she catalogued every corner, every hinge, every latch. "How does it work?" she asked.

Five minutes later, when the old man finished telling her how the illusion worked, and of its spectacular, fiery flourish, Lilly knew all she needed to know about the Fire Grotto. She also knew what was going to happen. Joseph Swann aimed to put her in the box, and set it afire. There was no doubt in her mind.

"You must remember the secret latch on the bottom," the old man said. "This is very important." The old man then held up another yellowed blueprint. "It is quite easy to get lost in Faerwood. There are many rooms here, many machines. If you do get lost, this will help."

Lilly took the old blueprint. She instantly memorized the dimensions, the details, where the doors and hidden stairwells were located, where the switches were. It seemed each room had a secret.

Before she could ask Karl Swann another question, Lilly heard the sound of a car engine. She looked out the barred window. Three stories below a van pulled into the driveway.

Lilly grabbed the blueprint and ran to the corner of the room, to the secret passage. The man stepped in front of her. He put something in her hand. "You will need this."

When she reached the opening, Lilly heard the old man add, "Remember the secret latch. Remember, Odette."

Lowering herself into the dark shaft, Lilly had no idea if she was returning the way she had come. She scrambled forward as fast as she could, banging her knees and elbows. Her hands were slick with sweat. The passageway seemed endless, and even darker than it had earlier. After a full minute she stopped, felt the sides, the ceiling. Had she passed Claire's room? She had no idea. She listened for any change in the hot silence. She heard only her pulse.

She continued onward. The sound of the classical music returned, this time louder. She *was* finding her way back. She was about to stop again when she saw the faint rectangle of light in the distance. She rumbled forward as quickly as she could, emerged through the panel, dashed into the room, gulping the fresh air. She heard footsteps in the hallway outside. A key turned in the lock.

Lilly grabbed her shoes from the opening, letting the panel slide shut. She bolted across the room and dove under the covers as the second key turned. As the door opened, Lilly noticed she had dropped the old blueprint on the floor. She grabbed it, pulled it under the comforter at the last second, her heart racing.

Joseph Swann.

The Fire Grotto.

Lilly did not know how she was going to get out of this, or if she would make it until morning, but she knew one thing for certain.

She could not allow Joseph Swann to get her inside that box.

EIGHTY-ONE

THEY HAD NEARLY ONE HUNDRED ADDRESSES OF PEOPLE NAMED SWAN, more than thirty for Swann. Uniformed officers from virtually every district were pounding on doors, calling in on police radios.

They had gotten word on the publishing house that handled David Sinclair's books. It was a small outfit in Denver. According to the senior editor, no one there had ever met Mr. Sinclair. Sinclair had sent an unagented proposal to them six years earlier, by mail. The editor had spoken to the man many times over the course of the writing and editing of the book, but Sinclair had never come to Denver. They corresponded with the author via a Hotmail account and a street address in Philadelphia, an address that turned out to be a drop box on Sansom Street. Their records showed that the man had rented the box by the year, sending a money order for a year at a time. There was a high turnover rate in employees, and the few who were contacted at this hour could not recall the man who rented box 18909. The initial form that was filled out appeared to be typed on an old IBM Selectric, and the street address and phone number listed were both phony.

Payments from the publishing house were made by company check, made out to David Sinclair. They had never been cashed.

The bookstore in Chester County had no address for him, just the cell phone number the detectives already had. It was a dead end.

At 3:20 AM a department car roared to a stop. It was Detective Nicci Malone. "We've got prints," she said. "They're on that Chinese box."

"Please tell me they're in the system," Jessica said.

"They're in the system. His name is Dylan Pierson."

THE TEAM DESCENDED on a run-down row house near Nineteenth and Poplar. Byrne knocked on the door until lights came on inside. He held his weapon behind his back. Soon the door opened. A heavyset white woman in her forties stood before them, her face puffed with sleep, last night's mascara racooooning her eyes. She wore an oversized Flyers jersey, baggy pink sweats, stained white terrycloth flops.

"We're looking for Dylan Pierson," Byrne said, holding up his badge.

The woman looked from Byrne's eyes, to the badge, back. "That's my son."

"Is he here?"

"He's upstairs sleeping. Why do you—"

Byrne pushed her aside, bulled through the small dirty living room. Jessica and Josh Bontrager followed.

"Hey!" the woman yelled. "You can't just . . . I'll *sue* you!"

Byrne reached into his pocket. Without looking back he tossed a handful of his business cards in the air, and stormed up the stairs.

DYLAN PIERSON WAS NINETEEN. He had long greasy hair, a feeble soul patch below his lower lip, way too much attitude for the time of night and Byrne's mood. On the walls were a mosaic of skateboarding posters: *Skate or Die; A Grind is a Terrible Thing to Waste; Rail Against the Machine.*

Dylan Pierson had been arrested twice for drug possession; had twice gotten away with community service. His room was a sty, the floor covered in dirty clothes, potato chip bags, magazines, questionably stained Kleenex.

When Byrne entered, he had flipped on the overhead light and all but lifted Dylan Pierson from his bed. Pierson was cowering against the wall.

"Where were you tonight?" Byrne yelled.

Dylan Pierson tried to comprehend how his little kingdom had suddenly been invaded by big scary police in the middle of the night. He wiped sleep from his eyes. "I . . . I have no idea what you're talking about."

Byrne took out a picture, a blowup of a computer screen capture of the Collector. "Who is this?"

The kid tried to focus. "I have no idea."

Byrne grabbed his arm, yanked. "Let's go."

"Wait! Jesus. Let me look." He turned on a desk lamp, looked more carefully at the photograph. "Hang on. Hang on. Okay. Okay. I know who this is, man. He looks different with that beard and shit, but I think I know him."

"Who is he?"

"I have no idea."

Byrne reared back, fists clenched.

"Wait!" The kid cowered. "I met him on the street, man. He asked me if I wanted to make some money. It happens to me all the time."

Jessica looked at Nicci Malone, back at Dylan Pierson, thinking, *You ain't all* that, *kid.* Still, he was young, and that counted for a lot on the streets of a city like Philadelphia.

"What are you talking about?" Byrne asked.

"I was hanging by the bus station, okay? On Filbert. You know the bus station?"

"We know the bus station," Byrne said. "Talk. Fast."

"He started talking to me. He pointed at this girl, maybe sixteen or so. Maybe younger. She looked like a runaway. He said if I would go up to her, give her some shit, and he came in like a white knight, he would pay me fifty bucks."

"When was this?" Byrne asked.

"I don't know. Two days ago?" The kid touched his cheek. "He burned my damn face. You should arrest this guy."

Byrne held up a photograph of the Chinese box. "How did your fingerprints get on this?"

"I have no idea."

"Say 'I have no idea' one more fucking time," Byrne said. "Go ahead."

"Wait! Let me think, man. All right. And this is *true*. When I met the guy I sat in his van for a while."

"What color was the van?"

"White. When I first got in he asked if I would move some of his things around in the back. This box was in there, I swear to God."

Byrne paced, kicking clothes and debris out of his way. "Then what happened?"

"Then I got out of the car, walked up to the corner, started talking to the chick."

"Then what? He burned your face?"

"Yeah. Like out of nowhere. And for no reason. When it was all over I met him around the corner and he gave me something."

"What did he give you?"

"A book. He put the fifty inside it."

"He gave you a book."

"Yeah," Pierson said. "I don't really—"

Byrne lifted the kid off the chair like he was a rag doll. "Where the fuck is it?"

"I sold it."

"To who?"

"The Book Nook. It's a used-book store. They're right around the corner."

EIGHTY-TWO

THE BOOK NOOK WAS A USED-BOOK STORE ON SEVENTEENTH STREET. The grimy front window haphazardly displayed comic books, graphic novels, a section of recent best-selling fiction, some vintage board games. There was a single light on inside.

Byrne knocked hard, rocking the glass door. Jessica got on her cell phone. They would find the owner. They did not have that much time, but protocol—

Byrne threw a bench through the door. He threw Dylan Pierson in afterwards, then followed him.

—was clearly not going to be followed.

"What was the name of the book?" Byrne yelled, flipping the light switch, turning on the fluorescents overhead. His fellow detectives scrambled to keep up.

"I don't remember," Pierson replied, picking bits of glass out of his hair. "I think it was something about outer space."

"You *think*?"

Dylan Pierson began to pace. He had no shoes on, and he was hot-footing on the glass. "It . . . it had a red planet on the cover . . . it was something about—"

"Mars?" Bontrager asked.

He snapped his fingers. "Mars. That's it. Mars something. Guy named Hendrix wrote it. I remember the name because I'm really into old school stuff like Jimi—"

Byrne ran down the Science Fiction aisle, found the shelf for authors whose last name begins with H. *Heinlein, Herbert, Huxley, Hoban, Hardin.* And then he found it. *Mars Eclectica.* Edited by Raymond Hendrix. He ran back to the main room. "Is this it?"

"That's it! That's the one! *Dude.* You are *awesome.*"

Byrne handled the book by its edges. He riffled through the pages. Then a second time. There was nothing. No notes inside. Nothing highlighted.

"Are you sure this is the book?" Byrne asked.

"Positive. Although, I gotta say that one looks a lot newer than the book this guy gave me."

Byrne reached for Dylan Pierson's throat. Josh Bontrager was able to step between them. Byrne then flung the book across the store. His eyes roamed the walls, the shelves, the counters. Behind the front desk were a pair of push carts. One of them had a sticky note pasted to the side, with a handwritten *New Books.*

Byrne vaulted the counter. He tore the books off the top shelf of the cart. Nothing. He ripped the books from the bottom shelf. And saw it. *Mars Eclectica.* It was a well-worn copy.

He flipped through the book. It didn't take long. In the table of contents there were two places where something had been cut out with a razor blade. They were sections of author's names.

_____ White, *The Retreat to Mars.*
Robert _____ Williams, *The Red Death of Mars.*

Byrne turned the book to Dylan Pierson. "What's missing here?"

The kid looked. "I have no—I mean, I don't know. I don't read that much."

One by one Byrne showed the page to the other detectives. "Anybody know these people?"

No one knew.

"*Fuck!*"

"The other copy," Jessica said. "Get the other copy of the book."

In a flash Josh Bontrager was at the back of the store, rummaging through the strewn books. He found the book in seconds, and was back.

He put it on the counter next to Byrne's copy. They looked at both versions of the table of contents.

With the missing names, the entries read:

Cecil B. White, *The Retreat to Mars*
Robert **Moore** Williams, *The Red Death of Mars*

"Cecil B. Moore," Byrne said. He looked at Jessica.
"The baseball field," she replied.
They'd found the diamond.

EIGHTY-THREE

THE BASEBALL FIELDS AT CECIL B. MOORE AVENUE AND NORTH Eleventh Street were deserted. The mahogany cabinet sat at home plate. Its glossy surface shone in the light thrown from the sodium streetlamps.

Byrne was out of the car before Jessica could stop it.

"God*damn* it!"

Byrne vaulted across the field, reached the box first. There was no hesitation, no stopping him. He opened the box, stared inside. And froze.

Jessica and Bontrager made it across the field. Jessica saw what her partner was looking at. Inside was a girl, wearing an antique white satin dress. It looked to be a wedding gown from the 1920s or 1930s. A veil covered her face. The bodice of the dress was soaked with her blood.

Byrne reached in, put two fingers to the girl's neck.

"She's alive."

EIGHTY-FOUR

THE AMBULANCE SCREAMED OFF INTO THE NIGHT. THE GIRL HAD LOST A lot of blood, but when the paramedics got her onto the gurney, her pulse was stronger, her blood pressure stable.

Jessica returned to the car, took the laptop out. She refreshed the killer's GothOde page. "It's up." She clicked on the new file. Same red curtains.

PART SIX: THE BRIDAL CHAMBER

She started the video. It already had sixteen viewings.

"Behold the Bridal Chamber," the killer said. He gestured to the mahogany cabinet, which was unquestionably empty, doors wide open. He closed the doors of the cabinet. "And behold the lovely Odette." He held out his hand. A teenage girl walked onto the stage wearing the old bridal gown. She was pretty and thin, with strawberry-blond hair cascading out from beneath her white veil. He kissed her hand, sent her offstage. He then turned the closed cabinet around three times, stepped back, drew a chrome revolver from his pocket and fired it into the cabinet. A moment later, he opened the cabinet to reveal the bride inside.

He waved a hand, and the screen went black.

AT 4:20 Byrne's cell phone rang. He checked the screen. Private number. He knew who it was even before he answered it. The communications unit had put "David Sinclair's" number on autodial, calling it every twenty seconds. They had not, of course, gotten an answer.

Byrne flipped open his phone, remained silent.

"Time is passing, Detective," the killer said.

"Would that were not true," said Byrne, trying to keep his rage in check. "Youth is fleeting."

"I never had a youth, I'm afraid."

"Why don't you stop down at the Roundhouse? We'll trade sob stories. You and me."

The man laughed. "Six Wonders down, one to go."

"Well, that's not exactly true."

Silence. "What do you mean?"

"The Bridal Chamber. Looks like you were left at the altar."

This time, a longer silence.

"We're at the diamond now—this is the diamond, right? The parallelogram part of the tangram puzzle?"

"What about it?"

He didn't deny it. They *were* right. "The girl is alive."

"That's not true. It can't be true."

"I don't make the weather, man. Besides, why would I start lying to you now? It might sully our beautiful friendship."

Silence again. Then the killer raised his voice. He was starting to crack. "It's *not* true. It's *not*. And wait until you see what's next, Detective Byrne. You will never forget it. Never."

The line went dead.

Byrne threw his phone halfway to center field. A few minutes later, Josh Bontrager jogged out to get it.

THEY HAD SIX of the tangram pieces—five triangles and one diamond. The killer had left the bodies of Caitlin O'Riordan, Elise Beausoleil, Monica Renzi, Katja Dovic, and a girl they had just identified as Patricia Sato—a runaway from Albany—in North Philadelphia parcels of land that were in the shape of a triangle. He had left his newest victim, as yet unidentified, still alive, on a baseball diamond. All that was left was the square. They had tried dozens of configurations with the pieces they had, trying to build the swan diagram. The horrifying truth was that just about every building in North Philly was either a rectangle or a square.

AT 4:28 Jessica's phone rang. They were still at the Cecil B. Moore scene. The crime-scene unit was processing the cabinet. It was Tony Park calling.

"Anything on the canvass?" Jessica asked.

"Nothing yet," Park said. "It's late, it's hot, we have a lot of pissed-off people named Swan or Swann in Philadelphia this morning."

"They'll get over it."

"I do have something interesting on what that magician fellow found. Something about Cygne."

"What about it?"

"There's a Galerie Cygne," Park said. "Spelled exactly the same way. It's the only listing in the city with a name even close."

"Where is it?"

"Twenty-fourth and Market."

Tony Park gave her the address. Jessica clicked off, told Byrne. "I'm going to go check on this," she said.

Byrne held up his handset. "Stay on channel."

"You got it."

EIGHTY-FIVE

4:30 AM

SWANN CARRIED THE BOX. IT WAS HEAVY. HE HAD FORGOTTEN HOW heavy it could be.

They were lying to him. It was a trick. *Their* trick. Claire was dead. She was in the Bridal Chamber. They would pay for this.

"*You have failed.*"

"I have not."

"*Acceptance is not enough, Joseph.*"

"It is not just acceptance. It is certainty."

Just about everything was in place for his grand finale. They would forever remember him. He would find a niche in the hierarchy of all things magic, all things puzzling, all things inexplicable. Even Thoreau believed that human beings *require* mystery.

"*People must believe the impossible.*"

"They will believe."

"*All magic is mentalism, Joseph. All magic makes people believe. The effect is in the mind.*"

He could no longer carry the box. He put it down, began to drag it.

"All magic is mentalism," he repeated. "All magic."

He got the box into position. He sat down next to it.

The effect is in the mind.

EIGHTY-SIX

JESSICA PARKED ON MARKET STREET. THE FACADE OF THE THIRTIETH Street train station loomed in the near distance, its lights reflected on the calm surface of the Schuylkill River.

She replayed the last video over and over in her mind. The Bridal Chamber. She thought of the way the girl looked in that antique dress, how frightened she had been. She thought of the blood. She had called the hospital on the way across town. The girl was being prepped for surgery.

Jessica was just about to get out of her car and enter the building when her phone rang. It was Byrne.

"What's up?" Jessica asked.

"We have him."

"We *have* him? What are you talking about? Where?"

"We got a call from the AV Unit two minutes ago. Three street cams saw someone dragging a big box across Nineteenth Street."

"Where on Nineteenth?"

"Right at Logan Circle."

Jessica realized the significance. "It's his square in the tangram puzzle," she said.

"It's his square."

When William Penn planned the development of Philadelphia in the 1600s, he designed five squares—one central square, with four others equidistant from the center. Today those squares are City Hall, Franklin Square, Rittenhouse Square, and Washington Square. The fifth square, located at the midway point between City Hall and the art museum, was originally called Northwest Square. Once a burial site and scene of public executions, the square was renamed Logan Circle in honor of William Penn's secretary James Logan. Logan Circle, Logan Square—it went by both names.

More important, at the moment, was the fountain at the center. Designed by Alexander Calder, it had a name of particular interest to the police right now.

Swann Memorial Fountain.

This is going to be spectacular. It will light up the night.

"Is he still there?" Jessica asked.

"Cams are locked on him. He's sitting at the edge of the fountain. Box is next to him. SWAT is getting into position right now."

Special Weapons and Tactics, headquartered in East Division, generally needed a twenty-four-hour notice for an entry. Getting them to mount an operation on the fly was rare, but it spoke to the urgency of the situation.

"You said there's a box?"

"Big box," Byrne said. "Right next to him."

"Bomb squad on scene?"

"Deploying now."

"Where are we setting up?"

"Nineteenth and Cherry."

Jessica looked at her watch. She hesitated for a moment, then said, "I'm on my way."

Byrne knew the tone. He knew *her.* "Jess. Are you—"

"I'll meet you there."

Before Byrne could say anything more, she folded her phone, and got out of the car.

EIGHTY-SEVEN

5:10 AM

LILLY HAD WAITED UNTIL JOSEPH SWANN LEFT HER ROOM. HE HAD NOT said a word, but he had paced, seemed agitated.

He left a dress for her, a velvet dress on a hanger. It was deep scarlet. Lilly recognized it as the dress the woman was wearing in the photograph Karl Swann had shown her. She imagined she was to wear it. She imagined she, like the other girls in the videos, was supposed to play the part of his assistant, an assistant who did not survive the trick.

She checked the door. Locked, of course. She tried to open the panel in the wall, but it did not work. Had Joseph known she left the room? Did he know she found his father? Had he sealed off her exit?

She glanced around the room. There had to be a dozen candles burning.

She put on the dress.

EIGHTY-EIGHT

5:11 AM

GALERIE CYGNE WAS LOCATED IN THE MARKETPLACE DESIGN CENTER at Twenty-fourth and Market streets. It was a large building, overlooking the Schuylkill River, home to more than fifty exclusive showrooms offering antiques, building products, AV systems, lighting, and wall coverings.

Jessica buzzed the night security guard. She badged him, he let her in. He was in his late fifties, ex-PPD. His name was Rich Gardener. He knew Jessica's father.

Cutting the cop dance short, Jessica got to the point. "What can you tell me about this Galerie Cygne?"

"Not much. Nice-looking stuff. Custom cabinetry, one of a kind furniture. Tables and dressers that cost what I make in a year. It's one of the smaller showrooms here."

"Can I see the place?"

Gardener squared his shoulders, then gestured to the elevators, looking pretty pumped about being back in the game. "Right this way, Detective."

JESSICA AND GARDENER stood in the hallway in front of the long glass wall that was Galerie Cygne. The interior was immaculately clean. The space was sliced with spotlights, highlighting cabinets, armoires, chairs, tables.

"Do you know the owner?" Jessica asked.

"Never met him."

"Have you ever seen him?"

"No. Sorry."

"Do you have a home address for him?"

The man hesitated. "I know you're on the job and all, but I have a job, too, right? I mean, I've run a few warrants in my time. Do you mind if I make a call?"

Jessica glanced at her watch. The team would be taking Logan Circle soon. She would be missed. "Please make it fast."

TWO MINUTES LATER, down in the lobby, Gardener looked up from his computer monitor. "Believe it or not, all correspondence with the owner goes to a post office box."

"There's no home address or other business address?"

"No."

"Is there a name at least?"

"No," Gardener said. "There's usually a page with emergency contact information, stuff like that. In case there's a fire, flood, act of God. But, for some reason, it's gone."

"Gone."

"As in erased. I know that there was an address here, because sometimes FedEx and UPS would have a delivery and the owner had to have it sent to his or her house."

"You're saying that the page has been deleted?"

"Yeah. But I've talked to one of the drivers who went out there once. Real horror-movie nut. Scared of his own shadow. Says the place is really spooky."

"Spooky how?"

"Said it's the old Coleridge place. I think they call it Faerwood or something. Said it's haunted."

"Where is this Faerwood?"

"No idea."

Jessica pointed to the monitor. "Can we get on the Internet?"

Rich Gardener looked at his watch, over his shoulder, back. "*We* are not supposed to. But seeing as you're Pete Giovanni's daughter and all."

JESSICA FOUND THE REFERENCE immediately on one of the wiki sites. Artemus Coleridge (1866–1908) was an engineer and a draftsman. He worked for the Pennsylvania Railroad. In 1908 he hanged himself from a roof beam at the huge North Philadelphia house he had built eight years earlier, a twenty-two-room Victorian mansion called Faerwood.

CLICK HERE TO SEE A PHOTOGRAPH OF FAERWOOD, the webpage teased.

Jessica clicked. The image ran ice through her veins.

She'd been there.

| 5:20 AM |

S WANN REMEMBERED A TIME WHEN HIS FATHER PLAYED A VENUE IN West Texas. The Great Cygne had performed a close-up routine at a honky-tonk called Ruby Lee's. When his father refused to reveal the secret of a card routine based on Dai Vernon's Cutting the Aces, he had been taken out back, beaten, his entire act stolen out of the car.

Twenty minutes later, perhaps in drunken remorse, the three men who'd assaulted the Great Cygne came outside with food for the man's young son. As his father lay unconscious in a dusty alley, Joseph ate chicken-fried steak and drank Coca Cola.

It had been this hot that night.

Swann put his hand on the box. Fire and water. Water and flame. There were many variations of the fire illusions. The cremation illusions. Some call the illusion Suttee, the term coming from the name of the goddess Sati who immolated herself because she could not stand living with her father's humiliation over her husband Shiva.

Some illusionists called the effect She, a title inspired by a strange little book by H. Ryder Haggard.

The Great Cygne called it the Fire Grotto. The effect was similar to the Sub Trunk, but that was the original version. This version would be different.

Swann sat in the shadow of the box. The red clock ticked. It was time. He would open the box and begin the final illusion of what the world would know, for as long as history was recorded, as the Seven Wonders.

| 5:25 AM |

T HE HOUSE SEEMED LARGER THAN IT HAD IN THE DAYTIME, MORE FOR-
bidding. Where the grounds had seemed merely unkempt in bright
sunlight, they now seemed populated with specters, with hunkering ap-
paritions in the darkness.

Jessica had printed out the photograph from the website. Faerwood, in 1908, was magnificent—sculpted hedges, a small well-tended
orchard, even a waterfall. Now it was a ruin.

Jessica had her handset live, an earphone in her ear. The SWAT
team had not yet moved in on Logan Circle. Any second now. The detectives and support personnel were assembled. Byrne had not yet
called her.

She had turned off her headlights halfway up the winding driveway,
cut the engine, drew her weapon, and approached the crumbling porch.
For the second time in as many days.

"I remember now. Last year a pair of policemen came around."

Jessica wondered how many places there were like this. Places hidden from view. Places where time had stopped. She put her ear to the
front window. At first it was cold silence, then she heard music. Someone was home. Was she chasing a ghost, or was this the place of a monster?

She rang the doorbell, stepped back, waited. No one answered. She shone her flashlight up the vine-covered wall. The sinister windows stared back. Next she tried the rusted iron knocker. Same result.

She rounded the house to the east, stepping through the tall brush, the high grass, skirting a small wooden gazebo. A multi-car garage was attached to the house. She stepped up to the doors, peered inside, saw a van, along with three late-model cars. One empty bay.

She continued around to the rear of the property. Crumbling stone benches squatted next to the path.

She looked at the back of the house, at the windows on the second floor. Half the windows were barred, even though there were no fire escapes. No way to get in.

They were not there to keep people from breaking in, she realized. They were there to there to keep people from breaking out.

A shadow danced behind one of the grimed windows. There was movement in one of the rooms.

Jessica stepped back, nearly stumbling over an ancient rusted sundial. She saw the curtains part. A figure emerged in the darkness. It looked to be a young girl.

Jessica got on her handset, hit the panic button. All PPD handsets were equipped with GPS, along with a little red button that, when activated, would call for every available cop in the division, along with their mothers.

Jessica could not wait. She looked around the immediate area, found a fist-sized rock, broke the window, reached inside, and unlocked the door.

She stepped into the house.

NINETY-ONE

LOGAN CIRCLE WAS DESERTED, EXCEPT FOR THE LONE FIGURE SITTING at the edge of the fountain, facing south, the large box next to him, like some strange tableau on Easter Island. The water pressure to the fountains had been cut. The lights were off. Byrne had grown up in Philly, had been to Logan Circle many times, starting with field trips to the art museum and the Franklin Institute as a child. Now the place looked like a Martian landscape, completely foreign to him. He had never seen it look so desolate, so vacant.

Sector cars and detective cars slowly approached from Vine Street, Race Street, North Nineteenth Street and Benjamin Franklin Parkway. All approaches to Logan Circle were blocked. Byrne was grateful for the time of night. If this was during the day, the traffic—and all the attendant problems of keeping people out of the way, and safe—would be myriad.

At 5:35 they got the go order.

Six SWAT officers approached the circle, AR-15 rifles raised. Even from a block away Byrne heard their commands to the suspect to get down on the ground. When the officers got within twenty feet or so, the man put his hands over his head, got down onto his knees. A few seconds later a pair of uniformed officers rushed in, handcuffed the man, and took him into custody.

This made no sense, Byrne thought. This was the Collector? This was their puzzle master? Byrne jogged up the block toward Logan Circle. Something was wrong. Before he reached the corner, Josh Bontrager raised him on the radio.

"It's not him," Bontrager said.

Byrne halted. "Say again?"

"It's some homeless guy. He says a guy paid him to drag the box here. A couple of the uniforms know who this guy is. They've seen him around."

Byrne looked through the binoculars. Protocol now called for the SWAT officers to clear the scene, and the bomb squad to investigate the suspicious package. Unless, of course, there was a young patrol officer on the landscape. An officer strikingly similar to the policeman Kevin Byrne had been more than twenty years earlier. At least attitude-wise. It was cowboy time. Or cow*girl* time, as the case may be.

Through the glass Byrne saw Officer Maria Caruso roar onto the scene, rip off the top of the cardboard box, then kick it halfway across Logan Circle. Shredded newspaper flew. There was nothing—and no one—inside.

They'd been taken by the puzzle master.

It was then Byrne heard the call for backup go out. His partner's call for help.

"Jess."

NINETY-TWO

SWANN OPENED THE BOX. THE BASEMENT WAS HOT AND DAMP AND CLOSE. He did not have a problem with confined spaces—he had been cured, forcibly, of this phobia at a tender young age.

The box had sat dormant for years. It had belonged to an Indian fakir, ostensibly, although Swann knew the man as Dennis Glassman, a slack-handed card man and part-time lawn-care consultant based in Reno, Nevada.

It was time for the Fire Grotto. The Seventh Wonder. With a twist, of course. This time the assistant would not get out of the cage.

Swann rolled the box to the center of the small stage. He adjusted his tie. Everything was arranged. Odette was upstairs. He had peered in on her. She was dressed in her lovely scarlet gown, just as he had planned.

He climbed the stairs to the third floor. The wall on the landing was activated by a key lock and a counterweight. He pushed aside the small painting, unlocked the door. It slid open. Beyond was a short, dark corridor leading to his father's room. Swann knew that his father had gotten out of the room a few times over the past twenty years— Karl Swann thought this was a secret—and each time Joseph had tightened security.

He edged open the door to the Great Cygne's foul lair. The old man was where he usually was, beneath the covers, sheets pulled up over his bony skull. Swann crossed the room, made sure the television was on. It was connected by a direct feed to the camera across from the stage in the basement.

It was time for Odette. Time for the Fire Grotto.

As Swann made his way through the maze, he considered how Faerwood had been built on a plot of land that had once been known as Prescott Square. He wondered if the police had arrived at Logan Circle yet. Logan Circle with its Swann Memorial Fountain.

Prescott Square, he thought.

The final piece of the tangram.

NINETY-THREE

Lilly had seen the woman in the backyard. She knew the woman had seen her. There was no time to waste. Lilly had to stop the woman before she got in the way of her plan. She looked at the blueprint. There was more than one way out of this room. She opened the closet door. To the right were a pair of tarnished brass hooks. She pulled down the hook on the left, then flipped up the one on the right. Nothing happened. Perhaps she had not done it fast enough. She tried again, quickening the process. She soon heard the counterweight fall, and saw a rectangular plate in the floor slide to the side, leading to a narrow spiral staircase. Lilly took off her shoes, twisted herself into the constricted opening.

She found herself in a corner of the great room. There was classical music playing, and almost a hundred candles burning. She knew she couldn't risk walking near the main stairs. She knew there was a narrow hallway at the rear of the room, a hallway that wrapped around to the solarium. She stepped into the corridor, turned toward the back of the house, and saw her reflection in a full-length mirror. Or was it? It seemed watery, rippling, like an image glimpsed through ice. She suddenly realized she was *surrounded* by mirrors, her reflection drifting into infinity. But there was no mistaking that it was not only *her* likeness she was seeing.

There was a woman at the end of the hall.

NINETY-FOUR

5:43 AM

THE HOUSE WAS ENORMOUS. JESSICA PASSED THROUGH A LARGE PANTRY, stocked floor to ceiling with dry goods. She tried a door off the pantry, perhaps to a root cellar. It was locked. She stepped through the kitchen. The floor was a black-and-white checkerboard tile; the appliances were all older, but highly polished and well maintained.

When Jessica stepped out of the kitchen and rounded the corner into the main hallway, she stopped. Someone stood just twenty feet away. There seemed to be a sheet of glass in the center of the corridor, a glass panel resembling a two-way mirror. Her first instinct was to step back and level her weapon, the classic police academy tactic. She caught herself at the last second.

The glass began to move, to pivot on a center pin. Before the mirror could rotate fully, Jessica realized that on the other side was a young woman in a scarlet gown. When Jessica stepped closer, the mirror stopped turning for a moment, shimmered. For an instant, Jessica's own reflection was superimposed on the figure on the other side of the silvered glass. When Jessica saw the composite image—a woman with long dark hair and ebony eyes, a woman who, in a parallel world, might have been her sister—her skin broke out in gooseflesh.

The woman in the mirror was Eve Galvez.

| 5:45 AM |

ALL AROUND HIM, FAERWOOD BEGAN TO BREATHE. SWANN HEARD THE sounds of running children, the sounds of hard soles on oak floors, the hiss of a 78-rpm record on a Victrola, the sounds of his father hammering and sawing in the basement, the noise of walls being erected, ramparts to keep separate the warring monsters of madness.

In his mind, he was transported back to the first time he had seen his father perform in front of an audience. He had been five years old, not yet part of the act. They were in a small town in Mississippi, a backwater outpost of a few thousand or so, a Sunday afternoon attraction at a county fair not far from Starkville.

In the middle of the Great Cygne's opening trick, Joseph looked around the room at the other children. They seemed mesmerized by the spectacle, magnetically drawn to this tall, regal man in black. It was at that moment that Joseph realized his father was part of the world outside the puzzle of his own life, and what he must do to change that.

He looked in the dressing-room mirror. The Great Cygne stood behind him. Joseph Swann dared not turn around. Though he could see and hear and smell the hot damp of the county-fair tent, he knew he had not traveled. He was in Faerwood, in *his* dressing room. He closed his eyes, wished it all away. When he opened them again the Great Cygne was gone.

As he slipped into his cutaway coat. Joseph recalled the day he had cut his father down from the rope hanging over the roof beam. He recalled the deep red welt at the base of Karl Swann's throat, the smell of vomit and feces. He had taken him to the back bedroom upstairs, not knowing what to do. When his father stirred, a half hour later, it all became clear to him. The Great Cygne was now trapped in his own device.

As dawn sought the horizon over the Delaware River, as Philadelphia stirred and stretched and rose, Joseph Swann ascended the stairs. It was nearing 6:00 AM, and the greatest of the Seven Wonders.

NINETY-SIX

WHEN THE MIRROR TURNED FULLY, AND A PAIR OF WALL SCONCES blazed to life, Jessica took a few cautious steps forward, her weapon lowered. She came face-to-face with the young woman whose image she had seen in the mirror.

"You're going to be all right," Jessica said. "I'm a police officer. I'm here to help you."

"I understand."

"What's your name?"

The girl stepped fully into the light. "My real name is Graciella," the girl said. "Some people know me as Lilly."

Graciella, mi amor, Jessica thought. It all began to make sense. She recalled the diary.

I still hide. I hide from my life, my obligations. I watch from afar.

Those tiny fingers. Those dark eyes.

These are my days of grace.

"Okay," Jessica said. She knew who she was talking to. "We have to leave. Now."

Graciella didn't move. "This man? This man who lives here?"

"What about him?"

"He calls himself Mr. Ludo, but his real name is Joseph Swann. He killed my mother. Her name was Eve Galvez. I'm going to kill him."

The girl held up a yellowed piece of paper. It looked like an old blueprint. "I got this from a friend of mine," she said. "Old guy. Wicked weird, wicked *old*. He used to be a magician, but his insane fucking son has kept him locked in a room for the past twenty years." She unfolded the paper. "There are things you should know about this house. Every room has a secret entrance and a secret exit to somewhere else."

"What are you talking about?" Jessica asked. "Let's go."

Graciella handed her the paper—the slight shake in her hands betraying her calm demeanor—then stepped away. "I'm not going with you. I'm not ready to leave yet."

"What do you mean you're not ready? Where is Joseph Swann? Where is he right now?"

Graciella ignored the question. "There's one more trick to come. It's called the Fire Grotto." The girl stepped back. She reached out and touched the switch plate on the wall, then touched her foot to the baseboard. "You've got to understand. I cannot let this rest. I *will* not let this rest. I'm going to kill him."

Graciella kicked the baseboard. To Jessica's left and right a pair of partitions dropped from the ceiling. She was suddenly enclosed in a six-by-six room. The only light was from the beam of her Maglite.

Jessica was alone.

NINETY-SEVEN

S WANN STEPPED INTO THE GREAT ROOM. ON ITS TATTERED CARPETING walked the specters of the past, the many treacheries of his childhood. On the worn, sturdy furniture reposed his victims:

Elise Beausoleil with her literary ramblings; Wilton Cole and Marchand Decasse and their thieving schemes. So many had come here, prying, threatening to expose him and the many riddles of Faerwood, so many had never left.

Swann heard conversation in the main hallway. It was not some phantom of the past. It was happening now. Before he could enter, a figure turned the corner. It was Odette, wearing her scarlet gown. She was as young and beautiful as ever.

"Are you ready?" Swann asked.

"I am."

"Tonight it is the Fire Grotto. Do you remember it?"

"Of course."

Swann offered his hand. Odette took it, and together they headed for the stairs.

NINETY-EIGHT

THE WALLS IN THE BASEMENT WERE DAMP AND CLAMMY. THE FLICKER OF the gas lamps drew their shadows in long, spindly forms.

Hand in hand, Graciella and Joseph Swann walked past many small rooms, twisting and turning through the labyrinthine halls. Some rooms were no more than ten-by-ten feet, bearing long oak shelves crammed with magic paraphernalia. Some were filled with steamer trunks, overflowing with memorabilia and mementoes. One was dedicated to smaller stage props—foldaway tables, production boxes, dove pans, parasols. Yet another room was devoted solely to the storage of stage clothing—vests, jackets, trousers, shirts, suspenders.

They eventually came to a long corridor. At the end of the passageway were bright yellow lights. As they approached the stage Graciella's heart raced. She thought of the night her mother phoned, the long dreadful night two months earlier when her world had been turned upside down. There had been so much Graciella wanted to say to her mother, years of confusion and frustration to unload. But by the end of the conversation she found that the hatred that had lived in her soul like a terrible fire for so long had simply vanished. Her mother had been not much older than she was when she'd had her baby, and she had given her up for adoption for all the right reasons. When Graciella hung up the phone she had cried until dawn. Then she had gone into her closet and opened all the boxes she had received over the years on her birthday and Christmas. She'd known who they were from all along.

Eve Galvez had loved her. That's why she walked away.

That night, via her cell phone, Eve had sent her a number of photographs. Photographs of Graciella at two and three and four years old, all taken from far away. Graciella playing lacrosse. Graciella hanging at the Mickey D's on Greene Road. The final photo was of this monstrous place. The last thing her mother had said was that there had been a girl named Caitlin O'Riordan, and that a man, a man who called himself Mr. Ludo—the man who lived here, the man she now knew as Joseph Swann—had killed Caitlin.

When the story of her mother's murder hit the newspaper, and all the flowers that had so recently been planted in Graciella's heart were ripped from the ground, she knew what she had to do. She made a promise to her mother's memory that she would finish the job.

But now that the end was in sight, she did not know if she could go through with it.

THE STAGE STOOD at the far side of the room. It was about fifteen feet wide. The floor was highly polished; there were velvet curtains drawn to the sides. A spotlight over the center of the stage cut through the blackness like a knife through necrotic flesh.

Joseph Swann offered his hand, and led Graciella into the wings.

Between them, the Fire Grotto awaited.

NINETY-NINE

J ESSICA PUSHED ON THE WALLS, BUT THEY WOULD NOT MOVE. SHE TRIED lifting one of the panels from beneath the chair rail, but it didn't budge.

There are things you should know about this house. Every room has a secret entrance and a secret exit to somewhere else.

She flipped on her Maglite, consulted the schematic the girl had given her. There were lines and notations all over the page. Once she found her bearings, she saw that in this part of the hallway, above the cold air return, there were a pair of dentils in the crown molding marked in red. Jessica pointed the Maglite at the ceiling. She saw that two of the dentils were a slightly lighter stain than the others. She pulled over a chair, stood on it. She pressed the dentil. Nothing happened. She then pressed the other, yielding the same result. She pulled both of them left, right. No sound, no motion. She pushed the two dentils in the center *toward* each other, and she suddenly heard the wall begin to move. Seconds later, it rose to the ceiling.

Jessica jumped down from the chair, gulping the air. She drew back to the wall, unholstered her weapon. In front of her was a short hallway with narrow stairs leading up. She climbed the stairs, and found a dead-bolted door at the top.

She slowly turned the lock, opened the door, and stepped through.

The room was pitch-black. She felt along the wall, found a light switch. Overhead a bronze chandelier blazed to life, illuminating a room time had forgotten.

She'd found the Great Cygne's prison.

GRACIELLA STOOD ON THE STAGE BENEATH HOT, GLARING LIGHTS. To her left was the Fire Grotto, a steel and smoked-glass cage about three feet by three feet by four feet high. The front had a door that opened out toward where the audience would be, if there had been an audience. The entire apparatus was on a short four-legged steel table with caster wheels. Hanging from the back was the hoop, a three-foot-diameter aluminum hoop attached to a cone of silk fabric.

It looked exactly like the drawings Karl Swann had shown her.

Remember the hidden latch.

Joseph Swann—dressed like his father, in full costume and makeup—emerged from a small room next to the stage. He stepped onto the stage, reached into his pocket, took out a small remote control of some kind, clicked it, then returned it to his pocket. Graciella looked across the room. She could barely make out the silhouette of a small camera on a tripod. She wondered if Karl Swann—the Great Cygne himself—was upstairs watching all of this.

His son Joseph waited a few seconds, then looked out into the darkness.

"Behold the Fire Grotto," he said. He turned to look at Graciella. "And behold the lovely Odette."

He reached over, opened the front of the glass-and-steel cage. He gestured to Graciella. She was supposed to get in. She looked inside, her memory overlaying the schematic drawing on the box itself. She glanced to the lower left corner. There, painted the same color as the smoked glass, was the hidden latch.

She stepped into the cage. In her hands was the item the old man had given her. She'd held on to it so long, so tightly, she'd almost forgotten she had it.

5:54 AM

THE ROOM WAS LARGE, HIGH-CEILINGED, CLUTTERED WITH OVERSIZED furniture from another era. Every inch of wall space was covered with yellowed news clippings, photographs, posters. Every surface seemed to yield memories of years spent in isolation.

In the corner was a large hospital bed, covered in grimy sheets. On the dresser was an absinthe fountain with two spigots. Next to it were filmy crystal glasses, sugar cubes, tarnished silver spoons.

Jessica crossed to the window, parted the velvet curtains. There were bars on these windows too. In the moonlight she could see she was on the third floor, just above the spiked railing that led around the rear porch. Jessica glanced at the bed. Attached to each brass post were a pair of rusted handcuffs. On the nightstands were a series of easel frames, aligned like timeworn headstones. In the photographs, a young man stood in various poses, all mid-illusion—linking rings, releasing doves, fanning cards.

She crossed the room, pulled down the bed sheets. The dead man stared up at her, his eyes rolled back in their sockets, his hairless skull veined and scabbed.

Jessica touched a finger to his neck. There was no pulse.

"And now the Seventh Wonder," a voice said. Jessica spun around, weapon raised. The television behind her was on. Ice-blue images flickered on the walls, the ceiling.

The scenario unfolding on the screen was identical to the other videos they had seen. But this time, Jessica knew who the man was. His name was Joseph Swann. The Collector. And he was somewhere in this house.

On-screen, Swann stepped to the side, and Jessica saw the steel-and-glass cage at the center of the stage. Inside sat Graciella. Swann closed the door, spun the cage twice, lifted a large conical silken drape overhead.

He then reached into his pocket, removed a small remote control, pressed a button. The camera angle widened, showing more of the stage. There was a ring of tower candles.

Swann picked up a small copper can with a spout, like a receptacle used for drizzling olive oil. He circled the silken cone, splashing the liquid from top to bottom, all the while mumbling something Jessica was unable to hear. When he finished, he placed the can on a side table, then walked behind the drape.

Jessica held her breath. For what seemed like a full minute, but was surely a much shorter period of time, there was no movement, no sound. The came a loud thud. The silken drapes billowed out, coming dangerously close to the candles. A few moments later a figure walked to center stage.

It was Graciella.

"Behold the Fire Grotto," she said.

She raised the hoop. The cage was closed, but Jessica could see something inside. It looked like a hand pressed against the smoked glass.

"And behold Mr. Ludo," Graciella added, gesturing to the box. "You may remember him from the Garden of Flowers, the Girl Without a Middle, and the Drowning Girl. You may remember him from the Sword Box, the Sub Trunk, and the Bridal Chamber." Graciella picked up a candle. "I remember him for another reason."

At this Graciella lowered the curtain, stepped behind. A few more seconds passed. The silk billowed again.

The world caught fire.

BYRNE PULLED INTO THE LONG DRIVEWAY, FOLLOWED BY JOSH BON-trager and Dre Curtis, along with seven or eight sector cars. It would only be a matter of time until every available officer in the district arrived. Jessica's Taurus was parked halfway up the drive. She was not in it. Byrne didn't see her anywhere.

The three detectives emerged from their cars. Byrne began to direct a perimeter. He and Josh Bontrager approached the front of the house. On the way in, Byrne had gotten on his cell phone to Hell Rohmer and gotten a brief background on the property. In the 1800s it had been known as Prescott Square. Byrne realized it was the final piece of the puzzle. He couldn't help feeling they were too late.

Byrne drew his weapon, chambered a round. Bontrager covered him as he peered through the leaded glass. Byrne couldn't see anything except the distorted flames of a hundred candles. Music came from inside. Byrne reached out, tried the knob. Locked.

The two detectives backed off the porch, their weapons lowered.

That's when Byrne smelled the smoke.

"Do you—" he began, just as the first flame licked the inside of the front window.

Three seconds later, an explosion rocked the world.

ONE HUNDRED THREE

IN THE DARKNESS, IN THE DEEP VIOLET FOLDS OF NIGHT, HE HEARS WHIS-
pers: *low, plaintive sounds that speak to him of his many crimes, his many
sins. As the voices overlap, as the pitch and timbre rise, so does the temperature
in the glass coffin in which he is trapped. He soon realizes that these are not the
voices of his past.*

It is the voice of fire.

*His head throbs with the effects of the chloroform. Where did Odette get
it? Why had she done this to him? He tries to calm himself. Panic is the enemy.
He slips his fingers into the secret latch in the corner of the box that is the Fire
Grotto. The catch is vertical. It does not move. Again he tries. This time the
metal is too hot to touch. Smoke filters in. He cannot breathe. He is once again
the Singing Boy. And once again he is locked inside a cabinet of his father's design.*

*He maneuvers his hand into his pocket, removes the small remote control.
He slides off the back panel, snaps it in two. He slips the hard plastic shard into
the slot at the bottom of the main catch and begins to turn the screw. The heat
is becoming unbearable. Sweat pools on the floor of the cage; steel hinges brand
his back. Turn by turn, the screw slowly loosens. Finally, the catch drops to the
floor of the cage. He pushes against the door. Nothing. He tries again. This
time it begins to move. He takes a deep breath, holds it, as the box is now filled
with smoke. His eyes and lungs burn as he rocks back and forth, forcing his
shoulder into the door. The glass panels of the Fire Grotto start to crack in the*

intense heat. He expands his chest, flexes his upper arms. The door flings open. He emerges from the cage to find the stage now covered in thick black smoke. He makes it to his feet. The backs of his arms and hands are scorched and blistered.

As the flames devour the curtains on either side of the stage, he looks into the wings. Through the miasma he sees the Great Cygne. It is not the broken man he knows, the man who has lived in his filth for almost twenty years. It is the young illusionist, the man who strode onto the stage, his magnificent cape billowing behind him, his eyes mesmerizing.

"Where dwells the effect, Joseph?"

"The effect," he says, each word burning his throat, "is in the mind."

The Great Cygne lifts his cape over his face. In an instant it drops to the floor.

The Great Cygne is gone.

Joseph Swann removes his false beard and eyebrows, his cutaway coat, and makes his way to the stairs, through the flaming inferno of the basement.

FIRE ENCIRCLED THE FIRST FLOOR OF THE HOUSE, AND JESSICA WAS trapped on the third floor. All the secret doors that had stood open were now closed, and she could not find the seams. There was no way out. As her handset crackled with static, a blast rocked the walls. The floor, the ceilings, rained plaster onto her head, and the concussive air sucked her breath from her lungs for a moment. The ornate clock on the wall behind her crashed to the floor, shattering its glass. The chandelier in the center of the room ripped from its plaster medallion.

She tore at the velvet drapes of one window, then the other. Both were barred.

She had to calm herself, to concentrate.

"There are things you should know about this house."

Jessica looked at the yellowed schematic. Half of it had been ripped away. It took her a few moments to orient the diagram. There were lines and notations all across the surface. She soon realized she had the southern and eastern sections of the house. Was she in the eastern section? She had no idea.

Smoke drifted under the door. Jessica heard glass shattering elsewhere in the house, popping like small arms' fire.

Her eyes danced over the yellowed page.

Where was she?

She found her location. Eastern wall. It showed three windows, but she only saw two, both of them barred. An arrow pointed to something on the wall, equidistant between the two windows. Jessica looked up. The only thing on the wall was a large wrought-iron sconce. She pulled on it. Nothing. She pushed. Nothing. She felt the heat in the very walls. The room was already thick with smoke up to her knees.

She twisted the sconce left, right, left, right, nearly tearing it from the wall. She was just about to give up when a panel slid down in front of her. Behind it was a round window. No bars.

Jessica looked around in the dense smoke. She found a heavy footstool. She lifted it and heaved it through the glass. Cool night air came rushing in. She was nearly knocked to the floor by the backdraft. Behind her, the door to the room slammed open and fire raged inside, devouring the brocade fabrics, the old dry furniture.

Jessica looked out the window. She could not see the ground. She recalled the sharp iron spikes along the railing. The flames raged ever closer. She could see part of the way down the hall, to the stairs leading up to the attic. The heat was so intense she felt as if her skin was about to peel from her face.

A figure emerged, clawing its way slowly up stairs. It was almost unrecognizable as human.

The figure paused for a moment, stared into the room. For a brief moment, through the flames, Jessica saw the man's eyes. And it was in this instant they knew each other. Hunter and hunted.

Jessica turned back to the window, to the smoke-thickened night air. Lungs fit to burst, she could wait no longer. As she climbed onto the sill she realized what she had seen in the charred and blistered apparition outside the door.

His eyes were silver.

She jumped.

6:00 AM

H E TURNS TO CLIMB THE FINAL FLIGHT OF STAIRS, JUST AS A PAIR OF *oil paintings melt and slide from the walls. On the landing, a burlwood collector's cabinet catches fire, its glass front cracking, its contents—a rare nineteenth century edition of* The Book of the Sacred Magic of Abramelin— *vaporizing in a burst of searing ash, coating his face and arms.*

He glances down the main corridor as doors are flung open. Through the dense smoke he sees each room. He recalls the lovely faces of Monica Renzi and Caitlin O'Riordan, of Katja Dovic and Elise Beausoleil, Patricia Sato and Claire Finneran.

He sees Lilly. His Odette.

As he drags himself up the staircase to the attic, the flesh from his hands is left behind on the white-hot iron railings.

At the top he finds Molly Proffitt, her delicate watery eyes now open in the Sea Horse tank, the gash in her head rent to expose her brain. Molly holds the door for him, the door leading to the attic and its massive roof beam.

Moments later Joseph Swann stands on a chair, the rope hanging loosely around his shoulders. He is framed by the large circular window that overlooks the front yard. At his feet, the old reel of film, The Magic Bricks, *bubbles and melts.*

He tightens the noose around his neck, the hemp rope pulling off the remaining flesh of his palms.

It is in this position that the flames find him, drawing him into their fiery embrace, into Hell, into the diseased heart of Faerwood.

IT WAS A FAMILIAR VOICE, BUT ONE SHE COULDN'T QUITE PLACE. WAS IT her father? Her brother Michael? It seemed to be filtered through a thick wad of wet cotton, like someone trying to shout through a mattress. For the moment she was underwater at Wildwood, her father yelling at her from the beach to watch out for the undertow.

But it couldn't be the beach. Something was *burning*. She had to—

"Jessica. You okay?"

Jessica slowly opened her eyes. It was Kevin Byrne. The world came swirling back. She nodded, even though she did not know the answer to this question.

"Can you talk?" he asked.

Another stumper. Jessica nodded.

"Who's inside the house?" Byrne asked.

Between gulps of oxygen. "An old man," she said. "A girl."

"What about our guy? What about the Collector?"

Jessica shrugged. Bright bolts of pain shot through her shoulders, her collarbone. She recalled falling from the window, falling. She didn't remember hitting the ground. "I don't know. I think they're all dead." She looked down the length of her body. "Broken?"

Byrne glanced at the paramedic, back. "They don't know. They don't think so. Your fall was broken by the hedges behind the house." Byrne patted her hand.

Jessica heard the sirens approaching. Moments later she saw the first ladder company arrive. She breathed more easily. Taking off the mask—over the objections of the paramedic—she slowly sat up. Byrne and Josh Bontrager helped.

"Tell me about Logan Circle," she said.

Byrne shook his head. "You don't want to know."

Jessica tried to smile. It hurt her face. "It's kinda my job."

JESSICA GOT UNSTEADILY to her feet. Even from across the road, the heat was intense. Faerwood was an inferno, flames shooting fifty feet or more into the sky. Somehow, Josh Bontrager found a cold bottle of spring water. Jessica drank half of it, poured the other half over the back of her neck.

Before she could make her way to the EMS van, she caught a shadow to her left; someone walking up the middle of the smoke-hazed street. Jessica was too shaken, too exhausted to react. It was a good thing she was surrounded by what seemed like the entire police department.

As the figure got closer Jessica saw it was Graciella. Her gown was covered with soot and ash, as was her face, but she was fine.

Kevin Byrne turned and saw the girl. Jessica watched the reaction on his face. It was the same reaction she'd had when she saw the girl in the hallway mirror. Graciella looked exactly like her mother, exactly like a young Eve Galvez. Byrne was speechless.

Graciella walked right up to Byrne. "You must be Kevin. My mom mentioned you." She stuck out her hand. It was bleeding.

Byrne gently took her hand in his. Sticking out of the young woman's palm were small shards of glass. The smell of a strong chemical filled the air.

"My name is Graciella," the girl added. At that moment the girl's legs gave out. Byrne caught her before she hit the ground. She looked up at him in a daze. "I think I need to lay down."

Labor Day weekend was a festive holiday in Philadelphia, including the annual parade along Columbus Boulevard and the Arden Fair just across the Delaware River.

For Detectives Balzano and Byrne there was little festive about it. They stood in the duty room, all but deluged by the paperwork related to the Collector case. They would piece together a preliminary report by the end of the long weekend.

When Eve Galvez learned of the Caitlin O'Riordan case, she became obsessed. She closely followed the investigation, and when she felt that detectives Pistone and Roarke were not doing their job, Eve decided to do it for them. She photocopied their files, going so far as to take the interview notes from the binder, the notes that mentioned Mr. Ludo.

Night after night, for two months, Eve went out on the street, talking to kids, looking for any trace of Mr. Ludo. She tracked Joseph Swann in city parks, bus stations, train stations, to runaway and homeless shelters. She finally caught up to him one night in June. As strong and resourceful as she was, he proved too much for her. He overpowered her and buried her in a shallow grave in Fairmount Park. Her exact cause of death was still undetermined.

On the night she was killed, Eve had called her daughter and told her everything. They had never spoken before. Every birthday and Christmas, Eve had sent her something.

That night Eve took a picture of herself in front of Faerwood with her camera phone, and sent it to her daughter. She had told Graciella of Mr. Ludo, and her quest for the truth about Caitlin O'Riordan, right before she disappeared.

Two months later, when Eve's body was discovered in a shallow grave in Fairmount Park, Graciella took what little money she had and came to Philadelphia.

Graciella had been adopted when she was eight weeks old, by a couple named Ellis and Catherine Monroe. Graciella had gone by the name Grace Monroe all her life, until the night she talked to her mother.

When Graciella was nine, her adoptive father had left, and her mother Catherine had sleepwalked through life after that. The woman had never been that close to her adopted daughter, leaving her to live in a world of her own. It wasn't until three days after Graciella had run away to Philadelphia that the woman reported her missing.

Joseph Swann could never have known that he had always been on a collision course with Graciella Galvez.

According to letters and journals found in Laura Somerville's strongbox, Laura had met Karl Swann, the Great Cygne, when she was only twenty-three. They had met in Baton Rouge and Laura agreed to become his assistant. They toured the southern United States in the sixties and seventies, and for years she had been Odette—playing nurse and mother to young Joseph, playing the occasional lover to Karl Swann, but more important, playing accomplice to young Joseph's murderous past. According to her diary, there were six young people found dead around the Great Cygne's traveling show over the years. Laura's journal detailed where they were buried. The District Attorney's office passed along this information to the state police departments in Texas, Louisiana, and New Mexico.

At least ten pages of Laura Somerville's diary were a confession. When Jessica and Byrne showed up at her apartment, she apparently believed her past had caught up to her. It was she who had made the calls about Shiloh Street after all, having shadowed Joseph Swann for months, hoping to anonymously tip the police.

When Karl Swann hanged himself in 1988, his son Joseph rescued him just in time, nursing him back to health, but locking the man in a dark, cold wing in Faerwood.

As far as the investigators could determine, Karl Swann never again left Faerwood. He had essentially lived in that room on the third floor for twenty years. It appeared his son had cooked for him and attended to his basic needs. In time, Karl Swann's mental illness brought him back to 1950 again. He lived through his son's re-creation of his world. He had watched, via television monitor, everything that happened downstairs on Joseph's secret stage.

If Eve Galvez had been obsessed with Caitlin O'Riordan, Joseph Swann was obsessed with the prism of his own madness—magic, puzzles, and the dark history of Faerwood.

In the days following the fire, investigators unearthed the remains of six other victims on the grounds of the mansion. All were as yet unidentified. All were buried in brightly colored boxes.

Fire investigators reported that the fire would have spread quickly enough through the old, mostly wood structure, but was accelerated by the explosion of the small oil furnace in the basement.

Joseph Swann's charred skeleton was found in the east wing of the attic. It appeared he tried to hang himself, but the ME's office believed the fire had gotten to him first.

His father, Karl Martin Swann, the Great Cygne, was found in his room on the third floor.

In his hand was a beautiful mahogany wand.

THEY LEFT THE CEMETERY AT NOON. EVE GALVEZ'S SERVICE HAD BEEN for family and coworkers only. Her family was small, but nearly a hundred people from the District Attorney's office had shown up.

JESSICA AND GRACIELLA stood near the river. It was only early September, but already the air whispered of the coming fall.

"Did you know your mother well?" Graciella asked.

"Not really," Jessica said. "She died when I was five."

"Wow. Five. That's pretty small."

"It is."

Graciella looked out over the river. "What do you remember most about her?"

Jessica had to think about this. "I guess it would be her voice. She used to sing all the time. I remember that."

"What did she sing?"

"All kinds of things. Whatever was popular on the radio, I guess." The songs came back, found their place in Jessica's heart. "What do you remember?"

"My mom's handwriting. She used to send things to my house. Birthdays, Christmas, Easter. I never opened the boxes. I was so mad at her. I didn't even know her, but I hated her. Until the night she called me and explained everything. She was sixteen when she had me. *I'm* sixteen. Geez, I can't imagine."

Jessica recalled the photographs in the photo cube at Eve's apartment, the high-school shot of Eve in which she looked heavy. She had not been overweight. She had been pregnant.

"When I hung up that night, after talking to my mom, I opened all the boxes she sent me. She sent me this." Graciella held out a sterling silver pendant on a fine chain. It was an angel.

"It's very pretty."

"Thank you." She slipped the pendant over her head, positioned the angel over her heart. "I wonder if you could take me someplace."

"Sure," Jessica said. "Anywhere you want to go."

"I'd like to go where my mother was found."

Jessica looked at the young woman. She seemed to have matured in the past few days. Her hair was brushed, her skin impossibly clear. She wore a white cotton dress. She'd told Jessica she'd worn nothing but black for years. She said she'd never wear black again. Graciella had given the police a full statement about the last moments she had spent in Faerwood. She said that after she stepped onto the stage, and saw the Fire Grotto, she didn't remember anything. All the video equipment had been destroyed in the fire. There was no record of what happened.

"You sure that's a good idea?" Jessica asked. "I mean, there's not much there. It's all been smoothed over. They've planted grass there."

Graciella nodded.

"Plus, you're supposed to meet with your uncle," Jessica added.

"My *uncle*. It sounds so weird," Graciella said. "Can he meet us there? In the park?"

"Sure," Jessica said. "I'll call."

They drove to Belmont Plateau in silence. Byrne followed in his own car.

JESSICA AND BYRNE watched the young woman cross the street, step into the shallow woods. When she stepped out, Graciella turned to someone on Belmont Avenue, waved. Jessica and Byrne looked.

Enrique Galvez stood next to his car. He wore a dark suit, his hair was trimmed and combed. He looked as nervous as Jessica felt, as fallen and needy as he had looked at the funeral.

When Graciella approached, the two embraced tentatively—strangers, family, blood. They talked a long while.

At noon, with an autumn moon already in the sky, Detectives Kevin Byrne and Jessica Balzano got into their cars, and headed to the city.

"Wow. I'M FINALLY INSIDE Casa di Kevin." They had stopped by Byrne's apartment on the way to the Roundhouse. Incredibly, he asked her if she wanted to come in.

"What are you talking about?" Byrne asked.

"I've never been here before."

"Yes, you have."

"Kevin. Between the two of us, who would you trust on this?"

Byrne looked at her, then out the window, onto Second Street. "You've never been here?"

"No."

"Man." He began to absently straighten up the place. When he was done, he got what he came home for—that being his service weapon and holster. "I have a date with Donna this Friday."

"I know."

Byrne looked coldcocked. "You *know*?"

"I talk to Donna now and then."

"You talk to my wife?"

"Well, technically, she's your ex-wife. But yeah. Now and then. I mean, we don't coffee klatch, Kevin. We're not swapping Rachael Ray recipes."

Byrne drew a long, rhythmic breath.

"What the hell was that?" Jessica asked.

"What was what?"

"That breath. That was yoga breathing."

"Yoga? I don't think so."

"I took yoga classes after Sophie was born. I know yoga breathing."

Byrne said nothing.

Jessica shook her head. "Kevin Byrne doing yoga."

Byrne looked at her. "How much do you want?"

"A thousand dollars. Tens and twenties."

"Okay."

Jessica's phone rang. She answered, took down the information. "We're up," she said. "We have a job. The boss wants us in."

Byrne glanced at his watch, back. "You go on ahead. I have a stop to make."

"Okay," she said. "See you at the house."

THE MAN STOOD NEXT TO THE RUIN. HE SEEMED THINNER THAN THE last time Byrne had seen him. All around him were the bulky brick entrails of another urban casualty. The city had taken the wrecking ball to the abandoned building on Eighth Street.

It was certainly no loss for North Philly. For Robert O'Riordan it was another story.

Byrne wondered how long the man would haunt this place, how long it would be until Caitlin said it was okay for him to go home. Everyone said it gets easier with time, Byrne knew. It never gets easier, it just gets later.

Byrne got out of his car, crossed the road. Robert O'Riordan saw him. At first, Byrne didn't know how O'Riordan was going to react. After a few moments O'Riordan looked at the broken building, then back at Byrne. He nodded.

Byrne walked up next to the man, stood with him, shoulder to shoulder. He didn't know if Robert O'Riordan was a religious man, but Byrne handed him something, a prayer card from Eve Galvez's service. O'Riordan took it. He held it in two hands.

Although they had never met in life, Robert O'Riordan and Eve Galvez were bound by something that would forever transcend this place, something that memory and time could erode, but never erase. Something found in the very heart of mercy.

And so Byrne and he stood, in silence, as the winds gathered leaves in vacant lots. Neither man spoke.

Sometimes words were not enough, Kevin Byrne thought.
Sometimes they were not even needed.

RICHARD MONTANARI is a novelist, screenwriter, and essayist. His work has appeared in the *Chicago Tribune*, *Detroit Free Press*, Cleveland *Plain Dealer*, and scores of other national and regional publications. He is the OLMA-winning author of the internationally acclaimed thrillers *Merciless*, *The Skin Gods*, *The Rosary Girls*, *Kiss of Evil*, *Deviant Way*, and *The Violet Hour*.